National Publication Foundation
国家出版基金项目

Planned by Zhuang Zhixiang   Edited by Pan Wenguo

READINGS OF CHINESE CULTURE SERIES

— ACADEMICS I —

Complete Works of Zhu Xi and Its Inheritance

Translated by Pan Wenguo

中国经典文化走向世界丛书

学术卷 一

庄智象◎总策划   潘文国◎总主编

潘文国◎译

上海外语教育出版社
外教社 SHANGHAI FOREIGN LANGUAGE EDUCATION PRESS
www.sflep.com

图书在版编目(CIP)数据

中国经典文化走向世界丛书. 学术卷. 一/潘文国译.
—上海：上海外语教育出版社，2018
ISBN 978-7-5446-5511-8

I.①中… II.①潘… III.①中国文学—综合作品集—英文
IV.①I211

中国版本图书馆CIP数据核字(2018)第162838号

出版发行：**上海外语教育出版社**
　　　　　（上海外国语大学内）　邮编：200083
电　　话：021-65425300（总机）
电子邮箱：bookinfo@sflep.com.cn
网　　址：http://www.sflep.com
责任编辑：李振荣

印　　刷：上海盛通时代印刷有限公司
开　　本：635×965　1/16　印张 15.75　字数 256千字
版　　次：2018年11月第1版　2018年11月第1次印刷
印　　数：1 100册

书　　号：ISBN 978-7-5446-5511-8 / B
定　　价：49.00元

本版图书如有印装质量问题，可向本社调换
质量服务热线：4008-213-263　电子邮箱：editorial@sflep.com

"Cherish one's own beauty, respect other's beauty, and when both beauties are respected and cherished, the world will become one", said Fei Xiaotong, a famous Chinese sociologist at a celebration party in honor of his eightieth birthday about thirty years ago. In a time of growing interest in intercultural communication today, these words sound especially wise and far-sighted. Translation, as one of the most important means for cultural communication, is usually done into one's mother tongue from other languages by native translators. This largely guarantees the quality of translated text, so far as the linguistic readability is concerned. However, this method implies a one-sidedness in correspondence, as only the translator's "respect for other's beauty" is concerned, regardless, though not completely, of how the local people look upon and cherish their own beauty. It should be compensated by translations on the other way, that is, works selected, interpreted, and translated by the local people themselves into languages other than their own. This approach may go directly against the prevalent views in modern translation theories but, in my opinion, is worthy of practicing. It is perhaps an even more effective way to bring about successful communication in cultures, and the beauties of the world can really be shared by the world's people. It is with such understanding that the Shanghai Foreign Languages Education Press is organizing a new series of books, entitled *Readings of Chinese Culture*, to introduce Chinese culture, past and present, to the world, with works selected and translated by the Chinese scholars and translators.

The series will cover a wide range of writings including but not restricted to works of different literary genres. For the first batch, we are glad to provide three books of essays and one book of short stories, all written by authors of the 20th century. They will be continued by a batch of serious academic writings on premodern Chinese classics in philosophy, literature, and historiography, written by influential scholars of our time.

Later, we will offer more books on classical Chinese drama, classical Chinese poetry, etc.

Some of the books in the series have been published before, but they have been revised and rearranged for the new purpose to meet the current needs of broader readers. We are looking forward to hearing comments and suggestions on the series for future improvement.

Pan Wenguo

CONTENTS

INTRODUCTION

Through years of efforts of the authors and translators, the Chinese-English Series of Pre-modern Chinese Classics and Traditional Culture has finally come under publication. The word *pre-modern* here refers to a specific period in Chinese history between *ancient* and *modern*, starting, as I propose, from the Song Dynasty.

The Song Dynasty is a very important period in China which, in a sense, marks the end of the classical China and the beginning of the pre-modern China. Before the Song Dynasty, China had always been a society of aristocrats when all important persons known to us, even the humblest ones like Tao Yuanming or Du Fu, had an aristocratic or noble background, whereas from the Song Dynasty on, common people from grassroots might have a chance to enter the elitist gentry; in fact, certain people from poor families had even become prime ministers or esteemed scholars in the Song Dynasty. The reason is that the imperial examination system which was founded in the Sui and Tang Dynasties was brought into full play in the Song Dynasty and yielded its best effect. "A muddy-footed farmer in the morning, an official in the emperor's court in the evening" became a realizable dream and the social strata became a convective and lively one. At the same time, thanks to the imperial policy which lay more emphasis on culture than on army, education and cultural undertakings were highly encouraged, which made the Song Dynasty the most wealthy and prosperous period in the history of China or even the world. What was described in the famous genre painting of *A Clear Bright Day on the River* by Zhang Zeduan and the famous tune-poem *Watching the Sea Tide* by Liu Yong, or recorded in the memoirs of *The Prosperous Days in Kaifeng* by Meng Yuanlao and *The Past Memories of Hangzhou* by Zhou Mi reflected the thriving and vigorous civil life never found in earlier dynasties, and gave us a direct impression that the Song and the Tang belong to two different epochs with the Song much closer to us. The much talked-about "four great inventions of China", with the exception of *paper*, were achieved in the Song Dynasty and introduced to the West, leading to the great Renaissance in Europe.

Culturally speaking, the Song Dynasty is an epoch of historic importance which creates the future by inheriting the past. This is a time when all the past cultural achievements were inherited and summarized; it is also a time when people made cultural achievements to influence the coming times till today in China as well as in East Asia. It might not be everybody's knowledge that the "traditional China" or "Chinese tradition" we talk about proudly today was not that of the Han, Tang or pre-Qin as we imagine or believe, but was actually created from the Song Dynasty, or reshaped by the Song people in the name of earlier periods. For instance, in the May Fourth Movement in 1919, people raised the banner of "Down with the Kong stash (Confucian doctrines)", but their criticism should actually be targeted at the "Zhu stash", as what they repudiated was not the doctrines of Kong Zi or Meng Zi, but the doctrine of Cheng Yi and Zhu Xi, only disguised as the former. And the Confucianism or neo-Confucianism many people have been advocating since the 1930s till today is actually a resurgence of the Song-Ming Principlism. Using the method of "elaboration instead of creation", Zhu Xi successfully transformed Kong ideology into Zhu ideology, which later became the dominant ideology especially since the Ming dynasty as it was adopted as the only authorized standard for imperial examinations. The methodology of Zhu Xi is a typical example of the Song scholars, which was adopted by other people in other fields as well. Everyone is familiar with the stories of "two Sima's". The former refers to Sima Qian in the Han Dynasty who created the chronological-biographical style in writing history, thus laying the foundation of the 25 orthodox histories in China, whereas the latter refers to Sima Guang in the Song Dynasty who, by continuing the tradition of *Spring-Autumn Annals* in the ancient time, revived the annalistic style in history writing, thus not only successfully inheriting the achievement of the past 17 *Histories*, but also opening a broader way for later history writing such as the event-focused style and the outline-focused style. Zheng Qiao of the Southern Song Dynasty found another new path by emphasizing the memorandum part of *Historical Records* and *History of the Han Dynasty* and spent his whole life finishing the book *Comprehensive Study of Memorandums,* a vital complement to Sima Guang's book which merely reorganized the biography part of *Histories.* The two books formed another tradition in historical studies, working side by side with the orthodox 25 *Histories* and impacting the historical study till today.

From the above examples we conclude that one cannot really understand China and Chinese tradition without studying the Song Dynasty and its cultural contribution. However, for a very long time in our translation and introduction of Chinese culture to the world, we lay too much emphasis on the pre-Qin part and neglect the Song Dynasty. The pre-Qin classics and philosophical works have had more than scores of translations while important books since the Song Dynasty, save poetry, plays and novels, have drawn little attention and translation. We translated *Confucian Analects* and *Mencius*, but did not know that the "feudal ideology" which had restrained the Chinese nation for centuries did not come directly from them but from the Song-Ming Principlism; we translated *Laozi* and *Zhuangzi* but did not know that what influenced the thoughts of intellectuals after the Song Dynasty was already an amalgam that merged Daoism, Confucianism and Buddhism, with the Chan Buddhism playing a very important role. Realizing this, we planned to do something to fill in the blank so as to draw attention from home and abroad to the introduction of the *pre-modern* cultural literature, of which the present series is the initial step.

The role of the Song Dynasty as a linkage between the ancient and the modern can be seen principally in the several "great" books or anthologies. In the early Northern Song period there already appeared the "four great works" of *Taiping Imperial Encyclopedia, Referential Records from Imperial Archives, Taiping Miscellany* and *Choice Blossoms of Literature*, three out of the four containing 1,000 volumes. These were doubtlessly the representative establishments of the Song culture. The *Kaibao Tripitaka* laid the foundation for the Buddhist pitaka compilation. The *Enlarged Rhyming Dictionary,* the

Collected Rhyming Dictionary, the *Enlarged Sinographic Dictionary* and the *Classified Sinographic Dictionary* marked new achievements in dictionary compilation. The *History as a Mirror for Governance* opened up a new path for historiography. The *Comprehensive Study of Memorandums* served as an important continuation in the formation of the ten *Comprehensives.* Hong Mai's *Miscellaneous Notes from the Tolerance Study,* Shen Kuo's *Pen Talk in the Dreamed Creek Garden* and Wang Yinglin's *Record of Observances from Arduous Studies* marked the beginning of pre-modern academic research. Although the *Complete Works of Zhu Xi* was compiled just recently, most of the works contained therein were already popular in the late Song Dynasty. Among them, the *Collected Annotations to the Four Books,* the *Close Reflections,* and the *Classified Analects of Zhu Xi* even became the most important textbooks of Principlism during the 700 years from the late Song Dynasty to the beginning of the 20th century. And from Zhu Xi one would naturally relate to Wang Yangming whose Mindology had played no less important role since the mid-Ming Dynasty. Thus we decided to introduce the pre-modern classics and their influence to Chinese culture by way of introducing some "great books" and their developments. In the present series we have chosen six books. They are respectively, the *Complete Works of Zhu Xi,* the *Records of Instructions and Reviews,* the *History as a Mirror for Governance,* the *Choice Blossoms of Literature,* the *Taiping Miscellany,* and the *Buddhist Tripitaka.* And we invited established experts in relevant areas to write concise, introductory books in the manner of "big heads preparing small pamphlets", before asking English experts with Chinese study background to translate them into English. Specifically, the authors and translators of the six books are:

> *Complete Works of Zhu Xi and Its Inheritance,* written by Fu Huisheng, annotated & translated by Pan Wenguo
> *To Attain Innate Knowledge — Records of the Instructions and Reviews and Yangming's Mindology,* written by Yang Guorong, translated by Gong Haiyan
> *History as a Mirror for Governance and Chinese Historiography,*

written by Zhuang Huiming, translated by Zhang Chunbai

Choice Blossoms of Literature and the Trends of Pre-modern Poetry and Prose, written by Chen Yinchi, translated by Zhang Deshao

The Buddhist Triptaka in Chinese and Its Cultural Concern, written by Li Xiangping, translated by Fu Huisheng

You may find in the list not a few names very familiar to the academic circles. For example, Professor Yang Guorong is the Changjiang Scholar of the State Ministry of Education and dean of the School of Humanities and Social Sciences of East China Normal University (ECNU), Professor Zhuang Huiming is the ex-vice-president of ECNU and dean of Meng Xiancheng Academy, Professor Chen Yinchi is head of the Department of Chinese Language and Literature of Fudan University and "Talent of the New Century" assigned by the State Ministry of Education, Professor Chen Dakang is the former head of the Department of Chinese Language and Literature, former head of the ECNU Library as well as member of the Discipline Appraisal Group of the Degree Committee of the State Council, Professor Li Xiangping is head of the Department of Sociology of ECNU and vice-chairman of Shanghai Society for Religious Studies, Professor Zhang Chunbai is the former dean of the School of Foreign Languages of ECNU and member of the Guidance Committee for Teaching Foreign Languages of the State Ministry of Education, as well as the vice chairman of the Shanghai Society of Foreign Languages, Professor Fu Huisheng is head of the Department of International Chinese Studies of ECNU and standing council member of China Association for Comparative Studies between English and Chinese, so on and so forth. Their participation is an important guarantee of the success of the present series. Here I would like to express my personal gratitude to these eminent scholars!

The plan for this series actually started a dozen of years ago and many authors handed their manuscripts rather early. It's mainly my delay and the difficulty in translation that had kept the process so long. Now, with the efforts of all the authors and translators, this series is finally under publication. Special thanks must go to Professor Fu Huisheng who personally took up the writing of one book and the translation of another two books. Besides, he has helped me to read over most of the manuscripts of translations. Without his persistence the series would not be successful.

Finally, I would like to extend my thanks to Shanghai Foreign Language Education Press and its president and editor-in-chief, Professor Zhuang Zhixiang, who has been unswervingly in support of the country's foreign languages teaching cause, and who, in recent years, has shown special concern for promoting the traditional Chinese culture to the world. Without their support, this seemingly unpopular title would not have an opportunity to go to the public.

Pan Wenguo
Shanghai
June 28, 2016

Chapter One

A Brief Introduction to *The Complete Works of Zhu Xi*

Zhu Xi[1] (1130–1200), a household name in China, is however a difficult philosopher to read. Yet he is also a monument which nobody can ignore if he wishes to learn and understand Confucianism and traditional Chinese culture. It is the intention of this pamphlet to give a brief and general account of Zhu Xi's Principlism and its legacy so as to draw us nearer to him.

Zhu was a prolific writer with many works written either by him alone or in cooperation with others. To understand why he was a synthesizer of Principlism and occupied such an important status in the development of Confucianism, one has to read through these works. *The Complete Works of Zhu Xi*, first published in 2002 and revised in 2010, provides us with the fullest written data for this purpose. Comprising a rich content with 27 books of his own work and 4 books of his edited work, *The Complete Works* is an accumulation of various publications of Zhu's works in 800 years. Here we will only discuss the formation of the great book from the three works in history, *The Collected Works of Zhu Xi*, *The Classified Analects of Zhu Xi*, and *The Complete Works of Zhu Xi*, through which we aim to get some fundamental knowledge of Zhu Xi's life, his work and his influence, and

---

[1] In the long history of China, Zhu Xi (1130–1200) has been referred to with many of his other names aside from his true name, such as Youlang or Jiyan, his child names; Yuanhui, Zhonghui, his courtesy names; Hui'an, Huiweng, Master Ziyang, Master Kaoting, Cangzhou Old Sickman, Yungu Old Man and Niweng, all his poetic style names; and Zhu Wengong or Master Zhu, his repected names. To make it easy, only his true name Zhu Xi and Master Zhu are used throughout the present book.

understand how these works were compiled and carried forward, so as to set up a foundation for further study.

1. *The Collected Works of Zhu Xi*

The Collected Works of Zhu Xi (henceforth *Collected Works*) was published when Zhu Xi was still alive, yet the title and the number of volumes it contained changed several times. As all the works it contained were written by Zhu Xi himself, the *Collected Works* is a valuable piece or even an encyclopedia for us to know Zhu's actual thoughts.

In the revised version of *The Complete Works of Zhu Xi* published in 2010, *the Collected Works* occupies six books from Book 20 to Book 25. Professor Liu Yongxiang pointed out in his *Collation Notes* written in 2001 that the *Collected Works* was already published in Zhu Xi's lifetime, no later than the year 1198. He found a letter *Reply to Hu Yong* in Chapter 63 of Zhu Xi's *Collected Works* in which Hu told Zhu about "your *Collected Works* printed in Masha[1]". Surely that selection had not been proofread by Zhu Xi. And what Hu had seen may be the *Zhu Xi's Selected Works* mentioned in the seventh chapter of *Tianlu-Linlang Catalogue*, now kept in Taiwan "National Palace Museum", which contains 11 volumes in the *First Collection* and 18 volumes in the *Second Collection*. If this is the case, then it is not as reliable as what the scholars since the Southern Song Dynasty had believed, as it had not been consented to by Zhu Xi himself.

Liu Yongxiang's *Notes* mentioned another *Collected Works* published during Zhu Xi's lifetime but not endorsed by him either — Wang Xian's block-print edition. According to the three letters *Reply to Liu Fu* (the eighth and the seventeenth to Liu in Volume 53, another in Volume 29 of *Collected Works*) and *Postscript to Wang Xinchen's Brief Biography* in Chapter 84, in 1198, Wang Xian insisted on carving three books of Zhu Xi's *Collected Works* despite Zhu's objection. On hearing that, Zhu advised him "to hurriedly store them and not to put them into publication", and finally this

---

[1] Masha is a place in Jianyang county, Fujian Province.

version did not appear later.

After Zhu Xi's death, three versions of *Collected Works* were recorded in certain documents. One is an 88-volume version compiled by Zhu Xi's fourth son Zhu Zai allegedly at his father's last wish (see *Brief Record of Mr Zhu's Life*, in Huang Gan's *Collected Works of Huang Gan*①, Vol. 36, and Zhu Yu's *Postscript* to *Zhu Xi's Complete Works Classified*). The other is a 150-volume version compiled by Huang Shiyi (see Wei Liaoweng②'s *Preface to Classified Analects of Zhu Xi*, in *Complete Works of Wei Liaoweng*, Vol. 53). And the third is a 165-volume version recorded in the *Bibliographic Treatise* of the *History of the Song Dynasty*, including the 40-volume *First Collection*, 91-volume *Second Collection*, 10-volume *Sequel Collection*, and the 24-volume *Extra Collection*. But all the three versions were lost in history.

The *Collected Works of Zhu Xi* we see today was first recorded in Vol. 18 of Chen Zhensun③'s *Zhizhai Annotated Bibliographic Records*, as a work of 100 volumes with no name mentioned of the compiler. The second part of Zhao Xibian's *Bibliographic Records: A Supplement* also recorded a copy of *Collected Works of Zhu Xi* in 100 volumes with a 10-volume *Continuous Collection*, noting that the *Works* was first carved by Wang Ye in Jian'an in 1239, completed and postscripted by Huang Zhuangyou later, and the *Continuous Collection* was published and prefaced by Wang Sui. And this version later became the origin of all versions published in Fujian and Zhejiang.

Liu's *Notes* made a careful study of the different versions published in Fujian and Zhejiang. He said, "The existing Fujian version was carved in 1265 in the Song Dynasty. According to Wang Sui's *Preface to the Continuous Collection* and Huang Yong's *Preface to the Extra Collection*, the first 100 volumes were exactly the same as those carved by Wang Ye. The *Continuous Collection* had one more volume than Wang Sui's version, but its contents

---

① Huang Gan (1152–1221), courtesy name Zhiqing and style name Mianzhai, is Zhu Xi's disciple and son-in-law.
② Wei Liaoweng (1178–1237), famous Song Dynasty scholar. His courtesy name is Huafu and his style name is Heshan, which was more often referred to in Chinese literature.
③ Chen Zhensun (?1183–?1262), famous Song Dynasty bibliographer. His courtesy name is Boyu, but he was more frequently by his style name Zhizhai.

were just the same as Wang Sui's except for a letter *To Liu Yundi* which was supplied by Xu Ji in 1250. So the Fujian version is no doubt originated from the copy recorded by Zhao Xibian, plus the ten volumes of *Extra Collection* compiled by Yu Shilu in 1263. As for the Zhejiang version, though slightly different in wording and the order of chapters, the collected pieces and even the omissions were the same as the Fujian version. There is no other explanation than to admit that these two versions were from the same source. Besides, a careful examination of the contents and wording of the two versions reveals that they had even made referential study from each other in checking the text, which is a sound proof that both versions were not the original one. As the Fujian version had twenty more chapters than the Zhejiang version, later publishers usually took the former as the foundation copy, and the latter as a reference.

"In preparing his collation, Liu Yongxiang used the *Collected Works* published by Zhang Dalun and Hu Yue in 1532 in the Ming Dynasty (a photoprint copy in the *Four Division Series*) as the foundation text, and collated it with the Fujian version (started from the Song Dynasty, continued in the Yuan and Ming Dynasties and now in the Shanghai Library collection), the Zhejiang version (published in the Song Dynasty, continued in the Yuan and Ming Dynasties and now in the National Library collection), the Tianshun version (published by He Shen and Hu Ji in the fourth year of the Tianshun Period (1460) of the Ming Dynasty and now in the Peking University Library collection), the Chunxi version (first printed in 1189 in the Southern Song Dynasty and now in Taiwan "National Palace Museum", a photocopy), and the Four Treasuries version (collected in *The Complete Library of the Four Treasuries,* the Wenyuange version, a photocopy). Sometimes he also used other materials such as He Ruilin's *Errata of Zhu Xi's Collected Works, Doubts Recorded,* and *Addenda to Errata and Doubts.*"

Throughout Zhu Xi's life, he worked profoundly and had publications on all four divisions of Chinese classics. In the Confucian classics division, he had *Collected Annotations to the Book of Poetry* and *Collected Annotations to the Four Books.* In the history division, he had *A Compendium of History as a Mirror for Governance* and *Words and Deeds of Famous Officials.* In the miscellaneous schools division, he had *An Explanation to the Book of Thorough Understanding* and *Close Reflections.* And in the collections division, he had *Collected Annotations to the Songs from the South* and *A Textual Study of the Complete Works of Han Yu.* But the 100-volume *Collected Works of Zhu Xi* does not include any of these monographs in the four divisions. Instead, it is a collection of Zhu Xi's poetry, essays, letters and miscellaneous writings relating Zhu's life, work and correspondence with others, thus it becomes a good source of notes and supplements to his monographs. All of them are reliable reference for Zhu Xi study since they were written by Zhu himself. The whole book contains four parts. Part one, volumes 1 to 10, is a collection of poetry, songs, music bureau songs, rhapsodies, *guqin* tunes, etc. Zhu is an ardent lover of poetry, partly because of the poetic education he received in his early life, partly because he himself was talented in poetry and had made an intense study of past poets, among whom Tao Yuanming and Wei Yingwu were his favorites. Zhu has left us with over 1,000 poems, of which some are very popular, such as those short poems entered in the *Anthology of Poems by 1,000 Authors.* In his *Selected Poems of the Song Dynasty with Annotations*, Mr. Qian Zhongshu praised Zhu Xi as "a great poet among the Principlists". Part two, volumes 11 to 23, is a collection of the reports and records relating Zhu Xi's career life and service for the imperial court, such as sealed memorial, suggestion memorial, gain-loss memorial, lecture on classics, official memorial, report, application, resignation and removal. And a few of them were manuscripts he prepared for his lectures. Part three, volumes 24 to 64, is a collection of letters, some of which were scholastic discussions — an important source for us to understand the evolution of Zhu Xi's philosophical ideas. Part four, volumes 65 to 100, is Zhu Xi's miscellaneous writings of all kinds, including prefaces, accounts, postscripts, inscriptions, exhortations, eulogies, memorials, comment memorials, notices, marriage contracts, beam-setting addresses, benisons, funeral address, tablet inscriptions, tomb commemorative accounts, epitaphs, brief biographies of dead persons, personal chronicles, biographies, and announcements. Zhu Xi had made painstaking efforts at essay writing which was so important for his personal career. He liked essays written by Han Yu and Zeng Gong. And his own essays were also praised by others. For instance, when pointing out that Zhu Xi's prose writing was influenced by the style of imperial examination writings, Li Guangdi[1] of the Qing Dynasty praised Zhu in his book *Analects of Rongcun: Continued*, saying, "Master Zhu, though not an accepted author as great as Sima Qian, Ban Gu, Han Yu or Liu Zongyuan, has a strong power in his reasoning, which makes him unbeatable in writing ability or literary force. Each sentence in his writing has something in it. And when he uses several phrases to explain one thing, not a single word is wasted." In reading the prose and poetry collected in *Selected Works* we can feel that they fully reflect Zhu's ability in writing as well as his Principlist ideas. The *Continuous Collection* comprises ten volumes of letters and dialogues. The *Extra Collection* consists of two parts. The first part, volumes 1 to 6, is a collection of letters, while the second part, volumes 7 to 10, is a collection of miscellaneous writings such as accounts, benisons, elegies, inscriptions, miscellaneous essays, applications, notices, and announcements. From above we can conclude that although the *Selected Works* is quite voluminous, it does not contain Zhu Xi's main philosophical monographs and annotations of classics. In a postscript written after the contents of a Ming Dynasty version of *Selected Works of Zhu Xi* published in 1532, Pan Huang explained,

> Presented here are 100 volumes of the *Collected Works of Zhu Xi*, 10 volumes of *Continuous Collection,* and 11 volumes of *Extra Collection*. Since the printing blocks were old and worn-out, Investigator Hu Yue and Vice Investigator Zhang Dalun successively reported to inspectors Yu Shouyu, Su Xin and Jiang Zhao to raise money for a new print to be kept in Fujian provincial inspector's office. I myself have read Mr Zhu's *The Original Meanings of the Zhou Book of Change, Collected Annotations of the Book of Poetry* and *The Four Books* and can

---

[1] Li Guangdi (1642–1718), famous Qing Dynasty scholar. His courtesy name was Jinqing, and his style names included Hou'an and Rongcun.

imagine what a man he was through these books. Now when I have access to these volumes, I came to realize how he was able to make a comprehensive and balanced study to reach such great achievements. Based on repeated investigation and years of accumulation, and profound discussion with his teachers and friends, he finally made consistent and systematic statements, complete and explicit enough to elaborate what he had discussed in his *Original Meanings*, *Collected Annotations*, and *Classified Analects*, and to penetrate into the minds of the ancient sages. Though how he worked on literature is no longer known now, judging from his remaining writings such as *Preface to Great Learning*, *Draft of White Deer Cave Rhyming-Prose*, and *Reply to Lü Zuqian*①, we can still see how he pondered and cogitated beyond words. What regret Mr Zhu must have had in his last years, when his books were officially banned and all his writings, even a slip of paper, were forced to be discarded! Whenever I read Zhu's *Reply to Zhan Tiren in a Request Not to Publish My Books* I would sigh over the letter, hating the mean behaviors of those persons. Forty years after Zhu's death, people began to collect his writings, but they were no longer his fourth son's first edition. Some articles such as letters to Mr Lu and Mr Wang and *Ode to Plum Flowers,* which were preserved in Wang Bai, Zhu Bohe or Yu Ji②'s families, were not included. And even those included were also doubtful. In this case, if we do not always keep in mind Zhu Xi's lofty ideas in theory and practice, it will not be easy for us to understand what his writings have left us, not to say those that were lost. I was told that at that time the books of Zhou Dunyi, Cheng Yi and Cheng Hao were relatively fresh from publication, yet the profound meaning in their subtle words was already hard to discern. Only Master Zhu found their works consistent with Kong Zi's and Meng Zi's doctrines, and earnestly wished to set

---

① Lü Zuqian (1137–1181), with a courtesy name Bogong, was more familiarly known as Master Donglai. He was one of Zhu Xi's best friends.
② Yu Ji (1272–1348), courtesy name Bosheng and style name Daoyuan, was also known as Master Shao'an. He was a very important poet in the Yuan Dynasty.

an evolutionary line of its development, so that people would not be confined to their poor knowledge. He believed that so long as one really set up a strong mind like Yi Yin and studied diligently like Yan Yuan, building a solid foundation with a bright wisdom, then he would better understand the three masters' teachings and be able to differentiate truth from doubtfulness. When Master Zhu worked so hard to continue with the past and open for the future, how shall we, persons hundreds of years after him, do? Will there be any scholars who would set up their minds and study as hard as Zhu's disciples Huang Gan and Chen Kongshuo did? They will feel the same when they read this! (*Complete Works*. Book 25. pp.5066–5067)

From the postscript we learned the banning of Zhu Xi's works during the Qingyuan period (1195–1200), and after that, even the *Collected Works* compiled by Zhu Xi's fourth son at his last words was not the original. That's really something regrettable. Yet, as works published before Zhu Xi's death, *Collected Works* is a valuable and reliable collection of data for us to understand Zhu Xi as a man, as well as his scholastic ideas.

2.   *The Classified Analects of Zhu Xi*

The Classified Analects of Zhu Xi (henceforth *Classified Analects*), different from *Collected Works*, is another collection of Zhu Xi's works as well as his words and deeds collected and edited by Zhu's disciples. It was arranged in books 14 to 18 in *The Complete Works of Zhu Xi*. The 8-volume version published by Zhonghua Book Company in 1994 reveals that the earliest version of *Classified Analects* was edited by Li Jingde and published in 1270, during the Xianchun period of the Southern Song Dynasty, 70 years after Zhu Xi's death. Before that, there had been at least 5 different versions of *Classified Analects*: 3 in the order of recorders and 2 arranged in themes. The former three versions are: (1) *Classified Analects of Zhu Xi*, a Chizhou edition by Li Daochuan in 1215; (2) *Continuous Classified Analects of Zhu Xi*, a Raozhou edition by Li Xingchuan in 1238; and (3) *Further More Classified*

Analects of Zhu Xi, another Raozhou edition by Cai Hang[1] in 1249. The latter two versions are: (1) *Classified Analects of Zhu Xi*, a Meizhou edition by Huang Shiyi in 1219, and (2) *Continuous Classified Analects of Zhu Xi*, a Huizhou edition by Wang Bi in 1252. Li Jingde first published the Jingding version of *The Classified Analects of Zhu Xi* in 1263 on the basis of Huang Shiyi's edition, and then, when Wu Jian published the Jianzhou version of *The Classified Analects of Zhu Xi, a Supplement*, he published the Xianchun version in 1270, by adding some new items from the *Supplement*.

From the prefaces of the above-mentioned versions, we can know how people of that time thought of the *Classified Analects*. For example, Huang Gan, Zhu Xi's son-in-law, wrote in the postscript of Chizhou edition:

> The dialogues between Mr Zhu Xi and his disciples were noted down by the latter privately when they withdrew from their master. They appeared in book form after Zhu passed away. Now these notes do not necessarily reflect the essence of the master's teachings, and the original meaning might get lost during circulation, to say nothing of possible change or omission that made the words unreadable. Li Daochuan was an official from Sichuan. He searched widely for the lost writings of Zhu Xi, and with the help of his friends, he obtained a lot of notes in their original form. Later he became a governor in Yizhen and an official in charge of granary section in Chizhou, and had a chance to meet those who had studied under Zhu Xi, such as Pan Shiju and Ye Hesun, collated different versions, dismissed the redundant ones, corrected the wrong ones, decided which to enter and which not, and finally edited them in volumes with certain order, covering 33 persons. When more versions were found later, they were added as attachment, so that they would not be lost again and could be known by more people.

---

[1] Cai Hang (1193–1259), courtesy name Zhongjie and style name Jiuxuan, was the second son of Cai Shen and grandson of Cai Yuanding. Both his grandfather and father were Zhu Xi's disciples.

Master Zhu was a prolific writer as well as an effective teacher who was good at guiding his students to understand the ultimate principles. Within a small room, teacher and students would discuss a matter to its most detail. The more they discussed, the more profound meanings they could draw from it. To read this book is a thrilling experience, just like standing at the teacher's attendance and hearing his voice. People of a thousand years apart are drawing near as if meeting in the same room, and words that were heard separately are now in the possession of a single person. The publication of this book is really invaluable. (*Classified Analects*. Book 1. p.2)

Obviously, as one of Zhu Xi's orthodox disciples, Huang Gan is serious in the genuineness of his teacher's works. His words "To read this book is a thrilling experience, just like standing at the teacher's attendance and hearing his voice" may assure us that the book after his careful review is genuine and reliable.

As to the content of the *Classified Analects*, Deng Aimin pointed out in his preface to *Zhu Xi and his Classified Analects* published by Zhonghua Book Company in 1994:

In the 140 volumes of the *Classified Analects of Zhu Xi,* the content of the *Four Books* occupies 51 volumes; the *Five Classics,* 29 volumes; philosophical topics such as Principle and Material Force, or knowing and doing, specific figures such as Zhou Dunyi, Cheng Yi, Laozi or Sakyamuni, and research methods, 40 volumes; history, politics, literature, etc., 20 volumes. Although Li Xingchuan said that should there be any difference between *Classified Analects* and the *Four Books,* it was the *Four Books* that was to be trusted, hinting that the *Classified Analects* were only of referential value, the fully understanding of certain problems did rely on the materials found in the *Classified Analects*. (*Classified Analects*. Book 1. p.10)

Clearly the *Classified Analects* is only a record of Zhu Xi's answers to the questions raised by his disciples on philosophical and scholastic problems; it's not Zhu's own academic writing. However, by providing different angles and more details, it helps us a lot to fully understand various respects of Zhu Xi's thought. Reading Huang Shiyi's *Postscript* to the *Classified Analects* and his explanation of the book's arrangement, one may have a basic understanding of the book, as well as a comprehensive grasp of Zhu Xi's philosophical ideas as a whole. He said,

When it is classified, it is possible to be arranged. I then would like to put forward some rules so as to put these materials in order. Extreme Ultimate comes before Heaven and Earth, which comes before Man and Matter, which calls for the names of Nature and Destiny, which ask for the Principles of Humanity, Righteousness, Propriety and Wisdom. And to learn is nothing but to acquire these Principles. Thus comes the order of Extreme Ultimate first, then Heaven and Earth, then the origin of Man and Matter, and Nature and Destiny, and then the set order of ancient learning. Next are the Classics, which clarify the Principles. Still next are Kong Zi, Meng Zi, Masters Zhou Dunyi, Cheng Hao and Cheng Yi who passed down these Principles. Then comes the repudiation of heterodox thoughts that would blind our understanding of the Principles. And it is our duty to repudiate them. Then starting from our dynasty we shall briefly touch upon monarchs, officials, laws and regulations, people and their viewpoints. These will show us how Principles, after Heaven and Earth are located, are working through ups and downs, order and disorder in history. And what cannot be classified will be placed at random. The book will be ended with the making of writings, since Dao is carried by writings. When the Principles are clarified and their meaning fully expressed, writings will naturally be well organized. In later years many scholars did not understand this and mistook writing itself for learning. Some even spent their whole lives playing with their ingenuous skills in an attempt to reach fame. But since their learning was on a wrong path without a clear understanding of

Principles, however hard they tried with their skills, their ideas would always betray themselves. The book is so arranged to show that writing is trivial while the understanding of the Principles is fundamental.

At first, some people absurdly suggested changing the way of classification. Their only reason was to avoid repetition. From today's point of view, there is only one Principle, but its manifestations can be many. Similarly, one question may be answered in various ways with different depths or details. When they are under the same title, they can help explain each other. As to the dialogues on the classics, they can inspire what is not mentioned in *Questions on the Four Books*, confirm what is not assured in *The Original Meanings of the Zhou Book of Change* and complement what is not finished in *Zhu Xi on the Book of History*. And with the help of these dialogues, what is regarded as lofty up to emptiness or inferior down to sheer profit in *Textual Analysis of the Great Learning* will be more clearly understood and not to be misled by similar sayings. I once said that Confucianism was brightened up by Zhou Dunyi and the Cheng brothers, and fully illuminated by Master Zhu Xi. From now on, even though the doctrine is not necessarily applied in the whole world, it will be read and studied by posterity. It will not be interrupted for another 1,500 years as it had been before. I am fully convinced by myself after reading and re-reading the volumes. (*Classified Analects*. Book 1. pp.6–7)

The confidence of the editor 700 years ago is now verified. For people today to understand Zhu Xi, his doctrine, and the development of Principlism, *Classified Analects* plays a very important role. A glance at the Contents arranged by Huang Shiyi and his explanation will help us more.

Principle and Material Force/Qi: Extreme Ultimate, *Yin* and *Yang*, what is given shape to images. 2 volumes.

Ghosts and Deities: They can be divided into three pairs: Relating heaven, they are *Yin* and *Yang* or natural forces; relating man, a man becomes a ghost after his death; relating sacrifices, it's what we talk about prophecy and deceased ancestors. The three are different, but they deal with the spiritual force just the same. Knowing both the difference and the similarity is the first step to talk about the principles of ghosts and deities. 1 volume.

Nature and Principle: "It's not complete to talk about Nature without mentioning the Material Force." So a volume is first given to the general discussion of the Nature of Man and things, and the Material Force bestowed by the Nature. Then, seeing that the ancient scholars found their study easy by first differentiating terminologies, and that the later scholars found it difficult to study because they paid little attention to the terminology and some were blind even for their whole life, to say nothing of bodily application, 2 more volumes are given to the terminologies. One for the terms of Nature, Emotion, Mind and Intention, the other for terms of Humanity, Righteousness, Propriety and Wisdom. This part contains three volumes in all.

Learning: First a volume of primary learning. Then a volume of approaches to learning. Then a volume of knowing and doing. Then two volumes on methods of reading in terms of how to acquire knowledge. Then a volume of maintaining personal integrity. Finally a volume of behavior. Altogether 7 volumes in all. This is actually the order in which Master Zhu taught his students, also the order of *Great Learning* from knowledge acquisition to sincere intention, mind rectification, personal cultivation, and then to family regulation, state government till what under heaven is set in peace. This is an order set by ancient sages and not to be changed whatsoever. In recent times there were certain people who were only good at playing with empty words but never tried to put them into practice. This is a fault on the learner's part who paid no attention on true acquisition of knowledge, not on the part of teaching itself. Should anybody find this a pity and try another alternative, say, practice before acquiring knowledge, then he might get some effect at first, but would eventually degenerate to heterodoxy in lack of proper reading, or at best, confined by his narrow sight, tend to be a mediocre conservative, unable to do anything great. This is not what one expects of Principlism.

Great Learning: 5 volumes.

Confucian Analects: 32 volumes.

Mencius: 11 volumes.

Doctrine of the Mean: 3 volumes.

Book of Change: This part strictly follows the original order of hexagrams. The division of chapters in *Survey I, Survey II, On the Trigrams, Sequence of Hexagrams* and *Mixed Hexagrams* is also done with reference to ancient annotations. Only the arrangement of three volumes of Outlines needs to be explained here. The Material Force/Qi and the Number are related to each other, but as the former appears before the latter, *Yin* and *Yang* takes precedence over the Number. As things were shaped by the Material Force and the Number, they are succeeded by the Map and the Script, which brought forth the *Book of Change*, so the sixty-four Hexagrams of Fuxi come after. As the *Book of Change* was originally written to teach people to divine, the divination with tortoise shells and yarrow stalks come next. And as the divination relied on odd and even lines as images to imitate good or ill luck, then Images follow. The above-discussed is Fuxi's *Change*, or as Zhu Xi put it, the original meaning, which occupies two volumes. In Fuxi's *Change*, there were not yet any explanatory words. The words were added successively by King Wen of Zhou, Duke of Zhou and Kong Zi, so the three sages' *Change* come next. Then, after a thousand years and more, Mr. Cheng began to explain the Principles of the *Change*, Mr Shao Yong[1] began to illustrate the Numbers in the *Change*, and Master

---

[1] Shao Yong (1011–1077), courtesy name Yaofu, was given a posthumous title Kangjie (meaning man with moral aspiration and self-restraint), when in his lifetime he called himself Master Enjoyment or Old man at Yichuan. He was an important philosopher in the Northern Song Dynasty.

Zhu Xi began to speculate the divination in the *Change,* thus the three masters' *Change* follows. After all these, there is a general discussion on how to read *The Book of Change,* and the significance of hexagrams and lines which can be inferred and understood, and it finally ends up with the discussion of human affairs, to show that the ultimate usage of *The Book of change* is to solve human affairs. Then there is a brief discussion of the gains and losses of later *Change* scholars for further reference. All above can be found in one volume. After the three volumes of Outlines, there are 4 volumes for *The Change* Proper I, 2 volumes for *The Change* Proper II, 3 volumes for the *Survey,* and 1 volume for *On the Trigrams, Sequence of Hexagrams* and *Mixed Hexagrams.*

The Book of History: 2 volumes.

The Book of Poetry: 2 volumes.

Classic of Filial Piety: 1 volume.

Spring and Autumn Annals: 1 volume.

The Book of Rites: 8 volumes.

The Book of Music: 1 volume.

Kong Zi, Meng Zi, Zhou Dunyi, Cheng Yi, Zhang Zai, Shao Yong and Zhu Xi: First there is 1 volume for Confucius/ Kong Zi, his disciples Yan Yuan and Zeng Shen, Mencius/ Meng Zi, up till Zhou Dunyi, Cheng brothers and Zhang Zai, as Zhou and others are successors of Kong Zi and Meng Zi. Then, there is 1 volume for Zhou's books and 3 volumes for Cheng Yi's books — 2 for those mentioned in *Close Reflections* and 1 for what is not mentioned and the rest in Cheng's *Works.* 2 volumes for Zhang Zai's books, also those that were mentioned in *Close Reflections.* 1 volume for Shao Yong's books. 1 volume for Cheng brothers' disciples. 1 volume for Yang Shi[1] and Yin Tun[2]'s disciples. 1 volume for Luo

---

[1] Yang Shi (1053–1135), courtesy name Zhongli and style name Guishan, Northern Song Dynasty philosopher, Cheng Hao's disciple.

[2] Yin Tun (1071–1142), courtesy names Yanming and Dechong, was Cheng Yi's disciple and a Song Dynasty philosopher.

Congyan[1] and Hu Hong[2]'s disciples. 18 volumes for Master Zhu Xi, among which 1 is on his lectures on how to study, 1 on his self-annotated books, 1 on his words during his official career outside the capital, 1 on his career in the capital, 1 on the way of governance, 1 on how to enroll scholars to be officials, 1 on his sayings on war and justice, 1 on his words on civil affairs and finance, 1 on officials, and 9 on teaching his disciples.

Lü Zuqian: 1 volume.

Chen Fuliang, Chen Liang[3] and Ye Shi[4]: 1 volume.

Lu brothers[5]: 1 volume.

Laozi: 1 volume.

Buddhism: 1 volume.

Present dynasty: 7 volumes.

Past dynasties: 3 volumes.

Philosophers of the Warring States, Han and Tang dynasties: 1 volume.

Miscellaneous: 1 volume.

Prose writing: 2 volumes. (*Classified Analects*. Book 1. pp.28–31)

From the prefaces, editing arrangement and layout of the book, we can see not only how his disciples and contemporaries thought of Zhu Xi, but also the evolution of Principlism in the Southern Song Dynasty. They are of important value in understanding Zhu Xi's philosophical ideas and

---

[1] Luo Congyan (1072–1135), courtesy name Zhongsu, and styled as Master Yuzhang. He was disciple of Yang Shi, and master of Zhu Xi's father. He was also the founder of the Yuzhang philosophical school.

[2] Hu Hong (1102–1161), courtesy name Renzhong, and nicknamed Master Wufeng. He studied after his father, famous scholar Hu Anguo and Yang Shi. And later became the founder of Huxiang philosophical school.

[3] Chen Liang (1143–1194), courtesy nme Tongfu and style name Longchuan. He was also a very famous Ci poem writer.

[4] Ye Shi (1150–1223), courtesy name Zhengze and style name Master Shuixin. He was an important poetry critic in the history of Chinese literature.

[5] The Lu brothers include three people: Lu Jiushao (1128–1205, courtesy name Zimei and style name Suoshan), Lu Jiuling (1132–1180, courtesy name Zishou and style name Fuzhai), and Lu Jiuyuan (1139–1193, courtesy name Zijing and style name Xiangshan). Of the three, Lu Jiuyuan was the most important one in the history of Chinese philosophy and the founder of the philosophical school of Mindology.

the response of the readers and scholars of his time.

3. *The Complete Works of Zhu Xi*

Although *Collected Works* and *Classified Analects* were both bulky publications themselves, they did not include Zhu Xi's main academic writings. From various sources we learned that his main academic writings were published in monographs from the Song down to the Qing Dynasties. According to the traditional method of bibliographic classification, *Classified Analects* and *Collected Works* belong respectively to the miscellaneous schools and collections divisions, while Zhu's works on Confucian classics and history divisions were included in the *Complete Works of Zhu Xi* (hence *Complete Works*) published in 2002.

The *Complete Works* tried all possible means to cover the entirety of Zhu Xi's publications. Although there was still something left out due to certain reasons, it already presents a magnificent view compared with all previous publications of Zhu. It is necessary and beneficial for us to have a comprehensive view of Zhu Xi, his life, thought, work as well as his time and the status when Priciplism reached its highest peak. Towards the end of 1970s and the beginning of 1980s, there appeared in the whole world a flourish of Zhu Xi studies. Under its influence, Zhu Xi study was also in full swing in China mainland since the 1990s. In May 1993, the World Federation of the Zhu Clan was established which actively supported the study of Zhu Xi. Zhu Jieren, the then director of the Institute of Ancient Books Collation of East China Normal University, proposed the compilation of the *Complete Works of Zhu Xi*, which immediately won enthusiastic response from the academic community as well as Zhu's decedents in and outside China. Wei Xinyi, the then leader of the Anhui Provincial Group for Ancient Books Collation and Planning, suggested the *Complete Works* be published collaboratively by Anhui Education Press and Shanghai Ancient Books Press. The *Complete Works* comprises 27 books proper and 4 books as complements. The above-mentioned two works, *Collected Works* occupies books 20–25, and *Classified Analects* occupies books

8–11. The rest of the works are introduced in the following in order of book arrangement.

Book 1 is composed of three works: *The Original Meanings of the Zhou Book of Change*, *A Primer of the Change Study*, and *Collected Connotations of the Book of Poetry*.

According to Zhu Xi, the writing of *The Original Meanings of the Zhou Book of Change* started from 1174 and lasted for more than 20 years. Its manuscript had been published and circulated before being completely finalized. There are now two Song dynasty versions of the book. One is kept in Beijing Library. It was an incomplete one, with no hints for the exact publishing date. The only thing we know is that it was doubtlessly a Song version and was earlier than Wu Ge's version. The other one, Wu Ge's version, was carved in 1265. Zhu Xi's study of *The Zhou Book of Change* had not been strongly influenced by *Cheng Yi's Commentary on the Book of Change*. He held his own view regarding the formation of the *Book of Change*. Firstly, he insisted the *Change* was originally a book of divination. Such a viewpoint led to his philosophical explanation of the book, which would be different from others. Secondly, he emphasized a stage-based viewpoint on the formation of the book, saying:

> The study of *The Book of Change* must be done separately. Fu Xi's *Change* was Fu Xi's, when there was not a single word of comment or judgment. Similarly, King Wen's *Change* was King Wen's, Duke of Zhou's *Change* was Duke of Zhou's, Kong Zi's *Change* was Kong Zi's. They must not be confused. (*Classified Analects*. p.1622)

This is a proof that Zhu Xi did not yield to the fashion of his time in the study of the *Book of Change*. He was a man of independent views, and his views represented a natural historicist perspective which had an enlightening effect on further research of the *Change*.

A Primer of the Change Study was published in the third lunar month of 1186, shortly after he wrote a preface for it. The book was a result of repeated discussions between him and Cai Yuanding. As a book for popularization, it was still based on Zhu's fundamental viewpoint that the *Change* was originally a book of divination.

The writing of *Collected Connotations of the Book of Poetry* took a fairly long time as Zhu Xi's understanding of the *Book of Poetry* changed quite a lot in the process of his study. The book was finished around 1186. The book has two versions at present, the 8-volume version and the 20-volume version. The former, according to researches, is a simplified version of the latter by deleting certain textual investigations and in-line annotations. And the existing Song version was most probably a copy of Cai Yuanding's edition carved at Xishan, a studio at Cai's home where he took the responsibility for carving and publishing books. In about 1189 he published Zhu Xi's *Textual Analysis of the Doctrine of the Mean, A Primer of the Change Study, Primary Learning*, and *Collected Connotations of the Book of Poetry*. Zhu Xi had a very good command of poetry and loved to compose poems himself. He advocated the appreciation of poetry from a humanistic point of view, emphasizing the function of influencing and educating people by poetry. He studied poetry from the angle of historical development and explained why they could play the role of education. This was consistent with his own worldview and attitude to life.

Books 2–5 is *A General Explanation to the Texts and Annotations of Rites and Ceremonies*, a synthesized recorder book of ancient rites with 1,300,000 Chinese characters, consisting of 37 volumes and 29 continuous volumes. Zhu Xi had long been expecting to write a comprehensive book of rites in his life, saying,

> The rites and music have been collapsed for more than 2,000 years, yet from a macroscopic point of view it is not so long. The problem is that they have now all been lost. How I wish that soon there will appear a great man who will sort and rearrange them! Yet I just don't know how long I shall wait. Nowadays the whole world is degenerating, but it's still possible that "the biggest fruit was left for later comers". (*Classified Analects*. Vol. 84. p.2177)

Zhu Xi studied ancient rites and sorted them in an attempt to serve his time and foster a good custom. He said,

The ancient rites were complicated and used frequently, but gradually became simplified and used rarely in later years. To practice ancient rites in today's life would seem against the custom. A better way is to make certain omission and addition in today's rites, to attain the same effect as the ancient rites in confined complicity, controlled frequency and equal authority, and that will be enough. The same is the case of ancient music which is not so easy to restore either. We can start from today's music, remove those gabbling noise, examine and adjust its pitches and tones, and ask the officials in charge of words to compose new melodies to cover briefly the content of Confucian lectures, hospitality, and his majesty's favor for the subjects. By singing these new melodies, it would be sufficient to create a tranquil atmosphere in society. According to the *Zhou Book of Rites* people were gathered at regular occasions to be read decrees. I don't know what "decrees" of that time were, but today we can compose a piece of work on virtues such as filial piety, fraternity, loyalty and fidelity, to be read to the people gathered in towns or countryside every three months or half a year, with detailed explanation for them to completely understand. Or to write it on the walls, which is beneficial too. (*Classified Analects.* Vol. 84. p.2177)

Zhu Xi knew clearly that it takes plenty of people and time to write such a great work, and had intended, when he was a lecturer of Confucian classics at the court, to make a report to the emperor in the hope that the work be done under the auspices of the imperial government. However, hardly had he set to write the report when the Qingyuan ban came, and he was forced to resign from his post in 1196 (the 2nd year of the Qingyuan Period). Then he went all out to compile the book all by himself. In two years the whole book began to take shape, except for the parts of funeral and sacrificial rites, and he started reviewing it. When everything was going on well, death suddenly fell upon him on the 9th day of the third lunar month of the year of 1200 (the sixth year of the Qingyuan Period), when the book remained unfinished. 17 years later, things changed all of a sudden. Zhu Xi was respected as a Confucian sage. And the unfinished *A General Explanation to the Texts and Annotations of Rites and Ceremonies* went to publication in 1217 in 37-volume format, among which 23 volumes had been reviewed by Zhu Xi and 14 volumes had not. The contents include: 5 volumes of *Rites in the Family*, 3 volumes of *Rites in the Local Community*, 11 volumes of *Rites in the School*, 4 volumes of *Rites in the State*, and 14 volumes of *Rites in the Royal Court*. His student Huang Gan continued to review the manuscripts of the parts of funeral and sacrificial rites, but soon he died, too. In 1223, the remaining 29 volumes were published, among which the last 14 volumes were still not reviewed. It was not until 1231 that the complete book of 66 volumes were published, thanks to Yang Fu, another of Zhu's disciples, who did the finalizing work. The book had different prints in later dynasties.

Book 6 contains two works, *Textual Analysis and Collected Annotations of the Four Books* and *Questions on the Four Books*.

Textual Analysis and Collected Annotations of the Four Books is the most widely published and most popular book of all Zhu Xi's works, and the most important representative thereof, which was continuously under revision throughout Zhu Xi's life. The Jianyang edition, published a few months before his death, should be regarded as the finalized version. However, those published before his death were all lost. A few published posthumously in the Southern Song Dynasty could still be seen. Zhu Xi inherited the Cheng brothers' view of considering the Four Books as an independent part among all Confucian classics, and did annotations for them respectively. His annotation for *The Great Learning* and *The Doctrine of the Mean* is called "textual analysis", whereas the annotation for *The Confucian Analects* and *The Mencius* is called "collected annotations", as it cites quite a number of sayings from the Cheng brothers, their disciples and others. The Four Books were later compiled into one called *Textual Analysis or Collected Annotations of the Four Books* or just *Collected Annotations of the Four Books.* This book is a historical summary of the Four Books studies proposed by the Cheng brothers and occupies an important status in Zhu Xi's Principlist system. Zhu spent enormous time and effort on the writing and revision of this book, with each revision shedding some light on new ideas.

Questions on the Four Books was not printed in Zhu Xi's life. Later, book-dealers in the Southern Song Dynasty secretly printed them in a single book, which was generally called Jianyang *dingyou* (or the year 1237) version. Chen Zhensun's *Zhizhai Annotated Bibliographic Records* has the following entries: *Questions on the Great Learning,* 2 volumes; *Questions on the Doctrine of Mean,* 2 volumes; *Questions on the Confucian Analects,* 20 volumes; and *Questions on the Mencius,* 14 volumes. From Zhu's *Classified Analects* we learned that the writing of *Questions* had undergone a long period. For instance,

> Zhang Rensou asked about *Questions on the Confucian Analects.* Zhu Xi replied: "it was written 50 years ago, so what it says is different from what I am thinking now. I intended to revise it, but stopped because of the heavy job."
>
> The master said that it was not necessary to read *Questions on the Confucian Analects.* When asked why, he replied that it was bitty. (*Classified Analects.* Vol. 105. p.2630)

Though for this reason or that, *Questions on the Four Books* was not published during his lifetime, Zhu Xi continued to make incessant revisions on the book, believing that it was beneficial to the readers. He said,

> I have been used to writing *Questions* in order that learners might understand what is orthodox. By reading this book, people will find which is worthy of differentiation and which is not. Removal of those worthless will make the orthodox more clearly. If one seeks too many explanations from outside, the orthodox ideas will be veiled. (*Classified*

Analects. Vol. 121. p.2928)

We believe that *Questions,* as an organic part of Zhu Xi's Four Books studies, will open a good window for us to peek into his thoughts.

Book 7 contains two monographs, *Essentials of Confucian Analects and Mencius* and *Household Rituals.*

Essentials of Confucian Analects and Mencius was written in 1172, recorded in Chen Zhensun's *Zhizhai Annotated Bibliographic Records* as a 34-volume edition. The book is mainly a collection of the Cheng brothers' explanations of the *Confucian Analects* and the *Mencius*, attached with comments of nine scholars Zhang Zai, Fan Zuyu, Lü Xizhe, Lü Dalin, Xie Liangzuo, You Zuo, Yang Shi, Hou Zhongliang and Yin Tun, and crowned with Zhu Xi's own preface. The book was also called *Essential Meaning* or *Collected Meanings* on other occasions. Although Zhu Xi wrote *Collected Annotations of Confucian Analects* and *Collected Annotations of Mencius* later, he never gave up *Essentials of Confucian Analects and Mencius,* claiming, "*Collected Annotations* is but the essence of *Essentials.*" (*Classified Analects.* Vol. 19. p.439) Obviously, *Essentials of Confucian Analects and Mencius* is an important reference for understanding the development of Zhu Xi's Four Books studies.

Household Rituals is a widely spread and influential ritual reader of Confucianism in China as well as in Southeastern Asian countries. The earliest known edition of *Household Rituals* was published by Liao Deming, Zhu Xi's disciple in Guangzhou in 1211. Different from *Rites in the Family* in *A General Explanation to the Texts and Annotations of Rites and Ceremonies* discussed above, *Household Rituals* does not talk about what is traditionally known as "rituals practiced by aristocrats", but those "rituals practiced by commoners" in the whole society which takes into account the life of ordinary families. This extension of ritual practice from "noblemen only" to common people meets the development of the society and the needs to educate the people to improve their lifestyle, and is surely beneficial to the society. The book consists of five parts: general ceremonies, capping ceremonies, wedding ceremonies, funeral ceremonies and sacrificial ceremonies.

Books 8–11 is the 59-volume *A Compendium of History as a Mirror for Governance* which records the history of China in 1,362 years from 403 B.C. (23rd year of King Weilie of Zhou Dynasty) down to 959 A.D. (6th year of Emperor Shizong of later Zhou Dynasty). It was an unfinished book upon Zhu Xi's death. Later, his fourth son Zhu Zai finalized it through careful study and published it in Quanzhou in 1218. The book is Zhu Xi's only historical work in an outline style and has many innovations in history writing. Zhu Xi held a contradictory view in history writing: on the one hand he insisted on the Principlism as the guideline, and on the other he advocated a straightforward writing style without hiding anything intentionally. It was for trying to solve this contradiction that he constantly revised this work to its best effect until his death.

Book 12 contains two works, *Words and Deeds of Famous Officials of Eight Imperial Courts* and *Source and Course of Principlist Scholars*.

Words and Deeds of Famous Officials of Eight Imperial Courts was published in 1172. It was a combination of *Words and Deeds of Famous Officials of Five Imperial Courts* and *Words and Deeds of Famous Officials of Three Imperial Courts*, and totaled 24 volumes, with a *Preface* written by Zhu himself, in which he said:

> In reading anthologies and other narrative books published in recent times, I found the words and deeds of the famous officials of his Majesty's court are much helpful to the education of people. But these records are segmented and unsystematic, lacking integrity and completion, and sometimes mixed with superficial and absurd tales. Dissatisfied with them, I tried to draw essence from them and compose this collection for memory. Due to the limited books I have, there must be much omission to be found and added later. (*Complete Works*. Book 12. p.8)

This work is an objective and comprehensive record of important men and their stories in the Northern Song Dynasty, and may be regarded as a brief dynastic history threaded by important figures. The "five Imperial Courts" refer to the five emperors of Taizu, Taizong, Zhenzong, Renzong and Yingzong of the Northern Song Dynasty, and the "three Imperial Courts" refer to the three emperors of Shenzong, Zhezong and Huizong of the same dynasty; only Qinzong, the emperor who lost his country, was left out. Since the book is a record of words and deeds which must be selected from other sources, the selection and compilation certainly reflected the editor's ideological tendency.

The 14-volume *Source and Course of Principlist Scholars* was not finalized until Zhu Xi's death though some unauthorized versions had been printed. The existing earliest edition was from the Yuan Dynasty. Zhu Xi edited this book to make a clear account of the origin and the development of the Principlist school, recording the words and deeds of 46 scholars including Zhou Dunyi, Cheng Hao, Cheng Yi, Zhang Zai, and their friends and disciples. The book has a far-reaching influence on later studies of the evolution of Principlism. *History of the Song Dynasty* took lead in arranging a section for *Biographies of Principlists*, with its facts and views mostly taken from this book. A 6-volume *Source and Course of Principlist Scholars: Continued* compiled by Xie Duo of the Ming Dynasty, and a 24-volume book of *Source and Course of Kaoting School* written by Song Duanyi and revised by Xue Yingqi of the Ming Dynasty both copied its title and layout. *Academic Case Studies of the Ming Dynasty* and *Academic Case Studies of the Song and Yuan Dynasties* compiled by Huang Zongxi[1] at the beginning of the Qing Dynasty were also under the strong influence of the book.

Book 13 consists of ten works: (1) *Illustrated Sacrificial Ceremony to Kong Zi Practiced at Prefectures and Counties in the Shaoxi Period*; (2) *An Explanation to the Extreme Ultimate Diagram*; (3) *An Explanation to the Book of Thorough Understanding*; (4) *An Explanation to the Western Inscription*; (5) *Close Reflections*; (6) *Questions and Answers at Yanping*; (7) *Must-knows for Children*; (8) *Primary Education*; (9) *A Textual Study of the Classic of Secret Revelation*; (10)

---

[1] Huang Zongxi (1610–1695), courtey name Taichong and style name Nanlei, but was more familiarly known as Master Lizhou. He was one of the most important scholars and historians at the turn of Ming and Qing Dynasties.

A Textual Study of the Concordance of the Zhou Book of Change.

Illustrated Sacrificial Ceremony to Kong Zi Practiced at Prefectures and Counties in Shaoxi Period is a book about local ceremony. Offering sacrifice to ancient sages and masters was an important ceremony in ancient schools which came into shape in the Zhou Dynasty. Zhu Xi wrote the book in the regret that in his time the local prefectures and counties lacked a sample of standard ceremony. The book was finalized in 1194, the 5th year of the Shaoxi Period. The original Song Dynasty edition cannot be found now. However, even in the Song Dynasty when the book was reprinted, there were already some alterations to meet the change of situations. Still more alterations would follow in later dynasties. What can be found now are only editions since the Qing Dynasty.

Early in the Southern Song Dynasty, *An Explanation to the Extreme Ultimate Diagram, An Explanation to the Book of Thorough Understanding* and *An Explanation to the Western Inscription* were already edited together as *Master Zhu Xi's Three Books* in one or three volumes. *An Explanation to the Extreme Ultimate Diagram* is Zhu Xi's explanation to Zhou Dunyi's 250-character essay *On Extreme Ultimate Diagram.* Zhu's ontological theory about the generation of universe sprouted from his understanding and study of Zhou's book, so this is a very important book to study Zhu Xi's thought. In his *Preface* to *An Explanation to the Book of Thorough Understanding* Zhu Xi said that the *Book of Thorough Understanding* was originally written by Zhou Dunyi under the title of *Understanding the Book of Change* and published together with *On Extreme Ultimate Diagram.* It was later introduced to the world by the Cheng brothers with their explanations. *Western Inscription* was a book written by Zhang Zai, and the Cheng brothers thought that it offered some new ideas which had never been mentioned by other sages before and was the most important theoretical finding since Meng Zi. By making annotations for the book, Zhu Xi extended Zhang's theory, emphasizing the Principlist ideas of "one Principle, multiple manifestations" and "Heaven and Man being one".

Close Reflections is a book co-edited by Zhu Xi and Lü Zuqian in 1175. They selected sayings from 14 books by Zhou Dunyi, Cheng Hao, Cheng

Yi and Zhang Zai, namely, Zhou's *Extreme Ultimate Diagram and Thorough Understanding*, Cheng brothers' *The Works of Cheng Hao*, *The Works of Cheng Yi*, *Cheng Brothers' Annotation of the Zhou Book of Change*, *Cheng Brothers on Confucian Classics*, *Posthumous Writings of Cheng Brothers*, *More Writings of Cheng Brothers*, Zhang Zai's *Correcting Strayed Ideas*, *Works of Zhang Zai*, *Zhang Zai on the Book of Change*, *Zhang Zai on Rites and Music*, *Zhang Zai on Confucian Analects*, *Zhang Zai on Meng Zi* and *Analects of Zhang Zai*. 622 quotations from these books were chosen to be organized into fourteen volumes as a primer for beginners. Zhu Xi said in its *Preface*:

> In this book learners can find the essentials of how to seek the beginnings and make efforts, and how to cultivate themselves and deal with others, as well as the outlines to differentiate the sages from the strayed doctrines. For those in the remote countryside or advanced in years who are determined to learn but lack good teachers or friends to guide them, the book will be adequate to initiate them into the studies. Starting from here, they can try to read the complete works of the four masters, study carefully and think repeatedly, reach the width then return to the essential. Then, the magnificence of the ancestral temples or the sumptuousness of the official buildings will all be possible for them to enjoy.

Zhu Xi's goal did not stop here. He actually regarded *Close Reflections* as a ladder to the Four Books, which are in turn a ladder to the six Confucian classics. Thus, he not only related the learning of the four masters with his Four Books studies, but clearly displayed his profound insight and lofty aspirations academically.

Questions and Answers at Yanping is a book edited by Zhu Xi in 1163 about the eleven years' correspondence between his Confucian teacher Li Tong and himself. On his way to career, studying under Li Tong was an important turning point in his change of thought from a Chanist/Zenist to a Confucian. Zhu's questions and Li's answers were all in the form of letters. This book was a memorial of his teacher Li Tong and a summary of Li's thinking, as well as a collection of precious data on the change of thought in Zhu Xi's earlier years.

We do not know when the *Must-knows for Children* was published, but the existing version was carved in the Yuan Dynasty. As it was merely a short piece, it generally appeared as a part of other books but not as a monograph. Zhu Xi paid due attention to education, especially the education at the initiate stage. He said at the beginning of the book:

> The initiate education of children starts from wearing dresses and costumes, then to conversation and daily behavior, then to cleaning oneself and the environment, then to reading and writing, then to all affairs, big and small. They are all listed here one by one under the general title of *Must-knows for Young Children*. As to the cultivation of oneself and rectification of one's mind, and other demands such as how to respect one's parents and deal with other people, or how to reach the thorough understanding of Nature and Principles, there are sages' writings and classics to be studied step by step.

If *Must-knows for Young Children* is only a collection of basic requirements in daily life and study, *Primary Education* fully displays Confucian ideas on child education and its content. *Primary Education* was compiled by Zhu Xi and his disciple Liu Qingzhi and published in 1187. It was in four volumes in the Song Dynasty, but after the Yuan Dynasty there were two different versions: a 10/11-volume version and a 6-volume version. Entered in the *Complete Works* is an 11-volume version. *Primary Education* is at the same time a Confucian classic and a primary textbook. The most important part of the book is the chapters of *Self-respect* and *Knowing the Ethics* in the *Inner Section,* especially *Knowing the Ethics,* as from the Principlists' point of view, human relations are a reflection of Heavenly Principles, which goes side by side with the Confucian concepts of "three cardinal guides and five constant virtues" as well as loyalty and filial piety. Shi Huang of the Ming Dynasty said,

The *Five Classics* takes the *Four Books* as the first step, without which one cannot enter the *Five Classics*. And the *Four Books* takes *Close Reflections* as the first step, without which one cannot enter the *Four Books,* and the *Close Reflections* takes *Primary Education* as the first step, without which one cannot enter the *Close Reflections*. To enter the hall of *Five Classics* one must take the steps of *Four Books*; To enter the hall of *Four Books* one must take the steps of Close *Reflections*; To enter the hall of *Close Reflections* one must take the steps of *Primary Education*. That is why *Primary Education* is the complete textbook for self-rectification of all generations and the base for great learning. To attain Confucian learning without setting such a base is like building a house without laying the foundation: how can the house be built? That's why Master Zhu purposely edited this book, so as to lay a foundation for everyone's learning and self-cultivation. (*Complete Works*. Book 13. pp.382–383)

A Textual Study of the Classic of Secret Revelation was included in the *Orthodox Daoist Scripture Canon* in the Ming Dynasty, with the annotator named as Zou Xin, the Daoist priest of Kongtong Mountain, while Zou Xin was known to be Zhu Xi's pseudonym when writing *Postscript to a Textual Study of the Concordance of the Zhou Book of Change*. There is no record in the bibliographical works of the Song and Yuan Dynasties about Zhu Xi's having done annotations for the *Classic of Secret Revelation*. The first record is found in the *Master Zhu's Existing Works* compiled by Huang Ruijie in the Yuan Dynasty, which includes an *Annotated Classic of Secret Revelation*, authored by Cai Yuanding and read and corrected by Zhu Xi.

A Textual Study of the Concordance of the Zhou Book of Change is a one-volume work which was recorded in both Chen Zhensun's *Annotated Bibliographic Records* and *Bibliographic Treatise* of the *History of the Song Dynasty*, and was printed when Zhu Xi was still alive. Zhu Xi claimed that the *Concordance* was not written to clarify *The Book of Change,* but just used the divination methods to guide actions. Based on such a viewpoint, he checked and corrected the text.

Book 19 contains two books, *Collected Annotations to the Songs from the South* and *A Textual Study of the Complete Works of Han Yu.* The former, consisting of an 8-volume *Collected Annotations to the Songs from the South,* a 2-volume *Songs from the South: Differentiation and Correction* and a 6-volume *Further Remarks on the Songs from the South,* is an epoch-making work which marks the turning of *Songs from the South* study from the Han-Dynasty style to the Song-Dynasty style. Zhu Xi set to work on the first two books in 1194, at the age of 65, and when he died in 1200, the third book was still not finished. In 1217, his son Zhu Zai put the three books in one and published it. The latter is Zhu Xi's monograph in the field of exegesis and textual studies. According to the editor's explanation in the *Complete Works of Zhu Xi,* during the reign of Emperor Xiaozong of the Southern Song Dynasty (1163–1189), Fang Songqing was editing *Works of Han Yu.* He studied and checked the texts by referring to other materials, such as 17 inscribed essays, other printed versions like the Linghu Cheng version of the Tang Dynasty, the Baoda version of the Southern Tang Dynasty, the imperial library version, the Hangzhou version of the Xiangfu reign (1008–1016), the Sichuan version of the Jiayou reign (1056–1063), Xie Kejia's version, Li Bing's version, and those books containing Han Yu's work such as *Literary Anthology* by Zhao De, *Choice Blossoms of Literature* by Li Fang et al, *An Anthology of the Tang Prose* by Yao Xuan, etc. Through comparison, differentiation and correction, he finished his work with a 10-volume *Corrigenda to the Works of Han Yu* and a one-volume *Corrigenda to Additional Works of Han Yu.* In Zhu Xi's late years, he found Fang's two *Corrigenda* unsatisfactory. On the basis of the two books, he started to search more materials for check and comparison, and finally wrote a 10-volume *A Textual Study of the Complete Works of Han Yu* in 1197.

Book 26 is *A Complete Collection of Zhu Xi's Lost Poems and Articles* which includes seven works: *Quatrains for Educating Children, Zhu's Family Genealogy at Chayuan of Wuyuan, Basics of Mencius, Collected Explanations of the Book of Poetry, Collected Analects of Zhu Xi, Collection of Master Zhu's Posthumous Writings,* and *Examination and Research of Zhu Xi's Lost Works.*

Quatrains for Educating Children contains the quatrains Zhu Xi wrote as notes on memorizing the Four Books when he was ill. Later they were used as textbooks to teach 5- or 7-sinogram poems to the children. In the Yuan Dynasty, the book was re-named as *Quatrains on Nature and Principles* as children's textbook. *Zhu's Family Genealogy at Chayuan of Wuyuan*, edited by Zhu Xi, was once thought lost but later found in the *Zhu's Family Tree at Yuetan of Xin'an* re-compiled in the period of Republic of China (1912–1949). In the preface to *Zhu's Family Tree at Yuetan of Xin'an*, Xu Yao'an pointed out that the book had undergone three compilations, first in the Song Dynasty, then in the Ming Dynasty, and finally in the reign of Qianlong of the Qing dynasty, over 200 years ago. Thus the book was a continuation of the Song-dynasty version, and the first volume written by Zhu Xi remained unchanged. Then there is *Basics of Mencius,* also called *Gist of Mencius,* whose present 5-volume version was selected and re-compiled from Zhu Xi's *Collected Annotations of Mencius.* Zhen Dexiu[1] said of the difference of the two books: To read *Collected Annotations of Mencius* one could get the full content, whereas to read *Basics of Mencius* one could taste the spirit, so that the book of *Mencius* could be more thoroughly understood. *Collected Explanations of the Book of Poetry,* originally a 20-volume book, was written by Zhu Xi in his early years to explain the *Mao-prefaced Book of Poetry.* But after 1177 he rejected *Mao's Prefaces* and started to write *Collected Annotations of the Book of Poetry.* At present the *Collected Explanations* was lost, and Professor Shu Jingnan searched in Lü Zuqian's *Study of the Book of Poetry at Lü's Family School,* Dan Changwu's *A Collection of Explanations to Mao-prefaced Book of Poetry* and Yan Can's *Collected Explanations of the Poetry* and collected the great part of Zhu Xi's *Collected Explanations of the Book of Poetry.* *Collected Analects* is a collection of 15 books mostly named "Analects", including *Questions and Answers between Teacher and Students, Fragments of Teacher's Instructions, Questions and Answers on Yuelu Mountain, Analects Recorded by Zhou Xian, Analects Recorded by Huang Youkai,*

---

[1] Zhen Dexiu (1178–1235), courtesy names Shifu, Jingyuan and Xiyuan, and styled as Master Xishan. He ws an important philosopher in the Southern Song Dynasty.

Analects Recorded by Huang Xianzi, Miscellaneous Records from Schoolmates, Analects Recorded by Lü Hui, Analects Recorded by Lü Deming, Analects Recorded by Cai Niancheng, What I Heard from Father, Analects Recorded by Zhou Biao, Analects Recorded by Lüqiu Cimeng, Zhong Tangjie, Lu Keji, Li Dezhi, Zhou Jie, Rao Gan, Li Jicheng, Zheng Zhonglü and Zhou Boshou and *Analects Recorded by Yang Yuli*, with no more comments. *Collection of Master Zhu's Posthumous Writings* is a collection of Zhu Xi's miscellaneous writings of all genres including rhymed prose, poems, reports, notes, letters, essays, prefaces, postscripts, narrations, inscriptions, exhortations, eulogies, elegies, stone inscriptions, tomb eulogies, biographies, with no more comments. *Investigation and Research of Zhu Xi's Lost Works* examines 90 pieces of poems and essays supposedly written by Zhu Xi, and with rich sources, does a very careful study of telling whether they are true or not.

Book 27 is *Appendix* with three referential materials about Zhu Xi: (1) Chronicles of Zhu Xi. In about 800 years, there have appeared 50 or 60 Chronicles of Zhu Xi, the earliest of which was made by Zhu's disciple Li Fangzi but is now lost. The existing Zhu Xi's chronicle was made by Du Zhang of the Yuan Dynasty. Included in this book are the following three volumes: *An Actually Recorded Chronicle of Zhu Xi* by Dai Xian of the Ming Dynasty, *Chronicle of Zhu Xi* by Li Mo of the Ming Dynasty, and *A Vetted Chronicle of Zhu Xi* by Wang Maohong of the Qing Dynasty. (2) Biographical data. Included are Zhu Xi's biographies, brief biographies and other sketches. (3) Prefaces and postscripts. Included are the prefaces and postscripts of books relating Zhu Xi throughout the 800 years after Zhu's death, a collection of diversified views towards Zhu Xi comprising descriptions, exemplifications, suggestions, attacks, and serious studies.

Beside the above 27 books which form the *Complete Works* proper, there are other 4 books as complements, which are works of other people but edited or compiled by Zhu Xi. To sort and edit other people's works is an integral part of Zhu Xi's writing, and is also an important aspect for us to better understand him.

Book I contains two works, *Collected Annotations of the Book of History* and *Digest of Explanations to the Doctrine of the Mean*. The former's author was Cai Chen, Zhu Xi's disciple, also his best friend Cai Yuanding's third son. In his last years, Zhu Xi wished to compile a *Collected Annotations of the Book of History*, similar to the *Collected Annotations of the Book of Poetry* he had already done. Having made a lot of preparations, he felt he was too weak, and decided to hand the work to Cai Chen, but he himself died the following year. After another ten years, Cai Chen finished the book. In its preface Cai stated clearly the foundation Zhu Xi had laid for the book:

> Since I committed myself to do the work, I immersed myself in reading to study the meaning. I collected different explanations for references, compared and digested them into a comprehensive understanding before I could compromise and offer my humble suggestion of the subtle essence. Many of my ideas were but a repetition of what I heard from my master. For instance, *The Canons of Yao and Shun* and *The Schemes of Yu* had been checked and corrected by the Master himself, and his handwriting remained fresh as yesterday. Alas! What sorrow! His personal correction was already included in the book. In certain places where he had pointed out the problems but did not have time to correct them himself, I would do it for him and include here. As the book itself was entrusted on me by my own teacher, it was not necessary to specify his words. (*Complete Works: Complements*. Book 1. pp.1–2)

It may be understood that this book serves in a certain aspect as an extension of Zhu Xi's own writing on history from the Principlist point of view. *Collected Explanations to the Doctrine of the Mean* was a book written by Zhu Xi's friend Shi Dun, for which Zhu had written a preface. Later Zhu Xi revised the book, deleted the redundant part and re-ordered it, re-named the book as *Digest of Explanations to the Doctrine of the Mean*. Zhu Xi's friend Zhang Shi said in the postscript to *Collected Explanations to the Doctrine of the Mean* which he helped to publish:

> Above are the two volumes of *Collected Explanations to the*

Doctrine of the Mean compiled by Shi Dun and published by me in the education office of Guilin. Shi Dun had followed my friend Zhu Xi's instruction when he edited the book, and his division of chapters and material selection were both in a reasonable order. And Zhu Xi had written a preface for him. (*Complete Works: Complements*. Book 1. p.125)

Zhu Xi himself had written several books on *The Doctrine of the Mean*. His active participation in the compilation of *Collected Explanations to the Doctrine of the Mean* and its continued deletion and revision was part of his effort to perfect his Four Books study.

Book 2 includes *Posthumous Writings of Cheng Brothers* and *More Writings of Cheng Brothers*. The former, completed in 1168 when Zhu Xi was 39 years of age, had 25 volumes and an appendix. Five years later, Zhu Xi searched and collected other unpublished sayings of the Cheng brothers to form the latter book in 12 volumes. These two books are records of the Cheng brothers' words and deeds, also a representative of their Principlist thought.

Book 3 includes 3 books: *Analects of Xie Liangzuo*[1], *Works of Zhu Song*[2] and *Poems of Zhu Gao*[3]. *Analects of Xie Liangzuo*, in three volumes, was a collection of Xie Liangzuo's speeches recorded by his disciples and edited by Zhu Xi. The Song-printed version of the book was lost, and the earliest existing one was published by Wang Zheng in 1513 in the Ming Dynasty. Xie was a disciple of the Cheng brothers and was reputed as one of the "Four Famous Students of the Cheng Brothers" with You Zuo, Lü Dalin and Yang Shi. *Works of Zhu Song*, published in 1199, was an anthology of prose and poetry of Zhu Song, Zhu Xi's father. The last book was a collection of poetry written by Zhu Gao, Zhu Xi's uncle.

Book 4 is *Works of Zhang Shi*[4]. The book was edited in 1184 by Zhu

---

[1] Xie Liangzuo (1050–1103), courtesy name Xiandao and known as Master Shangcai. He was disciple of the Cheng brothers and lay himself a foundation for Huxiang philosophical school.

[2] Zhu Song (1097–1143), courtesy name Qiaonian and style name Weizhai, Zhu Xi's father.

[3] Zhu Gao (c.1138), courtesy name Fengnian and style name Yulan, brother of Zhu Song and uncle of Zhu Xi.

[4] Zhang Shi (1133–1180), courtesy names Jingfu, Qinfu and Lezhai. He was best known as Master Nanxuan and was the most important scholar of the Huxiang philosophical school.

Xi at the request of Zhang Jin, brother of Zhang Shi, upon the latter's death. When Zhu Xi was provided the manuscripts, he found that they were far from enough and that many of Zhang Shi's writings were not included. So he made every effort to collect more materials, plus those letters that Zhang Shi had written to him, and finalized them in one book. During compilation he found that –

.... In the provided material many were discussed before but not decided later. On the contrary, many of his wonderful sayings in recent years that dealt with Confucian classics or current events and had incisive discoveries were not included. Although as a talent and an early learner, his achievements would have placed him among the best scholars of today, Zhang Shi was never satisfied with himself. In recent years he was even more diligent in reading classics and discussing it with friends, returning daily to his own mind and testifying by practice. It seemed to me that he never felt that he was already in an advanced age. That's why his views were always so fresh and boundless. When displayed in his words or writings, they always seemed so far-fetched yet so close to the reality. His wisdom in keeping balance between the far and the near, the shallow and the deep, left much for future scholars to consider. But if the material is not organized in good order so that some dismissed old views were mixed among fresh new ones, and the readers had doubts about the truthfulness and reliability of the texts, that would be my fault. So I tried to get all I had collected, made a careful comparison and study, and decided by his latest thought, to organize the book into 44 volumes. (*Complete Works: Complements.* Book 4. *Preface.* p.2)

From this we can also see how sincere Zhu Xi was to his friend, and how earnest he was towards true learning.

Although the *Complete Works of Zhu Xi* was compiled today, most of its content had been published in the Song Dynasty and continued in the following dynasties, so judging from historical and academic background it cannot be regarded as an utterly new one. From the above discussion we learned that when Zhu Xi was still alive, his works had been edited and published in various ways. In his late years, the Qingyuan ban was a great strike on him as well as his works. After his death, with the raise of his status, his works were sorted and published in a great number and came to a height in the Qing Dynasty. Many were published under the names of "complete", "anthology" and the like, among which *Complete Works of Zhu Xi Sponsored by His Majesty* was the most influential one. But clearly, none of them was a complete version compared to our version of *Complete Works*.

The fundamental reason for using *Complete Works* as the basic material to study Zhu Xi and his thought is the matter of representation. From the above discussion we can see the shortcomings of other resources: *Selected Works of Zhu Xi*, with the separate poems, essays, letters, cannot effectively reflect his achievements in philosophical studies; *Classified Analects of Zhu Xi,* merely a collection of his students' records, cannot be a reliable, rigorous and concentrated data to expound Zhu Xi's thought; and *Collected Annotations of the Four Books* or other monographs alone cannot reflect the comprehensiveness and integrity of Zhu Xi's contribution as a whole. The present book's intention to give a brief yet comparatively all-round account of Zhu Xi's philosophy and academic contribution justifies our choice of *Complete Works* out of all possible resources.

Chapter Two

Zhu Xi's Personal Character

Reading through *The Complete Works of Zhu Xi*, one would have a strong impression that from his childhood Zhu had had a strong aspiration for being a "sage", and there were ups and downs in his way to realize the ambition throughout his life. He finally succeeded in having his name inscribed in Chinese history as a great Confucian scholar of his time, though there did exist different opinions about it. He worked as an official for several times in his life, in an attempt to serve his country and people with all his love, but for most of the time he spent his life in reading, writing and educating students. Through his aspiration for being a sage, honesty in official service, and wholeheartedness towards learning, we see sincerity and practicality, the highlight of his personal character.

1. Aspiration for Being a Sage

In the several biographies contained in Book 27 of the *Complete Works*, we find quite a few passages relating Zhu's aspiration for being a sage. Three anecdotes were recorded in *A True Chronicle of Master Zhu Xi's Life* written by Dai Xian of the Ming Dynasty, relating Zhu's home visit for his clan and ancestral tombs in Wuyuan when he was 21 years of age:

> Master Zhu was accompanied by Dong Qi at a banquet held by his countrymen. When half drunk, everyone present was requested to sing a song. Zhu alone sang a tune from *Songs from the South* in a solemn voice, which at once brought a respectful atmosphere to the

occasion.

In a letter to his brother-in-law Cheng Xun on poetry, Zhu wrote, "A scholar's immediate task is not here. What is urgent for him is to cultivate his own personalities. He must pay enough attention to and be familiar with the *Confucian Analects* and *Mencius*, so as to really understand what they meant, memorize it and practice it whenever possible."

In Master Zhu's *Classified Analects* there is such a story: "In the county there is a Wutong Temple, the god of which was said to be strangely effective. On the day I returned, some people urged me to worship it but I refused. That evening after I drank some wine I suffered from diarrhea. And on the following day a snake appeared by the steps of my room. Many people ascribed these to my refusal to worship the temple. I replied, 'Luckily I have returned and live close to my ancestral tombs. It will be convenient enough to bury me near my ancestors if the god can really do me evil.'" This fully reveals Zhu's remarkable personal behavior. (*Complete Works*, Book 27. p.23)

From the above anecdotes we can see how Zhu Xi comported himself when he was 21 years old. At that time he had already passed the imperial examination and obtained the title of *Jinshi*, waiting to be assigned an official post when he had time to pay a home visit. His singing of the *Songs from the South* alone at a hometown banquet that surprised the audience presents us with an image of a brilliant young talent. His discussion with his brother-in-law about "a true scholar's immediate task is to return to cultivate his own personality" shows us the image of a future Principlist with a strong will and foresight. What's more, this future Principlist was both strenuous and down-to-earth for he realized the fundamental importance of *Confucian Analects* and *Mencius* as sages' books, which must be studied, fully understood, memorized and later practiced by young scholars. This unique and profound understanding is certainly mature beyond his age. His refusal to worship the Wutong Temple and his dismissal of unlucky trifles are the proof of his open-mindedness and generosity.

Such may be regarded as the first peak in Zhu Xi's life. It is really not easy for a fourteen-year-old fatherless boy to have such great achievements. It resulted from many factors, favorable or unfavorable, just as Zhu Xi said of himself, "I was overjoyed in my teenage when I read in *Mencius* that 'the sage and every one of us are of the same category', and thought it easy to become a sage myself. It is not until now that I realized its difficulty." (*Classified Analects,* Vol. 104, p.2611) The impulse to become a sage at teenage gradually turned into long-term solitary diligence later, tempered by reading and a hard life itself. However, throughout his lifetime, the perseverance in reading and studying the Four Books played an important role in urging Zhu Xi to realize his aspiration of becoming a sage, and the impulse of a young man became a constant impetus to strive forward. He taught his disciples, "Kong Zi said, 'Is benevolence far from us? So long as we aspire for it, it is here with us.' So everything depends on whether you set your hands on it. Meng Zi's words about Yi Qiu's two students playing the *weiqi* chess told us the same thing: one was striving at it, while the other took it for nothing. When I read this passage of *Mencius* at the age of eight, I was greatly inspired and decided that learning must be done in this way. I made up my mind at that time, without caring how the *weiqi* chess was exactly played. And from then on, I never stopped my endeavor." (*Classified Analects,* Vol. 121, p.2921)

Following the above description and what is found in Zhu Xi's biographies relating his career before the age of 21, we may divide Zhu Xi's life into three periods to understand how his character was forged. The first period started from 4 years old to 14 years old when his father passed away. Zhu Xi showed uncommon curiosity at the age of 4 when he asked where the sun or the sky was clinging to and what there was beyond the sky. He went to school at the age of 5 and seemed to have grasped the main theme of *The Classic of Filial Piety* at the age of 8 by writing eight words on the pages: "Failing to do this will make no Man." And, while playing with other children, he could draw the Eight Trigrams on the sand all by himself and sat there scrutinizing them silently. He was quite mature at the age of

10, not only knowing to study hard but also keeping his elders' teachings in mind and never forgetting them. His family and the environment also played important roles in his early maturity. When he was 11 years old, his father Zhu Song "hired Luo Zhongyan as his teacher, so Zhu Xi shared the same teacher with Li Tong; he heard the learning of Cheng brothers transmitted by Yang Shi, and thus successfully acquired the teachings of ancient sages. Later he made even stricter requirements on himself by dismissing superfluous words to reach what is essential. He studied *Great Learning* and *The Doctrine of the Mean* every day, laying emphasis on the practice of what was taught in *The Great Learning*. Thinking himself too quick-tempered which was harmful for pursuing Dao, he named his own study Pei Zhai, literary, the Study of Wearing Leather, as it was traditionally suggested that wearing leather was a symbol to change one's quick temper. This is a proof that Zhu Xi's learning is well founded." (*Complete Books*, Book 27, p.19) During this period, on the one hand, Zhu Xi was very diligent himself; on the other, his father's personal efforts in learning while constantly changing official positions also had a subtle transforming influence on the growing young child. The second period was a period of extremely hard study, spanning from 14 to 17 years of age. The death of his father when he was only fourteen years old caused great changes in Zhu Xi's life. According to his father's posthumous arrangements, he began to live and study with three scholars, Hu Xian, Liu Mianzhi and Liu Zihui. As recorded in *A True Chronicle of Master Zhu Xi's Life* written by Dai Xian:

> When Zhu Song was seriously ill, he wrote a letter in his own name, in which he entrusted all his home affairs to Liu Ziyu, said farewell to Hu Xian[1], Liu Mianzhi[2], and Ziyu's brother Liu Zihui[3], and

---

[1] Hu Xian (1085–1162), courtesy name Yuanzhong and known as Master Jixi, Principlist and educater, one of the three early techers of Zhu Xi.

[2] Liu Mianzhi (1091–1149), courtesy name Zhizhong and style name Caotang, and known as Master Baishui, one of the three early techers of Zhu Xi. He was also Zhu Xi's father-in-law.

[3] Liu Zihui (1101–1147), courtesy name Yanchong and style names Pingshan and Old Sickman, one of the three early techers of Zhu Xi.

told Zhu Xi, "Those three are my respected friends whose scholastic learning is profound. After my death, you should regard them as your own father and listen to them with no reservation." When Zhu Song died, Liu Ziyu built a house for Zhu Xi and his mother to live near his own residential area. And Zhu Xi, following his father's last wish, studied under the three scholars, whereas the latter treated him like their own son or son-in-law. Liu Mianzhi even married his own daughter to Zhu Xi. However, not long afterwards, the two Lius died within a few years. So Zhu Xi studied under Hu Xian's supervision for the longest time.

In his *Tomb Account for Mr. Liu Zihui*, Zhu Xi wrote: "When you were ill, I served in attendance as a pupil. One day I asked you about your procedure in reaching the Dao, and you told me gladly, 'I found my gate in *The Zhou Book of Change*. The words in the book "Go no farther than to return" are my motto which I would like to share with you.' In your *Decree Prayer* you said, 'Things hidden in the root make the tree bloom in the spring; things hidden in the body make a man full in his mind.' Again you said, 'If you cannot refresh yourself in virtue, that's my shame.' and, 'When speaking always think of amendment, when doing always be aware of tumble, and always remain in a state of alertness: these are qualities only the ancient masters Yan Hui and Zeng Shen could possess.' That is how you were expecting of me." In Zhu Xi's later years, he wrote a couplet on the gate: "Wearing the leather to follow my father's teaching; Hiding like a tree to carry on my teacher's legacy." This is the way to keep his father and teacher's words in memory[1]. In his *Tomb Account for Mr. Liu Mianzhi*, Zhu Xi wrote: "When you were studying at the Imperial College, you tried every means to learn from the Cheng brothers. You sought for their books to copy and memorize. When you heard that Qiao Ding had studied under Master Cheng Yi and excelled in the

---

[1] In ancient China to wear lether was a sign to make oneself patient. Zhu Xi's father therefore gave himself a style name "Weizhai", meaning "Study of Wearing Leather". "Hiding like a tree" was quoted from the above words by Liu Zihui.

study of *The Book of Change*, you went at once to study with him, and finally acquired all his knowledge. Then you quit the imperial college and returned. When you passed Nandu and Piling, you met Mr Liu Anshi and Mr Yang Shi respectively. You learned from both of them. You listened to their words, thought them over and practiced them seriously, thus became more powerful and well-learned daily." In his *A Brief Record of Mr. Hu Xian's Life*, Zhu Xi wrote: "He first studied after Mr Hu Anguo[1] and learned about the Cheng brothers. He also studied from Mr Qiao Ding who told him, 'Man's mind is smeared by the material world, thus unable to expose itself. Only through learning can it be re-illuminated.' Then he heaved a deep sigh and said, 'Is not the so-called learning actually a requirement to cultivate oneself?' So he decided to learn by himself without expecting to be known by others. He said goodbye to his fellow scholars and returned to his home mountains. Hu Anguo praised him as a gentleman with the virtue of a hermit." To speak briefly, the above is what Master Zhu Xi learned from his three teachers. (*Complete Works*, Book 27, pp.20–21)

The material in Dai's *Chronicle* was extracted mainly from the tomb accounts or life records Zhu Xi himself wrote for his three teachers. (see *Complete Works,* Book 24) Whenever he recalled his life in this period he would mention his deep impression of "arduous study". For example, he said: "When I was fifteen or sixteen years old, I read and found Lü Dalin[2]'s explanation of the paragraph 'Even a dull man will become wise and a soft character will become strong' so upright that it made its reader alert and highly motivated." (see *Complete Works,* Book 27) Also, "I started reading arduously since the age of sixteen or seventeen when I had no guidance around me and had to face all the difficulties by myself. It seems not

---

① Hu Anguo (1074–1138), courtesy name Kanghou and style name Qingshan, and was posthumously entitled Wending. He was more familiarly known as Master Wuyi and was an important scholar and official of the Northern Song Dynasty.

② Lü Dalin (1040–1092), courtesy name Yushu, style name Yunge, and known as Master Lantian. He was one of the four famous disciples of two Cheng brothers together with Yang Shi, You Zuo and Xie Liangzuo.

worthy of mentioning today, yet it was indeed a sweet memory of reading experience." (*Classified Analects*. Vol. 104. p.2612) From the above records and memorandums we may conclude that although Zhu Xi's father died when he was only fourteen years old, his father's arrangement for his life and study did have an ideal and positive effect, and the period of hard study did play an important role in his later success. The couplet "Wearing the leather to follow my father's teaching; Hiding like a tree to carry on my teacher's legacy" he wrote at his old age also tells of his sincere gratitude.

The third period was from eighteen to twenty-one years of age. He successfully passed the provincial examination at the age of eighteen and won high appreciation from the examining officer, who praised him when talking with others, "... Of all whose three essays were written as proposals on great events for the imperial court, that examinee would certainly become an uncommon person the other day." At the age of nineteen he passed the imperial examination and became a *Jinshi*.

Zhu Xi's early years were relatively smooth. The most important turning point in his life occurred in the summer of his twenty-fourth year of age when he became a student of Li Tong who finally guided him on the way to Principlism and the ambition of being a sage. As recorded in Dai's *Chronicle:*

> Li Tong was a student of Luo Zhongyan. When Yang Shi was advocating Principlism in the southeast area he had many disciples. But in terms of hard study, earnest practice and task shouldering, Luo could be proclaimed the only best one. And Mr Li was the only one who mastered what Mr Luo taught among all his fellow students. However, Li preferred truth aspiration than official service and was little known by others. Deng Di of the Shaxian County said of him, "Li Tong is like an icy bottle or the autumn moon, so clearly bright and spotless." Zhu Song thought it a good comment, which left a deep impression on Zhu Xi when he was young. Now that he had a chance to go to Tong'an, he decided to visit him.

At first Zhu Xi did not have a fixed teacher. He studied Confucian classics, and extended to Buddhism and Daoism for several years. It is after he met Mr Li Tong and reached a deep understanding of Principlism that he realized the errors of non-Confucians and could repudiate them. From then on he concentrated himself exclusively on the minute analysis of the subtle meaning behind the texts day in and day out, and the tradition of Confucian line thus found its connection.

Master Zhu Xi once said: "At first I studied from Mr Hu Xian and Mr Liu Zihui and got little knowledge about Principlism. Later I began to study after Mr Li Tong." Again: "After I met Mr Li Tong, I found the right path in my study, and realized my past mistakes in learning Buddhism and Daoism." And more: "When I met Mr Li first, I talked about many theories when Mr Li replied, 'How can you talk about so many theories in the air without the ability to explain the immediate facts right in front of you? Principlism is not something abstract or obtainable through the study of your daily life,' which I understood quite some time later. That's why I have some knowledge of Principlism today." And also: "I met Mr Li Tong at the age of 24 on my way to the official post at Tong'an. I told him about my study of Chan Buddhism. He just said, 'No.' I inquired repeatedly. Then he said, 'Why don't you try to read the works of the sages?' Then I put those Chan books on the shelf and turned to the Confucian classics. By reading day after day, I gradually found the teachings of the sages tasteful. When I returned to Buddhism once again, I found it full of mistakes and flaws." And again: "Mr Li told me to look for truth in the sages' books. I then studied intensively to acquire the true knowledge, and realized that all the previous scholars were wrong." And more again: "Shen Yuanyong asked Yin Tun, 'What's the key point in *The Book of Change Commented by Cheng Yi*?' Yin Tun replied, 'It lies in the same origin of principles and application, and the seamless relation between implicitness and explicitness.' When I mentioned this to Mr Li, he said, 'Certainly Yin was not wrong. But you have to know the exact meaning of all the 64 hexagrams and 384 lines before you can say so. Otherwise this answer may be harmful.' I was startled at hearing this and found that empty words without facts meant nothing. From then on I became more careful in reading."

In a letter to his friend Luo Bowen, Li Tong wrote: "Zhu Xi studies very hard. He takes delight in being benevolent and respects righteousness, a rare person among us." He said again: "This person (Zhu Xi) is very clever and tries every means to practice what he has learned. In his scholastic learning he goes so far as to the most subtle and delicate place. Whenever he argues, he uses your own weapon in your own room, and starts from his understanding at the very origin. It's really a pleasure to talk to him. In the past I used to discuss with Mr Luo. Later I found no friends to talk to and almost gave up. To talk to Zhu Xi is really beneficial. At first he had studied with Monk Daoqian and thought in the way of Buddhism. Through our discussion he found the reason in Confucianism and was able to point out the errors in Buddhism. I have seen nobody like him since Mr Luo." And again: "This student cares about nothing but his learning. When he first held discussion with me, he seemed restricted by theories. Now he is more broadminded and takes effort in explaining daily life. If he goes on like this, he will soon reach a good combination of principles and application. This can only be understood through daily practice. It will be wrong for one to know the principle when things are tranquil but become ignorant when things begin to move." (*Complete Works.* Book 27. pp.24–5)

The above paragraph, mainly extracted from *Classified Analects* and *Complete Works,* reflects such a fact: although Zhu Xi started to learn under his three early masters at the age of fourteen, he studied rather indiscriminately, from Confucianism to Buddhism and Daoism which were popular at that time. As a result, he learned a lot which was not exact enough. The greatest turn he took after he followed Li Tong was towards "practicality in learning" instead of empty talk. It was all the more the case when he told Mr Li Yin Tun's view about the key point of *The Book of Change Commented by Cheng Yi* being "the same origin of principles and application, and the seamless relation between implicitness and explicitness", in an attempt to corner Li; Li's reply made him alert that what was important in learning was to understand the meaning thoroughly first. Obviously, under the guidance of Li Tong, he began to concentrate himself on the study of Confucian classics and make successive achievements later. Li's emphasis on practicality was the impetus for his progress. In my opinion, Zhu Xi's study, especially after he became a student of Li Tong's, had a strong impact on his initial career as an imperial official, as well as his life-long scholastic study and aspiration for being a sage.

2.   A Practical Imperial Official

Zhu Xi became a *Jinshi* at the age of 19 and started his career as an official at 22. Throughout his life he had been an official in different provinces such as Fujian, Jiangxi, Zhejiang and Hunan before his final short service in the central government. From what is included in the *Complete Works* we can see that Zhu Xi was very earnest in performing his official duties. Here we will mention three aspects. First, he was eager in running schools and academies to popularize culture and train personnel, so as to put into effect his Confucian ideal of rite-music civilization. Secondly, he took genuine responsibility as a local official in solving people's fundamental difficulties in their daily life, which is a full manifestation of his humanistic idea in agricultural economy. Thirdly, he boldly expressed his opinions in his official reports, court answers and explanations to classical texts in the imperial court, in order to make known his political ideas.

At the age of 22, Zhu Xi was appointed chief secretary of Tong'an County, Quanzhou Prefecture, Fujian Province. He arrived there in the autumn two years later, and worked there for three years. As regards to his achievements in that period, Dai's *Chronicle* has such a record:

> He arrived at the post and worked diligently, minding every detail all by himself. His superior and other officials always depended

on him to make decisions. So long as something was good to the ordinary people, he would spare no efforts to do it. In the office there was a sitting room, which he renamed as Room for Brilliant Scholars, and decorated it with a big poster showing the responsibilities as the secretary. As schooling was also part of his duty, he would set himself as an example and make strict demands on the pupils, requiring them to be sincere and respectful in behavior and to embrace Confucian ideology in study. At first, the students, following their previous habit, would dismiss after they had finished the meals in the school. Master Zhu wrote an article to persuade and encourage them, saying, "A true scholar is always afraid of falling behind and never dares to lose time. That's why the ancient gentlemen were always so wearied in saving each day's time even to the minutes. But I was told that you students come to school in the morning and leave before noon. Is the way to 'save each day's time'? Nowadays students come to school for nothing other than to prepare for the imperial examinations, and if their study is enough to satisfy this purpose the students will use the rest of the time for all kinds of leisure. If the ancient gentlemen thought the same way, their learning was already far above taking part in the examinations. Why should they still study so diligently, saving each minute's time until their death? If you can understand that there are things beyond examinations, you will never find an end for study." Then he selected students from excellent ordinary people of the towns and discovered some good ones such as Xu Sheng. At that time there was a local teacher called Ke Han who always taught more than a hundred students and he was very strict and seldom yielded in behavior. Zhu Xi invited him to be a teacher in the county school. Thus the students dared not to play mischief. Later, finding that these were just means to prevent misbehavior and the routine texts were not pleasant enough to arouse their interest to correct their behavior, Zhu Xi proposed a new method of lecturing and discussion, making teachers and students engaged in them. Through discussions and disputes, their minds were broadened by the truth of the classical texts, and their behavior was successfully restricted by the school regulations. The students all happily followed him. And even the school houses, lecture rooms and students' dormitories got renovated. (*Complete Works*, Book 27. pp.25–26)

From the record we found Zhu Xi was very diligent in his first official post. Obviously, he left a strong impression in his successful rectification and improvement of the education in the county. By educating students, respecting teachers and establishing certain regulations, he not only improved education, but also perfected the work in other respects in the county. Besides, Zhu Xi did some concrete work for the healthy development of the county's education. The *Chronicle* records what happened in the third year of his first post:

He petitioned the Marshal and successfully made duplicates of all the books His Excellency kept in the house, to be stored in the Classics-and-Histories Pavilion specially built for the purpose. He also checked in the office the collection of books published a hundred years ago in the Zhiping period and selected about 200 volumes still readable to be placed in the pavilion for the scholars to read.

He set up a memorial temple for the late prime minister Su Song[1], as a moral and scholastic model.

The county school was accustomed to explaining the funeral ceremony with certain deeds by certain people. When Master Zhu arrived, he asked for a copy of *Zhenghe Period New Ceremonies for the Five Rites* but failed. He then drew a ritual diagram himself by making a cross-reference between *Zhou Rites, Ritual Ceremonies, Tang Rites of Kaiyuan Period*, and *Shaoxing Period Sacrificial Decree*, with detailed notes and explanations. By studying them daily, the responsible

---

[1] Su Song (1020–1101), courtesy name Zirong, prime minister of the Northern Song Dynasty, and at the same time a natural scientist and prolific writer in many fields. British historian Joseph Needham praised him as "one of the greatest naturalists and scientists in ancient China as well as in Middle Ages".

persons and students would make no mistakes when occasion came.

Master Zhu always regretted it was difficult for the literati and ordinary people in the prefecture and counties to practice ritual ceremonies at home, so he studied various funeral ceremonies and wrote to propose the adoption of *Zhenghe Period Ceremonies*. As for the general practice of the county's officials and people, he collected and edited another book called *Rites: An Abridged Version*, to be published and sent to the prefecture and county offices, which in turn copied and handed them out among the ordinary people. The prefecture and each county should choose some scholars who are earnest and fond of rites, cover their food and accommodation with school expenditure, and have them recite the teachings and practice the rites, so that people in need would know where to find examples. He even made designs of sacrificial utensils and costumes for the counties to copy and store. If the designs were not recorded in the ritual books, he would make serious study himself and draw pictures to illustrate them. The drawings were handed out with the books for people to keep at home. How sincere he is towards rites!

As recorded in *Classified Analects*, "At Tong'an, when I listened to the night bell, it often happened that my heart went astray while the bell was still resounding. That made me alert to the understanding that concentration was much needed in study." (*Complete Works*, Book 27. p.27)

The above paragraph recorded four things Zhu Xi did at his Tong'an post: (1) setting up a county school library filled with books he collected from various sources, together with a set of managing regulations for readers' convenience; (2) establishment of Su Song's Memorial Temple as a moral and scholastic model; (3) editing a diagrammed funeral ceremony book for the county school; (4) editing *Rites: An Abridged Version* as a reference for the prefecture and counties. When encouraging the students to study in one mind, he was vigilant himself to make progress every day.

He displayed the same enthusiasm towards education when he worked as Nankang prefect in Jiangxi Province, and made no less contribution. He proclaimed three notices when he arrived at Nankang prefecture at the age of fifty, two out of which were about local education management:

> (2) Let the scholars and elders of this locality gather at times during the year to educate the youngsters to study and practice those good virtues like filial piety, fraternity, loyalty and sincerity, so that they will be respectful to their parents, elders and superiors, sincere and generous to their relatives, and kind to their neighbors. With mutual help and assistance, a good custom will thus be formed.
>
> (3) Let the elders in this locality recommend and choose their youngsters who are determined for learning to attend schools. In my leisure time, I will work with the school teachers to explain the meaning of the classics, so as to help find and bring up the talents in due time. (*Complete Works*, Book 27. p.46)

It can be seen clearly that whatever post he held, Zhu Xi would pay due attention to education and personnel training. He did make certain achievements. He himself could, for example:

> ... go to the school every five days. He gave the first lecture on *The Great Learning*. Towards the end, he would ask the teachers to teach *Analects of Confucius*. If the students did not pass the tests, he would tirelessly explain the main idea of the classical texts. He respected those local people with morality or learning. And the local scholastic style improved greatly after his arrival. (*Complete Works*, Book 27. p.47)

Zhu Xi set up a memorial temple for Zhou Dunyi in the school, accompanied by Cheng Hao and Cheng Yi. He set up another "House for the Five Worthies" as models for the students to follow. Later he rebuilt the White Deer Academy in Lushan Mountain. At the age of sixty he was transferred to be the prefect in Zhangzhou and arrived there in the fourth month the following year. The first decrees he issued were:

> Zhangzhou had a good name in the past, but recently its custom was degenerating. Since the local people did not have a sense of rites, some even did not wear funeral costumes at their parents' death. Master Zhu educated them with rites and regulations of past and present. He then compiled and made known the ancient ceremonies concerning funerals and weddings, so that the local elders could train the youngsters. At that time, Buddhism was popular in the South. Local people, men and women, gathered at monks' residence to study Buddhist sutras. Unmarried girls even lived in the privately-built nunneries. Zhu Xi Banned all these and greatly transformed the custom. He would now and then go to the schools to lecture the students himself, just as when he was in Nankang. And people flocked to his prefecture residence for instructions. He also chose scholars with good behavior and moral integrity to be school teachers who could then serve as guides for students. In the school there used to be a temple in memory of Mr Gao Deng, who offended Qin Hui the vicious prime minister and was demoted to Rongzhou and died there. After writing a special article for the temple, Zhu Xi went on to apply and request a commendation from the emperor and was sanctioned. (*Complete Works*, Book 27. p.75)

At the age of sixty-five, Zhu Xi was dispatched to be the prefect in Tanzhou, Hunan. Hunan had a good tradition of education. "The scholars of Changsha loved learning. When Zhu Xi arrived, many students traveled hundreds of miles from different parts of Hunan to gather at Changsha for the lectures of Zhu Xi, who taught tirelessly, until there were no seats left inside the lecture and people had to sit outside. The audience often burst into applause of joy." Similarly, Zhu Xi spared no efforts in rebuilding the Yuelu Academy. According to the *Chronicle:*

> The Academy was originally designed by former Prime Minister

Liu Gong and Master Zhang Shi but had long been abandoned. He selected some honest people to repair and renovate it. He prepared a few extra quota for the students who had not passed the examinations, providing them food and accommodation just like the formal students at official schools. Later he found an open terrain and built a new campus.

In the daytime Zhu Xi was busy at dealing with the prefecture's routine affairs. In the evening he discussed with the students and was never tired of answering their questions. He often warned them to be practical — to start from things around themselves, and not to reach for what were beyond their control. His sincerity and eagerness greatly moved the audience. (*Complete Works*, Book 27. p.83)

Zhu Xi's practice of laying emphasis on education at whatever post he was assigned to did have an effect of changing local customs and habits, and greatly popularized the Confucian culture and ideas. At the same time, people around him were also educated and their work efficiency was improved.

Laying emphasis on education is only one of the characteristic in Zhu Xi's official career. He also displayed strong capability in solving practical problems. His economic idea of "sympathizing with the people" was brought into full play whenever he was assigned a post. In Nankang for example, the first document he issued when arriving at the post was *Proclamation of the New Prefect* in which he proclaimed his policy of management: "Popularize the culture and be considerate of the people". The first article of the *Proclamation* was:

This prefecture, with its barren land and scarce inhabitancy, has been suffering from numerous obligatory services and heavy taxes. The previous officials did try their best to lessen the burden of the people, but due to the requirement from the state government and the army they could do nothing but fulfill the immediate tasks set on them, leaving no room to solve the problem. That's why the people are getting poorer and poorer with each passing day, and some even are thinking of leaving their homeland. How miserable they are! I, being the prefect, can no longer see this happen again. Here I proclaim: if anyone under my governance, be he scholar or elder or Buddhist monk or Daoist priest or soldier, has any idea about the causes of the situation and knows the way to get rid of it, please write a detailed report and come to my office at the prefecture, whether in the morning or in the evening. I am eager to talk to him face to face, consider his proposals, and do my best to put them into practice, so that the number of households of the prefecture will rise and people and families here will become rich, to the satisfaction of His Majesty who shows great concern for his subjects. (*Complete Works*, Book 25. pp.4579–4580)

The above paragraph revealed Zhu Xi's open and broad-minded attitude towards the practical problems of Nankang. He was willing to find the causes by making investigations and sincerely hoped to solve them. In his *Notice to the Emigrants* we find a suitable case of how he thought and did to solve the economic difficulty in Nankang. He wrote:

When in service, former Prefect Zhao made an investigation and learned that the poor peasants in the three counties of this prefecture used to abandon their homes and ancestral tombs for other places in the event of poor harvests, which was indeed not their true intention. But hardly had the peasants left the border when the requests by local despots for the renting of the vacant lands they had left behind appeared on the county magistrate's desk. Many frauds could be found in these cases: some were applications without household documents, some were applications under false names, some pretended to have escaped for years to ask for exemptions, some presented household documents but could not find equivalents in the government, some, with exemption due, were applying under other names, some grabbed other people's lands but nobody dared to stop them, etc. And the responsible persons helped them to shield each other, thus the examination of taxes and rents reached no result. When the peasants presented complaints and asked for the return of their lands, they would meet numerable obstacles, either stopped by local officials or evicted by despots. Failing to manifest themselves, they had to quit and leave again. How pitiful they were! I have already spread notice to the subordinate counties. Considering that it may have been hidden or forgotten, I am sending it again. This notice is printed and circulated to the emigrant peasants. You can bring your applications or complaints to the prefecture office. Let it be known that all cases will be carefully examined and processed. (*Complete Works*, Book 25. p.4591)

On arriving at his post, Zhu Xi found that with the poor people being forced to leave their homes, local despots seized the opportunity to grab their lands and the local governments were unable to collect the taxes. He showed great pity and concern for the poor and was indignant with the rich. He on the one hand took some immediate measures to soothe the people, and on the other hand issued notice to encourage the peasants to return to their farm work. He even introduced to them certain farm techniques to improve the quality and efficiency of the agriculture. In his paper *An Encouragement to Agriculture* he wrote in great detail the whole process of farming, from the preparation of the paddy fields to their management, from the plantation of dry-land crops to the plantation of mulberries and hemp, in an attempt to ensure good harvests and farmers' improved living conditions. Thus, "the older generation may teach the younger ones to settle themselves on the proper work of farming to support their parents, free from such misbehaviors such as loafing, gambling, or drinking that hampered the proper work, and with the life improved, rites and righteousness were promoted." In Volume 16 of *Selected Works* we find many reports Zhu Xi made to the imperial court for tax exemption and disaster relief, e.g., *Second Report on Exemption of Taxes from the Xingzi County, Drought and its Result in Nankang Prefecture, Application for the Exemption of Taxes and the Allocation of Money and Rice from*

Army Provisions to the Relief of Disasters, More on the Drought and its Result in Nankang Prefecture, and *Application for the Detainment of Rice as Army Provision to the Relief of Poor People.* Huang Gan summed up what Zhu Xi had done in Nankang prefecture quite to the point in his *Anecdotes of Master Zhu*:

He cared for the difficulties of the people as if he himself suffered from the difficulties and was always ready to do things he thought favorable to them. Xingzi, one of his subordinate counties, was frequently suffering from bad harvest while it still had to pay heavy taxes. Master Zhu requested for its tax exemption or reduction by presenting as many as five or six reports. In case of a drought, he would study and discuss measures against natural disasters. His report to the court would always be done into the minute detail. When collecting offerings to the government, he would attend to it personally to decide whether they should be exempted or reduced. Relating the collection of taxes of rice shoots in autumn, harvest in summer, charcoals in winter, monthly storage, and *jingzhi* or *zongzhi* tolls, he would deal with them separately and make due reports several times until they were accepted. He would even apply to the provincial transport and storage & balance bureaus for retaining the army rations as a preparation for relief of starvation. He reiterated the prohibition of cutting the ways to ports or trades to neighboring provinces. When assigning officials, he would teach them how to estimate the severity of poor years, the number of households, the true storage of the warehouses, and the situation of trades of the relative places with practical methods, so that measures could be taken to help save the people. (*Complete Works*, Book 27. p.538)

Due to his successful policies in Nankang in the disastrous years, numerous people survived from starvation. This achievement led to his assignment to Director of Provincial Bureau of Storage & Balance in East Liangzhe Province in charge of tea and salt affairs during the great starvation in the east Zhejiang area. He "started right away" the day he

61

received appointment. At the post, he "formulated policies for disastrous years and readjusted official system", exposed several times the corrupt officials and cracked down on their criminal activities. He made several reports to the imperial court for certain exemptions of salt and wine taxes and obligatory services, and at the same time resumed and developed the production. The *Biography of Zhu Xi* in *The History of the Song Dynasty* highly praised his achievement in dealing with the natural disasters in the east Zhejiang area, and recorded the comment from the emperor as follows:

> As soon as he was appointed, he wrote letters to other prefectures for sending rice merchants to Zhejiang and agreed to exempt them from the taxes. So when he arrived, many rice boats were already crowding at the wharfs. He sought to know the hidden facts of the people's life. He made journeys around his prefecture always in a single cart without an entourage and arrived without people's knowledge. Fearing his righteousness, some officials of the prefecture and counties even chose to retire from posts. Whatever policies relating tolls, fare purchase, labor service, or wine sale monopoly, so long as they were unfavorable to the people, he would make some rectifications or even abolish them. In the course of relieving the disaster, he would at the same time plan for long and sustainable policies to develop the economy. On learning that certain people criticized Zhu Xi for being short of political capacity, His Majesty told Wang Huai[1], "I was quite impressed by what Zhu Xi had done." (*Complete Works*, Book 27. p.519)

As an official, Zhu Xi was not only a practitioner, but also a thinker with a broad mind and political foresight. In many of his reports or memorials to the emperors, he talked about the management of the whole country, thereby manifesting his understanding of how to run a country. In

---

[1] Wang Huai (1126–1189), courtesy name Jihai, was Prime Minister of that time.

1188 he presented a report to Emperor Xiaozong, suggesting six measures to rectify the malpractice of that time:

In my humble view, the world now is like a man with heavy sickness, ill from heart and stomach inside and four limbs outside to all the hair on the surface. Although he could still eat and drink as usual, the seriousness of his sickness has already frightened away many experienced doctors. Only such top-class doctors such as Bianque or Hua Tuo with their magic medicine to cleanse his stomach and wipe out the root cause of his illness may finally make him safe. Otherwise, with the sickness getting heavier without the patient's knowledge, it will be too dangerous for ordinary doctors to treat. That's why my previous reports always cited the saying that if the medicine is not strong enough the illness will not be cured. However, I have still more to say. There are too many things in the world worthy of discussion, but I have no time to talk about them all but will come straight to the most fundamental in the world and the most urgent affairs facing us today. What is most fundamental in the world is Your Majesty's mind. And the most urgent affairs facing us today are the following six things: (1) assistance for the crown prince; (2) selection and appointment of main ministers; (3) upholding fundamental moral principles; (4) changing the social customs and habits; (5) cherishing and fostering people's productive forces; and (6) rectification of military and political management. I will talk about these in detail and hope to have Your Majesty's attention.

Thus, Zhu Xi earned more understanding and appreciation from Emperor Xiaozong and became even more famous. In the following year, Emperor Xiaozong abdicated and handed the throne to Emperor Guangzong. Zhu Xi wrote a report to the new emperor, presenting an all-round illustration of his political ideas and administrative policies:

To study Confucian classics to upright the mind, to encourage the cultivation of self to regulate the family, to keep lackeys far away to make room for upright persons, to restrain private favors to uphold justice, to promote correct principles to repudiate sinister or supernatural ideas, to choose good masters to assist the crown prince, to select and appoint right persons to establish a good official system, to uphold moral principles to improve the folk customs, to practice frugality to lay a solid foundation for the country's economy, and to make a better governance for resistance against foreign aggression: the above ten items are all worthy of Your Majesty's attention, not a single one of which should be neglected. (*Complete Works*, Book 20. p.618)

Zhu Xi went into detailed explanations for all the above ten points. (1) To study Confucian classics to upright the mind. Zhu Xi regarded the mind of the emperor as the most fundamental thing in running a state. When that is ensured, everything can be done. (2) To encourage the cultivation of self so as to regulate the family. That shows the importance of self-cultivation and family regulation in governing a country. (3) To keep lackeys far away to make room for upright persons. That is a suggestion for the emperor to associate with the right persons. (4) To restrain private favors to uphold justice. That is a suggestion for correct appointment of posts. (5) To promote correct principles to repudiate sinister or supernatural ideas. That is to make policy out of correct principles instead of vicious or supernatural deception. (6) To choose good masters to assist the crown prince. That tells the importance of early education to the crown prince, the future emperor. (7) To select and appoint right persons to establish a good official system. That is about the importance of selecting suitable ministers to help run the country. (8) To uphold moral principles to improve the folk customs. That is to encourage good behaviors to establish the good customs among the people. (9) To practice frugality to lay a solid foundation for the country's economy. That is to keep balance of the economy and develop production. (10) To make a better governance for resistance against foreign aggression. That is to emphasize that internal affairs are the basis for a successful and effective foreign policy. Anyway, to recover the lost lands is always in the mind of every monarch in the Southern Song dynasty.

In general, Zhu Xi was earnest in his official career, and his political ideas are the true manifestation of a Principlist of his time. This earnest, sincere, and practical attitude, however, decided that there would be no smooth path for him in his official career, but full of twists and turns.

3.   A Diligent Pursuer of Learning

Zhu Xi was a diligent learner throughout his life, which provides us an understanding to further study his personality. By reading through his *Complete Works*, we realize how he was pursuing the truth through learning, and at the same time learn something about his character. First, he had a clear aim in learning by setting a target to be a sage at a very young age. Secondly, he was diligent and always concentrated himself on learning. Thirdly, he paid much attention on the method of study, emphasizing that the ultimate aim of learning was self-improvement in morality. And fourthly, he strove hard for academic innovation and all-round development.

Zhu Xi set up his mind to be a sage at a very young age and knew its realization depended on tireless study. So when he was told about —

> Lu Jiuyuan's view that by "restraining oneself to return to the rites" one not only needs to restrain his selfish desires but also to restrain his ambition to be a sage, Zhu at once retorted: "Such words are just like children playing games with lofty standards. The true Confucians can never agree with it. To set one's mind to be a sage is a very good idea. If this is to be denied, then Sages Yao and Shun's 'being wary and fearful', Duke Zhou's 'thinking of the three ancient kings', Kong Zi's 'being fond of antiquity and earnestly seeking it', Master Yan Hui's 'anyone working hard can be like him (i.e. Sage Shun)', and Meng Zi's 'wish to take Kong Zi as my example' should all be denied."
> (*Classified Analects*, Book 7, p.2619)

With the ambition to be a sage, one must work very hard. So Zhu Xi studied very diligently. Lu's words about restraining the ambition to be a sage invoked his refutation with many citations from ancient masters, which proved that he was keen on his ambition at all times, a pursuit from his childhood.

Zhu Xi knew very clearly from his childhood that to realize his ambition to be a sage he could rely on nothing but his own efforts. That explains why he studied so diligently all his life. In his last years, he summed up the hardship he had experienced in study:

"I would advise you to set aside other business and concentrate yourselves on study. I began to study in my twenties and believed that I might know much in the end. Now so many years have passed and I suddenly find that I am thus old. Yet what I have gained is so little. That time flies so quickly is really dreadful."

He then continued to talk about the difficulty in study. "You might think that these books are too simple and easy to be studied. However, I used to spend much effort on them. It was just like crossing a narrow bridge when a misstep was fatal. My brain effort failed me after the age of fifty. Often the Principle was merely a hair's breadth, yet I could not reach it. That's why all my study on classics like *The Great Learning, The Doctrine of the Mean, The Confucian Analects* and *The Mencius* was finished before I was fifty: after that age not much improvement could be made. But today there are so many people who are so careless in their study. Even in literary writing our forerunners did spend a lot of effort. Should these efforts be transferred to truth-seeking, what great achievements they would have made! Just look at Han Yu's *A Reply to Li Yi* and Su Xun's *A Letter to His Excellency Ouyang Xiu* — how hard they worked! Those masters never did their work in a casual way. Ouyang Xiu was always polishing his essays until complete satisfaction. Su Xun did not set out to write until everything was considered over and over again in his brain.

What a pity they spent so many efforts in writing! What outstanding achievements they would make if they transferred their efforts to study Principlism! It seems that the ancient masters tend to do the dullest work with the cleverest talent while people today were trying to do the cleverest thing with their dullest minds. So they can never catch up with the ancients. Kong Zi said that 'Zeng Shen was always slow'. We should do things in this way." (*Classified Analects,* Book 7, p.2621)

Zhu Xi understood that hard work must be combined with ceaseless perseverance. In his later years he still worked strenuously though suffering from poor health and illness. He thought,

"Man's bloody energy may be strong or weak, but not his will. If he always keeps a strong will, nothing can stop him even when his bloody energy is getting weak. Take myself for example. Old and weak as I am, I know very well that to get up a little later in the morning will help me in keeping good health. But then my heart would not agree. Every morning at three o'clock or so I would wake up and could not fall asleep again. From this I concluded that a man with will would not be influenced by his bloody energy, and he who was moved by bloody energy was merely self-deceiving."

Master Zhu, suffering from backache, beriberi and diarrhea, was advised to get up later in the morning. He replied, "I could not get up late by nature. I have to get up in the morning the minute I notice a glimpse of light, and start to consider reading. It makes me uneasy if I get up a little late and feel guilty for being poisoned by laziness. Only getting up early can give me the sense of invigoration." (*Classified Analects,* Book 7, p.2623)

Zhu Xi was a true and diligent scholar till his old age. When someone advised him to write less, he replied, "It was unreasonable for a man to idle away his time after he had eaten his food." Fang Shiyao suggested that he could write more outlines instead, but he refused, saying, "Outlines are not enough because any small mistake could cause a great error." (*Ibid.* p.2623)

Zhu Xi often told his pupils and disciples about his study method and writing experience. Once he said, "When I make any change of words in the classics, I never did it without reasons. You must think hard to understand why I did so." "When I made comments on the classics, I weighed every word I used." (*Ibid.* p.2626) Such an attitude of his gives us a hint to analyze what seems contradictory in his writings; namely, we must not take those words and explanations that are different from others as ignorance or careless mistakes, but try our best to seek a reasonable explanation. Just as Fu Cheng said, "Neither Zhang Zai nor the Cheng brothers made their meanings very clear in their writings. It was not until Master Zhu that everything became clear." Zhu Xi said:

> They were all talents with a quick mind, so they could talk in a free way. Yet when I made my notes, I had to study the original meaning first. When a sage said something, even his immediate follower, be he another sage, might not understand him completely, as his words were related to a special time or event which the late comer did not have the chance to know about. Thus his explanation might not be the same as what the first sage meant. For example, Cheng Yi's explanation of the classics was based on his understanding at his time, which did not have to be the same with the original meaning of the classic, though the explanation itself might be a very good one. Take *yuan-heng-li-zhen* 元亨利贞 in the *Book of Change* for example. Originally it just meant that "great" (*yuan*) "success" (*heng*) was "favorable" (*li*) for "correctness" (*zhen*). A "success" which could not lead to "correctness" is of no use. These words written by King Wen of Zhou were just for the use of divination, so there was only "great success" and "favorable for correctness", not vise versa. Later Kong Zi explained the four characters as four virtues, first in his *Tuanci* 彖辞, then in his *Wenyan* 文言, and since then everyone understood *yuan-heng-li-zhen* as "four virtues" and no one cared about "great

success being favorable for correctness". *The Book of Change* was fundamentally a book about divination as *The Zhou Book of Rites* clearly pointed out that the divination officer was in charge of three books of changes: *Lianshan* or *The Xia Book of Change*, *Guizang* or *The Shang Book of Change*, and *Zhouyi* or *The Zhou Book of Change*. In ancient dynasties, posts were set at the court to be in charge of divination task and several persons had been appointed. Qin dynasty was not far from the ancient time and when the First Emperor burnt political books, the *Book of Change* was retained as it was only a book of divination. Nowadays the idea of *The Book of Change* being a book of divination would be regarded as disgracing the book, and it can only be a book of philosophy as Kong Zi brought forth many philosophical conclusions from the book. People did not know that behind *ji*吉 (fortune), *xiong*凶 (evil), *hui* 悔 (repentance) *and lin*吝 (regret) in the book there did exist some reasons and lecturing content. Kong Zi's explanation of them as four virtues did have some good intent but frankly it did not go with King Wen's original idea. If you now say to a diviner that "*yuan* is chief of goodness, *heng* is gathering of excellence, *li* is harmony of righteousness, and *zhen* is the stem of events", he would only be puzzled. To sum up, King Wen meant what he meant, which did not hinder Kong Zi's understanding, whereas Kong Zi, though not criticizing King Wen, did not understand him, and his explanation only meant what he intended to mean. (*Classified Analects*, Book 7, pp.2625–26)

This is a good proof that Zhu Xi had already established a concept of historical context, not only in understanding his predecessors' works, but also in his own works of annotation. The understanding of *The Zhou Book of Change* at various times is a most typical example. To a certain extent, Zhu had already had a sense of hermeneutics, and like King Wen, Kong Zi and Cheng Yi, he would boldly bring forward his own understanding in explaining the classical texts, though he did not announce it too openly due to this or that reason. As a matter of fact, his explanations of *Three Books* *by Zhou Dunyi and Zhang Zai*① were not brought to public until rather late. Such a hard-working scholar eight hundred years ago is a high-level, earnest researcher even by today's standard. This also reminds us of the debate between him and Lu Jiuyuan brothers on the relation between The Ultimate of Nothingness and The Ultimate of Extremity, at which Zhu Xi was so persistent in his viewpoints. Though some of his defense sounded irrational from a general reader's stand, his viewpoints were reasonable if you looked from his angle and explained in his way. Zhu Xi's diligence and concentration in study won praise from Li Tong, his teacher, who commented:

> This student always concentrates himself on study, caring for nothing else in life. At beginning he used to be restrained in other people's sayings, but now he began to have a broader mind and spend more efforts on daily usage. If he keeps on he will reach a state of combining theory and practice. (*Complete Works*, Book 27. pp.24–25)

Reading through his *Complete Books,* we can feel that Zhu Xi had always kept an earnest and persistent spirit in his work and study until his death. Whatever classic books he read, he would bring forth some fresh ideas that are different from his predecessors and contemporaries. That also explains why Zhu's viewpoints attract the scholars after him.

There were many Principlists in the Song Dynasty, but few could be like Zhu Xi who was so keen on study methods and could pass them to others. To study with a clear aim and initiative is one thing, and to know how to study well with more efficiency is another thing. Thus, starting from the Principlist's stand that the Principle lies in everyone himself, Zhu Xi held that the aim of study is to help one to find it — that is also what is meant in *The Great Learning*'s "to illuminate illuminating virtues". So he said, "The so-called learning can only be attained through oneself whereas

---

① The three books are *The Extreme Ultimate Diagram* and *The Book of Thorough Understsnding* written by Zhou Dunyi, and *The Western Inscription* by Zhang Zai.

reading is of secondary importance. All Principles lie in Man himself and are not added from outside." If this is accepted and all one needs to do is self-examination and self-inspiration, then why should we read books, especially books written by sages? Zhu Xi replied: "Although the Principles lie in ourselves, they could only be attained when combined with personal experience, just as what the sages taught us. What the sages taught us was what they had experienced themselves." That is to say, though Principles lie in everyone's mind, the books written by sages with their own life experience can help the people to master them. Zhu Xi emphasized that it was not the only way for a man to acquire knowledge while growing up, for one has to master the Principles of the world and of the world affairs even when there were no sages, saying, "Learning is something that has to be mastered by everyone no matter he is wise or foolish, young or old, rich or poor. Don't they have to learn if there were no sages, nor books, nor their thoughts? They still have to!" However, since there did exist so many books written by sages, it provided opportunities for people to study by themselves, as well as for their teachers and friends to help them, as Zhu Xi put it: "Now there are sages' sayings and writings, so why don't we study them? Teachers and friends can only offer their discoveries. But if we do not work hard ourselves, how can they help us?" Therefore, before reading, one should know the "Principles":

> Reading is of secondary importance. Principles of human life are already complete in everyone. The reason why one should read lies in his lack of experience. The sages had rich experience, which they recorded in their books. To read is to find their experience and the Principles they drew from it. When you thoroughly understand it, you'll find that all these Principles are actually your own, not imposed on you from outside. (*Classified Analects,* Book 1, p.161)

Taking it as a universal truth, Zhu Xi insisted that for reading, the first and foremost is to read the sages' books, as sages were men among men and by reading their books one would receive a boost in one's overall quality. "The books of the sages must be read, recited and pondered upon constantly," so that the reader may "know the sages' thoughts, and from those find the Principles of the nature." The aim of reading sages' books is to raise one's ability of understanding the world with the help of the words:

> The most critical point in reading is to know how the sages taught people to behave as a man. It is like curing a disease with medicine: one must know how the disease starts and what prescription to take. And with the prescription, one must know which herbs to be used, what dose each ingredient is to be allotted, how the medicine is processed, prepared and administered, etc.
>
> The way of study has been fully discussed in the sages' teachings. Generally speaking, a learner must be critical in reading. Learning and studying is a great event, as it teaches men to be men. When reading, one must read again and again, to understand each paragraph and each sinogram, with the reference of other people's notes, comments and explanations, and finally match the Principles with what exists in one's own mind. After all, reading must be matched with one's own understanding. Du Yu[1] said: "Take it leisurely, and let them read it by themselves; enrich the content, and let them seek satisfaction themselves; and like the overflowing of waters or moistening of rains, the annotations will explain the difficult points and help them to grasp the principles underlining the texts. Then everyone will get what they want." (*Classified Analects,* Book 1, p.162)

Thus, to study classics is to learn from the sages, and through them to know the world, and more importantly, to know oneself as well as others. One must think with his own mind what to learn, how to do learning and how to do true learning. Zhu Xi had his own idea in this respect together

---

[1] Du Yu (222–285), courtesy name Yuankai, was a famous historian of the the Jin Dynasty, specially well known for for his annotations to *Zuo's Narration of the Spring and Autumn Annals.*

with his own method. For him, reading intensively is more effective than reading extensively:

> Reading broadly and extensively is not as good as reading intensively and thinking carefully. (*Classified Analects,* Book 1, p.168)
>
> To read is to investigate. One must read very carefully, paragraph by paragraph, over and over again. Spend one day or two just on one paragraph until complete mastery. Then move on to a second paragraph. By and by, you will find that all the principles are clear. One must ponder on the text at any time, whether sitting or walking, or return to what is already understood, which might lead to new discoveries. Either the structure or the content, once you spend time on it, each time you will get a fresh finding. Sometimes after reading you will change your idea, and another time you will be more confirmed of your original idea. That's why I say reading extensively is not as important as reading intensively. But anyway one must strive forward and never turn back.
>
> Books must be read intensively. Intensiveness leads to more familiarity, which will naturally lead to more understanding. It is like eating a fruit. One cannot eat a fruit with just one bite. Only after chewing and chewing can one taste the fruit, whether it's sweet or bitter or sour or hot. (*Classified Analects,* Book 1, p.167)

Of course reading intensively does not mean reading less. It's just like Francis Bacon's words about certain books "to be chewed and digested". "Intensive reading" is applied to the few important classics. Based on these books and a good habit of reading, one can read more widely. And as we know, Zhu Xi himself was a man of wide interest and broad reading, and he was amazingly knowledgeable.

Zhu Xi's emphasis on reading and reading methods is closely related with his Principlist ideology. For him, learning and mind-training is one thing:

Fundamentally, to learn is to imbue something to the mind to be expressed through body.

By incessant reading, a man can control his mind and keep it in place. Master Zhang Zai said: "Reading is what is used to maintain the mind. Once relaxed, the morals will be out of control. So how can one do without it?" (*Classified Analects,* Book 1, p.176)

The most important goal of reading is not the acquisition of knowledge, but moral accomplishment. Thus:

Reading requires whole-hearted concentration of both mind and body without considering any outside affairs. Then some principles may be acquired. "To learn widely and be steadfast in your aspiration, inquire earnestly and reflect on what is at hand," so why then "benevolence lies in it"? That's because if one keeps his mind in reading and does not go astray, then Principles will surely stay there. Now many people read with their minds wandering elsewhere. That's but a waste of time. I would advise them to lay aside their books until they can focus their minds. (*Classified Analects,* Book 1, pp.177–178)

In addition to keeping a good habit of reading, one must also examine how the sages and other scholars read and draw experience from them for his own improvement.

All in all, reading is for one's own sake. One's own affairs can only be coped with by oneself. Yin Tun wished to read his teacher Cheng Yi's *Recorded Sayings,* and Cheng Yi said: "I am here. Why read this?" When asked about this, Zhu Xi commented:

When Master Cheng was there, it might be unnecessary to read his *Sayings*; but if he is not there, how could his disciples stop reading that? Only the *Sayings* were compiled by his students, who had different understandings of the teacher's words to be discerned by the reader himself. Some older scholars said that it was sufficient to read *Survey to the Book of Change* and similar classics, and there was no need to read Cheng Yi's *Sayings* or other books. That viewpoint could not stand. If that is true, then it will be sufficient for people to read *Six Classics* only, and there was no need to read *The Confucian Analects* or *The Mencius*. All things under Heaven, be it high or low, great or small, if you study them in close relation to yourself, every gain is yours; if no efforts are paid, then any choice of the books will prove to be of no use. (*Classified Analects,* Book 7, p.2479)

Zhu Xi was an ambitious, diligent and earnest scholar who had a grand plan for his study, which was basically fulfilled in his life. It is because of his diligence in reading, down-to-earth attitude towards writing, and his aspiration to be a sage, that he could successfully make progress on his road of academics and finally became a great Principlist in history.

Chapter Three

Subjective Characteristics of Zhu Xi's Philosophy

Master Zhu Xi's *Three Books* of *An Explanation to the Extreme Ultimate Diagram, An Explanation to the Book of Thorough Understanding* and *An Explanation to the Western Inscription*, his cognitive mechanism of governance of Mind over Nature and Emotion, and his *Textual Analysis and Collected Annotations of the Four Books* jointly constitute the main content of his Principlist hermeneutics, which may be explained with adequate thoroughness in three perspectives: the combination of Principle and Material Force, the governance of Mind over Nature and Emotion, and knowing/doing and sincerity/reverence.

1. The Combination of Principle and Material Force

Zhu Xi laid special emphasis on Zhou Dunyi's *Extreme Ultimate Diagram* and *Book of Thorough Understanding*, and Zhang Zai's *Western Inscription*, and used his personal interpretation of the three books as the ontology of his own philosophical system. This conclusion is made from the fact that there is certain difference and distance between his explanations and the three original books, as if they were only used to illustrate his own ideas. This kind of interpretation of classics brought him not only disapproval from scholars of his time, but also criticism and censure from later scholars. However, Zhu insisted on his own practice and made self-defense. In the Southern Song dynasty, Zhu Xi's interpretation of the three books, *An Explanation to the Extreme Ultimate Diagram, An*

Explanation to the Book of Thorough Understanding and *An Explanation to the Western Inscription*, were already published and jointly known as *Master Zhu's Three Books*. In the Ming and Qing Dynasties *Master Zhu's Three Books* was successively printed. It may well be said that these three books made a foundation of Zhu Xi's Principlist philosophy. Here we will sketch Zhu's philosophical ontology of the combination of Principle and Material Force through a textual analysis of *An Explanation to the Extreme Ultimate Diagram* as well as the other two books.

The Extreme Ultimate Diagram written by Zhou Dunyi was regarded as "an illustration of the origin of the Heavenly Principle and an exploration into the beginning and end of things". *(History of the Song Dynasty*, Vol. 427. p.9273) Zhu Xi agreed with that viewpoint and further claimed that the 40-chapter *Book of Thorough Understanding* was originally entitled *Thorough Understanding of the Book of Change* and published together with *The Extreme Ultimate Diagram,* and the two books were made known to the world by the Cheng brothers at the same time. "The two books complemented each other to explain the separation and integration on one Principle, two Material Forces and Five Phases, to record the delicacy of Dao as an entity, and to decide the choice of justice, words or profits, so as to raise the general level of ordinary studies. They gave cordial and concrete words when talking about methods to become moral and means to deal with the mundane. Their grand outline and great function had surpassed the Confucians since the Qin and the Han Dynasties, and the refinement of their arrangement and the profoundness of their meaning were not to be easily caught up by contemporary scholars." In his *Postscript to the Book of Thorough Understanding,* Zhu Xi said: "The most marvelous part of Mr Zhou's learning to be known can all be readily found in his *Extreme Ultimate Diagram*, and the *Thorough Understanding* is but a further illustration of it." *(Complete Works,* Book 13, p.130) Zhang Zai's *Western Inscription* is a book of great importance in the history of the Song Dynasty Principlism. It was praised by the Cheng brothers as having said something never mentioned by previous sages or other scholars since Meng Zi. By making an interpretation of the book, Zhu Xi developed its meaning, laying emphasis on the Principlist theory of "one Principle, multiple manifestations" and "Heaven and Man being one". In this way, Zhu Xi integrated his annotations and interpretations of the three books to a single entity as the foundation of his own philosophical thought.

There are only 249 Chinese characters in Zhou Dunyi's *Extreme Ultimate Diagram,* which is actually a mixture of Daoist priests' alchemy diagram with the *Appendices to the Book of Change,* woven into a cosmological system composed of Heaven, Earth and Man. If we read it carefully and compare it with Zhu Xi's explanations, we will find that Zhu has practically made certain revisions to Zhou's view in his overall explanation. That is to say, Zhu Xi was actually using Zhou's book as a means to establish his own cosmology and ontology. His *Explanation* is in reality a deviated version of the original book. Let's examine it more closely:

First, in explaining the very first sentence in Zhou's book that "the Ultimate of Nothingness is at the same time the Ultimate of Extremity", Zhu Xi said,

> What the great Heaven embraces, free from sound and smell, is the pivot of universe and the foundation of things of all varieties. That's why it is said that the Ultimate of Nothingness is at the same the Ultimate of Extremity. It does not mean that there is another Ultimate of Nothingness outside the Ultimate of Extremity.

Obviously, Zhou's original text didn't make it ambiguous that the "Ultimate of Nothingness" was the foundation of the universe. But Zhu Xi's explanation created a difference between the monist view of "the Ultimate of Nothingness being at the same time the Ultimate of Extremity" and the dualist view of "from the Ultimate of Nothingness to the Ultimate of Extremity". Now this difference is in essence the difference between the Confucian monism and the Daoist dualism, which is of great importance in Chinese philosophy. Zhu Xi's explanation is on the side of monism, which at once aroused heated debates. Lu Jiuyuan, for instance, argued with Zhu Xi and held that Zhou Duyi's *Extreme Ultimate*

Diagram was from Daoism. If we compare this saying with Lao Zi's words, we may indeed find that it is very similar to Lao Zi's basic terminology of Existence and Non-existence. Yet Zhu Xi here insisted on the monist stand and directly excluded the possibility of dualism. It must have some relation with his intention to establish his own ontology of Principlism or the fact that he had already a Principlist ontological understanding in his mind. In establishing the Confucian Principlist ontology, there would be no room for the typical Daoist ideology. From his entire explanation of the *Diagram*, Zhu Xi seemed to have found a suitable traditional philosophical basis for the establishment of his own Principlist ontology. By just making a few revisions, explanations and extensions, he might happily attain his goal. And so he actually did. Such a practice of his is very similar to Kong Zi's practice of composing *Appendices to the Book of Change* by explaining and extending the thoughts in the *Zhou Book of Change*. Through his explanation, Zhu Xi seemed to have removed the traces of Daoism and made the *Extreme Ultimate Diagram* an ideal and complete discourse of Principlist ontology. In his reply to Lu Jiuyuan's letter Zhu Xi insisted on the Confucian stand in *Appendices to the Book of Change* and further expounded his monist view regarding the Extreme Ultimate. This may be considered his most important expression in establishing the Principlist ontology:

> In *The Survey* of *The Zhou Book of Change*, we found that "The metaphysical realm is called the Way", and also that "The alternation between Yin and Yang is called the Way". Does it mean that Yin and Yang belong to the metaphysical realm? No. It actually tells us that although Yin and Yang belong to form or vessel, the alternation of them is the function of the Way. So when we talk about the Ultimate of the Way, we call it Ultimate of Extremity; when we talk about the motion of the Ultimate, we call it the "Way". It is one thing with two names. When Master Zhou called it Ultimate of Nothingness, he was emphasizing that Ultimate has no form or dimensions. If anyone suspects why it exists before things appear and also after

things appear, stands outside Yin and Yang and also moves inside Yin and Yang, permeates in everything and everywhere and yet has no sound or smell or any affection, he is confusing himself with the differentiation of vessel and the Way. Somebody even said that "beyond the metaphysical realm there is the Ultimate of Extremity", implying there is something beyond the Way. That is utterly wrong.

As quoted above, Zhu Xi insisted not only on his statement that the metaphysical realm was the Way, but also that what was said in the *Survey* about the metaphysical realm being the Way and the alteration between Yin and Yang being the Way were the same with Zhou Dunyi's statement at the beginning of his *Extreme Ultimate Diagram*. Obviously, this explanation lowered the philosophical level of the statement of "The alteration between Yin and Yang is the Way", as Yin and Yang were only regarded as the vessel or the movement of Ultimate. From the historical point to judge the development of Principlism, the task of getting rid of the influence of Daoism and Buddhism was not fulfilled by Zhou Dunyi and the Cheng brothers. It was not until Zhu Xi that his *An Explanation to the Extreme Ultimate Diagram* made an important step forward towards the clear statement of Principlist ontology. That is why he insisted so stubbornly on his view. In Zhu Xi's later statement, the Ultimate of Extremity was the Principle itself. He said, "The Extreme Ultimate is the ultimate Principle of Heaven, Earth, and myriad of things. In Heaven and Earth there is the Extreme Ultimate. So is in the myriad of things. However, the Principle exists before Heaven and Earth. That movement generates Yang is the Principle, and that Tranquility generates Yin is also the Principle." He used Principle to replace the concept of Extreme Ultimate and considered movements, tranquility, Yin and Yang to be one with Principle, which brought abstractness and uniformity to the expression of his ideas.

Secondly, he did not align himself with Zhou Dunyi when he explained the latter's generation of the universe: "The movement of the Extreme Ultimate generates the Yang. When the movement goes to extreme, it becomes tranquil. Tranquility generates the Yin. When tranquility goes to extreme, it begins to move again. Thus movement and tranquility alternate and are the roots of each other, respectively generating Yin and Yang, and the Two Modes are thus established." About this Zhu Xi said:

That the Ultimate has both Yin and Yang aspects is the result of the movement of the Heavenly destiny, as seen in that "The alternation of Yin and Yang is the Way". Sincerity is the foundation of the sages, the beginning and end of all things, and also the Way of destiny. The movement of destiny means the penetration of sincerity. To be followed by goodness means that all things thus begin to appear. The tranquility of the destiny means the return of sincerity. To be completed by Nature means that everything adjusts its own Nature and destiny. "Extreme movement leads to tranquility", "extreme tranquility returns to movement", "alternation of movement and tranquility are roots for each other" — all these are explanation of the movement of the destiny. "Movement generates the Yang", "tranquility generates the Yin", "by different generation of Yin and Yang, the Two Modes are established" — these are explanation of the ever-flowing of the destiny. The Ultimate of Extremity is the original state of immensity, whereas the movement and tranquility are the opportunity it takes. The Ultimate is the Way at the metaphysical realm, whereas Yin and Yang are vessels at the physical realm. Thus, judging from what is obvious, movement and tranquility do not happen at the same time, and Yin and Yang do not occupy the same place, yet the great Ultimate exists wherever and whenever. And judging from what is subtle, empty and tranquil without signs though it seems, the Principle of movement or tranquility, Yin or Yang, permeates all the time. Even so, looking back, we cannot see their combination at the beginning; looking forward, we cannot see their departure in the end. That's why Master Cheng said, "Movement and tranquility know no beginning, and Yin and Yang know no starting." If not a man of Dao, how can he utter these words?

At the very beginning of the paragraph, Zhu Xi stated "That the Ultimate has both Yin and Yang aspects is the result of the movement of the Heavenly destiny", thus changing the relation between the Ultimate and Yin and Yang in Zhou Dunyi's original words that "the movement of the Ultimate generates Yang", as the original meaning of the latter implied the self-movement of the Ultimate. Zhu Xi placed the Ultimate in the metaphysical realm where it did not move itself, and moved Yin and Yang from the metaphysical realm to the physical realm, where they moved under Heavenly destiny. This change, as the change in the first sentence, clearly showed the difference between Zhu Xi and Zhou Dunyi, and Zhu was using Zhou's words to establish his own Principlist ontology. Further, Zhu Xi used "sincerity", "penetration of sincerity" and "return of sincerity" to illustrate the relation between the Extreme Ultimate and Yin/Yang and movement/tranquility respectively. What he called "the foundation of the sage", "the beginning and end of all things" and "the Way of the destiny" was the same as the great Ultimate. And he explained "the alternation of Yin and Yang is the Way" as a synonymous expression of "the movement of the Heavenly destiny". Yin and Yang were degenerated to the vessels at the physical realm, while movement and tranquility were respectively "followed by goodness" and "completed by the Nature" in the process of "the penetration of sincerity" and "the return of the sincerity", causing everything to appear and adjust their Nature and destiny. It is in fact not an explanation of Zhou Dunyi's text, but a mixture of Zhu's own understanding of the Qian hexagram with its exposition in the *Zhou Book of Change* and his explanation of Zhou Dunyi's *Book of Thorough Understanding*. In the exposition of the Qian hexagram we find, "Great is the virtue of the Qian hexagram, depending on which everything begins to appear. Clouds float, rain falls, and all things take their shape and are distributed naturally. The Way of Qian changes, adjusting the Nature and destiny of all things." And in Part I of the first chapter "Sincerity" in Zhou Dunyi's *Book of Thorough Understanding* we find, "Sincerity is the foundation of the sage. 'The Way of Qian changes, adjusting the Nature and destiny of all things.' And sincerity is thus established. Therefore, 'the alternation of Yin and Yang is called the Way. It is followed by goodness and completed by the Nature.' Origination and prosperity point to the penetration of sincerity, whereas benignancy and perseverance point to the return of sincerity," and what followed was about the relation between the Ultimate and Yin/Yang. They gave us a clear picture of how Zhu Xi was different from Zhou Dunyi in his ontological understanding. In Zhu Xi's succeeding description from both the "obvious" and the "subtle" angles, the Ultimate occupied the place of "Principle" and "oneness" whereas Yin/Yang and movement/tranquility had the place of "Material Force" and "difference", thus laying the foundation for later statement of "One Principle, different manifestations". "Looking back, we cannot see their combining at the beginning; looking forward, we cannot see their departing in the end" reveals the mysterious Nature of the combination of Principle and Material Force, and the inseparable state of myriad different things, as well as the no-beginning, no-ending Nature of movement/tranquility and Yin/Yang.

Thirdly, Zhou Dunyi's original text reads, "The Yang changes and unites with the Yin to generate the Five Phases of water, fire, wood, metal and earth. When the five Material Forces are distributed in harmonious order, the four seasons run their courses." Obviously, Zhu Xi's explanation here again made his own reform on the traditional theory about Five Phases and expressed his new idea, following Zhou's words.

There is the Extreme Ultimate. Its movement and tranquility create Two Modes. There are Yin and Yang. Their transformation and union bring forth the Five Phases. But the Five Phases, while their substance remains on the earth, their Material Forces are running in the Heaven. Talking from the angle of substance, their order of generation is: water, fire, wood, metal, earth, among which water and wood belong to Yang whereas fire and metal belong to Yin. Talking from the angle of Material Force, their order of running is: wood, fire, earth, metal, water, among which wood and fire belong to Yang whereas metal and water belong to Yin. Generally, the Material Force belongs to Yang and the substance belongs to Yin. And alternatively, movement belongs to Yang and tranquility belongs to Yin. For there is no limit to the transformation of the Five Phases, but wherever they go, they follow the Way of Yin and Yang. And as to Yin and Yang themselves, wherever they go, they always follow the original Nature of the Extreme Ultimate. There is no possibility for any slight deviation.

It can be clearly seen that in his concrete explanation of the text, Zhu Xi has added something of his own. For example, the transformation and union generate the Five Phases. And the Five Phases can be ascribed to Heaven and Earth, to the Material Force and the substance. Both are different not only in order, but also in their attributes in Yin or Yang. At the same time Yang (movement, Material Force) and Yin (tranquility, substance) are also the theoretical and substantial foundation for people and things to acquire different qualities. In the end, both the transformation of the Five Phases and the change of Yin and Yang are the Nature of the Extreme Ultimate.

Fourthly, Zhou Dunyi's original text reads, "The Five Phases constitute the Yin and Yang; the Yin and Yang constitute the Ultimate of Extremity; and the Ultimate of Extremity has originated from the Ultimate of Nothingness. The generation of the Five Phases is each to its own Nature." As to this, Zhu Xi explained:

When the Five Phases were generated, everything that the universe needed for creation was ready. Based on this he dated back further to prove that the integrated whole was a reflection of the subtlety of the Ultimate of Nothingness, and the subtlety of the Ultimate of Nothingness existed in everything. Although the Five Phases were different substances and the four seasons were different Material Forces, they could not exist outside Yin and Yang. Although Yin and Yang were in different position and movement and tranquility were alternate in time, they could not exist without the

Ultimate of Extremity. And the Ultimate of Extremity itself, soundless and smellless, was the expression of its own Nature and substance. Is there anything under the Heaven that can exist without Nature? Thus, the generation of the Five Phases differs from each other in accordance with their particular substance and Material Force. That's what is called "each to its own Nature". Since each Phase goes to its own Nature, the integrated whole of the Ultimate of Extremity also exists in every Phase. And that Nature exists everywhere is proved here.

As a matter of fact, there is a clear hierarchical relationship of the three pairs: the Five Phases/Yin and Yang, Yin and Yang/Ultimate of Extremity, Ultimate of Extremity/Ultimate of Nothingness, found in the first three sentences in Zhou's original text. Yet, Zhu Xi purposely erased the difference between the Ultimate of Extremity and the Ultimate of Nothingness, insisting that the two were the same. His emphasis on "an integrated whole" was to expose that "the Ultimate of Nothingness exists in everything", which led to "each to its own Nature". In Zhou's original text, "each to its own Nature" meant that the generation of the Five Phases creates different Nature for each, but Zhu Xi explained that "the integrated whole of the Ultimate of Extremity exists in every Phase and Nature exists everywhere", which is an expression of his "one Principle, multiple manifestations", and also a deviation from the original.

Fifthly, Zhou's original text reads, "The truthfulness of the Ultimate of Nothingness, and the essence of Yin and Yang and the Five Phases, join together mysteriously into an integration". Here he did not mention the concept of "Nature". But Zhu Xi's explanation to this is:

> There is nothing in the world that exists without Nature and Nature permeates in everything. That's why the Ultimate, the Yin and Yang, and the Five Phases can be fused so closely, or "mysteriously". "Truthfulness" relates to Principle, meaning non-inappropriateness, and "essence" relates to Material Force, a name with no other explanation. Integration means joining together, or that the Material

Forces join into a form. Here Nature is the core, woven intricately by Yin and Yang, the Five Phases and others, and each joins into a form according to its own type.

Here Zhu Xi introduced the concept of Nature directly. Its synonymous expressions in this context were "truthfulness", "Principle" and "non-inappropriateness", but basically, it meant the Nature of concrete things, which was closely related to the Nature of human he was to further illustrate. In Zhu's *Classified Analects*, the general title for volumes 4, 5 and 6 was called Nature and Priniple, whereas the separate titles for each chapter were respectively "Nature of human and things and of Material Force and substance", "Terms and meaning for Nature, Emotion, Mind and Intention" and "Terms and meaning for Humanity, Righteousness, Propriety and Wisdom". Thus we can see that Zhu Xi's own theory was focused on Nature and Principle. The synonyms for Yin, Yang and the Five Phases here were "essence" and "Material Force". The formation of myriad of things was based on Nature, woven intricately by Yin, Yang and the Five Phases through "mysterious integration". This was a fundamental explanation of Principlism to the formation of all things, and helped to set the cognitive basis for the recognition of the formation of Man at the Principlist period.

Zhou Dunyi said in his *Extreme Ultimate Diagram*, "The Way of the *Qian* trigram brought forth the male. The Way of the *Kun* trigram brought forth the female. The two forces affected each other and generated myriad of things. The generation and regeneration of myriad of things caused endless change and transformation." Upon this Zhu Xi commented:

Yang and the vigorous brought forth the male, which is the Way of the father; Yin and the obedient brought forth the female, which is the Way of mother. The two marked the beginning of the human beings: both were generated by the Material Forces. The Material Force was condensed into a form. Force and form worked with each other and brought forth generation after generation of human beings and other things. From the point of view of male or female, either had a Nature of itself and they together formed an Ultimate. From the point of view of the myriad things, each had a Nature of itself and they together formed an Ultimate. To speak generally, the myriad of things were of one Ultimate. To speak separately, each thing possessed an Ultimate itself. When we said that there was nothing outside the Nature and Nature permeated everywhere, here we see the full explanation. Master Zisi said, "When the gentleman talked about the greatness, nothing could load it; when they talked about the smallness, nothing could split it." He was actually talking about the above-mentioned fact.

Following the principle of "basing mainly on the Nature, the essence of Yin/Yang and the Five Phases joined together mysteriously into integration", the Yang brought forth the male and the Yin brought forth the female and the two formed the Ways of father and mother respectively. However, Zhu's further inference about "Nature and Material Forces working together" could not be found in Zhou Dunyi's original text, and it was Zhu's own idea to implant his own concept of "one Principle, multiple manifestations" into the interpretation of how things came into being at the beginning of the universe. From our knowledge and logic, we can see no direct deductive relation among what he described as "one Principle, multiple manifestations" that "male and female have different Nature of their own and together they form one Ultimate", "myriad things have different Natures of their own and together they form one Ultimate", and "talking separately, everything has an Ultimate in itself". We can only conclude that this was Zhu Xi's own presupposition, as this presupposition of "one Principle, multiple manifestations" was extremely important for him to explain the formation of humans and things and his way of investigating things to acquire knowledge. And the Nature was born at the same time with Material Forces and forms with no exceptions.

Zhu Xi went on to explain the part of the generation of human Nature in Zhou's *Diagram*, which is very important for us to understand the main concepts in his own theory about Mind and Nature and its development. We will make some comparisons in the next three sections.

Sixthly, Zhou Dunyi said, "Man was bestowed the highest excellence and became the most intelligent. When his form came into being, his spirit developed consciousness. The five virtues in his Nature were aroused. And good and evil could be distinguished and human affairs took place." In his explanation Zhu Xi added something of his own:

> This is to say that all men possessed the Principle of movement and tranquility, but with too much lavished on the former. The birth of either Man or things was following the Way of the Extreme Ultimate. Yet Yin/Yang and the five phases, the Material Forces and substance worked alternatively, and the best was bestowed upon Man. So his Mind was the most intelligent and could keep the completeness of his Nature. That's what is called the Mind of Heaven and Earth or the purist quality of Man. However, form was shaped from the Yin and spirit was developed from the Yang, and the Nature of the Five Phases was aroused by the outside things. The Yang/good and Yin/evil could be distinguished from their types, and the difference among the Five Phases was separated into myriad of things. The two Material Forces and the Five Phases affected each other to generate myriad of things. This was the manifestation of the Principle in Man. Had it not been the sages who pointed it out from the completeness of the Ultimate, the purist quality of Man could not have been established, for various desires would be aroused and passions would overcome them and, attacked by gains and losses, men would not be far from the beasts.

Here we notice: 1) The use of "Principle of movement and tranquility" as the synonym of "Nature", and "the Way of the Extreme Ultimate" as the flowing of the "Ultimate" and "Principle" were added by Zhu Xi, to emphasize the inborn existence of the "Nature" and the "Principle" inside the human beings. 2) To claim that among all things generated, Man's

"Nature" was bestowed the highest excellence was clearly an intentional elevation of human Nature. 3) There were many different descriptions regarding the functions of the "Mind" in Zhu Xi's theory, among which "empty and intelligent" was worthy of special mentioning, because "The birth of either Man or things was following the Way of the Extreme Ultimate" and "his Mind was the most intelligent and could keep the completeness of his Nature". These sayings, though commonplace, were the starting point of Zhu Xi's doctrine about Mind and Nature. 4) Yin/Yang and the Five Phases affected each other to generate myriad of things. Yang/good and Yin/evil could be distinguished by their types, and of these Man was not an exception. This did not contradict with the previous discourse as that was a general principle, or related specifically with the sages who possessed the "completeness of the Nature" and "the Way of the Ultimate", and was the "Mind of Heaven and Earth" or the "purist quality of Man". Whereas for ordinary people, their "various desires would be aroused and passions would overcome them and, attacked by gains and losses, Man would not be far from the beasts". Thus Zhu Xi laid a foundation for his theory that the numerous people with the exception of the sages need to extinguish their desires and make an exhaustive study of the Principle.

Seventhly, for what was said about the Nature of the sages expressed in Zhou's book that "the sage settled his Way with the Mean, Correctness, Humanity and Righteousness, laid emphasis on tranquility, thus setting up the purist qualities for Man. Therefore, the sage identified his virtue with Heaven and Earth, his brilliance with the sun and the moon, his order with the four seasons, and his good or evil fortunes with the ghosts and deities," Zhu Xi explained:

> This is to say that the sage was complete with the virtue of movement and tranquility, with his basis always setting on the latter. While Man was born with the excellent force of Yin/Yang and the Five Phases, the sage was born with the most excellent of the excellence. So his action was in accordance with the Mean, his behavior Correctness, his thinking Humanity, and his judgment

Righteousness. His movement and tranquility were completely in accordance with the Way of the Extreme Ultimate without any loss. Then, what was previously discussed about "various desires being aroused, passions overcoming and men being attacked by gains and losses" would find its settlement. Yet tranquility marked the return of the sincerity and the perseverance of the Nature. If the Mind was not tranquil and silent without any desire, how could one cope with the constant changes of the things and to regulate all the movements under Heaven? So the sage kept in the Mean, the Correctness, the Humanity and the Righteousness. The movement and tranquility altered around him with the latter always being the fundamental. He positioned himself on the Mean, and neither Heaven and Earth, nor the sun and the moon, nor the four seasons, nor the ghosts and deities could betray him. Only when the substance was established could the function be displayed. Master Cheng said in relation to the movement and tranquility of the universe, "No concentration, no straightforwardness; no gathering, no dispersal." He meant the same.

1) Zhu Xi had planted a hint at the beginning of the previous paragraph about the difference between the sage and the rest of the people. His words that "all men possessed the principle of movement and tranquility, with too much lavished on the former" did not have any equivalent in the original text and were only his own inference. They formed a sharp contrast with the words at the beginning of the present section that "the sage is complete with the virtue of movement and tranquility, with his basis always setting on the latter", highlighting the sage as "the most excellent of the excellence", or in other words, a standard model for all men. Thus, "to set the basis on tranquility" became an important concept in Zhu's theory about Mind and Nature.

2) As the standard model, his movement and tranquility were "completely in accordance with the Way of the Extreme Ultimate without any loss", then what are those standards? It seems that Zhu was imitating Confucius, who split the two words *yuanheng* and *lizhen* in the original

Book of Change into four virtues of *yuan, heng, li* and *zhen*, and split the four sinograms in Zhou's original *zhong* (the Mean), *zheng* (Correctness), *ren* (Humanity), and *yi* (Righteousness) into four ways: his action is in accordance with the Mean, his behavior Correctness, his thinking Humanity, and his judgment Righteousness. Thus, the Mean, Correctness, Humanity and Righteousness also became important concepts in Zhu's own theory of Mind. Among them, Humanity was still more important, about which Zhu had many sayings.

3) Viewing movement and tranquility from the angle of Mind and Nature, tranquility was in the dominant position and was the foundation of the movement. Tranquility, being the necessary prerequisite for "the return of the sincerity and the perseverance of the Nature", obviously occupied an important position in Zhu's theory of Mind and Nature.

4) It required two conditions to cope with the myriad changing things and regulate the movements: silent tranquility and desirelessness. Thus, silent tranquility and desirelessness also became two important topics in Zhu's theory of Mind and Nature. While keeping to the Mean, Correctness, Humanity and Righteousness, and letting the movement and tranquility alter around him, the sage must stick to tranquility as the foundation for the movement, so that he could cope with everything. This goes along with Master Cheng's view about the movement and tranquility of the universe.

Eighthly, for Zhou's conclusion that "the superior man cultivates these qualities and enjoys good fortune, whereas the inferior men violate them and suffer from evil fortune", Zhu Xi explained:

> The sage embraced the completeness of the Extreme Ultimate, so wherever he went, by movement or tranquility, he arrived at the extremity of the Mean, Correctness, Humanity and Righteousness, as a natural behavior, free from cultivation. Unable to get at that stage, the superior man had to cultivate those moral qualities to enjoy good fortunes. And not knowing those qualities, the inferior men violated them and suffered evil fortunes. To cultivate or to

violate, the difference was also the difference between reverence and unscrupulousness. Sticking to reverence, one would know fewer desires and more reasons. When one desired for fewer and fewer things until nothing, the state of tranquility, emptiness, movement and uprightness of the sage could be strived for.

There are only two sentences in Zhou Dunyi's original text. Obviously Zhu Xi was using this opportunity to propagate his own theory of Mind and Nature again. 1) The Nature of the sage was superb, and so was his entity of the Extreme Ultimate. Both his movement and tranquility naturally met the standards of the Mean, Correctness, Humanity and Righteousness, without the need for any cultivation. In comparison, the superior man who followed and cultivated these standards would enjoy good fortunes, and the inferior men who neglected and violated them would suffer evil fortunes. So after all, he was persuading people to carry out self-cultivation to extinguish their desires to preserve the Principle. 2) The only requirement for self-cultivation was *reverence*, which became a key word in Zhu's theory of Mind and Nature, and around which many could be said and much could be done. 3) Fewer desires meant more understanding of the Principle. When desires came to nil, the movement and tranquility could match that of the sage. So sage could be emulated through self-cultivation.

Ninthly, Zhou's original reads, "So it is said that 'Yin and Yang were set as the Way of Heaven; firmness and yieldingness as the Way of Earth; and humanity and righteousness as the Way of Man'. It is also said that 'Tracing back to the beginning and investigating the ending one would understand what is life and death.'" Zhu Xi explained:

Yin and Yang formed the Image, which was how the Way of Heaven was set; firmness and yieldingness formed the substance, which was how the Way of Earth was set; Humanity and Righteousness formed the moral standards, which was how the Way of Man was set. The Way was one but manifested itself in different cases, here in the three cardinal forces. And in each of the force difference lay between entity and function. But after all they were all under one Extreme Ultimate. Yang, firmness and Humanity referred to the beginning of things whereas Yin, yieldingness and Righteousness referred to the end of things. If able to trace back to the beginning to know life, one would be able to investigate the end to know death. This is the untold mystery of the universe throughout past and present. The *Book of Change* written by the sages meant the same and could be quoted as evidence.

Zhou's original text was actually the original text from *The Zhou Book of Change*. Zhu Xi's explanation lay emphasis on the differentiation between entity and function, as well as such concepts as the Extreme Ultimate, Yin and Yang, and tracing back to the beginning and investigating the end. This shows that his understanding of *The Extreme Ultimate Diagram* was the same as his understanding of *The Zhou Book of Change*. Although the concepts of the Ultimate and Yin/Yang as he understood had some subtle change, he was still on the line of the historical, cultural tradition.

Tenthly, Zhou Dunyi's original text said, "Great is *The Book of Change*! Here lies its extreme excellence!" Obviously, Zhou was paralleling his *Diagram* with the *Book of Change*. Zhu Xi said in his explanation:

As a book, *The Zhou Book of Change* is comprehensive and complete. But to talk of its extreme excellence, only this diagram can fully illustrate it. This is indicative. I was told that when the Cheng brothers studied after him, Master Zhou drew the diagram himself and gave it to them. The Cheng masters' talk on Nature and Heavenly Way was mostly derived from it. However, they never showed the diagram to others. There must have been something behind it. The scholars should know that.

On the whole, we cannot say that Zhu Xi's *Explanation to the Extreme Ultimate Diagram* was Zhou Dunyi's understanding of the *Diagram*. Rather, it is Zhu Xi's own understanding of the *Diagram* with Zhou's explanation as he attempted to establish his own ontology and theory of Mind and Nature. His aim was to set up a foundation for his own Principlism. Even in this sentence, though he admitted that the Extreme Ultimate originated from Zhou Dunyi and was continued and extended by Cheng brothers, what's more important was to prove that his own theory had good sources.

Zhu Xi regarded *The Book of Thorough Understanding* and *The Western Inscription* as supporting explanations to *The Extreme Ultimate Diagram*. He said that *The Book of Thorough Understanding* was originally named *Thorough Understanding the Book of Change* and published together with *The Extreme Ultimate Diagram*, and that "All that was said in *The Book of Thorough Understanding* was about the essence of the *Diagram*." However, his words were doubted both at his time and later. Now let's see how Zhu Xi did his *Explanations to the Book of Thorough Understanding*. There were 40 chapters in *The Book of Thorough Understanding*. They were:

1. Sincerity. Pt.1	2. Sincerity. Pt.2
3. Sincerity, subtlety, virtues	4. Sagehood
5. Caution in action	6. The Way
7. Teachers	8. Fortune
9. Thought	10. Will to learn
11. Harmony and transformation	12. Government
13. Rites and music	14. Devotion to actuality
15. Love and reverence	16. Movement and tranquility
17. Music. Pt. 1	18. Music. Pt. 2
19. Music. Pt. 3	20. Learning to be a sage
21. Impartiality and understanding	22. Principle, Nature, destiny
23. Master Yan	24. Teachers and friends. Pt.1
25. Teachers and friends. Pt.2	26. Mistakes

27. Tendencies	28. Literary expressions
29. Implications of the sage	30. Refined implications
31. Hexagrams of *Qian, Sun, Yi* and action	32. Hexagrams of *Jiaren, Kui, Fu,* and *Wuwang*
33. Wealth and honor	34. Vulgarity
35. Consideration and deliberation	36. Punishment
37. Impartiality	38. Kong Zi. Pt.1
39. Kong Zi. Pt.2	40. Hexagrams of *Meng* and *Gen*

From the titles of the chapters we cannot see the similarities or differences between *The Book of Thorough Understanding* and *The Extreme Ultimate Diagram*. But if we take it as a whole from the philosophical angle of Confucian tradition, it is also not easy for us to deny the close relation between the two books. Zhu Xi reminded us at the end of his *An Explanation to the Book of Thorough Understanding*:

The depth of Master Zhou's learning, if to understand by images, was fully expressed in his *Extreme Ultimate Diagram*. And his *Book of Thorough Understanding* was written to expose the implications of the *Diagram*, especially the chapters of sincerity, movement and tranquility, Principle, Nature and destiny. The books of the Cheng brothers were all further extensions of his idea, especially in their chapters of *Epitaph of Li Zhongtong, Eulogy to Cheng Duanque,* and *On Master Yan's Love of Learning*, which even copied Zhou's words. That's why Pan Xingsi placed the *Diagram* on top of all Zhou's writings when he wrote a eulogy for Zhou's tomb, followed by other writings such as *On the Book of Change, Thorough Understanding of the Book of Change,* etc., as he fully knew its importance.

Notes:

According to Zhu Zhen, *The Extreme Ultimate Diagram* was passed down from Chen Tuan to Zhong Fang, who passed it to Mu Xiu, who passed it to Master Zhou. And according to Hu Hong, what Master Zhou received from Zhong Fang and Mu Xiu was only part of the teachings he learned, and not the most important one at that. And Qi Kuan said that the *Diagram* was only a drawing painted by Master Zhou to teach the Cheng brothers, not a book. All the three were wrong as they did not see Pan Xingsi's *Eulogy*. Hu Hong didn't even know about the depth of Master Zhou's learning, which had never left this diagram. For quite a long time Master Zhou's *On the Book of Change* was not seen by people. The two versions that appeared in the past were not the real ones. One of the two, *On Hexagrams*, was written by His Excellency Minister Chen[1]. The other, *On the Survey of the Book of Change,* was full of stale talks of Buddhism and Daoism. Some were rather ridiculous. For instance, it said, "*The Book of Change*'s pretending to know the Way under Heaven was just like the macaque master's deception of the macaques." Such a book could never be written by Master Zhou. *Thorough Understanding of the Book of Change* might be the other name of *The Book of Thorough Understanding*; only it was not known when "the Book of Change" in the title was taken away. If *On the Book of Change* made annotations to the classic book itself, then the *Thorough Understanding* talked about the general theme of the classic without following its text. Now almost all present versions attached *Thorough Understanding* to it, misleading people to believe that this was the last chapter. And Master Zhou's subtle intention of setting up the diagram was obscured. When people talked about the *Thorough Understanding*, they didn't even know that the general outline was indeed hidden in this book. (*Complete Works. Book 13. pp.131–132*)

The above paragraph shows that Zhu Xi knew very clear about the Daoist origin of Zhou Dunyi's *Extreme Ultimate Diagram* pointed

---

[1] May refer to Chen Junqing (1113–1186), famous upright official and Prime Minister of the Southern Song Dynasty.

out by others, yet he insisted on his own explanations. He had similar opinion about the *Thorough Understanding*. The statement that *"Thorough Understanding of the Book of Change* might be the other name of *The Book of Thorough Understanding"* could not be proved in terms of wording. And that the "subtle intention" of the *Thorough Understanding* corresponded with the *Extreme Ultimate Diagram* was only his own understanding from a special angle and level. Even the order was changed. In this way, let's further look at the chapters of sincerity, movement and tranquility, and Principle, Nature and destiny which he thought were the most demonstrative of the implications of the *Extreme Ultimate Diagram*.

There are four chapters relating "sincerity".

Chapter 1:

Sincerity is the foundation of the sage. "Great is the virtue of origination of the Qian hexagram. All things of creation depend on it for their beginnings." It is the source of sincerity. "The Way of Heaven changes constantly, bestowing on all things their own distinctive Nature and life." In this way sincerity is established. It is pure and perfectly good. Therefore, "Alternation between Yin and Yang is called the Way. To spread and carry on it is of goodness and to perfect and persevere in it is of Nature." Origination and prosperity demonstrate the smoothness of the sincerity, and benignancy and perseverance demonstrate the recovery of the sincerity. Great is the Change, the source of Nature and life!

Chapter 2:

Sagehood is nothing but sincerity. It is the foundation of the five constant virtues and source of all activities. When in tranquility, it is nothingness; when in movement, it is existence. It is perfectly correct and clearly penetrating. Without sincerity, five virtues and all activities will be wrong, astray or obstructed. With sincerity, little effort is needed for definite result with no difficulty. Therefore it is said: "Once the master himself is restrained and the rites recovered, all under Heaven will arrive at Humanity."

Chapter 3:

Sincerity needs no action. Subtlety refers to good and evil. The virtues: love means Humanity; suitability means Righteousness; reasonability means Propriety; understanding means Wisdom; keeping to one's words means faithfulness. Doing things by Nature and with ease is called a sage. Doing things with recovered Nature and with perseverance is called a worthy man. One whose subtlety is not to be seen and his force is not to be exhausted is called a spiritual man.

Chapter 4:

Utterly motionless is called sincerity; moved to smooth action is called spirituality; moved but not to be sensed between action and non-action is called subtlety. Sincerity is pure therefore clear-sighted; spirituality is responsive therefore mysterious; subtlety is delicate therefore excluded. One who possesses sincerity, spirituality and subtlety is called a sage. (*Complete Works.* Book 13.)

From the description of *sincerity* in the above four chapters we can see that this book had some relation with Zhou's *Diagram* and the *Survey* in the *Book of Change.* *Sincerity* was abstracted as a category to a high degree, similar to many of our familiar concepts such as the *Way* and *non-action,* and was expressed as *sagehood, virtues, spirit, subtlety* and *the sage.* At the same time we found that although the sincerity in the *Thorough Understanding* had some similarity with the explanation of the term in Zhu Xi's *An Explanation to the Extreme Ultimate Diagram,* they are not entirely the same, as the meaning of sincerity here is ambiguous, overlapping with other terms as the Way, the Change, and the Nature. It seems sincerity is used here to replace the *Change.*

Chapter 16 is an acknowledgement and description of the state of myriad of things in their movement, tranquility, growth or extinction, combining some terms used in Zhou's *Diagram,* as well as in the *Survey* and *Laozi*.

> To move without being tranquil, or to be tranquil without movement, that is the thing. To move without movement, or to be tranquil without tranquility, that is the spirit. To move without movement or to be tranquil without tranquility does not mean being neither moving nor tranquil. Things cannot penetrate each other, whereas the spirit can create miracles in everything. Water, belonging to Yin, is rooted in Yang. Fire, belonging to Yang, is rooted in Yin. The Five Phases are nothing but Yin and Yang. And Yin and Yang are finally the Extreme Ultimate. The four seasons are running their courses. The myriad things all have their beginnings and ends, integrating and separating infinitely. (*Complete Works*. Book 13. pp.112–113)

Chapter 22 Principle, Nature and destiny. The original text is:

> Whether obvious or subtle, only the intelligent can expose it. The firmness can be either good or evil, as is the yieldingness, and only the Mean is the final choice. The two Material Forces and the Five Phases transform and generate myriad of things, the five creating differences and the two giving them entities. And the two forces are ultimately one. This is to say that myriad things are fundamentally one, and the one has myriad manifestations. And either the myriad or the one has its own justness, big or small. (*Complete Works*. Book 13. pp.116–117)

In this chapter Zhu Xi talked about the relation between the Principle, the Nature and the destiny. To a certain extent, it accorded with what he said in his *An Explanation to the Extreme Ultimate Diagram*. At the end, Zhu Xi put a note saying that this chapter shared the same view with Chapter 16. But by comparison, we find that they were just similar, not the same.

If we read *The Thorough Understanding* carefully, we will find that Zhou Dunyi was really familiar with the Confucian classics such as *The Zhou*

Book of Change, The Confucian Analects and *The Mencius.* Using the style of speech recording, he expressed his understanding of Heaven, Earth, and the human life, with *The Extreme Ultimate Diagram* as the ideological background. To a certain extent, we may share the views and understanding with Zhu Xi on this book.

As the third one of Zhu Xi's *Three Books, An Explanation to the Western Inscription* is his inspection and abstraction of Zhang Zai's *Western Inscription* based on his other two books. There are only 253 Chinese characters in Zhang's *Western Inscription.* Through his interpretation of the book, Zhu Xi developed its meaning, laying emphasis on the Principlist ideas of "one Principle, multiple manifestations" and "Heaven and Man being one". Here is the full text of the *Western Inscription:*

Qian trigram (Heaven) is my father and Kun trigram (Earth) is my mother. And I, a small creature, find a place amidst them. Therefore, what fills between them is my body, and what governs them is my Nature. All people are my siblings and all things are my companions. The great ruler is the eldest son of my parents, and the ministers are his stewards. Respecting the aged is to treat the elders as elders. Loving the orphaned and the weak is to treat the youngsters as youngsters. The sage is the integration of all good virtues, and the worthy is the most outstanding one. Those suffering from various diseases or deformities and those losing their spouses or children are all my brothers in distress and need. To protect them when time comes is my duty as the son of my parents, and the purist filial piety is to make my parents happy and free from care. To disobey the duty is to disobey the good virtues. To harm humanity is called an injurer. To assist the evil is called an unlike son. Only those practicing good virtues in every act are the like sons. Those who know changes are good at recording their deeds, and those who thoroughly understand their spirit are good at inheriting their will. Being self-alert at the darkest house brings no disgrace. Keeping Mind to nourish the Nature needs untiring effort. The Great Yu attended his parents by hating pleasant wine. Ying Kaoshu extended his love to his folk by educating the talents. Working incessantly is Great Shun's way to please his parents. Waiting for punishment without escaping is Shen Sheng's way to be reverent to his father. Keeping his body intact and sound to return it to Heaven, is he not Zeng Shen? Following his father's order to dare the wilderness, that is Yin Boqi. Wealth and honor are what enriches my life; poverty and sorrow are what helps my fulfillment. I will live to follow and die at peace. (*Complete Works*. Book 13. pp.141–145)

From this short essay we see a Confucian's expression of his general knowledge about the relation between Heaven, Earth and Man, in a style like Zhuang Zi's *Enjoyment in Untroubled Ease*. Zhu Xi gave a comment after his annotations:

Comment:

Between Heaven and Earth there is only one Principle. Yet, since "the Way of the *Qian* trigram brought forth the male, the Way of the *Kun* trigram brought forth the female, and the two forces affected each other and generated myriad of things", the myriad things are of different sizes and different degrees of closeness and cannot be equal to one another. If not for the sage and the worthy men, who can join all the differences into commonness? The *Western Inscription* is actually written for this purpose. Master Cheng claimed that the statement "one Principle, many manifestations" could cover the whole picture. Heaven being father and Earth being mother suits everything that has life. That is what I call "one Principle". But people and things have different births and different degrees of closeness among themselves, so their manifestations must be different. Because one is many, the whole world is governed by one family and the whole country one person, but there will not be the disadvantage of universal love. Because many are one, people are of different closeness in relationship and different degrees in richness, but no one should be confined to serve himself alone. This is the main idea of the *Western Inscription*. From his extension from the closeness in treating one's own parents and children to the selfless Mind for public service, from the sincerity in respecting one's own parents to the Way of following the Heaven, we see that nothing can be outside the saying of one Principle with many manifestations. We don't need to take "treating people as my siblings, elders and youngsters as elders and youngsters" as the one Principle and memorize it in heart in order to understand the many manifestations. What's more, if we have to "weigh all things before distributing them evenly", we need to weigh things first. If there is no weighing beforehand, how can one decide whether the distribution is even or not? The second letter of Yang Shi had an intention to express this idea but did not do it. I follow him to say the above words. It is my hope that friends with same aspirations will discuss it with me. (*Complete Works*. Book 13. pp.145–146)

Enlightened by Cheng Yi's *A Reply to Yang Shi on Western Inscription*, Zhu Xi forwarded his opinion and turned the understanding of Zhang Zai's text into a consensus of Principlists as well as a philosophical summary, with special emphasis on the Principlist cosmology of "one Principle, multiple manifestations" and "Heaven and Man being one". The Song-dynasty Principlist paid more attention on the "different manifestations". Zhu Xi was no exception.

Zhu Xi's *Three Books* inherited the thoughts of Zhou Dunyi, the Cheng brothers, Zhang Zai as well as views of their disciples such as Yang Shi, but elaborated more of his own understanding, development and comprehension. In this way his *Three Books* may be regarded as the Principlist explanation in his own way, thus forming the foundation of his own cosmology and ontology.

2. Governance of Mind over Nature and Emotion

The basic concepts and contents of the epistemological part of Zhu Xi's Principlism lie mainly in volumes 4, 5, and 6 of the *Classified Analects of Zhu Xi*, their titles being respectively: Nature & Emotion 1: Nature of men/things and Nature of Material Force/substance; Nature & Emotion 2: Names and meanings of Nature, Emotion, Mind and Intention; Nature & Emotion 3: Names and meanings of Humanity, Righteousness, Propriety and Wisdom. They can also be seen in his letters to his friends and his miscellaneous writings, as well as in his connotations to the Four Books, especially *The Doctrine of the Mean*. Here we shall discuss Zhu Xi's epistemology from the cognitive mechanism of governance of Mind over Nature and Emotion, to know how Zhu Xi sees and understands this world from his Principlist Mind. The discussion will be carried out in five respects:

1. The development of the concept of governance of Mind over Nature and Emotion;

2. The nature of the concepts of Mind, Nature and Emotion;

3. The mechanism of governance of Mind over Nature and Emotion;

4. The Mean, mean and harmony, and the arousal and not-arousal;

5. Notes and annotations to the *Doctrine of the Mean* relating the governance of Mind over Nature and Emotion.

Firstly, the governance of Mind over Nature and Emotion is an expression of the cognitive mechanism of the Song dynasty Principlism, shaped by many scholars with their relative contributions, big or small, and finalized by Zhu Xi. Zhu Xi himself admitted that this viewpoint was not created by him but had its own origin and development:

Zhang Zai put it most directly: "It is the Mind that governs the Nature and Emotion." Meng Zi said, "The sense of compassion is the beginning of humanity. The sense of shame is the beginning of righteousness." How well he talked about the relation between Nature, Emotion and Mind! By Nature no one is ungood. The arousal of the Mind is called Emotion, which may be ungood. But to say that ungood is not from the Mind is also untrue. In a word, Mind as an entity is always good, but influenced by Emotion it may be ungood. Nature is the integral name of the Principles, while either Humanity,

Righteousness, Propriety or Wisdom is just the name of one of the Principles of Nature. And the sense of either compassion, shame, modesty, or right-wrong is the name of the Emotions aroused. These are Emotions from the Nature and are good. Their beginnings are subtle and originate from the Mind. That's why we say that it is the Mind that governs the Nature and Emotion. Nature is not something beyond the Mind but Mind itself possesses Nature and Emotion. When the Mind is out of control it sometimes does things ungood. For example, "I want Humanity, and here comes Humanity"; but if I want inhumanity, and humanity will disappear. Similarly, "Yan Hui has not violated Humanity for three months" means he might violate it in other times. "One never knows the time when it comes or goes, neither does he knows its direction." Keep cultivation and concentrate on oneness — that will be good enough. (*Classified Analects*. Book 1. p.92)

We may understand Zhu Xi's words at three levels: 1) The viewpoint of "governance of Mind over Nature and Emotion" is best explained by Zhang Zai and most completely expressed by Zhu Xi himself. 2) The origin of the viewpoint may be traced back to the pre-Qin Confucians. Kong Zi was the first one to talk about the relation between Mind and Humanity. On the one hand, Mind is good and humane, and by Nature is humane, and Mind itself possesses Humanity, and on the other hand one's speech and behavior must not violate Humanity and lose its good Nature. However, sometimes the Mind would violate Humanity. Possession and violation of goodness are both the Nature of Mind. 3) Meng Zi mentioned the Nature of the Mind and their expressions, that the sense of compassion was the beginning of Humanity and the sense of shame was the beginning of Righteousness. The former reflects the Nature of the Mind and the latter the Emotion of the Mind. Of course, this paragraph does not clarify the relation of the relative elements in the statement about the governance of Mind over Nature and Emotion. Zhu Xi himself could not fully understand and apply this statement at first but had experienced a process of research. He said:

> I first read Hu Hong's works and found that he only related
> Mind with Nature and there was no place for Emotion. Later I
> learned Zhang Zai's doctrine about the governance of Mind over
> Nature and Emotion, and its contribution in introducing the term
> Emotion. In Meng Zi's words "the sense of compassion is the
> beginning of Humanity", Humanity is the Nature and compassion
> is the Emotion. That is to see Mind through Emotion. He also said,
> "Humanity, Righteousness, Propriety and Wisdom are all rooted in
> the Mind." That is to see Mind through Nature. So the Mind can
> govern Nature and Emotion. Nature is the entity and Emotion is the
> function. The written form of Mind is only one sinograph (心 or 忄),
> whereas the characters of Nature (性) and Emotion (情) both use it as
> a radical.

By comparing Hu Hong's viewpoint which contains only Mind and
Nature with Zhang Zai's governance of Mind over Nature and Emotion,
Zhu Xi concluded that Zhang's point was more convincing and more
balanced between Mind, Nature and Emotion. And at the same time he
emphasized the similarity of Zhang's viewpoint with that of Meng Zi's. It
is a historical analysis which confirms the inheritance and development of
Meng Zi's idea by Zhang Zai.

Secondly, Zhu Xi's summery of the historical development of the
statement of governance of Mind over Nature and Emotion also means
that he had his own understanding of the elements contained (Mind,
Nature, Emotion) and their relations. In Zhu Xi's Principlist theory, Mind
was an important concept with rich content. Briefly speaking, Mind was
deep and clear, empty and bright, perceptual, combined with both spirit
and substance, dominant in the whole body, prevalent and generative,
while at the same time had some ethic features such as goodness, evil,
humanity, sincerity, human Mind, Mind of the Dao and the Principle.

For Zhu Xi, the Mind had a material side as well as a spiritual side, or was the combination of both. So, when asked about the metaphysical and physical realms of the Mind, he replied, "Mind, different from the heart, is one of the five internal organs of the substantial body. It is mystic, controlling life and death. As an organ, heart can be cured with medicine when ill, yet the Mind cannot be cured by any medicine." When he was further asked if the Mind was metaphysical, he replied, "Mind is more traceable than Nature, and more natural and spiritual than the Material Force." Thus, Mind is perceptual. (*Classified Analects,* Book 1. p.87) "When the Principle is combined with the Material Force, it will be perceptual. Just like a candle, when added with fuel, it will have more fire." When asked if what generated the Mind was the Material Force, he replied that it was nothing more than the perception. (*Ibid.* p.85) For him, the Mind is empty and bright, something with the spirit, and dominator of the body. He said, "The substance of the human Mind is empty and bright and is the dominator of the whole body. Happiness, anger, worry and fear, aroused by different feelings, are indispensible factors of its function. However, one must first acquire knowledge, be sincere in Intention without selfish considerations, then when not affected by outside things the substance of the Mind will remain still, blank as a mirror, balanced like a scale; when affected by the outside things the Mind will respond automatically, depending on whether the things are beautiful or ugly, heavy or light — all depending on themselves. And the Mind itself actually does not do anything. That's why the Mind, both its substance and its function, can always be on the right side and dominate the whole body."(*Collected Works.* Book 5. p.2512) He regarded the Mind as the viewer or the listener which was blank in itself and had no image, whereas the object it looked at or listened to had an image. So he drew an analogy: "The human Mind is like a mirror which has no image at first. When it is used on people or things, they are reflected in the mirror, beautiful or ugly. If there were already an image in the mirror, how could it be used to reflect things? The human Mind is just the same. It is blank at first. Only when things come to affect it will we by response know whether they are high or low, heavy or light. When things are gone, the Mind will return to blankness as before." (*Classified*

Analects. Book 2. p.347) His description of the mysteriousness of the Mind was rather impressive when he said, "the human Mind is extremely mysterious. A thought may occur thousands of miles away or hundreds of years ago, but it can arrive here in an instant. How mysterious it is!" Again he said, "The human Mind is so mysterious that it can sense things to the very minute details. The whole universe can be perceived. A thought of millions of years ago can be perceived now, and a thought of today can be perceived millions of years later in the future. It is really mysterious!"(*Ibid.* p.404) For Zhu Xi the human Mind has two main characteristics: prevalence and generativeness. More concretely, he said, "The meaning of 'Mind' can 'be summarized with one word — generativeness'. 'The greatest virtue of Heaven and Earth is generativeness.' Man was born with the Material Force of Heaven and Earth, so his Mind must be humanistic and therefore generative.""... Must be understood with both prevalence and generativeness, as Master Cheng said, 'Humanity is the Mind of Heaven and Earth which generate things.' Heaven and Earth are vast and things are pervasive and generative." (*Classified Analects.* Book 1. p.85)

From what is described above, Zhu Xi was trying to give a reasonable explanation of the Mind. Based on that, he also tried to enrich it with certain ethic features such as goodness, evil, humanity and sincerity. Someone asked about the good or evil of the Mind: "As a thing the Mind possesses all virtues. Goodness is no doubt from the Mind. Is evil, which is out of man's selfish desire, also from the Mind?" Zhu replied, "Yes, it is, though it's not the Mind's substance." One asked again: "Is it also the human Mind?" "Yes," was the reply. "Then does the Mind possess both good and evil qualities?" "Yes, both." (*Classified Analects.* Book 1. p.86) Another one asked, "Does the Mind possess both good and evil qualities?" Zhu Xi replied from his Principlist stand: "Mind, as something active, of course has both the good and evil sides. Sympathy, for instance, is good. If one shows no sympathy when he sees a child falling into a well, then it's evil, for to leave good is evil itself. As substance, Mind is good. But you cannot say that evil has nothing to do with the Mind. For without the Mind how can one do evil? For ancient people, to study means to exhaust the Principles and acquire knowledge, trying his best to get rid of the evils, and goodness will gradually come back. So distinguishing good from evil is something to be done later than actually doing good or evil." The man asked again: "How do we understand and choose goodness?" Zhu replied: "To make a choice itself is understanding. There are five good things and five evil things here for you to choose. The right choice you make means the right understanding you have reached. If you cannot make a right choice, how can we know that you have understood it?" (*Ibid.*) Humanity was first proposed by Kong Zi, and sincerity was discussed in *Doctrine of the Mean* and *The Mencius*. Zhu Xi developed both terms. He held that humanity and sincerity were not the same thing: "Humanity is humanity, sincerity is sincerity; they must not be confused. Understand one thoroughly, and understand the other thoroughly, then you will understand both." (*Ibid.* p.104) If Humanity and sincerity are two things, then what's the relation between them? So someone asked: "Is it that sincerity is the substance and Humanity the function?" Zhu Xi replied: "Their Principle is one. For it is substantial, we call it sincerity. Substantially, it is manifested as compassion, shame, reverence, or right and wrong. "(*Ibid.*) In fact, in his *An Explanation to the Book of Thorough Understanding* and *Annotation to the Doctrine of the Mean*, Zhu Xi talked a lot about sincerity. We shall cite just one example here. There is a passage in the *Doctrine of the Mean* which reads: "From understanding to sincerity is called Nature; from sincerity to understanding is called instruction. Sincerity leads to understanding and understanding leads to sincerity." Zhu Xi explained: "The virtue of the sage is from Nature which is substantial and illuminating. This is the Way of Heaven. The learning of the worthy man is from instruction, which is to understand goodness first before putting it to practice. This is the Way of Man. By sincerity nothing cannot be understood; understanding can lead to sincerity." (*Complete Works.* Book 6. p.49) He emphasized that sincerity meant truthfulness: "Sincerity is what is truthful, and is the Nature of the Principle of Heaven. To be sincere is to make something untruthful truthful, and is the effort of Man." (*Ibid.*) In his *On Humanity* Zhu Xi made a clear distinction between Mind and Humanity:

Heaven and Earth take living things as their Mind, while Man and things when born take the Mind of Heaven and Earth as their Minds respectively. The virtue of the Mind, though inclusive and pervasive, can be summed up in one word: Humanity. Let me illustrate it. The Mind of Heaven and Earth has four virtues of originality, prosperity, benignancy and perseverance, among which originality governs all others. The running order of four seasons is spring, summer, autumn and winter wherein the Material Force of spring is penetrating. Likewise, the Mind of Man has four virtues of Humanity, Righteousness, Propriety and Wisdom, among which Humanity is all inclusive. The expression and function of the Mind is the four Emotions of compassion, reverence, suitability and differentiation wherein compassion is throughout all others. So when talking about the Mind of Heaven and Earth, the mere mention of originality can cover all others; when talking about the human Mind, the mention of Humanity can cover all others. The Way of Humanity stands for the Mind of Heaven and Earth which generates everything and exists in everything. When Emotions are not aroused, their substance is already there; when they are aroused, their function has no limit. If one really understands and keeps to it, he will find that the origin of all goodness and behaviors is here. That's why Confucianism insists on all his learners to strive for Humanity.

Zhu Xi's view on the relation between Mind and Humanity from the angle of Humanity may be regarded as a comprehensive and macroscopic explanation of the Mind, thus complementing and completing the Principlist investigation into the Mind. In fact Zhu has many macroscopic considerations on the concept of Mind. Here we will give three examples.

1) Zhu Xi held that "the Mind has no match". That means in Zhu's Principlism the Mind had no counterpart or anything corresponding to it. When his disciples asked about "Mind being the Great Ultimate" and "Mind possessing the Great Ultimate", we found the following dialogue:

The master replied: "It is very delicate and hard to say. The Mind has both moving and tranquil sides. Its substance is called the Change. Its Principle is called the Way. Its function is called mystery." Huang Gan withdrew and told other students: "Our teacher was so familiar with the Principles and it seems so easy for him to make his point so clear." Ye Hesun asked: "He said, 'Its substance is called the Change,' then what is the substance?" Huang Gan replied, "Substance is not the same as 'body'. Principle is the same as Nature. Such problems must be dealt with in a flexible way according to different situations. For instance, when Meng Zi said, 'Humanity is human Mind,' Humanity is the Mind itself, a Principle. When the *Analects* said 'Master Yan's Mind would not violate Humanity for three months,' Mind is a dominator which will not violate the Principles. All these must be read with flexibility." Huang went on to say: "Master Zhu said in his *An Explanation to the Extreme Ultimate Diagram* that movement and tranquility are opportunities to take. Only Cai Yuanding was clever enough to understand what it meant and praised the saying as exquisitely put. The Great Ultimate is the Principle at the metaphysical level whereas Yin and Yang are the Material Forces at the physical level. The Principle has no shape while the Material Forces are traceable. If the Material Forces have the two sides of movement and tranquility, so does the Principle they support." He further cited from the *Chapter of Movement and Tranquility* of *The Book of Thorough Understanding*: "Movement without tranquility or tranquility without movement, that is the ordinary thing; movement without movement or tranquility without tranquility, that is the spirit. Movement without movement or tranquility without tranquility does not mean that it is neither moving nor tranquil. Only ordinary things cannot go between the two sides while the spirit can go through all things. So movement and tranquility are opportunities to take." Master Zhu then said: "Usually I was quite apt to make such distinctions. Now it gradually became difficult for me to do so." "Once as I was climbing up the

Yungu Mountain I met a heavy rain and was drenched through. After I arrived at my destination I thought to myself: 'What filled up the Heaven and Earth is my body, and what governs the Heaven and Earth is my Nature.' At that time Cai Yuanding and another student were also there. I asked them to explain the two sentences I had just said, and I myself also made an explanation. Later I found what I said had some reasons. From then on I started to make explanations to *The Western Inscriptions* and other books." (*Classified Analects*. Book 1. p.84)

The above dialogue exposed to us the source theory and historical foundation of the concept of the Mind. It is coherent with the first part of the present chapter, i.e. the discussion about Zhu Xi's *Three Books*. Based on the understanding that the Mind has both moving and tranquil sides he made considerations of a comprehensive framework of substance, Principle and function. Whenever he said that the Nature was the Principle or the Humanity Mind was the Principle, he was making one thing clear, i.e. his understanding and expression of the Mind had its historical origin and a process of research and consideration based on the words of his predecessors. The above passage may lead to the conclusion that "the Principle of the Mind was the Great Ultimate, and the movement and tranquility of the Mind was Yin and Yang". In other words, the Mind is consisted of both the metaphysical and physical realms.

2) As to the difference between the Mind of Man and that of the Way, Zhu Xi said: "The mystery of the Mind, to be understood from Principles, is the Mind of the Way; to be understood from the desires, is the Mind of Man."(*Zhu Xi's Works*. Book 5. p.2863) However, he insisted that either the Mind of the Way or the Mind of the Man referred to the same Mind: "The same Mind, to be understood from the desires of the eyes, ears, etc. is the Mind of Man; and from the Principles, is the Mind of the Way." (*Classified Analects*. Book 5. p.2009) He insisted on the idea of one Mind, refusing to be led astray by other sayings. So he said: "If one says that 'the Mind of the Way is the Mind of Heaven' and 'the Mind of Man is the set of men's desires', it is to say that there are two Minds. Man has one Mind only.

When sensing the Principles, it is the Mind of the Way; when sensing the sound, color, odor and taste, it is the Mind of Man. There is nothing more. To say 'the Mind of Man is the set of men's desires' is not correct, although even the worthiest man cannot be utterly free from them and the saying is not entirely wrong. Lu Jiuyuan also said this to other people. There are not two Minds. Just one Mind, with two senses." (*Classified Analects*. Book 5. p.2010)

3) As to the relation between the Mind and Principle, Zhu Xi regarded Principle as part of the Mind when he used the following metaphor: "'The Mind and Principle are one thing. Principle is not something beyond the Mind. It is inside the Mind. Only the Mind cannot control it, and it will manifest itself when things occur.' He then smiled, saying: 'It may seem funny. The Mind is like a sutra store. When the sutras are removed and a lamp is lit, the whole place will be illuminated. It's a pity that few people can see this.'" (*Classified Analects*. Book 1. p.85) At the same time, he emphasized that the Mind was the dominator of the whole body.

Someone asked: "*Questions on the Four Books* said, 'Though the Mind is the dominator of body only, its mystery can govern the Principle throughout the world; though the Principle is manifested in myriad of things, its function does not go beyond the Mind of one man.' Is the function the Mind's function?" The master replied: "The Principle has its function, which is not necessarily the Mind's function. The substance of the Mind possesses the Principle, which is pervasive and exists everywhere. But the function of the Principle still cannot go beyond the human Mind. It is because though the existence of the Principle is in things, its function lies in the Mind." He said again: "The Principle is pervasive between Heaven and Earth but is governed by the Mind. That's why its function cannot go beyond the Mind. So we say that the existence of the Principle is in things whereas its function lies in the Mind." The next morning the Master said again: "I said that because we regard our own body as the subject and other things as object. In one word, saying that the Principle lies in the subject is the same as saying that it lies in the object." (*Classified Analects. Book 2. p.416*)

After the above discussion on the concept of the Mind, we will go on to talk about the other two main concepts of Nature and Emotion in the mechanism of the governance of Mind over Nature and Emotion.

Thirdly, Nature and Emotion are the two main components in the mechanism of the governance of Mind over Nature and Emotion. The Nature should be understood from two sides of Nature and partial Nature. According to what is discussed in volume 5 of *Classified Analects* about Nature: 1) The relation among the four concepts of Heaven, Destiny, Nature and Principle can be seen like this: Heaven is natural; Destiny is the running and bestowal of Heaven; "Nature is what the myriad things get as life in general" (*Classified Analects. Book 1. p.82*); and Principle is the rule for respective things and objects. 2) Heaven is the substance of the Principle, and Destiny is its function. Nature is the Principle and Destiny that Man receives, and Emotion is the function of Nature. 3) Further accounts about Destiny as what Heaven gives and Nature as what things receive: "Destiny gives, and the Material Force is being given; Nature receives, and the Material Force is being received." So, "Nature is the many ways and Principles born from Heaven." The Way is Nature, which in turn is the Principle. "Nature is the Principle scattered at various places." 4) To speak more concretely, "Nature is the exact Principle, comprising Humanity, Righteousness, Propriety and Wisdom." 5) The only characteristic of Nature is goodness, and no Nature is ungood. "To carry it on is goodness and to perfect it is Nature." As to the distinction between Nature and goodness, Zhu Xi said:

"… Compassion is the goodness of Humanity and shame is the goodness of Righteousness. On returning to tranquility from extreme movement, it is Principle again." One asked again: "Goodness is the Way of Nature. Is it to be seen here?" The master replied: "It must be looked at from the instant. 'To carry it on is goodness and to perfect it is Nature.' For Heaven and Earth, goodness goes before the Nature. What is expressed is goodness; what is generated is Nature. For man, Nature goes before the goodness." When someone mentioned Meng Zi's saying about Nature being good, the Master replied: "Here the word Nature is a noun while good is an adjective. They are not counterparts. In reading one must read carefully. What fits there does not necessarily fit here. If one rigidly transfers what fits there to here, then mistakes occur." (*Classified Analects*. Book 1. p.83)

As manifestations of the Principle of the Nature, goodness may be that of Humanity, of Righteousness, etc., and finally is the Principle again when the extreme movement returns to tranquility. Goodness is Principle, and Nature is also Principle; their distinction lies in that, speaking from Heaven and Earth, goodness goes before the Nature, whereas speaking from Man, Nature goes before goodness. So the discussion of Nature and goodness in the *Extreme Ultimate Diagram* is different from the discussion of Nature being good in the *Mencius* in that they have different emphasis and implications. In practical recognition and experience, Nature does not appear as an independent thing for aspiration and exists only in "exhaustion of the Principle and investigation of the objects". So Zhu Xi concluded that the reason why the past Confucians had different sayings about the concept of Nature is not that they could not distinguish goodness from evil, but that they had not found a suitable place to locate the term Nature, and there would always be the case when people could not do so in their heated contending. Only the sage could recognize the Nature and he then seldom talked about it.

Concerning the partiality of the Nature, Zhu Xi's answer is sometimes incoherent:

> When talking about the myriad things having the same origin, it seemed that the Principle was the same but the Material Forces were different; however, when looking at the various manifestations of the myriad things, it seemed the Material Forces were close yet

their principles were utterly different. The difference of the Material Forces lies in the difference of purity and impurity. The difference of principles lies in the difference of completeness and partiality. (*Zhu Xi's Works*. Book 4. p.2222)

As to your doubt about the partiality of the Principle and the Material Force, if speaking from their origin, the Principle exists before the Material Force and we must not talk about the completeness and partiality of the Principle; but if speaking from natural endowments, it is the Material Force that comes before the Principle. Thus, when there is a certain Material Force, there is the certain Principle; when there is no Material Force, there is no Principle; when there are more Material Forces, there are more Principles; when there are few Material Forces, there are few Principles. Then why can't we talk about completeness or partiality? (*Zhu Xi's Works*. Book 5. p.3078)

Zhu Xi's discussion on Emotion is always related to Nature. 1) In item 53, volume 5 of his *Classified Analects*, he said very clearly: "Nature is the Principle of Mind; Emotion is the movement of Nature; and Mind is the dominator of Nature and Emotion." He talked more concretely in item 56: "Nature is hard to describe. So, to say Nature is good is to see whether the four beginnings like compassion, shame, etc. are good, just like the clearness of stream water can prove the clearness of fountainhead. The four beginnings are Emotions. Nature is Principle. Its expression is Emotion and its origin is Nature, just like shadow and shape." 2) In volume 3 of his *Annotations to the Mencius* Zhu Xi made a clear description of the four beginnings: "Compassion, shame, modesty, and right-wrong are Emotions. Humanity, Righteousness, Propriety and Wisdom are Natures. Mind is the governor of Nature and Emotions. Beginnings are hints of the Emotions. When Emotions are expressed, they give hints to the Natures." It further told us that Humanity, Righteousness, Propriety and Wisdom referred to compassion, shame, reverence and right-wrong respectively.

Fourthly, when we are familiar with the conceptions and definitions of the component parts of the mechanism of the governance of Mind over Nature and Emotion, we can see it is concentrated on the discussion of silence and affection, of arousal and non-arousal, and of the Mean and Harmony. Zhu Xi took the four virtues of origination, prosperity, benignancy and perseverance and the four seasonal processes of birth, growth, harvest and storing in the *Zhou Book of Change* as examples to describe the relation between Nature and Emotion, thus illustrating comprehensively the working status of the mechanism of the governance of Mind over Nature and Emotion:

> Origination, prosperity, benignancy and perseverance are Natures; birth, growth, harvest and storing are Emotions; to give birth with origination, to grow with prosperity, to harvest with benignancy, and to store with perseverance are governed by the Mind. Humanity, Righteousness, Propriety and Wisdom are Natures; compassion, shame, compromise and right-wrong are Emotions; to love with Humanity, to hate with Righteousness, to compromise with Propriety, and to know with Wisdom are governed by the Mind. Nature is the Principle of the Mind; Emotion is the function of the Mind; and Mind is the governor of Nature and Emotion. When Master Cheng talked about substance being called the Change, Principle being called the Way, and its function being called mystery, he was actually referring to this mechanism. (*Zhu Xi's Works*. Book 6. p.3512)

Now let's further see how this mechanism works in the context of real movement or tranquility:

1) Silence and affection of the Mind is Zhu Xi's Principlist development on the basis of what is talked about in the *Survey to the Book of Change*. In the tenth chapter of the *Survey* it reads: "The *Change* does not think or move. It remains silent and tranquil. But when affected it penetrates through all things under Heaven." If this statement is somewhat deific or mystic, Zhu Xi's explanation is entirely a rational thought based on Principlism. He used this passage for further considerations:

Thoughtless and actionless, it remains in the state of silence and tranquility while being affected all the time. When it is being affected, it remains silent and tranquil all the time. This is the completion of the Heaven's destiny and extreme uprightness of Man's Mind, or what we say about the same origin of substance and function, or restless streaming of water. It seems unable to be coped with by division of the time. When it is not aroused, we see the substance of affection; when it is aroused, we see the function of the silence and tranquility: it just suits the different occasion but never separates. (*On Silence and Affection in the Book of Change, Collected Works.* Book 6. pp.3257–3258)

2) The movement and tranquility of the Mind was generally referred to as "arousal and non-arousal", as seen in the text of *The Doctrine of the Mean:*

Pleasure, anger, sorrow and joy, when not aroused, are in a state of the Mean; when aroused and conforming to the measure, they are called Harmony. The Mean is the grand foundation under Heaven, and Harmony is the most passable Way under Heaven. When the state of the Mean and Harmony is reached, Heaven and Earth will find their places and the myriad of things will be generated. (*Complete Works.* Book 6. p.33)

Zhu Xi did not discuss the problem of arousal and non-arousal in *The Doctrine of the Mean* simply, but referred to the philosophical consideration on the work of the Mind. This is a good example to show that Zhu Xi, though seemingly offering no original views of his own, did think about the problem deeply over and over, for he demonstrated his effort and ability in doing research with new discovery and development, and his explanation would always be reasonable and sound. In his *Explanation to the First Chapter of the Doctrine of the Mean* he gave a full explanation to the above passage:

The Heaven's destiny is called Nature. This is just a general statement. To speak separately, its substance is the Mean, and its function is Harmony. The Mean is what Heaven and Earth have established, and that's why it is called the grand foundation; the Harmony is how the change and generation has been working, and that's why it is called the most passable Way. Such is the complete statement of the Heaven's destiny. What man receives cannot be out of it. When pleasure, anger, sorrow and joy have not been aroused, it is in the state of the Mean; when they are aroused and conforming to the measure, it is called Harmony. However, Man may be allured by things and cannot control himself, so the grand foundation may not be established; the arousal may not conform to the measure, so the great Way may not be passable. With the grand foundation not established and the great Way not passable, though the Heavenly Way was still running incessantly, for me it may have stopped. Only the Gentleman knows that the Way is not to be left aside even for a second. Its substance and function are there, so there must be some way to attain it, and bring it to its fullest play. The reverence makes one upright inside, then pleasure, anger, sorrow and joy cannot go astray, so the Mean can be attained; the righteousness sets examples outside, then pleasure, anger, sorrow and joy can be adjusted, so the Harmony can be attained. When reverence and righteousness work together on one, he cultivates and inspects himself, keeping alert and careful all the time; then, he will have all the virtues in himself before those sentiments are aroused, and when those sentiments are aroused, the virtues will help him to arrive at tranquility and movements without interruption. Thus the Mean and Harmony are inside oneself and nothing stays between Heaven and Man — that is called "the Heaven and Earth will find their places and myriad of things will be generated".

3) The governance of Mind over Nature and Emotion is the theoretical

foundation of Zhu Xi's Principlist study on the Four Books.

Zhu Xi's Principlist explanation on the governance of Mind over Nature and Emotion can be regarded as part of his theoretical foundation of his study on the Four Books, especially *The Doctrine of the Mean*. The words in his *Preface to the Textual Analysis of the Doctrine of the Mean* may be taken as a summary of the above comment:

> I used to say that the mysterious and knowing Mind is only one. That the differentiation of the Mind of Man and the Mind of the Way comes from the understanding that the former was born from the individual form and the Material Force and therefore is dangerous, while the latter was born from the uprightness of the Nature and destiny and therefore is mysterious. Yet every one has a shape, so even the wisest has the Mind of Man, and every one has a Nature, so even the most stupid has the Mind of the the Way. Only the two has a very narrow gap between them. If not correctly coped with, the dangerous will become more dangerous, and the mysterious will become more mysterious, until at last the justice of the Heavenly Principle cannot conquer the privacy of Man's desires. Only with carefulness can one distinguish between the two and will not confuse them, and only with oneness can one keep to the Mind's uprightness and never leave it. Constantly keep at this without interruption, and the Mind of the Way will always be one's governor and the Mind of Man will always obey it. Thus the dangerous will be safe, and the mysterious will be apparent. Then either in motion or in tranquility, in speech or in action, one will not risk shortage or over-practice.

Therefore, with the basic knowledge of the theories of "combination of Principle and the Material Force" and "governance of Mind over Nature and Emotion" to examine Zhu Xi's study of the Four Books, we can understand to a great extent its true aim and significance. Some people, Lu Jiuyuan for example, criticized Zhu's study of the Four Books as merely textual explanations because they did not really understand Zhu

Xi's *Annotation to the Four Books*. By reading this book, we can see Zhu Xi's rich knowledge of language and culture, and come to a comprehensive understanding of his way to express his own exploration and aspiration for being a sage through long years of study and annotation of the Four Books, and with the *Annotations* itself, to reach his aim of "illuminating the luminous virtues, rejuvenating the people, and arriving at the best of bests".

3. Knowing/Doing & Sincerity/Reverence

The core of Zhu Xi's philosophy lies in the emphasis on both knowing and doing, with knowing in the key position. This explains why it is so important to acquire knowledge or thorough understanding by investigating things. And in the process of knowing and doing, an attitude of sincerity and reverence is required. These views are all closely related with Zhu Xi's theory on the study of the Four Books. Here we try to approach his study in six aspects: (1) the Four Books are an organic whole; (2) the three guidelines and eight items in the *Great Learning* are actually the aim and direction of being a man; (3) the cases in the *Confucian Analects* and the *Mencius* are standards and norms to turn the three guidelines and eight items into practical actions; (4) to acquire knowledge and get thorough understanding by investigating things is the prerequisite for practical action, for a full understanding of the objects and a good knowledge thus acquired are necessary for effective practice and actual results; (5) in the process of knowing/doing, the attitude of sincerity/reverence is critical, which should be cultivated through practice; (6) the aspiration for the *Doctrine of the Mean* is a superb or ideal process as well as a result at a high level, a state for life-long pursuing, because understanding and mastery of the *Doctrine of the Mean* can enhance the understanding of the *Great Learning*, the *Confucian Analects* and the *Mencius*, and guide everyone's practice more conscientiously.

Firstly, at the core of Zhu Xi's philosophy is the study of the Four Books, which are an integrated whole. Zhu Xi said about the completeness of the Four Books: "In reading one can start from the easiest and simplest ones such as the Four Books of the *Great Learning*, the *Doctrine of the Mean*, the *Confucian Analects* and the *Mencius*, which are so clear-cut in reasoning. Only people do not read them. If these Four Books are understood, what other books cannot be read! What reasoning cannot be attained! What affairs cannot be coped with!" (*Classified Analects*. Book 1. p.249) Obviously he regarded the Four Books as easy and simple instead of difficult and hard to read. The question is that people should regard them as core classical books for life-guidance, read and understand them thoroughly, so as to understand the principles under Heaven and to find a way to be a sage. He raised the Four Books to the level of sacred books. Thus, to read the Four Books is to read the sacred books of Principlism, the Bible of Confucianism. For Zhu Xi, the Four Books have already surpassed the traditional Five Classics of the *Book of Poetry*, the *Book of History*, the *Book of Change*, the *Book of Rites*, and the *Spring and Autumn Chronicles*, and become the sacred books for the new Principlism. Zhu Xi had more words on the Four Books, for instance:

I told people to read the *Great Learning* first, so as to know the whole structure; to read the *Confucian Analects* next, so as to set up the foundation; to read the *Mencius* still next, so as to see the development; then to read the *Doctrine of the Mean*, so as to see the subtlety of the ancient people. The *Great Learning* brings the grades and order together and is easy to understand, so it should be read first. The *Confucian Analects* is rather practical, but the teachings are scattered in different places, and it might not be easy for beginners. The *Mencius* could arouse and irritate people. The *Doctrine of the Mean* is a little difficult, and is suitable to read after finishing the other three books. The order of study should start from the *Great Learning*, then the *Confucian Analects*, then the *Mencius*, then the *Doctrine of the Mean*, the last being carefully written on a grand scale. Just read the *Great Learning* first, then the *Confucian Analects* and the *Mencius*, then the *Doctrine of the Mean*, and they should be read carefully and minutely, to the details of every word and every sentence. If these are thoroughly understood, your life will benefit to no bounds. If you do not study hard, all the ancient books you have read — no matter how many — will turn out to be of no use. Books are for enlightenment, leading you to do as the sages in the books did. So when these Four Books are read, other books will be easy to understand. (*Ibid*.)

The above passages lay emphasis on careful and thorough reading of the Four Books, in order to get enlightened and to do as the sages in the books do. By so doing, all other questions will be solved easily. Here, "get enlightened" and "do as the sages do" obviously refer to knowing and doing. Zhu Xi valued practice and emphasized it throughout his Principlist ideology and the whole process of his annotation to the Four Books. And his annotations to the Four Books can help us to understand the philosophical thoughts in the Four Books Study system.

Secondly, the way of the great learning, or the three guidelines and eight items as expressed in the *Great Learning*, are the aim and direction of the actions the Confucians educated the people to do. Zhu Xi held that the 205 sinographs of the first chapter of the *Great Learning* were Kong Zi's words quoted by Zeng Zi. And the next ten chapters were Zeng Zi's ideas written down by his disciples. The text, though fixed by Cheng Yi, had some passages in disorder, in Zhu Xi's opinion. So he re-ordered the whole text. Against this historical background, Cheng Yi gave a new explanation to the second guideline 親民 in the *Great Learning*, which Zhu Xi further annotated:

Master Cheng said: "親 should be read as 新."
"Great learning" is to learn to be great. 明 is to illuminate. "Luminous virtues" are what man got from Heaven, which is mysterious, full of wits and can be used to cope with various affairs. Restrained by personal Material Force or covered by Man's desires, they may be dimmed sometimes. However, their inner brightness is always there. So the learner should learn to re-illuminate them, so as to return to their original. 新 means to refresh or rejuvenate. When

one's own luminous virtues are re-illuminated, he should extend it to refresh others to get rid of the old dirtiness. "Stop" means to arrive at some place and never leave again. "Best of bests" is the place where all things and objects are at their best. That is to say, the effort at illuminating the luminous virtues and rejuvenating the people must stop at the best place and never leave again. One must strive to exhaust the extremes of the Heavenly Principles and be free from any Man's personal desires. These three are the guidelines of the Great Learning. (*Complete Works.* Book 6. p.16)

It can be seen that Zhu Xi is explaining the three guidelines from his own ontology and epistemology so as to establish the ultimate aim for the way of Great Learning. According to the three guidelines, there are two kinds of men: self and others. What one needs to do first is to cultivate one's own mind, which is mysterious, full of wits and can be used to cope with various affairs, and which is always covered by desires and needs to be illuminated now and then so as to return to the original. Then one must help others to illuminate their virtues. When both arrive at the best state, it should be kept unchanged. Nevertheless, to illuminate virtues has its own aims and courses, which are the so-called eight items: cause tranquility under Heaven, bring order to the state, regulate the family, cultivate the personality, rectify the mind, make the will sincere, acquire the knowledge, and investigate things. From the son of Heaven to ordinary people, everyone should do these eight things, and know why, what, and how:

Knowing where to stop, one will have determination. Determination leads to calmness. Calmness leads to tranquility. Tranquility leads to deliberation. Deliberation leads to attainment. Things have their roots and branches. Affairs have their beginnings and ends. To know which comes first and which comes afterwards is close to the Way. The ancient who wished to illuminate the luminous virtues under Heaven would first bring order to his state; he who wished to bring order to his state would first regulate his family;

he who wished to regulate his family would first cultivate his own personality; he who wished to cultivate himself would first rectify his mind; he who wished to rectify his mind would first make his will sincere; he who wished to make his will sincere would first acquire the knowledge; he who wished to know the knowledge would first investigate things. Things investigated, knowledge is acquired; knowledge acquired, will is sincere; will sincere, mind is rectified; mind rectified, personality is cultivated; personality cultivated, family is regulated; family regulated, state is in order; state in order, all under Heaven is in tranquility. From the son of Heaven down to an ordinary person, all must regard the cultivation of personality as the root. It has never been the case when the root is confused while the branches are in order; nor has it been the case when what is treasured becomes slighted and what is slighted becomes treasured. (*Ibid.* pp.16–17)

Thirdly, Zhu Xi regarded the cases in the *Confucian Analects* and *Mencius* as the standards and norms to turn three guidelines and eight items into practical actions. He said: "The *Confucian Analects* and *Mencius* are just the foodstuff of the *Great Learning*. All these, simple or detailed, are cross-referential. If the *Great Learning* is not used as a framework, the relation is not easily found." (*Classified Analects.* Vol. 19. p.48) This reveals that Zhu Xi's understanding of the *Confucian Analects* and *Mencius* was to put them in the framework of three guidelines and eight items in the *Great Learning*. To a certain extent, the *Great Learning* symbolized the two works in the Principlist way. From such an angle, "*Confucian Analects* is a fragmentized collection of questions and answers. Water is water, whether it is in the sea or in a ladle. So no matter how many times or words have been said, the Principle is the same one. When you understand it thoroughly once, you can understand it on other occasions." He said again: "What the sage and the worthy man said is just one thing. For instance, on the concept of 'choosing what is good to follow', the *Confucian Analects* would say 'study and practice it in due time', while the *Mencius* would say 'to understand goodness to make oneself sincere'. They used different precise words but eventually meant the same." (*Ibid.*) At the beginning of his compilation of the *Collected Annotations to Confucian Analects and Mencius*, he wrote a paper *How to Read Confucian Analects* and *Mencius* in which he cited eight quotations from Master Cheng. One of them is, "Master Cheng said, 'Studying *Confucian Analects* and *Mencius* first is like using a ruler or a scale, with which one can measure or weigh things and get to know their length or weight." Another one reads, "Master Cheng said, 'Learners should regard *Confucian Analects* and *Mencius* as the foundation. When the foundation is laid, the Six Classics can be understood without too much effort. In reading, the learners should try to know why the sage would write the classic, what he was intending, and how the sage became a sage, to be compared with why we could not attain where he had attained and what we are lacking. Reading and pondering day and night, setting the mind at ease, changing the material force and leaving what was doubtful, then the sage's intention could be seen." (*Complete Works.* Book 6. p.61)

The understanding of the *Confucian Analects* and *Mencius* by Zhu Xi and his disciples follows this way of thinking. For example,

Tong Boyu asked: "The words of *Confucian Analects* are all-inclusive, but what it reveals to people is only the essence of holding, remaining, moistening and nourishing. The intention of the *Mencius* is all exploratory, but what it reveals to people is mostly the beginning of self-experience for extension and expansion." Master Zhu replied: "Kong Zi was a man with a broad vision. Whatever he said has profound meaning. Meng Zi only told people what he found on the spot, unlike Kong Zi who was standing on the basic foundation. That's why Master Cheng said of him as 'a man of talent but lacking a solid foundation'. In a word, what Kong Zi said can cover Meng Zi while what Meng Zi said cannot go beyond Kong Zi. Kong Zi did not make everything clear but just told people what to do and the humanity was already there. For instance, he said: 'Be respectful in everyday life, be reverent in handling affairs, and be faithful when working with others.' When these are practiced, the mind is already there. Meng Zi is different. He said: 'The mind of compassion is the beginning of humanity. Anyone seeing an infant falling into a well will have a sense of apprehension and compassion.' This is to teach people to make inference from concrete facts." Yang Daofu asked: "Is Meng Zi's 'seeking the strayed mind' and 'born from accumulated righteousness' not standing on the basic foundation?" Master Zhu replied: "Sometimes he did so, but was always too general." Yang went on: "Did he just tell people what he himself was doing?" Master Zhu replied: "Yes, he did. It's also the way he saw things. From later people's eyes, Kong Zi and Yan Hui were like Emperor Wen of the Han dynasty who cultivated himself in tranquility and eventually abolished nearly all the punishments, whereas Meng Zi was like Emperor Taizong of the Tang dynasty who took care of everything under Heaven and also eventually abolished nearly all the punishments." (*Classified Analects. Book 2*. pp.430–431)

The *Confucian Analects* and *Mencius* respectively recorded the words and deeds of Kong Zi and Meng Zi, which result in different explanations as to their history and texts. Zhu Xi expressed his own ideas by citing Cheng Yi's opinion and inspired later readers to start from the stand of three guidelines in the *Great Learning*, and set its eight items as their aim of life and the cases in the *Confucian Analects* and *Mencius* as their standards of behavior.

Fourthly, Zhu Xi's emphasis of the *Great Learning* mainly lies on the four words of *ge-wu-zhi-zhi* (investigating things to acquire knowledge). "This idea is directly related to the method of learning, which is the focus of all Principlist theories." (Chen Lai. *A Study on Zhu Xi's Philosophy*. p.284) Zhu Xi said: "Investigating things to acquire knowledge. What is taught in the *Great Learning* is no more than 'A sovereign should stop at Humanity, and a subject should stop at reverence', which the ancients all have learned in their primary schooling. But things are not so simple. Inside 'stopping at Humanity and at reverence' there are many things, such as why Humanity and reverence should be practiced. Then we came to the detailed teachings about investigating things and acquiring knowledge. It is like going to the academy. If you just arrive at the gate of the academy, it is also 'arriving' or 'investigating things to acquire knowledge'. But if you do not come into the building of the academy, it is not 'investigating things to acquire knowledge' after all." "Others taught people to practice with standards set up by themselves. And there are certain people with good quality who can be free from exhausting the principles, investigating things and acquiring knowledge. Now the sage wrote the *Great Learning* as we see today, for the purpose of letting everyone enter the domain of the sage." "The *Great Learning* is the general outline of learning. Study it first to know the outline and you will find that the contents of other classics are cluttering in it. When the *Great Learning* is understood and you start to read other classics, you will find that a certain part is about investigating things to acquire knowledge, another part is about the cultivation of oneself, and a third part is about regulating the family, re-ordering the state, or bringing what under Heaven to tranquility." (*Classified Analects.* Book 1. p.252)

According to Zhu Xi's annotation to *ge-wu-zhi-zhi* in the text of the *Great Learning,* "*ge* means exhaust, *wu* means things. The whole phrase means to exhaust the principles in things to extremities." (*Complete Works.* Book 6. p.17) Thus, the concept of *ge-wu* consists of three stages, approaching things, exhausting principles and attaining extremities, among which the stage of exhausting the principles is most critical. Several points can be discussed: 1) It is not that after one thing is investigated, then all Principles are understood. Even Yan Hui could not do so. Only by investigating things one day after another, by accumulation of knowledge and experience, can one reach a certain point where all things are understood. 2) From the body of one person to the Principle of myriad of things, there is a lot for one to understand, and the day will come when he suddenly arrives at enlightenment. 3) To exhaust the principles does not mean to exhaust all the principles under Heaven, nor does it mean to exhaust the principles of one thing. It can only be understood through accumulation. 4) To investigate things does not mean to investigate all things in the world. Having exhausted the principles in one thing, one can extend it to other things. If a certain thing cannot be exhausted, one can start from other things, from easy to difficult, or from shallow to deep, as all things share the same Principle and all principles are from one origin and can be inferred from each other. 5) All things have principles and must be investigated. 6) Take filial piety for example: the Way of filial piety must first be realized. One must know what to offer suitably to one's parents and how to keep the house suitably warm or cool according to the seasons, etc. first before he can really practice the filial piety. There's more than simply prattling filial piety. 7) To observe things and examine oneself does not mean whenever one sees a thing he has to examine himself. As things and men share one Principle, knowing this may shed light on the other. This can be explained by the way of in and out. When talking about the largeness, one can extend to the height and thickness of Heaven and Earth; when talking about the smallness, one can go deep into the origin of one small thing. These should all be under a scholar's consideration. 8) If starting from Nature and Emotion, one is really starting from oneself. But it should be known that even a grass or a tree has its own Principle which is worthy of investigation. 9) The key of knowledge acquisition is to know the whereabouts of the best of best virtues. Failing at this by vainly investigating the principles of myriad things is like the troops roaming without destination. 10) The best way to investigate things is to examine oneself at the same time, which may bring you true feeling and knowledge.

Fifthly, the attitude of sincerity and reverence plays a key role in the process of knowing and doing. And this attitude should be nurtured in daily practice. There is a comprehensive analysis of sincerity with Zhu Xi's explanation in *The Doctrine of the Mean*. In *Questions on the Great Learning* Zhu Xi talked about the importance of reverence in study:

> Question: I have already known why there should be reverence at the beginning of study, but should there also be reverence at the end of study?
>
> Answer: Reverence is the dominator of the Mind as well as

myriad of things. Know where to make your effort, and you will know why primary learning must start from here; know primary learning's dependence on it as the beginning, and you will know why great learning must also depend on it as the ending — to keep consistency. When the Mind is set up, you can exhaust the Principles by investigating things to acquire knowledge, which is called "paying respect to virtuous nature and working on the way of learning"; you can also cultivate yourself by making your will sincere and rectifying your mind, which is called "establishing the big and not missing the small"; you can also regulate your family, re-order the state or even the world, which is called "cultivating oneself to calm the people, and being earnest and respectful to lead all under Heaven to tranquility". All these never leave reverence for a single day. Is reverence not of key importance from beginning to end in the sage's doctrine? (*Completed Works*. Book 6. pp.506–507)

Reverence is a quality necessary for all beginnings and endings, as well as an important condition for the success of all study and self-cultivation.

Zhu Xi's description of knowing/doing, sincerity/reverence, and investigating things for knowledge acquisition was rather complete, yet the sayings and words of other people which he cited were comparatively fragmented. So, from his own Principlist angle, he made a new and more comprehensive summary for this problem, revealing more of his own development:

The Heavenly Way is running its course and making generations. Whatever filled up Heaven and Earth with sounds, colors, looks and images are all things. As things, they cannot but have certain rules inside them, which were all bestowed by Heaven and not created by Man. Talking from what is closest to us, Mind as a thing is the dominator of our body. Its substance consists of the Natures of humanity, righteousness, propriety and wisdom; its function includes Emotions like compassion, shame, reverence and right-wrong, which

129

are mixed inside us, ready to be aroused by different senses with no confusion. Next, for what our body possesses, we have the usage of mouth, nose, ears, eyes and four limbs; for what our body contacts, we have the constant relations of sovereign/subject, father/son, husband/wife, elder/younger, and friends. These, similarly, cannot but have certain rules inside them, which we call the Principle. Outside me to other people, the Principle of other people is not different from that of mine; far from me to things, the Principle of things is not different from that of Man; to the largest, the running of Heaven and Earth and the change from ancient to present cannot go outside the Principle; to the smallest, space as tiny as a dust or time as short as a breath cannot go without it. This is the goodness bestowed by Heavenly God and the constant virtue held by common people, or what Master Liu called "between Heaven and Earth", what Confucius called "Nature and Heavenly Way", what Zisi called "Nature of the Heavenly destiny", what Meng Zi called "Mind of Humanity and Righteousness", what Master Cheng called "the Mean born from Nature", what Master Zhang called "the origin of myriad things", what Master Shao called "the shape and entity of the Dao", etc. But substance and Material Forces are different in clarity and partiality, and desires are different in depth and thickness, so the difference between Man and things, between the worthy and the unworthy, are also great and cannot be regarded as the same. Because the Principle is the same, the Mind of one man can know the Principle of the myriad of things under Heaven; because their qualities are different, the Principle cannot be exhausted for certain reasons. The Principle being unable to be exhausted is a proof that the knowledge is not complete enough; knowledge being incomplete, what the Mind has aroused cannot be purely reasonable but is mixed with selfish desires. In this case, his will is not sincere, his mind is not rectified, his personality is not cultivated, and neither the family, the state, nor all under Heaven can be brought into tranquility.

In the past the sage was worried about this and resorted to

education. He established primary learning, and did all he could to let the pupils be familiar with sincerity and reverence so as to regain their strayed minds, and cultivate their virtuous Nature. On entering the stage of great learning, he made them face the things and objects, extending the Principle they had already learned to make investigation to extremities, so that their knowledge would cover everything widely and profoundly. As to the methods of strenuous study, it may be researching the facts, or pondering over the subtle thoughts, or analyzing the sinographs, or attending lectures and discussions. Thus, they could, whether in the virtues of Mind and body and of Nature and Emotion, or in the constants of daily life and relations, or even in the change of Heaven and Earth, ghosts and deities, or in the adaptations of the birds, beasts, grass and trees, find in anything something which was inborn and subject to no change. They would understand thoroughly, both outside and inside, rough and delicate, and could make deduction, so that one day they could suddenly get everything through. Then everything in the world could be studied to the utmost subtlety and man's intelligence and wisdom could be used to display the Mind itself to infinity. (*Complete Works. Book 6. pp.526–528*)

Here Zhu Xi is adopting his methodology of "combination of Principle and Material Force" and "governance of Mind over Nature and Emotion" to make an analysis of the problem of "investigating things to acquire knowledge". It is based upon the viewpoint of "one Principle, many manifestations". At the same time, he fully realized that the problem was not explained fully and to its extremity. So he asked himself a question as a complementary remark: "However, you made your study not from the Mind but from the traces, not from inwards but from outwards. I am afraid that the learning of the sage and the worthy was not so shallow and segmented." He then answered the question himself:

Learning for man is just for the sake of Mind and Principle.

Although the Mind is the governor of only one body, its substance is mysterious enough to govern the Principle of the entire world; although the Principle is scattered in myriad of things, its function is so subtle that it does not go beyond one person's mind and cannot be discussed only from inside or outside, with roughness or delicacy. But if one does not know the mystery of the Mind and where to put it, then the Mind will be dim and disturbed, and unable to exhaust the fineness of the Principles. And not knowing the fineness of the Principles and the way to exhaust it, he will remain partial and stagnant, and cannot keep the wholeness of the Mind. It proves that the Principle and the momentum can promote each other. So the sage set up education to make people, on the one hand, memorize the mystery of the Mind and place it in the solemn tranquility and oneness as the source for exhausting the Principle; and on the other hand, know the subtlety of the Principles and exhaust them through study, consideration and debate, so as to work the Mind's function to full play. Large and small, active and tranquil, both contain and nourish each other. At first there is no choice for inside or outside, rough or delicate; later when truth and force are accumulated through a long time, thorough understanding is reached and the integrated oneness is found, there is no need to talk about inside or outside, roughness or delicacy. Now if you really think that this is shallow and segmented, and wish to hide the shape and shadow and create a deep and faraway, difficult and abstract theory, so that the learners will place their minds outside the words and discussions, and stress that the Dao can be reached only in this way, then it's most seriously influenced by the recent miscreant Buddhism. If you wish to transplant this to our ancients' learning that taught us to illuminate luminous virtues and rejuvenate people, you are utterly wrong! (*Ibid.*)

In the process of investigating things to acquire knowledge and exhausting the Principle, Zhu Xi quoted the Cheng brothers' words extensively and talked a lot about the Principle of things, but at the same time he also emphasized the importance of exhausting the Principle of the Mind. Only the method and process were slightly different with those of things. Obviously he did not agree with Lu Jiuyuan's psychological method.

Knowledge acquisition and Principle exhaustion must finally be realized in practice, so Zhu Xi repeatedly emphasized the parallel of knowing and doing and their mutual promotion. For instance, he said: "Knowing and doing always promote each other, like eyes cannot walk without feet and feet cannot see without eyes. In terms of sequence, knowing comes in advance; but in terms of weight, doing is heavier." "In relation to knowing and doing, he said, 'Knowledge not yet practiced, this knowledge is still shallow; only after personal practice can this knowledge become clearer, unlike that of days before.'" "Knowledge acquisition and forceful action are not to be biased. When one side is inclined upon, the other side will be injured. Master Cheng said, 'Self-cultivation needs reverence; study promotion ends with knowledge acquisition.' He was dividing them into two. What he needed is to differentiate first and second, or light and heavy." "When the sage or the worthy talked about knowing, he was at the same time talking about doing. In the *Great Learning,* 'Like cutting then filing, it is indicating the course of learning' is immediately followed by 'Like chiseling then grinding, it is indicating the course of self-cultivation'. In *The Doctrine of the Mean,* 'study, inquiry, meditation, discrimination' is followed by 'practice'." (*Classified Analects.* Book 1. p.148)

Sixthly, what *The Doctrine of the Mean* aspires is an ideal, superb process and effect of knowing/doing and sincerity/reverence at a high level, a life pursuit for man. The understanding and mastery of *The Doctrine of the Mean* can help improve our understanding of *The Great Learning, Confucian Analects,* and *Mencius,* as well as the general level of knowing and doing. To put it in short, there is a passage on sincerity in *The Doctrine of the Mean:*

> Sincerity is the Way of the Heaven; to attain sincerity is the Way of Man. Sincerity means hitting the point without effort, getting the idea without consideration, and leisurely walking on the Way of the Mean: this is the sage. To attain sincerity means to choose goodness

and persistently hold on to it. He must study broadly, inquire carefully, meditate cautiously, discriminate clearly and practice earnestly. (*Ibid.* p.48)

Zhu Xi's annotation to the above passage may be regarded as the starting point of his Principlism, as well as the focus of his philosophical ideas. He said:

Sincerity means truth without any mistakes. This is the Nature from the Heavenly Principle. To attain sincerity means to get something that is not perfectly true and endeavor to make it perfectly true. This is what the Man should aspire for. The sage's virtues are completely Heavenly Principles, and are true without any mistakes. He leisurely walks on the Way of the Mean, or the Way of Heaven, without having to make consideration. Not yet to the stage of sagehood, one cannot be free from human desires and what he does cannot be all true. Unable to get anything without consideration, he has to make a choice of what is good before he takes any action. Choosing goodness is something relating to study, and persistently holding on to it is something relating to action.

The next five points are to Zhu Xi the steps to attain sincerity. He even said, "Study, inquiry, meditation and discrimination are the process for choosing goodness: it is getting knowledge by learning. Earnest action is persistency in practicing Humanity: it is applied for action. Master Cheng said, 'Removing any one from the five, it is not true learning.'" That's why knowing/doing and sincerity/reverence emphasized by Zhu Xi in his Four Books Studies became the starting point for us to understand Zhu Xi's thoughts.

Chapter Four

Synthesizer of the Song Dynasty Principlism

At the age of 48, in his correspondence with Zhang Shi, Zhu Xi mentioned the topic of "synthesis". Although in his letter he just talked about the meaning of synthesis and its development, by reading through his *Complete Works,* we find that the general framework of his Principlist synthesis had already formed. In the next 23 years of his life (Zhu Xi lived to 71 years old), though his academic thoughts developed at a slower pace and he published fewer academic works, he still made some improvement to his synthetic work. Using his own standard "collection and systemization" for synthesis to examine his Principlism, we can see that throughout his life he was strenuously working on the realization of this aim. Here we will discuss it in three aspects: 1) His agreement with Cheng Yi in their minds. The compilation of *Posthumous Writings of Cheng Brothers* and *More Writings of Cheng Brothers*, the annotation to *Master Zhu's Three Books,* and the edition of *Close Reflections* all revealed his exploration to the origin of Principlism. 2) The Principlist approach to the Four Books Studies, the Principlist explanation of the Five Classics, the reconciliation of the four branches of Confucian classics, histories, miscellaneous schools and collections, the sorting of the Song dynasty Principlist legacies such as *Source and Course of Principlist Scholars* and *Analects of Xie Liangzuo,* and the Principlist explanation of a series of historical works like *A Compendium of History as a Mirror for Governance* and *Words and Deeds of Famous Officials of Eight Imperial Courts* — all these showed his capacity of academic synthesis. 3) His correspondence with contemporary scholars all had some relation to the development or defense of the Principlism. The representative scholars were Zhang Shi, Lu Zuqian, Lu Jiuyuan and Chen Liang. Superficially, all his viewpoints were inherited and developed from his predecessors, but judging more profoundly, Zhu Xi was an independent scholar himself. With his perseverance and persistent work, he collected the segments and passages of Principlist ideas, the individual scholars and their words and works, and put them together through scrutiny, analysis and selection into an organic integration with his own explanation and development, thus resulting in the Principlism with Zhu Xi's name.

1. Communication with Cheng Yi through Minds

Zhu Xi was regarded as the synthesizer of Principlism by later scholars, and his theory was called Cheng-Zhu Principlism. Why should it be called Cheng-Zhu Principlism? It is mostly due to Zhu Xi himself. As a matter of fact, the core of Zhu Xi's philosophical ideas, or ontology, was the explanation and interpretation to *The Extreme Ultimate Diagram*, *The Book of Thorough Understanding*, and *The Western Inscription*, written respectively by Zhou Dunyi and Zhang Zai. And his theory of "governance of Mind over Nature and Emotion" was also from Zhang Zai. In this way, it is not so reasonable to call his theory Cheng-Zhu Principlism. But from the construction of the Four Books Studies, he mainly inherited the academic legacy of the two Cheng brothers. From Zhu Xi's *Postscript to the Posthumous Writings of Cheng Brothers* we see that both Cheng Yi and Zhu Xi emphasized the importance of communication of minds through writings. And the main part of Zhu Xi's Principlism was his development and extension on the Chengs' discourses. The relation between Zhu Xi and Cheng Yi provides an illustrative case for the study of Zhu Xi's synthesis.

After formally acknowledging Li Tong as his master, Zhu Xi studied more diligently on Confucian classics and won Li Tong's praise. After Li Tong's death, Zhu Xi wrote *Preface to Perplexed to Learn and Afraid of Hearing Too Much: Miscellaneous Writings*, which in a way exposed the broad mind of a Confucian and can be regarded as Zhu's version of Cheng Yi's work *What Sort of Learning Does Master Yan Like* in the new era. This matching of their thought can be regarded as the "communication through minds" in

Principlism. Zhu Xi said:

> Master Kong said: "those who are born learned are of the highest grade; those who learn to become learned are of the next; those who are perplexed and want to learn are of the still next; those who are perplexed and refuse to learn are at the lowest." Those "born learned" are Yao, Shun and Kong Zi himself; those who "learn to become learned" are Yu, Ji and Yan Hui. Perplexity is having difficulty in action. Feeling perplexed and starting to learn to make himself more capable is lower than the above two. However, being able to do so, he may make achievements not far behind those gentlemen; being unable to do so, he may be demoted to the lowest class. The difference between the two lies in whether he takes up learning. He must be encouraged! He must be encouraged! I used to name my living-room "Perplexed to Learn", and tell everyone who came its meaning. Now I entitled my anthology of miscellaneous writings as *Perplexed to Learn and Afraid of Hearing Too Much: Miscellaneous Writings,* the second phrase of which was taken from the meaning of Zilu in *Confucian Analects* who was afraid of hearing too much in case he was unable to act upon all of them. In my opinion, those who are "perplexed to learn" should take this attitude in their endeavor. If people, reading my book, will worry about being degenerated to lower grades and being unable to act upon all they have heard, it will be a great help for me in practicing my humanity. (*Complete Works.* Book 24. p.3617)

The preface should have some relation with his teacher Li Tong. Because of Li Tong's death, Zhu Xi's promising study of Confucianism came to a pause and he felt anxious about it. This anxiety, expressed in that preface as a proclamation of ambition, was similar to the sentiments expressed in Cheng Yi's work *What Sort of Learning Does Master Yan Like* written at his young age. To a certain extent, the two papers matched with each other and formed a "communication through minds". The background of Cheng Yi's paper was: "Cheng went to study at the State

Academy at about twenty. Hu Yuan tested the students and was surprised at seeing Cheng Yi's paper. He at once received him and asked him to be a teacher at the academy." This paper, which had surprised Hu Yuan, must have also attracted Zhu Xi's attention:

Among the sage's 3,000 students Yan Hui was the only one recognized as good at learning. When the six arts like *Book of Poetry*, *Book of History*, etc, were studied by all 3,000 students, what, then, was the branch of learning specially favored by Master Yan? It must be the learning that led to being a sage.

Can one learn to be a sage? The answer is "Yes". Then what is the proper way of learning? The answer is: Heaven and Earth accumulated the essence of the universe and bestowed the fineness of the five phases upon Man, who, by origin, was true and tranquil. When not aroused it possessed the five Natures of humanity, righteousness, propriety, wisdom and fidelity. When its shape was formed and aroused by outside things, its core was stirred and seven Emotions were aroused, called pleasure, anger, sorrow, joy, love, hatred and desire. When emotions were flamed and became agitated, the Natures were challenged. Then the awakened would restrain their emotions to the Mean, rectify their Minds and nourish their Natures. This is called Nature overcoming Emotions. The dull did not understand this. They would let go of their Emotions until they went astray and fetter their Natures until they were lost. This is called Emotions conquering Nature. The way of learning is nothing but rectifying one's Mind and nourishing the Nature. Abide by the Mean and be sincere, and he will be the sage. For a gentleman to learn, he must first understand the Mind, know what to nourish, then practice hard to reach the extremity. This is called from understanding to sincerity. So the learner must exhaust his Mind. With Mind exhausted, Nature is known. When Nature is known, he can return to sincerity and be a sage. That's why the *Grand Norms* said: "Thinking means wisdom; wisdom begets sage." The way to be sincere lies in the depth of fidelity in the Way. Deep fidelity leads to the effective result of action. The effective result of action makes one keep to it more resolutely. The humanity, righteousness, faithfulness and fidelity must never leave the Mind, sticking to it in haste, sticking to it in turmoil, and sticking to it out or at home, in speech or in silence. As time passes they will never get lost and Man will live peacefully with it and all his actions and behavior will fit the requirement of rites, and there will be no room for crooked ideas to spring up.

So what Master Yan followed was "not looking at anything that is against the propriety, not listening to anything that is against the propriety, not saying anything that is against the propriety and not doing anything that is against the propriety". What Kong Zi praised of him was "Whenever he got hold of something good, he would keep it to his heart and never lose it," and "He never vented his anger on others or repeated an error for the second time. For things not good he never failed to know, and never did it again if he did know." This proves how profoundly he was fond of learning and how diligently he learned. Whatever he looked at, or listened to, or said, or did, was in accordance with the rules of propriety. The difference between him and the sage lies in that the sage was born learned and needed no strenuous effort to hit at the point and took on the way of Mean at ease, while Master Yan had to think before gaining, and work strenuously before hitting at the point. So the gap between Master Yan and the sage is only a hair's breadth. Meng Zi said: "Filling up with substance and brilliance is called great. Great with transforming power is called a sage. A sage to an unknown extent is called a deity." Master Yan is at the stage of "filling up with substance and brilliance". What he was still lacking is that his power is just to keep to it but not to transformation. Since he was so fond of learning, if given years, he would soon reach the stage of transformation. That's why Kong Zi said: "It is a pity that he died at so young an age." He was sorry that Yan was unable to reach the stage of being a sage. Transformation refers to the ability of being mystic and natural, to gain without thinking and to hit at the point without paying effort. It is also what Kong Zi said about "At the age of seventy, I did everything according to my mind and never violated rules."

Somebody asked: "Sages are those who were born learned. Now you say we can become sages through learning. Is there any reason?" I replied: "Yes. Meng Zi said: 'Yao and Shun are by Nature whereas Tang and Wu are by turning back.' By Nature means born learned, and by turning back means to learn to be learned." I said again: "Kong Zi was born learned. Meng Zi was learned through learning. Later people did not know that and thought that sages were born learned and could not be attained through learning, thus losing the way of learning. Instead of turning back to make requirements of themselves they sought ways outside and praised those with strong memories or writings with flowery words. They spoke highly but seldom attained the Dao. So what the scholars like today is quite different from what Master Yan liked at his time." (*Works of Cheng Hao and Cheng Yi.* pp.577–578)

In this paper Cheng expressed an idea of making the Four Books of *The Great Learning, The Book of the Mean, The Confucian Analects* and *Mencius* as the foundation of learning. At the same time he criticized the study atmosphere of his time and encouraged a practical and rational spirit of learning to be a sage. This happened to be the same aspiration and ideal which Zhu Xi fostered at his young age. This matching of minds later led to Zhu Xi's action in compiling *Posthumous Writings of Cheng Brothers* and *More Writings of Cheng Brothers*. In Vol. III of his *New Philosophical Studies of Master Zhu*, Qian Mu made a comment when talking about Zhu's compilation of *Posthumous Writings of Cheng Brothers* and *More Writings of Cheng Brothers*: "The *Posthumous Writings of Cheng Brothers* was compiled at the fourth year of Qiandao period (1168 AD) when Master Zhu was 39 years old. The Cheng brothers' doctrines were highly valued and worshiped at that time and the compilation of the *Posthumous Writings* was exquisite in selection and careful in arrangement, presenting a good order for learners to follow. This was Master Zhu's great contribution to the Principlist circle of that time." (p.126) "The *More Writings of Cheng Brothers* was edited at the ninth year of Qiandao period (1173 AD) when Master Zhu was 44 years old, five years later after the previous book. This is an exhaustive collection of two Chengs' unpublished works. He further discussed the errors in Hu Anguo's version of *Chengs' Collected Works*, which I will discuss in detail in my *On Master Zhu's Emendation Studies*, thus creating a credible and readable version of Chengs' works. This was also Master Zhu's contribution. If the scholars at that time were like Chengs' own disciples, paying little attention to the ancient classics on the one hand, caring even less about ancient literature and history on the other, leaving their teachers' works and teachings in disorder, contenting themselves with citing a few isolated sentences as having included all the essence of their teachers' theory and learning, then after one or two generations, the doctrine would unavoidably decline." (*Ibid.* p.128) This is indeed the case in history. For Zhu Xi, what he gained is the "communication of minds" throughout the process of compilation. He acknowledged in the two postscripts of the books:

> The book *Posthumous Writings of Cheng Brothers* with 25 chapters of questions and answers between teacher and students were all notes recorded by the disciples of the two Cheng masters. At first the notes were recorded and later published separately after their teachers' death. There was not a unified version between them and sometimes the individual recorders would even make some revisions for their own sake. Years passed and there have been not a complete book. I used to have some copies at home stored and passed down by my ancestors, which, with recorders' names on them and coherence in content, were quite reliable for having not been altered by other hands. Later I tried to search for more of the same kind and finally got 25 chapters. Then I re-ordered them by the sequence of recording time, retaining their original titles and making a new copy so as to see the reasons for classification. Nevertheless, once I heard a story

that when Master Cheng Yi was still alive and healthy, his pupil Yin Tun got a note taken by Zhu Guangting and showed it to the master. The master replied: "I am still alive. What's the use of reading the notes? If it did not get my mind, it is only the recorder's idea." Since then Mr Yin dared not read the notes again. Now the two Cheng masters propagated Principlism a thousand years after Kong Zi and Meng Zi's death and brought it to new prosperity, and their disciples were all elites of the time. They studied under their teacher so closely and their notes should have been able to record the true essence and be passed down to others, yet Master Cheng was still so alert lest they be distorted. He must be worried that the scholars might not know the importance of "mind communication" and rest on the surface of the language. Should there be a slight deviation, the errors it caused might be beyond imagination! Not to say that I myself live several scores of years after them; by just collecting the segmental remainders and hearsays that are hard to tell right or wrong, I am really uncertain that these material could lead us to the delicate truth of their teachings. However, the general idea of the masters' learning can be known. If the readers of this book can set up the foundation mainly on reverence and understand the Principles to exhaust the knowledge so that with the foundation established and knowledge cleared up, the Dao may be understood and the foundation be more solid, then they may attain the mind of the master in their life, and be able to make judgment between truth and doubt. Besides, there are more copies from different hands which were mostly separate parts or amendments, not the original. In the future, if I can find the originals, I will add into the present version; if not, I will discard the redundant and edit the rest into another book for future scholars. (*Complete Works: Extra Volumes*. Book 2. pp.10–11)

After the appendix to the *Posthumous Writings of Cheng Brothers*, Zhu Xi said:

The volume on the right is an appendix of eight papers about Master Cheng Hao's brief biography and others, including an elegy and a report of Cheng Yi, both in the original. Only there was no book written about Cheng Yi's life in the past. I tried to find texts from the *True Records* and *Selected Works*, collected and compared them with things mentioned in other books, and finalized into a personal chronicle. I dared not exaggerate, nor could I promise that every record was correct. All I could do was to add a note to every item to show its source. Now I combined them together into one volume as an attachment to the 25 chapters. Alas! If only we can examine the words to find his mind, investigate his deeds to see his application, and get something from both! Can we then possibly say that his Dao has already been passed on to us? (*Ibid.* p.12)

We can clearly see that Zhu Xi was re-ordering the two Chengs' works in such a careful and down-to-earth way that on the one hand he was earnestly inheriting the Principlist thought of his predecessors, and on the other hand he was continuously finalizing his own ideology through the process of learning and editing. As quoted above, "to know mind communication" and "to find the mind" which he emphasized twice were the true academic target he was aspiring for. For example, in editing *Essentials of Confucian Analects and Mencius*, the outline was exactly the essence extracted from the words of the two Chengs about the two classics. And on certain points he would carry out a focal study and write a defining essay. Here is one example in *Master Cheng on Nourishment and Examination:*

Question: "Master Cheng said: 'The retaining (of Nature) and cultivation (of Mind) is better done before the arousal (of Emotions).' He said also: 'A good examiner examines the arousal (of Emotions).' What does he really mean?"
Answer: "This means reverence must penetrate through movement and tranquility. In your quotation from Master Cheng, before arousal, things were already there. That is called conception in tranquility,

or the revealing of the Mind of Heaven and Earth as related in the Fu hexagram; when already aroused, things were to be examined along with their development. That is called seeking tranquility through movement, or stopping at the right place as related in the Gen hexagram. But without reverence, what else can shape the form of movement in tranquility, or examine the tranquility in movement? That's why the Master said again: 'It is better for the learner to care for reverence first, and then all of them will be known.' In this case, learners should not seek ways other than this." (*Complete Works*. Book 23. p.3269)

Zhu Xi met his dilemma in his academic development when Li Tong died. After repeated consideration and exploration, he made up his mind to follow a way of handling perplexity with learning, to learn to assist Humanity and finally to be a sage. This is quite similar to Cheng Yi at the time when he wrote *What Sort of Learning Does Master Yan Like,* or we may say this is to a certain extent a communication of minds or an agreement between minds. Zhu Xi turned his goal to action and took up the work of sorting the Cheng brothers' philosophical works. This not only benefited the popularization of the Chengs' doctrine, but served to open up a new path for his own academic career.

2. The Synthesized Principlist System of Zhu Xi

The synthesized Principlist system is a good portrayal of Zhu Xi's life-long endeavor for learning to be a sage. His "synthesis" can be summarized in the following four features: 1) The establishment of the Four Books as the new core canon of Confucian classics. The Principlist annotation and explanation done by Zhu Xi to the Four Books made it a new composite and specialized learning, which demoted the traditional Five Classics to the secondary place, and later formed a new Confucian tradition consisting of the Four Books and the Five Classics, which lasted till today. And Zhu Xi's Principlist annotation and explanation displayed new features of his own hermeneutics. 2) *Master Zhu's Three Books* of *An Explanation to the Extreme Ultimate Diagram, An Explanation to the Book of Thorough Understanding,* and *An Explanation to the Western Inscription,* created by making annotation and explanation to Zhou Dunyi and Zhang Zai's original works, and the Principlist hermeneutic system which is the combination of substance and function, knowing and doing, sincerity and reverence, formed on the basis of the mechanic of governance of Mind over Nature and Emotion, which was inherited and developed from the *Doctrine of the Mean,* the *Mencius,* Zhang Zai down to Zhu Xi. 3) The sorting and study of the source and course of the Yi-Luo school (i.e. the two Chengs and their disciples) not only provided rich material for the study of the above two aspects but also left a precious legacy for later generations about the development of Principlism, which had a far-reaching influence. 4) The combined historical and philosophical study broadened Zhu Xi's academic view, and the all-round research in the four branches of Confucian classics, histories, miscellaneous schools and collections revealed his aspiration to be a sage through broad study, constant ambition, tireless learning and close consideration.

Zhu Xi studied the Four Books all his life. His latest revision of the *Great Learning* was done just one month before his death. His works about the Four Books could be divided into five groups: 1) *Textual Analysis and Collected Annotations of the Four Books.* This is the core classic. In the process of making annotation and explanation to the Four Books, Zhu Xi combined the Han dynasty methodology of textual study and the Song dynasty methodology of ideological interpretation. This approach was praised even by the compilers of *The Complete Library of the Four Treasuries* in the Qing Dynasty, who strictly distinguished these two schools of learning. Among the Four Books, the annotation to *The Great Learning* and *The Doctrine of the Mean* were called *Textual Analysis* while those to *The Confucian Analects* and *Mencius* were called *Collected Annotations,* as the latter had quoted many words from the two Cheng masters as well as their disciples and others. 2) *Essentials of Confucian Analects and Mencius* and *Digest of Explanations to the Doctrine of the Mean.* Though the latter book was just his compilation, Zhu Xi did play a leading role in the making of the final version. The book selected the explanations of *The Doctrine of the Mean* from ten scholars: Zhou Dunyi, Cheng Hao, Cheng Yi, Zhang Zai, Lü Dalin, Xie Liangzuo, You Zuo, Yang Shi, Hou Zhongliang and Yin Tun, in the same editorial policy as the former book, which selected explanations of *The Confucian Analects* and *Mencius* from eleven scholars: Cheng Hao, Cheng Yi, Zhang Zai, Fan Zuyu, Lü Xizhe, Lü Dalin, Xie Liangzuo, You Zuo, Yang Shi, Hou Zhongliang and Yin Tun. People used to think that with the publication of the *Collected Annotations of the Four Books* and *Questions on the Four Books, Essentials of Confucian Analects and Mencius* might be unnecessary to go around. But Zhu Xi insisted on it, saying that "*Collected Annotations* was the essence of the *Essentials*". So we may regard the *Essentials* as an indispensible part of Zhu Xi's Four Books Studies. 3) *Questions on the Four Books.* This is his more detailed explanation and comment on the Four Books. 4) Miscellaneous writings in *The Collected Works of Zhu Xi.* They are prefaces, discussions on the main or difficult points in the Four Books, and letters about the topic. 5) Questions and answers in the *Classified Analects of Zhu Xi.* Reading through *The Complete Works of Zhu Xi*, we can not only get a comprehensive understanding of Zhu Xi's system of his Four Books Studies, but also sense his profound knowledge in his Four Books Studies and carefulness in researching the traditional culture. Zhu Xi had many writings on the Four Books. Having a good understanding of his Principlist ideology may be an easy way to approach them.

Zhu Xi also made systematic annotations and explanations to the five traditional Confucian classics and wrote *Collected Annotations to the Book of Poetry*, *Collected Annotations of the Book of History*, *A General Explanation to the Texts and Annotations of Rites and Ceremonies*, and *The Original Meanings of the Zhou Book of Change*, though the second one was not finished and the third one was not published in his life. He did not write annotations to the *Spring and Autumn Chronicles,* but we found in his *Classified Analects* that he was very familiar with this book and its three *Comments,* and had a plan to write on it. Zhu Xi's *Collected Annotations to the Book of Poetry* was full of Priniplist spirit. When asked why he did not explain the *Prefaces to the Book of Poetry*, Zhu Xi replied:

When I began to read *The Book of Poetry* at the age of twenty, I found those *Little Prefaces* meaningless. After discarding them, I found the reading of the *Poetry* more tasteful. I asked many home teachers about it and they all replied that the *Prefaces* should not be abandoned. Yet my doubts had never been removed. When I was thirty years old I resolutely concluded that the *Little Prefaces* were concocted by the Han dynasty Confucians on no ground and were absurd beyond words. (*Complete Works.* Book 17. p.2750)

From this we can see Zhu Xi's Principlist spirit in reading, i.e., the historical view of contexts, the careful perusal of texts, the accumulation of investigation, and the independent and rational judgment. So in his Preface to his *Collected Annotations to the Book of Poetry* he followed his own Principlist way when he talked about the objects and significance of *The Book of Poetry*:

Man was born tranquil — that was Heaven's Nature; Man was moved by the influence of the things — that was the desire of the Nature. Desires led to thoughts, which led to words, which, when words themselves were not enough, would lead to chants and songs with natural rhythms — that was how the poetry came into being.

Poetry was what remained when human mind was moved by things to words. The movements of minds might be good or evil, so the words it formed might be right or wrong. Only the sage was on top of every one and his movements were all good, so his words could be used as teaching material. Sometimes his movements were so complicated that one had to make a choice when he heard the sage's words, and the wiser men would return to themselves and learn lessons, which was also a sort of teaching. When the Zhou dynasty was in its prime time, up from the royal court and down to the lanes and villages, all words they uttered were correct and were set to music by the sage to influence the country and people. And the poetry of the different states was also displayed to be examined as a reference for promotion or demotion when the king went on an inspection tour over the country. After the reigns of King Zhao and King Mu the country began to decline. Down to the Eastern Zhou period, the custom was totally given up. Kong Zi was living at that period but was not in the position like kings to play the role of inspection or promotion and demotion. What he could do was to collect and study the lost classics, discard the redundant, adjust the confusing, and remove those good ones yet not enough to set as examples and evil ones yet not enough to use as alerts, thus creating a version for readers to know the gains and losses, to learn from the good and to overcome the evil. So although his politics was not adopted at his time, his teachings are enlightening for thousands of years. (*Complete Works*. Book 1. pp.350–351)

What Zhu Xi gave to the traditional classics was not only a Principlist interpretation, but also detailed annotations and explanations based on the profound study of the notes of the predecessors, which brought new experience and insights to the readers.

For the study of *The Zhou Book of Change,* Zhu Xi wrote two books, *The Original Meaning of the Zhou Book of Change* and *A Primer of the Change Study*, and the former became one of the classics in the history of *Change* studies. Zhu Xi said in a letter to his friend:

Your metaphor about reading the *Change* was a good one. The book was written for divination and the words were used according to the images and numbers to decide luckiness or unluckiness. Its methodology no longer existed later, so all the later talks about images and numbers were far-fetched and all the later talks about meaning and theory were groundless. That's why the book is not easy to read, and also the reason I should have written the *Original Meanings* and the *Primer* for it. (*Complete Works*. Book 23. p.2886)

Here we can see the sincerity and practicality of Zhu Xi's scholarship. On the one hand, he tried to clear up the development of *The Zhou Book of Change*; on the other, he was also popularizing the book. Different from the Song Dynasty tendency of *Change* research which aimed at elaborating theories through the book, Zhu's research laid emphasis first on the inheritance of the classic and tradition, and the development of new ideas from it. He investigated the development of the book with a historical view. One of his well-known opinions was that "*The Change* was originally a book for divination". He reiterated that "Fuxi's *Change* was Fuxi's *Change*, King Wen's *Change* was King Wen's *Change*, and Kong Zi's *Change* was Kong Zi's *Change*"; (*Complete Works.* Book 16. p.2211) he emphasized that the book was a result of accumulation, which should be read in relation with different historical periods when new things were created and added. There are many differences between Zhu Xi's *Zhou Change* study with that of his contemporaries, and his study of images was more enlightening to later scholars. He said, "Mr Cheng Yi said that images were just metaphors. But there should be images as they were; only we cannot guess them out." (*Ibid.* p.2203) And he did point out in several places certain ancient meanings possibly implied in the images of the book. He worked hard on the classics in a down-to-earth way, and rejected empty talk. He did not blindly follow Cheng Yi whom he respected so much. He said:

> Mr Cheng Yi said that images were just metaphors. But I am afraid that the sage would not be willing to write a book of metaphors. Zhu Zhen often used implied hexagram or alternates to explain Yin and Yang. When he talked about Yin, he could extend it to Yang, and vice versa. For him Qian could become Kun and Kun could become Qian. These were too absurd. Recently Lin Li developed another concept of "tumbling alternate", with which one hexagram could change to eight. How ridiculous! In my opinion, the sage wrote the *Change* just as a book for divination. Only later Confucians were reluctant to admit the fact and tried every means to evade from the topic. That's why they were so difficult. Today we shall only add the meaning of divination to

it, and everything will be easy to explain. (*Ibid*. p.2218)

Here we see that Zhu Xi never followed others blindly, nor did he worship the ancients or authorities blindly, and he was good at finding problems in reading and offered his doubt. This is the true academic spirit of a Principlist, which was vividly displayed in his *Zhou Change* study and worth learning from.

Zhu Xi attached great importance to the study of rites and ceremonies. He wrote *A General Explanation to the Texts and Annotations of Rites and Ceremonies*, a huge book with 66 volumes and 1.3 million sinograms, which was not published in his lifetime. He started to study rites and rite systems very early, which was abundantly recorded in his *Classified Analects* and *Collected Works*. The *Illustrated Sacrificial Ceremony to Kong Zi Practiced at Prefectures and Counties in the Shaoxi Period*, which he compiled for local schools, was a practical and useful pamphlet of rites. The *Household Rituals* he edited was also a simplified and applicable rites book for ordinary people and had a wide influence. In our classics study we used to neglect the study of rite systems, dismissing that as already out of date. But after reading this *General Explanation*, we might change our mind; we can not only acquire certain knowledge in this branch of traditional culture, but have a new view of Zhu Xi's synthesized Principlist system as well as his personal ambition.

He said: "It is over 2,000 years since the system of rites and music collapsed, but judging from a grander angle, it's still a short period. However, most of the rites are already little known. It is expected that some very great man in the future will make a thorough study of them, but I don't know when he will appear. Now the world is changing rapidly, but I believe there is still the principle of 'the biggest fruit remaining uneaten'." (*Complete Works*. Book 17. p.2876) These words showed that he was really a far-sighted Principlist, who regarded the study and practice of rites and rite systems as an important aspect in ruling the country and a social practice of the Four Books Studies. This not being done, like the biggest fruit remaining uneaten, would make him feel sorry. From a Principlist angle he said: "'Heaven regulates the decrees. It bestows upon us five decrees to make our relations thick. Heaven regulates the rites. It makes us follow five rites as constants.' This is Heaven's bestowal, not to be added or subtracted. Only the sage's mind is in accord with that of Heaven, and the rites he sets entirely agree with Heaven in every detail. They were created by the sage not in vain, but out of Heaven's decree. The later people's minds might not be the same as the sage's mind, so if they did as the sage had done and passed the practice down to their posterity, that would be good enough and go along with Heaven and the Principle." (*Ibid.* p.2885) This explains why, despite his old age and poor health, he insisted on compiling the book. However, he thought that the rites he studied and re-ordered should be applicable. But the applicability depended on certain objective conditions. And the most ideal conditions were: "Understanding the Zhou rites is the first step, but to apply them needs the position of the prime minister, who must fully understand the good result. However, even the prime minister needs an emperor as wise as King Wen or King Wu to fully put his will to action." (*Ibid*. p.2879)

He fully understood that for the realization of his ideal, it needed "a very great man", and the sorting and reform of rites classics also needed "a very great man" to "make a thorough study", which meant reforming the traditional rites and rite systems to suit the needs of different times, and establishing Principlist new norms for an ideal country with the developed classics. So he said:

> "For the rites, time is the most important factor." If the sage or the worthy were asked to make the ceremonies, he would not make them all in the ancient way. Most probably he just made some adjustment on the ancient rites to make them suit the present custom, and suggested some restrictions so that the rituals would not be too simple. Judging from Kong Zi's approval to those "first entering the stage of rites and music", and "adopting the Xia Dynasty calendar, riding the Shang Dynasty chariot", it could be seen that he was making subtractions of the Zhou Dynasty's rites to return to the

ancient simplicity. The *Ritual Book* we compiled is similarly a brief collection of ancient system for people to make their own subtraction for application. If all must be done following the ancient custom in great details in such things as clothing, caps and shoes, it surely will not do. (*Ibid*. p.2886)

From this understanding Zhu Xi claimed that among the three classics about rites, "*Rites and Ceremonies* is the canon, and *The Book of Rites* is an explanation to it. For instance, there was a chapter of *Capping Ceremony* in the former, and correspondingly, there was a chapter of *Meaning of Capping Ceremony* in the latter; similarly, there was *Wedding Ceremony* in the former and *Meaning of Wedding Ceremony* in the latter. Rites about feast, archery, etc. were all the same, with the exception of *Meeting Ceremony of Gentlemen* in the former, which had no correspondent 'Meaning' to it in the latter." (*Ibid*. p.2899) At the same time, "Rites books such as *Rites and Ceremonies* is still complete like other classics." And, for Principlism, "*Rites and Ceremonies* was not a planned book of the ancients. It started from certain ideas to be practiced and copied. Later it became popular and welcomed and the details were regarded as very considerate and meaningful, and were finally recorded by the sage as a book." (*Ibid*. p.2898) Zhu Xi called *The Zhou Book of Rites* "the *Zhou Officialdom*" for it recorded the official system of the Zhou Dynasty. So he said: "Talking about books of systems, only *The Zhou Book of Rites* and *Rites and Ceremonies* were reliable. *The Book of Rites* was not so reliable." (*Ibid*. p.2912) Based on such understanding, Zhu Xi set up a framework for his *A General Explanation to the Texts and Annotations of Rites and Ceremonies*, i.e., "taking *Rites and Ceremonies* as the main thread, connecting it with recordings of rites in *The Book of Rites* and other miscellaneous books including classics and histories, then adding notes and comments of various Confucian scholars". (*Complete Works*. Book 2. p.25) By such a "thorough study" and reform, he set up a Principlist system of rites, including: 1) *Household Rituals* in two volumes; 2) *Neighborhood Rituals* in three volumes; 3) *Learning Rituals* in eleven volumes; 4) *States Rituals* in four volumes; 5) *Royal Court Rituals* in fourteen volumes; 6) *Funeral Rituals* in sixteen volumes; 7) *Sacrificial Rituals* in fourteen volumes. This ritual system, based on the eight items from the *Great Learning* and together with its Principlist spirit of practicality, provides us with more understanding of Zhu Xi's academic thoughts and feelings.

Zhu Xi had had an in-depth study of *The Book of History* and had planned to write a *Collected Annotations to the Book of History*, similar to the *Collected Annotations to the Book of Poetry*, as in his *Collected Works* and *Classified Analects* we can find many of his writings and his dialogues with his students regarding the study of the book. However, realizing that he could not finish the book himself in his life, he entrusted the work to his pupil Cai Chen, son of Cai Yuanding. In the first book of Zhu Xi's *Complete Works: Complements*, we did find *Collected Annotations to the Book of History* authored by Cai Chen, who said clearly that Zhu Xi had entrusted the work to him in the winter of 1199 and died the following year. It took Cai Chen ten years to fulfill the task. He admitted that he had received guidance from Zhu Xi, and his edition included certain parts written directly by or revised under the advice of Zhu Xi. A short comment on *The Book of History* in Cai's preface might have expressed Zhu Xi's Principlist spirit:

> The government of the two emperors and three kings was based on Dao, which in turn was based on the Mind. Only when the Mind is known can Dao and government be discussed. Why? Subtlety, oneness, and keeping to the Mean were the methodology of Mind passed down between Yao, Shun and Yu. To establish the Mean and to establish the top norm was the methodology of Mind passed down between King Tang of Shang and King Wu of Zhou. The terms they used may be different: virtue, or humanity, or reverence, or sincerity, but they all meant the same principle, and their difference just revealed the delicacy of the Mind. When speaking of Heaven, one should be solemn because it was where the Mind was born; when speaking of the people, one should be modest, because they were what the Mind was applied to. Rites, music and education are

the expression of the Mind. Canons, systems and classics are the production of the Mind. Family regulation, state government and world tranquility are the extension of the Mind. How marvelous is the property of the Mind! Existence of the Mind leads to peace; non-existence of the Mind leads to turmoil. Peace or turmoil depends on the existence or non-existence of the Mind. Future rulers with the intension of attaining the two emperors and three kings' government must search for their Dao; to search for their Dao, they must search for their Mind. The essence of their Mind exists nowhere but in this very book! (*Complete Works: Complements.* Book 1. p.1)

Reading through *Collected Annotations to the Book of History*, we can understand the effort Cai Chen spent on it during the ten years. His annotation and explanation can basically follow Zhu Xi's Principlist ideology. To a certain extent, this work of Cai Chen's can be included in Zhu Xi's Principlist system of Five Classics interpretation and became one of its organic components.

Zhu Xi did not write any book about *Spring and Autumn Chronicles.* He said in the first year of Shaoxi reign (1190) when he was 61 years of age:

My deceased father loved *Zuo's Comments* and every evening he used to read one volume before going to bed. So the book was familiar to my ears even before my schooling began. When I grew older, I asked about its layout from my teachers and elders and did see a few important points, but after all I did not have enough faith in understanding its Mind. So I never wrote anything about it except for some impressions in its most important relations between sovereigns and subjects, and between fathers and sons. Recently I published the three classics of *Change, Poetry* and *History* in my prefecture. For the *Book of Change*, I used the Lü's version of 12 chapters. For the *Book of Poetry* and the *Book of History,* I moved the prefaces to the end of the classics so as to see the original form of the books, instead of being restricted in the ideas of later Confucian masters. The classic of three

Rites was too bulky to be ordered and corrected. Only the teachings in *Spring and Autumn Chronicle* had been adjusted by the sage and must not be neglected. And Mr Shao Yong in his *Supreme Norms Governing the World* regarded the four classics of *Change, Poetry, History, and Spring and Autumn* as the necessary learning for emperors and kings, so the book is by no means to be excluded. So I printed the Zuo-commented version of the classic separately to follow the other three classics. As for the other two versions, Gongyang's and Guliang's comments, their difference with the Zuo's lay only in the names of persons and places, not in what relates to the principles. Therefore they could be excluded. In the future if anyone could follow Mr Lü's example to make pronunciation research of the three comments, he would be fulfilling my will. (*Complete Works.* Book 24. pp.3890–3891)

It seemed to us that Zhu Xi had a good family education in the classic of *Spring and Autumn Chronicle*, which could be proved in his familiarity of its details in his dialogues with the students and his familiarity with the past researches. But in the above passage he clearly expressed his reluctance in writing a book about it, though he did pay attention to it by printing the *Zuo's Comments*. And he expected that someone in the future would do some pronunciation research for the three *Comments* of the *Chronicles*. Here we collect what he said to the students in the *Classified Analects* to see that his hesitation in writing the book was not because he didn't want to, but because of the academic problems in it:

For *Spring and Autumn Chronicles*, there were certain places I didn't really understand, and was not sure whether they were really the sage's words.

Spring and Autumn Chronicles is difficult to read, at least for my life. About Kunwan the Duke of Zheng for example, there were many different versions.

Spring and Autumn Chronicles was a collection of true happenings of the time recorded by Kong Zi on bamboo slips. Later scholars was not so learned and all explained it with their own understanding or guessing, just as Zhang Zai pointed out, "Their comments were mostly farfetched because they didn't quite understand the meanings and the principles." Cheng Yi said that this book was "the great law for governing the whole world". He really got the essence of it. However, there are many issues in the book which were improper and were difficult to deal with. (*Ibid*. Book 17. pp.2870–2871)

Nevertheless, some of his words proved that he had his own views on the *Chronicles*:

> To read the *Chronicles*, one must first read through the *Zuo's Comments* to know the whole story. Then one may understand why the sage should make such revision and the significance of the events at that time. (*Ibid*. p.2836)
>
> What the *Chronicles* recorded, such as someone doing something, was written after the original historical record of the Lu state with certain revision. People now confirm that certain words were used specially for criticizing certain people. Then Kong Zi was revealed as a man making comments out of personal opinion and praising and criticizing wantonly. In reality Kong Zi just made direct record of the facts and the good or evil would expose themselves. If people today insisted on their reading practice, they should find the original text of the Lu history and make a comparative study between the similarities and differences. But is it possible? (*Ibid*. pp.2833–2834)
>
> The fault of the *Zuo's Comments* lies in that it made decisions of right and wrong not from the justness of principles but from the success or failure. I used to say that Mr Zuo was a slippery man and a time-server. (*Ibid*. p.2838)
>
> 80–90% of the facts recorded in the *Zuo's Comments* may be correct. *Gongyang's Comments* and *Guliang's Comments* focused on explaining the meaning of the classic. The events recorded in their books were mostly guesses. (*Ibid*. p.2840)

Thus we can see that on the whole Zhu Xi would like to make annotations on the *Spring and Autumn Chronicles*, but there were too many problems, and some were very hard nuts to crack as relevant historical materials were lacking.

In general, Zhu Xi's study of the Five Classics in the spirit of Principlism, combined with his study of the Four Books, reflected his endeavor to interpret the Four Books and the Five Classics coherently in the spirit of Principlism. Indeed, he achieved a good result. In the entire history of Confucian studies, he was the one who tried to synthesize all the Confucian classics, and was basically successful at that, though not superb. Failing to write an interpretive book about the *Spring and Autumn Chronicles,* Zhu Xi wrote two other books, *A Compendium of History as a Mirror for Governance* and *Words and Deeds of Famous Officials of Eight Imperial Courts*, marking his unique accomplishment in the field of historical studies.

In his preface to *A Compendium of History as a Mirror for Governance* Zhu Xi mentioned that Sima Guang was first entrusted to compile the *History as a Mirror for Governance* and later condensed it into a 30-volume *Contents.* In his last years, finding the original book too detailed and the *Contents* too simple, he decided to write an 80-volume *Extracts* of the original. He left the world before finishing the book, and based on his posthumous manuscript Hu Anguo wrote *A Supplement to the Extracts of the History as a Mirror for Governance*. Zhu Xi read this book in Hu's house and regretted that the book could not provide an outline for memorization. So, based on all the above-mentioned four books, he made a new layout, and by addition, subtraction and extraction, he compiled a new book *A Compendium of History as a Mirror for Governance*. Despite what he said, what he actually did was

> … Mark the year to record the history, attach to it the dynasty, use big sinographs to outline the main event, and add notes to make narration complete, so that the history is clear and through like looking at one's own palm despite the long years passed, the

countries being united or disintegrated, the records being detailed or sketchy, and the comments being similar or divergent, then entitle the book *A Compendium of History as a Mirror for Governance* in several volumes, to be kept in my own bookcase for personal reference. I dare not say that I have understood both Mr Sima and Mr Hu's intention in writing their books, but now, with years marked, the Way of Heaven is clear; with dynasty attached, the Way of Man is put in order; with outline summarized, lessons and warnings are manifested; and with details described, all subtleties become obvious. Thus scholars dedicated to the study of investigating things to acquire knowledge will also be moved by this. And the two masters' intention might also be learned and kept in mind.

Obviously, Zhu Xi wrote his Principlist ideology into his history and historical comment. This was realized through the *Layout* he planned for the book. Wang Bai said in his *Postscript to the Jigutang Version of "A Compendium of History as a Mirror for Governance" Published in Xianchun Period of the Song Dynasty*, "If not for the layout he planned and carried throughout, how could his compiling intention be clear, his warning and advice be understood? And how could the great law, which supported the Heavenly relations, restrained human desires, and measured the hundreds of kings' statutes to set up standards for thousands of years, be directly expressed?" (*Complete Works.* Book 11. p.3504)

The layout of Zhu Xi's *Words and Deeds of Famous Officials of Eight Imperial Courts* is similar to that of his *Essentials of Confucian Analects and Mencius*, indicating that he had had a thorough study of the history of the Northern Song Dynasty. Li Weiguo said in his *Statement for Checking and Punctuation:*

Words and Deeds of Famous Officials of Eight Imperial Courts extracted a great amount of material from private and official works, including more than a hundred of official history memoirs, privately compiled histories, miscellaneous histories, anthologies and casual notes, and another hundred of tablet inscriptions or brief biographies, among them many were already lost in history. For instance, *Words and Deeds of His Excellency Wang Zeng*, a 37-item memoir recorded by Wang Gao, had 25 items cited by Zhu's book, and *Words and Deeds of His Excellency Fan Chunren* had 21 items cited. Other sources included *Fan Zuyu's Family Records, Hu Anguo's Family Records, His Excellency Wang Anshi's Daily Records, Wang Yansen Chronicle*, and sixteen or so others. Some historical material like casual notes, though still available today, were incomplete and could be complemented by Zhu's book.

A Compendium of History as a Mirror for Governance and *Words and Deeds of Famous Officials of Eight Imperial Courts* together represent Zhu Xi's study on the entire history and have the effect of "the thousand years of history to be checked readily like one's palm". Having summarized Zhu Xi's achievements in the Confucian classics, the histories and the miscellaneous schools, let's now turn our eyes to the fourth branch, the collections. In this branch, Zhu Xi had two weighty works, *Collected Annotations to the Songs from the South* and *A Textual Study of the Complete Works of Han Yu*.

A Textual Study of the Complete Works of Han Yu is a masterpiece of Zhu Xi's in exegesis and textual criticism. It makes reference of over 10 books. *The Complete Works of Han Yu* was compiled by Fang Songqing of the Southern Song Dynasty. In his later years, Zhu Xi found that many of Fang's revision did not go along with Han Yu's original meaning, so he decided to make a re-revision. In the beginning of the first volume of his book he said:

I made a close research into the similarities and differences of the various versions, and made decision according to the coherence of the texts, principles of the meaning, and other resources. If correct, even the newly emerged copies from grassroots would not be neglected; if doubtful, even the official versions, ancient versions or stone-rubbed versions would not be trusted. I detailed the discussions into 10 volumes of the *Textual Study*.

From this we see many advantages and innovations in Zhu Xi's textual study. He tried to collect as many different versions of the text as possible, then made decisions according to facts and principles without being restrained in any set frames. As a great literary writer himself, he had a solid linguistic foundation which was well beyond ordinary people. Based on Han Yu's principle of "eliminating obsolete words with great effort" in writing, his revised version is far superior to Fang Songqing's in terms of language. This version established Zhu Xi's position in Han Yu studies as well as the history of textual study.

From *The Chronicle of Zhu Xi* and the poems he wrote, we learned that Zhu Xi had a very good foundation of *The Songs from the South* from a young age, and working as officials in the southern land before the frustration in officialdom at his last years may be the reason why he should take up writing the *Collected Annotations to the Songs from the South*, which was later regarded as the turning point of the *South Songs* study from the Han Dynasty style to the Song Dynasty style. This book also marked his establishment in the *South Songs* study as well as in the history of literary studies. Zhu Xi made a clear statement about this book in an additional comment of the *Contents of the Collected Annotations to the Songs from the South*:

> Qu Yuan's deeds, though having surpassed the border of the Mean and not to be learned as a model, are all from his sincere patriotism. Qu Yuan's words, though having degenerated to weirdness and resentment and not to be taken as an example, are all from his true love and sorrow which were difficult to control. Though he did not know how to learn the way of the Duke of Zhou and Kong Zi from the north and satisfied himself with galloping at the lower stream of poems, which might let the pure Confucians feel ashamed, his poems could still move those exiled subjects, forsaken sons and abandoned wives to tears or happen to be heard by the kings, fathers and husbands; then, natural goodness would have been found and

their relation would have been improved, thus help making the three guidelines and the five canons more weighty among people. This is why I always find his poetry tasteful and don't want to simply label it as "wordy poet's work". (*Completet Works*. Book 19. p.16)

As a Principlist, Zhu Xi directed the study of Qu Yuan into the realm of Principlism. He praised Qu Yuan's sincere patriotism and thought that Qu's moving works could reveal the Heaven's Nature of ordinary people and improve the understanding and popularization of Principlist ethics. Though his criticism of Qu Yuan may sound strange to us, his research method and open mind did mark an epoch-making change in the history of the *South Songs* study:

It was not a long time from Qu Yuan writing his poetry to the Han Dynasty, and the critics had already lost the theme of the work; even Sima Qian was no exception. And the books written by Liu An, Ban Gu and Jia Kui were all lost. Till the Sui and Tang Dynasties, there were still five or six interpreters of the book. A monk called Daoqian could even read it with the southern pronunciation, though it was also lost and we are not sure whether his pronunciation was right or not. Only the *Textual Analysis of the Songs from the South* written by Wang Yi of the Eastern Han Dynasty and the *Complementary Annotations to the Songs from the South* written by Hong Xingzu exist today, and their explanations of the names and things are already detailed. But there remained many questions in Wang Yi's book for his choice and discussion of the titles, and Hong's book could offer no answers. As to the significance of the poetry, both did not study very closely by repeated recitation to find the meaning behind the words, but just hurried to propose new arguments, with far-fetched proofs. Thus, either too pedantic to understand the true emotions, or too hasty to arrive at the principles, they both failed to get the essence of Qu Yuan's work which was already covered in obscurity. (*Ibid*. p.17)

This brief account tells us about the historical development of *South Songs* study in general as well as Zhu Xi's contribution to it.

Among Zhu Xi's great number of synthetic academic works, the *Close Reflections* and the *Source and Course of Principlist Scholars* are of special importance. They represent a Principlist research plan combining an inner, microscopic view with an outer, macroscopic view. The former collects 622 quotations from 14 books written by Zhou Dunyi, Cheng Hao, Cheng Yi and Zhang Zai, and is divided into 14 volumes. The fourteen source books are: 1) Zhou Dunyi's *The Extreme Ultimate Diagram*; 2) *The Works of Cheng Hao*; 3) *The Works of Cheng Yi*; 4) *Cheng Brothers' Annotation of the Zhou Book of Change*; 5) *Cheng Brothers on Confucian Classics*; 6) *Posthumous Writings of Cheng Brothers*; 7) *More Writings of Cheng Brothers' Works*; 8) Zhang Zai's *Correcting Strayed Ideas*; 9) *Works of Zhang Zai*; 10) *Zhang Zai on the Book of Change*; 11) *Zhang Zai on Rites and Music*; 12) *Zhang Zai on Confucian Analects*; 13) *Zhang Zai on Mencius*; and 14) *Analects of Zhang Zai*. And the content of the fourteen volumes as recorded in volume 105 of Zhu Xi's *Classified Analects* are respectively: 1) the substance of Dao; 2) an outline for learning; 3) investigate things to attain thorough understanding; 4) keep cultivation; 5) correct errors and strive for goodness, restrain oneself and restore the rites; 6) the way to regulate the family; 7) the way to be in position or not, to be promoted or demoted, to accept or reject ; 8) the way to govern the state and bring the whole country to peace; 9) systems; 10) the gentlemen's way to deal with affairs; 11) the way of teaching and learning; 12) correct errors and diseases of man's mind; 13) heterodox doctrines; and 14) the atmosphere of the sage and the worthy. In his preface to the book Zhu Xi briefly talked about his purpose of compilation:

> Mr Lü Zuqian from Dongyang came to my Cold Fountain Study and stayed with me for about ten days. We studied the works of Master Zhou, Masters Cheng and Master Zhang together, and sighed at their greatness and vastness — as if with no limit — and were afraid that the beginners did not know where to start. So we worked together to select those quotations concerning the general

principles and usable in daily life to make this collection. The key points that a scholar needed to start the good virtues or cope with the relation between himself and others, and the basic points for identifying heterodox doctrines and understanding sages can all be seen here. Those in the remote countryside who were determined to learn Confucianism but had no guidance from good teachers or friends could find a gate to enter if they could get this book and study carefully. Then if they continue to study the complete works of the four masters diligently and repeatedly, arriving at their broadness then returning to their essence, the magnificence of the ancestral temples and the richness of the variety of mansions could also be exhausted.

Although the book was a cooperative compilation of Zhu and Lü, in general Zhu Xi had a grand plan of his own. His words about "returning from broadness to the essence" revealed his ambition of a great plan for profound researching as well as writing, and a comprehensive and detailed mastery of the academic thoughts of the four masters.

During the 800 years and more from the publication of the *Close Reflections* in the Song dynasty till now, the book was widely read and had a great influence. The number of its prints was only next to that of the *Textual Analysis and Collected Annotations of the Four Books,* which was the officially authorized textbook for imperial examination. Zhu Xi used to say, "The four masters are the ladder to the six classics, whereas the *Close Reflections* is the ladder to the four masters." "The great method of self-cultivation is sufficiently found in the *Primary Education.* The essence and the subtleness of the principles are to be found in the *Close Reflections."* (*Classified Analects.* Book 105. p.2629) The title of the book comes from a passage in the *Confucian Analects,* "Zixia said: 'Learn broadly and determine your mind, inquire earnestly and reflect closely, and you need to go nowhere else to look for Humanity.'" which means that one should study and reflect from daily affairs close at hand. Later people study Song dynasty Principlism mostly from *Close Reflections.*

For the purpose of clearing out the source and development of Principlism, Zhu Xi wrote *Source and Course of Principlist Scholars*, which recorded words and deeds of 46 people from Zhou Dunyi to Cheng Hao, Cheng Yi, Zhang Zai, and their friends and disciples, to show clearly their relationship as masters and disciples. The book consists of 14 volumes as following:

1) Mr Zhou Dunyi (brief biography; 14 anecdotes)

2) Mr Cheng Hao (*Brief Biography* by Mr Cheng Yi; memoirs and prefaces by disciples and friends)

3) Mr Cheng Hao (*Postcript to Brief Biography* by You Zuo; *Lament* by Lü Dalin; *Tomb Commemorative Account* by Wen Yanbo; *Eulogy* by Chen Tian; 27 anecdotes)

4) Mr Cheng Yi (personal chronicle; elegy; an abridgment from Hu Anguo's *Report*; 21 anecdotes)

5) Mr Shao Yong (*Epitaph* by Mr Cheng Hao; *Brief Biography* by Zhang Min; 15 posthumous notes)

6) Mr Zhang Zai (*Brief Biography* by Lü Dalin; *Lament for Mr Zhang Zai* by Mr Cheng Hao; *On Posthumous Titles* by Sima Guang; 19 anecdotes), Zhang Jian (*Brief biography* by Lü Dalin; 5 posthumous notes)

7) Lü Xizhe (brief family biography), Fan Yiyu (5 anecdotes), Yang Guobao (elegy; 5 anecdotes), Zhu Guangting (*Tomb Eulogy* by Fan Yiyu; elegy; 4 anecdotes)

8) Liu Xuan (*Epitaph* by Li Yu; *Elegy* by Mr Cheng Yi; 5 anecdotes), Li Yu (*Elegy* by Mr Cheng Yi; *Elegy* by Lü Dalin; 2 anecdotes), Lü Dazhong and Lü Dajun brothers (brief biographies; *Epitaph* by Fan Yu), Lü Dalin (elegy; *A Tourist Note to Yongzhou* By Mr Cheng Yi; 11 anecdotes)

9) Su Bing (*A Recommendation to the Imperial Court* By Lü Dalin on behalf of his brother; 3 anecdotes), Xie Liangzuo (anecdotes), You Zuo (*Epitaph* by Mr Yang Shi; 5 anecdotes).

10) Yang Shi (*Epitaph* by Mr Hu Anguo; A discussion on the epitaph to Yang Shi; *A Reply to Chen Yuan*; *A Memoir of Mr Yang's*

Appointment as a Business Officer by Chen Yuan; *Brief Biography* by Lü Benzhong; 9 anecdotes)

11) Liu Anjie (*Epitaph* by Xu Jingheng; anecdotes), Yin Tun (*Epitaph* by Lü Jizhong; 10 anecdotes)

12) Zhang Yi (3 anecdotes), Ma Shen (*Brief Biography* by He Dui; *A Continued Note* by He Gao; 3 anecdotes), Hou Zhongliang (3 anecdotes), Wang Pin (*Epitaph* by Zhang Xian)

13) Hu Anguo (brief biography)

14) Cheng brothers' disciples with no memoirs: Wang Yansou; Liu Lizhi; Lin Dajie; Zhang Hongzhong; Feng Li; Bao Ruoyu; Zhou Fuxian; Tang Di; Xie Tianzhong; Pan Min; Chen Jingzheng; Li Chudun; Meng Hou; Fan Wenu; Chang Zhongbo; Li Pu; Chang Dayin; Guo Zhongxiao; Zhou Xingji; Xing Shu.

Here we copied down the title of each volume with respective content to show that Zhu Xi was very earnest in doing the research. His exploration was exhaustive, and all his materials were based on reliable facts. Some of the people mentioned in the book had no record at all; it had to be inferred from other sources that they were disciples of certain masters.

Source and Course of Principlist Scholars was largely an unfinished draft upon Zhu Xi's death. He might have received different answers when he asked his friends for opinions, which he treated carefully. For instance, Wang Yingchen did not agree that Zhou Dunyi was the master of the two Cheng brothers. And Lü Zuqian suggested that the publication could wait for some more years until some facts were more clear and complete. Zhu Xi discussed these problems in his letters to Lü Zuqian. But the book was published without the author's knowledge. *Source and Course of Principlist Scholars* made a clear account of the relations between Principlist scholars, and is therefore a convenient reference for later people to learn and study. And it had great influence for similar studies in later time, such as *Biographies of Principlists* in the *History of the Song Dynasty* compiled in the Yuan dynasty, *Description of Source and Course of Principlist Scholars* written in the Ming Dynasty, and *Academic Case Studies of the Song and Yuan Dynasties* and *Academic Case Studies of the Ming Dynasty*, both written in the Qing Dynasty.

From what is discussed above, we can see that Zhu Xi was a genuine synthesizer of Principlism: his Four Books Study, which he carried out for the great part of his life, established the central position for Four Books Study in traditional Confucian classics while demoting traditional Five Classics Study to the second place of importance, and at the same time founded the Principlist Hermeneutics for Four Books and Five Classics; his sorting of the source and development of the Song dynasty Principlism, especially the two Cheng brothers and their followers, laid a solid foundation for his own Principlist studies and left precious materials for later scholars to understand Principlism; by making interpretation and explanation to the Song Principlists' works such as *An Explanation to the Extreme Ultimate Diagram, An Explanation to the Book of Thorough Understanding* and *An Explanation to the Western Inscription*, he set up his own Principlist ontology and epistemology to guide his study and application; the comprehensive study of the history equipped him with a capacity of combining both history and classics in research, a quality seldom found in ordinary scholars; and at the same time he tried to make himself an all-round scholar in all the four branches of the Confucian classics, the histories and historiographies, the miscellaneous schools, and the collections.

3. Development and Defense of Principlism through Correspondence

Zhu Xi had academic relations with many people in his life. From the angle of his academic development and spreading influence, apart from his Confucian master Li Tong, there were four people who had many letters or other written messages with him. They were Zhang Shi, Lü Zuqian, Lu Jiuyuan and Chen Liang, who marked respectively four nodes in Zhu's academic life. When Li Tong died, Zhu Xi was lucky enough to make friends with Zhang Shi and Lü Zuqian. What he gained most through correspondence with Zhang Shi was to learn of the general academic level of Huxiang school, the orthodox Principlism in the south, headed by Zhang Shi. In his over 40 letters to Zhang Shi we found that what he discussed most at that period was Humanity, Mind, Mean and Harmony, arousal and non-arousal, and the Doctrine of the Mean. And his mechanics of governance of Mind over Nature and Emotion found better understanding and expression through their correspondence. This was his biggest gain from his friendship with Zhang Shi. His friendship with Lü Zuqian resulted in a joint compilation of the book *Close Reflections*. And many of his other books were also written in full consideration of Lü's opinions. I personally think that Lü's family background of scholarship and experience in sorting historical literature also had some influence on him. Lü's wide range of contacts helped Zhu Xi in getting acquainted with Lu Jiuyuan brothers and Chen Liang. When Zhu Xi was 52 years old, the deaths of Zhang Shi and Lü Zuqian had a great impact on him, and to a certain extent cut off his relations with outside academic circle. Although he was modest and had some contacts through lecturing, his academic relation with others declined to a state of debate and confrontation, and he was generally on the unfavorable side. That was because in comparison with him, Lu Jiuyuan was younger and more aggressive, and the Lu brothers' criticism of Zhu Xi was a kind of purposeful misreading or misunderstanding of Zhu Xi's academic views which had appeared unacceptable in the academic context of that time. As to his debate with Chen Liang on the way of king or despot, between righteousness and profit, we found that he was gradually lagging behind the time in situational awareness and the way of expression.

In the *Academic Case Studies of the Song and Yuan Dynasties: Zhang Shi*, Quan Zuwang remarked, "Zhang Shi was like Cheng Hao and Zhu Xi was like Cheng Yi. Should Zhang Shi lived longer, who knows how much achievements he would have made!" (Book 2. p.1609) Huang Zongxi spoke highly of Zhang Shi: "The Hunan school was most popular at that time but lacked a leisurely manner. Only when Zhang Shi emerged and had discussion with Zhu Xi that they complemented each other perfectly and the exaggerated words got readjusted. The words in the Gu hexagram that 'the son can accomplish his father's cause and there is no harm' seems most suitable to Zhang Shi's case." (*Ibid.* p.1611) From the above two comments about Zhu Xi and Zhang Shi we can see that both Zhu and Zhang were well learned but had different characters: Zhang was more reserved whereas Zhu was more outgoing. What Zhu Xi got most from his correspondence with Zhang Shi was the establishment of the mechanics of governance of Mind over Nature and Emotion in his Principlist system through their detailed discussion, to the end of describing the mechanics in a distinct and complete fashion. This was important not only in constructing his Principlist system, but also in applying it to his various explanations of classics. Volumes 30, 31 and 32 of the *Collected Works* contain Zhu Xi's 49 letters to Zhang Shi, among which 33 were about *The Doctrine of the Mean* or the governance of Mind over Nature and Emotion. Here we just discuss his letters on the two concepts of Humanity and the Mean and Harmony. In Volume 32 there were 6 letters concerning Humanity which benefited them both. In one of the letters Zhu Xi said:

> Your *On Humanity* was simple and clear, better than mine. But you just mention Nature and leave out Emotion and the permeation of Mind in Nature and Emotion. It seems to me that you just relate Nature with Mind. If that is the case, then your quotation of Meng Zi's "Humanity being Man's Mind" would be going against your other words above. Can you elaborate it more?
>
> Again you said, "When selfishness is conquered, what remains is vastly public, which will then penetrates the blood vessels of Heaven, Earth, and the myriad of things. The Principle of love is obtained inside, whereas its function is expressed outside. Then nothing between Heaven and Earth is not my Humanity. This is the Principle existing inside my nature, not anything forced." I am afraid these words were not well put. When selfishness is conquered and the vast public permeates everywhere, nothing can then cover the substance of Humanity. When the Heavenly Principle is not covered, the blood vessels of Heaven, Earth, and the myriad of things will naturally be

penetrated, and the function of Humanity will naturally be pervasive. So the Principle of love, existing originally in my own nature, exposes itself because of the great publicity, not after the great publicity; it reaches everywhere because of the penetration of the blood vessels, not after the penetration of the blood vessels. There was some confusion in your paper. Please reconsider it. The saying that the Principle of love is Humanity is also insufficient as it does not consider Heaven and Earth. The substance of Humanity is known here, and then we can say its function is all pervasive when the blood vessels of Heaven, Earth and the myriad of things are penetrated. The Principle itself was simple, but became confusing when mixed with others like Heaven, Earth and the myriad things. Kong Zi's answer to Zigong's question about patronizing extensively and helping many was like this, too. And it could also be in the words of "exposing the Mind of Heaven and Earth" in the Fu hexagram, as the appearance of the first Yang line was already self-sufficient to expose the Mind of Heaven and Earth, requiring nothing from outside. Further, Mr Zhou Dunyi once said, "It's the same as mine." In your explanation, there would be only "the same" but no "mine".

You words that "nothing between Heaven and Earth is not my Humanity" are also doubtful. We can say that "all under Heaven are IN my Humanity", but cannot say that "all under Heaven ARE my Humanity", as thing is thing and Mind is Mind. How can we regard things as Mind?

And you said, "This is the Principle existing inside my nature, not anything forced." Obviously you wished to elaborate the idea that Humanity does not have to wait for anything else, but your sentence does not make it clear. In one word, both the above sentence "Nothing between Heaven and Earth is not my Humanity" and this sentence are superfluous. Please reconsider it, will you?

If we compare the above passage with the final version of *On Humanity* in *Works of Zhang Shi* edited by Zhu Xi, we can see that Zhang Shi did accept

Zhu Xi's suggestion and made some revisions:

Man's Nature comprises four virtues of Humanity, Righteousness, Propriety and Wisdom. The Principle for love is Humanity, for suitability is Righteousness, for modesty is Propriety, and for knowledge is Wisdom. The four virtues do not have outward shapes, but their principles are rooted here, and here is their substance. The Nature comprises only the four and its completeness includes all the four. But the so-called Principle for love is actually the Mind of Heaven and Earth which generates the myriad of things and which itself was born from Heaven and Earth. Therefore, Humanity is the dominator of the four virtues and embraces the four. The four virtues in the Nature, when expressed to Emotion, are the beginnings of compassion, shame, right-wrong, and modesty, while the sense of compassion goes through all of them. That's why the relation of Nature and Emotion is that of substance and function, and the Way of the Mind is to govern Nature and Emotion. When one is covered by his own selfishness, he will lose the Principle of his Nature and do evil things, or even be jealous or brutal. Is it Man's true Emotion? How deep is he trapped or drowned! So what is most important in doing Humanity is to conquer one's own selfishness. Selfishness being conquered, the vast public will permeate, and the Principle of love which was originally in the Nature will not be covered. That Principle of love, free from coverage, will penetrate the blood vessels of Heaven, Earth, and the myriad things, and its function can be applied everywhere. So, regarding love as Humanity runs the risk of losing its substance — the same as Master Cheng's regarding love as Emotion and Humanity as Nature — and the Principle of love is Humanity. Regarding public as Humanity runs the risk of losing its truthfulness — in Master Cheng's words, that Humanity is difficult to describe, and that it is close to public but cannot be straightly called public — while being public can make Humanity humane. In tranquility exists the substance of Humanity, Righteousness, Propriety and Wisdom, whereas in movement the beginnings of compassion, shame, modesty, and right-wrong start. Their names and order must not be alternated. Only the Humanity can arrive at suitability by deduction, which is the location of Righteousness; the Humanity can be modest and restricted, which is the location of Propriety; the Humanity can perceive things without being blinded, which is where the Wisdom is located. It proves that only the Humanity is all-capable and can permeate the others. That's why Meng Zi spoke generally of Humanity as "Humanity is the Mind of Man". It is just the same as the fact that the four virtues of originality, prosperity, benignancy and perseverance in the Qian and Kun hexagrams were generally mentioned as Qian originality or Kun originality in *The Book of Change*. Nevertheless, a scholar can neglect the importance of aspiring for the Humanity, but if he does, he must not neglect to take self-restraint as the fundamental way. (*Complete Works: Complements*. Book 4. pp.287–288)

Comparing the two texts, it is obvious that Zhang Shi had accepted Zhu Xi's suggestion and made some revision in wording, which made his idea simpler and clearer. During their correspondence, Zhu Xi himself made repeated revisions and adjustments in his own statements. So the improvement was mutual. The clearer definition of Humanity laid a solid foundation for the recognition of governance of Mind over Nature and Emotion, especially its key concept of the Mean and Harmony.

The concept of the Mean and Harmony was raised by Zhu Xi after repeated consideration. Here we shall cite his five quotations on the concept to show his progress through his correspondence with Zhang Shi. In his first reply to Zhang, he said:

Man began to have knowledge the day he was born. Things happened all the time around him and it was difficult for him to attend to all. He had to change his ideas again and again till his death, with no time left for rest. It was true to all men in the world. Yet in the sage's teachings there was a concept of the Mean that referred to the period of non-arousal and tranquility. Was it possible that what was prevalent in daily life meant "aroused" and what was being done in a short break without contact with the outside world meant "not aroused"? Based on such understanding I had tried to look for something, only to find that when I was in the senseless state everything was in the dark or being blocked, unlike anything substantial corresponding to things; whereas in a dim state when I seemed to realize something it was already "aroused" and no longer in tranquility. The harder I tried, the less I found. Then I retreated to test in daily life and found that whenever I was moved or touched there would be something integrally corresponding to things. That was the running of the Heavenly destiny, the trigger for ceaseless generation. It might appear and disappear ten thousand times a day, but its fundamental tranquility would remain tranquil. The so-called non-arousal was actually like this. Is there another thing restricted in a special time and place that can be called "the Mean"? (*Works of Zhu Xi*. Book 3. p.1290)

Above was what Zhu Xi got by his own experience when he found doubt in reading. But soon he had a new idea:

What you found in my previous several letters was only a dim image of "great root" and "universal path" which I insisted on stubbornly, without thinking deeply on the sentence about "when the Mean and Harmony were attained". Thank you for constantly reminding me to hurry to the understanding of Humanity lest there is not a foundation to make efforts. I used to see the atmosphere of a restless surging sea and feel myself driven by the waves, knowing nowhere to stop. As I used to think like that, I was courageous in coping with routine affairs, but lacked a natural and graceful spirit. I knew it was not good, but didn't know where it was from. Now I see that in the vast universe anyone has a home of his own where he can settle his life and destiny and which can dominate his perceptions.

This is also the central place for setting up the great root and walking on the universal path, as well as the place where substance and function find the same origin, and no gap exists between the implicit and the explicit. My previous opinion of coming and going seemed too hasty. It was like trying to take a distant path while the destination was near. It was really ridiculous. (*Ibid*. p.1372)

His experience of tranquility led Zhu Xi to the realization of the significance of self-awareness. So he made new progress after further reading and consideration:

Thanks for agreeing to my various remarks, especially my viewpoint on the essence of non-arousal. How I felt relieved! However, compared with the viewpoints of my predecessors, my viewpoint seemed lacking a guiding line. Pondering over it once more, I realized that this principle must be discussed on the basis of Mind, and then the virtues of Nature and Emotion and the wonder of the Mean and Harmony will all find their right places. Now in a man's body, perceptions and actions are none but the function of Mind, which is in fact the governor free from the interference of movement or tranquility, speech or silence. When in tranquility, things had not happened and thoughts had not occurred, and only Nature was integral with all its content; this was the state of the Mean when Mind was the substance in silence without any motion. When in movement, things happened alternatively and different thoughts emerged, then the seven sentiments showed up in turn for different purposes. This was the state of Harmony, which was the function of Mind, aroused by outside things. But Nature in tranquility still had to move, and Emotion in movement must be restricted, so the substance and function of Mind had never left each other even when it was aroused from silent tranquility and ran throughout. If a man possessed the Mind but did not aspire for Humanity, then there would be no place to expose the wonder of the Mind; if he aspired for Humanity but did not show reverence, then there would be no chance to show the attainment of Humanity. As Mind was the governor of body free from the interference of movement or tranquility, speech or silence, so the man of virtue, when displaying reverence, was also free from the interference of movement or tranquility, speech or silence. When not aroused, the reverence was already kept in cultivation; when aroused, it constantly ran between inspection and reflection. In cultivation, thoughts had not emerged but perceptions were not covered, which could be called "movement in tranquility", or "exposing the Mind of Heaven and Earth" as in the Fu hexagram. Since "movement in tranquility" was governed, silence must not necessarily be untouched; since "tranquility in movement" was examined, the touch might also be silent. Thus silent but constantly touched, touched but constantly silent, the Mind ran through and was all pervasive while there was not a moment when Humanity was not there. (*Ibid*. pp.1303–1304)

Here we can see that Zhu Xi had already sorted out his mechanic of governance of Mind over Nature and Emotion by making a description of the concepts of silence, the Mean, Harmony, and the working system thereof, though his expression was still not clear enough, which means that his thoughts were not yet smooth. Zhu Xi summarized in his *First Letter to Friends in Hunan on the Mean and Harmony:*

In relation to the meaning of arousal and non-arousal in the *Doctrine of the Mean*, my previous understanding was that Mind was in the state of arousal whereas Nature non-arousal, as I thought that Mind was the running substance, and believed in Master Cheng's words that "Mind usually referred to arousal". But later I found that it was not in accordance with most of Master Cheng's other works. After thinking over it again, I found that the definitions of Mind and Nature was improper and the mistake was beyond textual study, as the daily practice was totally out of consideration. According to *Works* and *Posthumous Writings* of the Cheng brothers, the period of thoughts yet to emerge and things yet to happen was often regarded as the non-arousal state of pleasure, anger, sorrow and joy. At that period, Mind was the silent, motionless substance, and Nature of Heavenly destiny existed there. As it neither went beyond nor fell short, with no inclination to either side, it was thus called the Mean. When it was affected and penetrated all things in the world, then Nature of pleasure, anger, sorrow and joy was aroused and the function of Mind was thus manifested. As they were all attained at a due degree and none was abnormal, it was thus called Harmony. (*Works of Zhu Xi.* Book 6. p.3383)

This time, Zhu Xi realized the importance of daily practice through the reconsideration and discussion with Zhang Shi. After continuous correspondence and debate, Zhu Xi finally reached his own conclusion. In his *Preface to the Previous Sayings on the Mean and Harmony* he summarized his previous thoughts:

In my early years I studied *The Doctrine of the Mean* under Mr Li Tong for the true sense of the non-arousal of the sentiments of pleasure, anger, sorrow and joy. He died before I got the essence. I pitied myself for being so slow and found myself homeless like a poor man. Later I learned that Zhang Shi had inherited Mr Hu Hong's scholarship and went to Hunan to inquire. Zhang told me what he heard from Mr Hu but I still did not understand. I withdrew and pondered myself; sometimes I even forgot to sleep or take meals, until one day I sighed to myself: "A man's life from cradle to grave may have different periods of speaking or silence, movement or tranquility, but in general they are aroused. The so-called non-arousal is just the state when it has not been aroused." From then on I did not trouble myself with further doubt whether I had got the true sense of the *Doctrine of the Mean*. Later in Hu Hong's writings I found his *Letter to Zeng Jifu on Non-Arousal*, where he expressed a similar idea which made me even more confident. Even when I found Master

Cheng's words did not agree with it, I would not believe it, thinking that his true sense was lost in history. Sometimes I told other people my findings, but no one seemed to understand it thoroughly. In the spring of 1165, I told this to my friend Cai Yuanding, and during our conversation I suddenly had a doubt of myself: though my idea came from my own meditation, it should be told to others, then why was it so difficult for me to explain it clearly or for the listener to understand it quickly, since the fundamental principle of the *Change* was simple and easy, and a generally agreed viewpoint should not be like this? And Master Cheng's words were passed down by his excellent disciples and should not be all wrong. Was it possible that what I had insisted on was an obstacle to myself? Then I retook Master Cheng's works, calmed myself and carefully read it again. Just a few lines and all my problems were solved, and I realized that the original meaning of Nature and Emotion, and the subtle ideas of the sage were actually so plain. And what I obtained through the shallow reading the other day was so unwarranted as to mislead myself. And on that wrong basis I even made deductions to extremity. How dangerous it was, beside the loss in getting the true meaning! I was a little frightened and hurriedly wrote to tell my feeling to Zhang Shi and other friends who had engaged in our discussion. Only Zhang Shi replied and fully agreed with me, while others either believed or doubted or hesitated for years till now. The shortcoming of man's thinking, sometimes too far and sometimes too near, or tired of too common and afraid of too fresh, would be like this. Should we be alert against it! At my leisure time I checked previous letters and made a collection of relative letters. I entitled it *Previous Discussions on the Mean and Harmony* and wrote a preface revealing the whole story and my former mistakes, so that the future learners may draw from my lessons. My only regret is that I cannot ask Mr Li Tong about it. But from what he had already said, we can infer what he would say, and it should not be far away. (*Works of Zhu Xi*. Book 7. pp.3949–3950)

Truly, Zhu Xi's untiring spirit of pondering on the same question again and again and finally reaching a reasonable conclusion is worthy of Li Tong's praise and sets a good example for the later scholars.

One more result of Zhu Xi's correspondence with Zhang Shi is his compilation of the *Works of Zhang Shi*, which remains a much-told story in the academic history.

There are three aspects in Zhu Xi's correspondence with Lü Zuqian, which are worthy of our attention. The first is their academic friendship. They discussed certain problems, and Zhu Xi often sent his new writings to Lü for his opinion, and received replies concerning not only the works in general but also in wording details. Their joint compilation of *Close Reflections* is a good proof of academic cooperation. The second is that, with Lü's connection, Zhu got to know Lu brothers and Chen Liang, representatives of the Jiangxi school and the East Zhejiang school, to learn about their views and exert his influence on them. The third is that Lü's academic background helped him in raising his interest and ability in studying history.

The co-editing of the *Close Reflections* by Zhu Xi and Lü Zuqian was a much-told tale about their academic cooperation. Zhu himself looked highly upon that book, regarding the book's quotation of Zhou Dunyi, Cheng Hao, Cheng Yi and Zhang Zai's sayings as a ladder to the four scholars, which in turn was a ladder to the Four Books and Six Classics. This cooperation shows, to a certain degree, Zhu's trust of and reliance on Lü Zuqian.

Toward the completion of the compilation, they had some difference in the order of contents. Zhu Xi asked Lü Zuqian to explain his points, and Lü replied directly:

> After the *Close Reflections* was completed, somebody suspected that the first volume concerning Yin/Yang, Change, Nature and Destiny was not suitable for the beginners. I, however, have been engaged in the planning of the order: If the beginners knew the origin of the Priniciples too late and too sudden, they would be lost in the fog

and didn't know how to continue. To place it at the beginning of the book will let them have some idea on the first day they start and they will then be yearning for it. The method of study and the practice in daily life discussed in the other chapters are all in a reasonable order. Following this order, the study will be from lower to higher or from nearer to farther, which is really the editors' attempt. If one looks down upon what is close at hand and craves for something high and far, skipping the normal steps, it will only lead to emptiness and leave nothing to rely on. It goes against the concept of "close reflections". I hope the readers will understand this. (*Ibid*. p.165)

Such an understanding should be attributed to his family's academic background. From his *Postscript to Studying the Book of Poetry at Lü's Family School* we even learn that Zhu Xi had some literary contacts with Lü Zuqian's father. He said:

Lü's *Family School* is a book of synthesis which covers miscellaneous views, big or small, in a consistent narration, which, on the one hand, quiets down the quarrel on different versions, and on the other, is a coherent and idiosyncratic statement of its own. It is prudent in laying down any definition of a word or a matter. Its judgments, many having surpassed those of the predecessors, are raised in a modest way, showing respect for the forerunners. Alas! Man like Zuqian's father can be said to have attained the doctrine of gentleness and honesty. Through reading this book, students may understand better Kong Zi's comments about the *Poetry*'s function of socialization and complaint. But, what was mentioned in the book as Mr Zhu's point was actually my humble viewpoint at my young age which was accidentally adopted by Zuqian's father. Some years later, I found my views not so well thought-out, like that about *Ya, Zheng,* or orthodox and strayed, and made relevant changes, while Zuqian's father, surprisingly, did not put up any objection. I wished to discuss the matters with him when he suddenly passed away. Ah! Gone is Zuqian's father! As I am old and my health is declining, I am not sure whether I can make further progress to solve the debates. His father's brother Lü Zujian entrusted the book to his friend Qiu Chong, who put it to publication so that the book would last forever, and Qiu wrote to me requesting a preface. I could not refuse and wrote briefly about the process, and presented the doubting viewpoints for further discussion among the public, while at the same time as a memorandum recording my sorrow and regret. (*Works of Zhu Xi*. Book 7. pp.3970–3971)

Perhaps out of the previous reasons, Zhu Xi asked Lü Zuqian to be his son's teacher. Lü was a man of profound learning, the creator of the Jinhua or Wu school. He was especially famous for his historical study, which included *The Book of History, Tang History as a Mirror, History as a Mirror for Governance*, and *Historical Systems*. He was also the author of the 200-volume *True Records of Emperor Huizong* and the 150-volume *Literary Anthology of the Song Dynasty*. So Zhu Xi often sent his writings to Lü Zuqian for criticism. For example, he sent the contents of his work on rites to Lü, saying: "That order of contents might not be very good. Pray study it and give me your opinion." (*Works of Zhu Xi*. Book 7. p.3886) When he set to edit *Source and Course of Principlist Scholars*, he asked Lü to help search material and write a preface. Lü Zuqian read part of the draft and offered his opinion but did not write a preface for he thought the draft might be immature yet. It remained so till Zhu Xi's death, which shows to a certain extent his respect for Lü. In my opinion, concerning historical study and writing, Zhu Xi was undoubtedly influenced by Lü Zuqian.

Lü Zuqian had a sharp eye to discern able people. When he was in charge of provincial examination, he discovered Lu Jiuyuan. And when he was an examiner in the palace examination, he enrolled Ye Shi and other two scholars from Yongjia. They all became his personal connections. Lü was also on intimate terms with Chen Liang. All his friends later developed academic relations with Zhu Xi, thus creating an environment for him to know the scholars in Zhejiang and Jiangxi provinces and carry out academic discussions with them. When he had academic divergence with Lu Jiuyuan brothers, it was Lü Zuqian who organized the Goose Lake meeting for them to solve their differences.

The debate with Lu Jiuyuan brothers let Zhu Xi find, for the first time in his life, true academic rivals. Both of them displayed hardness and softness and did not yield to each other. Even after Lu Jiuyuan died, Zhu still would not pardon him and went on to criticize him. The debate between Zhu and Lu seemed uninterrupted until the publication of *An All-round Discussion on Master Zhu's Last Years* by Li Fu in the Yongzheng reign (c. 1723–1735) of the Qing Dynasty, lasting over 500 years. Historically speaking, this is a very important problem which we will discuss in more detail in Section 3 of our next chapter. Here we just give a brief introduction about the concepts of the Ultimate of Nothingness and the Ultimate of Extremity.

In explaining the expression of "the Ultimate of Nothingness is at the same time the Ultimate of Extremity" in his *An Explanation to the Extreme Ultimate Diagram,* he denied the existence of the concept of the Ultimate of Nothingness as that of the Ultimate of Extremity. From the stand of cultural tradition, such a negation was groundless. So Lu Jiushao, Lu Jiuyuan's elder brother, wrote to Zhu Xi to point it out. Yet Zhu Xi insisted on his own stand and repudiated him. Lu Jiuyuan supported his brother and criticized Zhu Xi, saying:

> Master Zhu suggested that Zhou Dunyi's *Extreme Ultimate Diagram* was from Mu Xiu[1] who was a disciple of Chen Tuan[2]. There must be some story behind it. Now Chen's scholarship was that of Lao Zi. The term Ultimate of Nothingness was from the 28th chapter of *Laozi*, which could not be found in Confucian classics. The first chapter of *Laozi* said, "Namelessness is the beginning of Heaven and Earth; name is the mother of the myriad of things," and at the end of the chapter, he identified both as the same. This is Lao Zi's view.

---

[1] Mu Xiu (979–1032), courtesy name Bochang, scholar in the early Northern Song Dynasty.
[2] Chen Tuan (879–989), courtesy name Tunan, style name Fuyaozi, was granted a name "Master Xiyi" by the emperor. He was a famous Daoist and a legendary immortal.

"The Ultimate of Nothingness is at the same time the Ultimate of Extremity" is the same as it. (*Works of Lu Jiuyuan.* p.24)

From Lu brothers' understanding of the Daoist cultural origin and the relevant material, they were absolutely right about this matter. From Zhu Xi's own words, we know that Zhu was also very familiar with Daoism and Buddhism and should be familiar with these materials as well. But Zhu kept on defending himself. He said in his *Reply to Lu Jiushao:*

Thanks for telling me the mistakes in the *Extreme Ultimate Diagram* and the *Western Inscriptions* and your own points. I dared not make any comment on the two books before. It is not that I followed the predecessors blindly or attached myself to the school, but because I found that it was a truth beyond any suspicion after repeated reading. Starting from my own understanding to make explanation, I was afraid that I was unable to find its profundity but might distort the original, so how dare I claim to make any contribution to it? After carefully reading your letter and reflecting what I said before, I am afraid that you may have neglected the original and were too confident of yourself. You did not place yourself in his position and rebuked him from your own stand rashly. Take the first sentence in the *Extreme Ultimate Diagram* for example, which was fundamentally repulsed by you: if the Ultimate of Nothingness was not mentioned, then the Ultimate of Extremity would become an ordinary thing, insufficient to be the root of myriad changes; if the Ultimate of Extremity was not mentioned, the Ultimate of Nothingness would be empty talk and could not be the root of myriad changes. This single sentence proves how accurate and delicate Master Zhou was in arranging his words. (*Works of Zhu Xi.* Book 3. pp.1566–1567)

In his letter he expressed clearly that his explanation was not made out of nothing but was a result of careful reading and consideration. He criticized Lu Jiushao for hasty objection without careful reading. Lu

Jiushao, thinking that he was too stubborn and aimed at winning the debate only, did not write any answer. And Lu Jiuyuan continued the debate. To speak objectively, Lu Jiuyuan was young and vigorous, having a profound learning background and a precise way of thinking, and gained the upper hand in the debate. The two scholars' debate reached no conclusion in the end, and they no longer had any correspondence later.

In my opinion, there are many things behind the debate about the Ultimate of Nothingness and the Ultimate of Extremity, in terms of academic development. Here I would like to mention three points. First, the essence of the debate was to exclude the influence on Confucianism by the Daoism and Buddhism. From the negative side, Lu Jiuyuan held that it was improper to place the Daoist theory of Nothingness Ultimate/Extreme Ultimate as the foundation for Confucian resurrection. So Zhu Xi's explanation appeared segmental and redundant, while Zhu Xi's explanation was a reformative creation. He judged the problem from the Principlist angle and tried to make it the theoretical foundation for the establishment of Principlism, in the same way as transforming the divination judgments *yuanheng* "great success" and *lizhen* "favorable for correctness" to the four virtues of origination, prosperity, benignancy and perseverance in the history. Zhu and Lu had the same destination but different paths, and finally reached different conclusions. Secondly, the expression of the Ultimate of Nothingness and the Ultimate of Extremity is closer to the Principle of things than to the Principle of the Mind, which made Zhu and Lu contradictory to each other. Thirdly, the above two points marked a turning point of the historical development of Principlism toward the end of the Song dynasty, which saw the rapid rise of Lu Jiuyuan's School of Mind. This was a new progress in the development of Chinese philosophy. From Zhu Xi's governance of Mind over Nature and Emotion to Lu Jiuyuan's Mind itself being the Principle, Man's Mind was getting liberated to a certain degree, and the Buddhist and Daoist ideology based on the Mind, in combination with Confucian Mind-Nature theory and the tradition of the *Survey of the Book of Change*, turned out to be the foundation of the new Confucianism.

The debate between Zhu Xi and Lu Jiuyuan made it impossible for Zhu's Priniplism to dominate the academic stage of the time. After Lü Zuqian died, the Jiangxi and Zhejiang schools came onto stage. Lu Jiuyuan's School of Mind and the discussions on profit and righteousness of the Zhejiang scholars became popular. Among the Zhejiang scholars, Chen Liang became a focal point because of his distinct viewpoints. In the *History of the Song Dynasty* Chen Liang was described as "born with a bright sight, highly talented, fond of military affairs and quick at writing." (*History of the Song Dynasty*. Vol. 436. p.9475) His works include: four *Reports to the Emperor, Pondering over the Past,* and *Five Essays on Reviving the Country.* He was on good terms with Lü Zuqian, and in turn became a friend of Zhu Xi's. But for Zhu Xi, Chen was more like an object to influence and transform. We can see this attitude in his letter to this little friend, in which he made some descriptions:

> Your new theory is grand, extraordinary and full of original ideas. Having not recovered from my surprise, I cannot haste a comment. I will give it when I read more. (*Works of Zhu Xi*. Book 3. p.1587)
>
> Your long letter is grand and majestic, full of imagination, which is difficult to face. Even if Meng Zi were still alive, he would be unable to say a word, not to mention a silly and stupid me, whom you regarded as a mean Confucian. What do I have to say? (*Ibid*. p.1597)

Because of such an attitude, when Chen Liang was wrongly imprisoned, he gave his advice:

> Please consider my suggestion that you discard your ideas about accepting both righteousness and profit and practicing both the king's and the despot's way of reigning, and engage yourself in controlling one's anger and restraining one's desires, as well as in overcoming one's evils to change for the good. If you can practice self-discipline in the way of a pure and mature Confucian, it will not only exempt yourself from man-made disaster, but also lay a solid foundation of

orthodox Confucianism for you to bring your talent into full play in the other day. (*Ibid*. p.1590)

But in reply to Zhu Xi, Chen Liang said frankly, "The path in the world is getting narrower, and you are the only one leaving me some hope," expressing no wish to turn to Confucianism. Here we quote part of the letter Zhu Xi wrote to Chen Liang, in which he tried to persuade him to accept Principlism. He first summed up Chen Liang's opinion:

> You talked quite a lot in your letter. But your general idea was no more than to elevate the status of the Han and Tang dynasties, equaling them to the three ancient dynasties; and to belittle the three ancient dynasties, equaling them to the Han and Tang. This idea is based on the supposition that the past and the present are different, and what the sages and the worthy people did may not be examples for today. So long as one has the will to save the world and successfully extinguish the social chaos, he can be a hero of the time, even if what he does might not go along with the principle of righteousness. But you do not like the principle of righteousness, so you say that when Heaven, Earth, and Man stand side by side equally, it is not that Heaven and Earth can run independently while Man must be dependent. Since Heaven and Earth are lasting forever, the emperors of the Han and Tang can fulfill any great cause if they did so and so. And even Heaven and Earth can rely on them till now. You said quite a lot, but mainly you were trying to prove such a point. (*Ibid*. p.1597)

Then Zhu Xi analyzed a key passage in the letter, concentrating on the above mentioned three aspects: 1) The Mind of Man and the Mind of the Dao. 2) The kingly reign and the despotic reign, by righteousness and by profit, of the three ancient dynasties and the Han and Tang dynasties. 3) The way to become a Man.

Firstly, Zhu Xi emphasized the distinction between the Mind of Man and the Mind of the Dao, between Heaven's Principle and Man's desires. Surely Man cannot be without desires, but he must possess the uprightness of Heaven and Earth. And the teachings of the ancient sages have been to get rid of Man's desires and return to Heavenly Principle, as summed up in the "mind-to-mind inheriting method": "The Mind of Man is in danger; the Mind of the Dao is in subtlety. Keep to sincerity and oneness and stick to the middle way." This heritage had been passed down from Yao, Shun, Yu, Tang of Shang, Wu of Zhou, down to Kong Zi, Yan Yuan, Zeng Shen, Zisi and Meng Zi, then was lost in history. Discarding Confucianism and the learning of the sages to yearn for wealth, position, fame, etc. was utterly wrong. The Mind of the Dao must be set as the base.

Secondly, Zhu Xi held that the difference between the three ancient dynasties and the Han and Tang dynasties was actually the difference between the Mind of the Dao and the Mind of Man. Because the Mind of the Dao expressed in three ancient kings' rules and Kong Zi and Meng Zi's teachings were not inherited, the emperors of the Han and Tang dynasties might sometimes happen to coincide with the Mind of the Dao, but in general they put profit and desires at the highest place, which created a gap between them and the three ancient dynasties. If people wished to connect the two historical periods as Chen Liang had hoped, the Mind of the Dao must first be established.

It may be better to study the mind-communication inheritance method of Yao, Shun, Tang and Wu, setting it as a criterion on oneself, while examine the subtleties of the minds of Emperor Gaozu of the Han dynasty or Emperor Taizong of the Tang dynasty: accept what they coincidentally did in accordance with the ancient kings and look for where it came from, and dismiss what they did against the ancient kings and search for its origin. In that case, the constant norms between Heaven and Earth and the general truths throughout the history will become my own quality. It would not do just by sitting back and talking about the past events, covering up the mistakes already made, or taking the coincidences as the overall facts in the belief that they were the same as the ancient sages. (*Ibid*. pp.1600–1601)

Chen Liang disagreed with these sayings about the Mind of the Dao or the sages, so he raised another debate about the way to become a Man. Zhu Xi thought Chen Liang's view "that learning to be a Man not necessarily in adherence to the Confucian way, and melting gold, silver, copper and iron into a vessel for practical use, proved that his foundation of setting up the Mind was for profit and gain", and proposed that "following the Confucian way one could finally become the Man as Kong Zi defined." Otherwise, free from norms and standards, one could be neither superior man nor inferior man, the gold, silver, copper and iron would all be damaged and could not make a vessel. To speak objectively, Zhu Xi's historical view of returning to the best practice of the three ancient dynasties was problematic, and definitely could not convince Chen Liang whose historical examination and expression were comparatively objective. In spite of this, Chen Liang highly respected Zhu Xi in person. He not only asked Zhu to write a poem of *baoxiyin* (leisurely seated song), but constantly sent greetings to Zhu with small gifts. He even wrote a praise for Zhu Xi's portrait: "His body is of manly purity. His breath embraces correct sentiments. He is bright in the face and the back, and I don't know why he is so joyful; he sits upright with deep thought, and I don't know what he is worried about. You cannot confine him to seclusion; neither can you fix him in officialdom. He has been in the world for so long, awaiting the Heavenly god's decree." However, the world is changing. In time of peace, the Confucian tranquil cultivation may persuade people to a certain extent, but towards the turbulent social reality of the Southern Song dynasty, and in the popularity of the Theories of Mind and of profit and righteousness, Zhu Xi's persuasion sounded pale. Later Chen Liang was appointed by the emperor himself to be an officer, a proof that his theory was suitable to the society. Unfortunately he died of disease before he could arrive at his post.

Chapter Five

Inheritance of *The Complete Works of Zhu Xi*

Part of Zhu Xi's works was already in circulation at his lifetime. After the ban against his works was lifted towards the end of the Song Dynasty, his works received more attention and were spread more widely; the inheritance of his learning thus started. In all the three dynasties of the Song, Yuan and Ming, Zhu Xi, as well as his learning, was highly respected, though because of different reasons. The dominant status of Zhu's Principlism was established in the Yuan and Ming Dynasties. The development of the Mindology in the Ming Dynasty brought about competition between the theories of Zhu Xi and those of the Mind. *The Final Verdict of Master Zhu's Last Years* written by Wang Shouren[1] at the Ming Dynasty and *An All-inclusive Discussion of Master Zhu's Last Years* written by Li Fu[2] in the Qing Dynasty both claimed that Zhu Xi's thought at his last years was the same as Wang Shouren's or Lu Jiuyuan's Mindology. This was a disputed problem in the inheritance of Zhu's learning, and has been unsolved till today and worthy of further study. The status of Zhu Xi's study as an official learning was strengthened and consolidated at the turn of the Ming and Qing Dynasties.

---

[1] Wang Shouren (1472–1529), courtesy name Bo'an, and was posthumously granted the title of Wencheng (literally cultural achievement), but was more widely known as Master Yangming or just Wang Yangming. He was a great thinker, literary writer, philosopher, and militarist in the Ming Dynasty, and the great synthesizer of Mindology.

[2] Li Fu (1675–1750), courtesy name Julai and style name Mutang, a scholar in the Qing Dynasty.

1. The Inheritance of Zhu Xi's Principlism in the Song, Yuan and Ming Dynasties and the Establishment of Its Dominance

After Zhu Xi's death, his status as a great scholar was recognized by the government, and he was highly respected at the last period of the Song Dynasty. At the end of *Zhu Xi's Biography* in *The History of the Song Dynasty*, there was a summary of Zhu' learning, through which we might learn about its status at that time:

> Zhu Xi craved for learning at a young age. His father, Zhu Song, told him when seriously ill, "Hu Xian, Liu Mianzhi and Liu Zihui are my esteemed friends who have very good family learning background. After my death you can go to respect them as your teachers and listen to them one-heartedly." Zhu Xi did as his father told him, so when he took up learning he studied hard at the classics on the one hand, and widely acquainted himself with scholars of the time on the other. Li Tong, who had once studied under Luo Congyan, was old and retired to his hometown. When Zhu Xi heard this, he walked several hundred miles to see Li Tong.
>
> Generally speaking, his learning was to exhaust the Principles to acquire the knowledge, and return to himself for practice, with a focus on keeping to reverence. Once he said that the inheritance and spreading of the sage and the worthies' Dao was through the books. If the meaning of the books was not discovered, then the inheritance would be in dark. So he exerted all his energy to study the sage and the worthies' teachings. His monographs include: *The Original Meanings of the Zhou Book of Change, A Primer of the Change Study, Yarrows Divination: Examination and Correction, Collected Annotations to the Book of Poetry, Textual Analysis of the Great Learning and the Doctrine of the Mean, Questions on the Four Books, Collected Annotations to Confucian Analects and the Mencius, An Explanation to the Extreme Ultimate Diagram, An Explanation to the Book of Thorough Understanding,*

An Explanation to the Western Inscription, Collected Annotations to the Songs from the South, The Songs from the South: Examination and Discussion, and *A Textual Study of the Complete Works of Han Yu.* His edited books include: *Essentials of Confucian Analects and Mencius, Basics of Mencius, Digest of Explanations to the Doctrine of the Mean, An Erratum on the Classic of Filial Piety, Primary Education, A Compendium of History as a Mirror for Governance, Words and Deeds of Famous Officials of Eight Imperial Courts, Household Rituals, Close Reflections, Posthumous Writings of Cheng Brothers* and *Source and Course of Principlist Scholars.* All of them had been published. When Zhu Xi died, his interpretations of *The Great Learning, The Doctrine of the Mean, Confucian Analects,* and *Mencius* were officially set up as school textbooks. His book, *A General Explanation to the Texts and Annotations of Rites and Ceremonies,* though unfinished, was also set up as school textbooks. Throughout his life, his written works went up to 100 volumes, his dialogue with his students contained 80 volumes, and his relevant records amounted to 10 volumes.

In the later years of Shaoding period (c. 1220s), Librarian Li Xinchuan proposed that the seven scholars Sima Guang, Zhou Dunyi, Shao Yong, Zhang Zai, Cheng Hao, Cheng Yi and Zhu Xi be listed among the persons who had the honor of sharing sacrifice with other worthies in the Confucian Temples but received no reply. In January 1241, the emperor visited the Imperial Academy and wrote an edict on spot to let the five people Zhou Dunyi, Zhang Zai, Cheng Hao, Cheng Yi and Zhu Xi be listed among the persons to share sacrifice in the Confucian Temples.

Huang Gan said, "The orthodox doctrine of the Dao needs the right people to pass to later generations. Since the Zhou dynasty, only a few people could take up the task and carry it forward, and only one or two persons could carry it forward and bring it to more brilliance. Kong Zi, Zeng Zi and Zisi could carry it forward, but only Meng Zi could bring it to more brilliance. After Meng Zi, Masters Zhou Dunyi, Cheng Yi and Zhang Zai could carry it forward, but only Zhu Xi could bring it to more brilliance." His words were widely acknowledged by learned people. (*Complete Works*. Book 27. pp.532–533)

The above biography in the *History of the Song Dynasty* pointed out Zhu Xi's "learned family background" as well as his aim of learning. At the same time, it briefly related the history of the official endorsement of Zhu Xi and his learning at the end of the Song Dynasty. It fully revealed that in the Southern Song Dynasty people had already realized Zhu Xi's contribution in carrying forward the Confucian cultural tradition, and what's more, even the emperor had found the value of Zhu Xi's Principlism in serving his own purpose.

As the son-in-law of Zhu Xi, Huang Gan thought himself an inheritor of Zhu Xi's doctrine, which he passed to his disciple He Ji, thus Zhu Xi's thought was continued and glorified. In his preface to *The Case Study of the Four Masters of North Hill* in *Academic Case Studies of the Song and Yuan Dynasties,* Quan Zuwang[①] suggested that "Huang Gan's heritage was glorified in Jinhua". The four masters of North Hill in Jinhua county were respectively Huang's disciple He Ji, He's disciples Wang Bai and Jin Lüxiang, and Jin's disciple Xu Qian.

He Ji was a native of Jinhua. His father was the deputy magistrate of Linchuan county while Huang Gan happened to be the magistrate. He seized the opportunity and made his two sons to be Huang Gan's students. Huang Zongxi wrote:

> Huang Gan told him that the aim could be attained only by diligent and down-to-earth study. He Ji listened with respect. Then he studied hard and thought deeply, keeping calm and patient, to wait for some day of thorough understanding of the Principle. He never thought himself higher than others by offering different opinions or slightly changed his ideas to comply with others. The books he

---

① Quan Zuwang (1705–1755), courtesy name Shaoyi, style name Xieshan, important historian and literary writer of the Qing Dynasty.

read were full of red and black marks, which clearly revealed their meanings and intentions without further explanation. When Wang Bai became his student, he taught him with Hu Hong's words: "Set up will to make the foundation firm, and keep reverence to sustain the will. Will was set up on the surface of things while reverence was flowing between things." Mr He Ji had a collected work of 30 volumes, including 18 volumes of argumentation with Wang Bai. Often they would exchange dozens of letters to discuss one matter, and He Ji would not change his viewpoint. In 1264 he was appointed instructor of Wuzhou prefecture and director of Lize Academy, but he refused. At the first years of Xianchun period (1265–1275) he was appointed collator in the History Section and instructor of the Chongzheng Palace, then changed to secretary of the Construction Office, in charge of Xiyue Temple. Later he stayed at home, never leaving again. (*Academic Case Studies of the Song and Yuan Dynasties*. Book 4. p.2726)

He Ji strictly followed his teacher's words and studied very hard. His will of "learning on a firm will, of a large scale, at constant practice, and with persistence until death" fully revealed Zhu Xi's spirit. He claimed, "The study of the Four Books should be focused on Master Zhu's *Collected Annotations* and complemented by *Classified Analects*, for the latter was a result through many hands and might not be exactly the same as the original. It would be better to complement the subtlety of the former with the elaboration of the latter, and to understand the complicacy of the former with the details of the latter." (*Ibid.* p.2727) Such a study method was the characteristic of the Zhu Xi school. Therefore Huang Zongxi commented: "He Ji's idea was that it was enough to read and memorize the Four Books. He said in his late years that 'the *Collected Annotations* was self-sufficient in meaning and principles, and it was superfluous to add other explanations.' He said so because since the Jiading period (1208–1224) when the ban against Zhu Xi was lifted, many people used Zhu Xi as a tool for their own purposes. But they loved daily enjoyment more than the pleasure of philosophical study. So their achievement was less every day. Many even stole or copied other's sayings or believed in hearsay to establish their own fame. He Ji was a prominent scholar even among his fellow learners, but he was still not satisfied, saying, 'It's a pity that I do not have a good health as Mr so-and-so who could accept all offers for him. But I am afraid that his work did others no good but only made himself busy on the way. Why? Because he was not at all familiar with the Four Books.' He Ji strictly followed his teacher and could be said to have the style of the Han dynasty Confucians." (*Ibid*. p.2727)

Unlike He Ji, Wang Bai, Jin Lüxiang and Xu Qian did not follow Zhu Xi's tradition so strictly. Wang Bai was also a native of Jinhua. His grandfather Wang Shiyu was a disciple of Yang Shi and his father Wang Han was a disciple of Lü Zuqian. Huang Zongxi talked about how Wang became a student of He Ji: Wang admired Zhuge Liang in his young age and named himself Changxiao (long whistling, something always done by Zhuge Liang when he was a hermit). When he was 30, he read the Four Books with his friend Wang Kaizhi. He took up *Collected Annotations to Confucian Analects and Mencius*, copied them with different colors of red, yellow or black, in order to understand Master Zhu's decision of selection. He found that Huang Gan's *General Interpretation* lacked the part of questions and answers, and complemented it with extracts from *Classified Analects* and called it *General Understanding*. One day when he read the part of "being respectful in daily life and reverent in coping with affairs", he suddenly realized that "long whistling was not the way to be reverent" and changed his name to Luzhai. Later he met Yang Yuli and was told that He Ji had learned from Huang Gan and obtained all Zhu Xi's doctrines. He at once went to He Ji, asking to be his student. He Ji wrote *Advice for Wang Bai* to him, encouraging him to set up will and keep reverence. From then on, Wang studied even more diligently and carefully and used different colors to mark his understanding. (*Ibid*. p.2730)

Huang Baijia[1] made a general comment on him: "Wang Bai had a

---

[1] Wang Baijia (1643–1709), courtesy name Zhuyi, style name Bushi, was the third son of Huang Zongxi, the famous historian and scholar in the early Qing Dynasty. He helped his father together with Quan Zuwang to finalize the book *Academic Case Studies of the Song and Yuan Dynasties*.

deep faith in Zhu Xi. However, for the *Great Learning*, he believed that the part about investigating things to acquire knowledge had not been lost and was unnecessary to be complemented; for the *Doctrine of the Mean*, he suggested that since there was a record of 'two books on *The Doctrine of the Mean*' in *The Bibliographic Treatise of the History of the Han Dynasty*, the section starting from 'perception resulting from sincerity' in the present version should be another book; for *The Extreme Ultimate Diagram*, his opinion was that the first sentence should be understood around the diagram itself, and that the Ultimate of Nothingness did not mean shapeless and the Ultimate of Extremity did not mean reasonable; and for Zhu's explanation of the books of *Poetry* and *History*, he proposed his own complements. Does it mean that he purposely showed his difference with Zhu Xi? Master Ouyang said, 'The classics are books beyond one time. Errors during inheritance are not mistakes of one person. And corrections and complements are not to be done by one person. Scholars should all give their opinions for the wise people's choice and finally for the emergence of a new sage. The later followers of Zhu Xi cannot go to its inside world and would rather keep to its superficial meaning by reciting his notes. They do not know the whys of Zhu's theory and deem it an attack if there is one word different from Zhu's. With such understanding, could Wang Bai be another attacker of Zhu Xi? Alas, how unscholarly today's scholars are!'"(*Ibid.* p.2733) Wang Bai's opinions may not necessarily be correct. As times are different, so must be the study of Zhu Xi's philosophy. And it's too normal for scholars to offer different opinions.

Jin Lüxiang, a native of Lanxi, was a man with extensive interest in astronomy, topography, rites and music, fields, military affairs, Yin-Yang and calendar. People of that time commented that He Ji was as honest as Yin Tun, and Wang Bai was as upright as Xie Liangzuo, while Jin Lüxiang shared both qualities in one person. Many of his books, *Pre-part of the History as a Mirror for Governance*, *Explanations to Textual Analysis of the Great Learning*, *Textual Study of the Collected Annotations to Confucian Analects and the Mencius*, *A Tabular Annotation to the Book of History* and *Annotations to the Book of History* included, seemed to be products after reading Zhu Xi's

193

books. That's why Huang Baijia said, "Jin Lüxiang wrote a book entitled *Textual Study of the Collected Annotations to Confucian Analects and the Mencius*, in which he had many findings not mentioned by Master Zhu and some were even contradictory to Zhu's view. It was not because he wished to prove himself higher by intentional difference; instead, he had a mind to illuminate Principlism just like Master Zhu. And Master Zhu himself was not a man who hated criticisms. Those who engaged themselves in imperial examinations tended to follow Master Zhu's words into minute details. It reminds us that true inheritance of scholarship is quite another thing." (*Ibid*. p.2738)

Xu Qian was also a Jinhua native and learned to be a scholar all by himself. He started his career as a teacher at the age of thirty. When he heard that Jin Lüxiang was lecturing at Lanjiang, he went to see him at once. The latter's words impressed him greatly: "Our Confucian doctrine emphasizes one Principle with multi manifestations. The difficulty lies not in the one Principle but in the many manifestations." Also, "The sage's doctrine is nothing but the Mean." Huang Zongxi talked about Xu Qian's learning process: "He started from differentiating the many manifestations and finally arrived at the oneness of the Principle. And he tried hard in finding the Mean in everything and practiced it. Several years later he learned all Jin's theory and merged it with his own." Xu Qian was a teacher for forty years and taught about a thousand students. He talked about the Four Books: "The aim of learning is to become a sage. We must first know the sage's mind before acting in the sage's actions. The sage's mind can be found in the Four Books. And the meaning of the Four Books is fully expressed in Master Zhu's annotation. Judging from its rich meaning in succinct description, can it be attained in an easy way?" Huang Zongxi summed up: "'Talking about one Principle with multi manifestations, the difficulty lies not in the one Principle but in the many manifestations.' This was what Li Tong told Master Zhu. At that time Master Zhu was still enchanted by non-Confucian doctrines. Li's words were like medicine to cure his sickness directly. In Jin Lüxiang and Xu Qian's time, scholars in Zhejiang and neighboring provinces all belonged to the Cihu school[1], which argued that Mind itself was to be studied, and things were not important. They did not understand that there was no Mind apart from things. So Jin Lüxiang re-cited the words to correct the erroneous understanding of the time. These words were really the blood vessel of five generations from Li Tong down to Jin Lüxiang[2]. As to later scholars who did not understand the Principle and focused their interest on individual things separately, that might be called learning without a sound foundation or falling ill because of the medicine. This is not the fault of these words." (*Ibid.* pp.2756–2759)

Huang Baijia said, "Apart from He Ji, Rao Lu was also Huang Gan's student. Among Rao Lu's disciples, Wu Zhongxing and Zhu Gongqian also had some fame, and there were no more influential people after them. But in He Ji's line, Wang Bai, Jin Lüxiang and Xu Qian had obtained Master Zhu's essence, and Liu Guan, Wu Shidao down to Dai Liang, Song Lian[3] and others were influenced by Master Zhu. How prosperous! It can well be said that the line of Zhu Xi's inheritance was right in Jinhua." (*Ibid.* p.2727)

When Rao Lu went to study under Huang Gan, the latter asked, "The *Confucius Analects* first talked about 'timely practice', what does that mean?" Rao answered, "It has two meanings: one is to understand by careful thinking, and the other is to practice by familiar understanding." The answer was highly appreciated by the teacher. Wu Cheng once said, "In Master Zhu's *Textual Analysis of the Doctrine of the Mean* and *Questions on the Four Books*, the selection is accurate and the discussion is detailed. But excessive accuracy leads to minuteness and too many details lead to superfluity. For the simple-minded people, minuteness makes their heads break; for the bright-minded people, superfluity makes them

---

[1] Cihu School was a Mindology school founded by Yang Jian (1141–1226), a student of Lu Jiuyuan, who lived by the lakeside of Cihu Lake.

[2] The "five" generations are successively Li Tong – Zhu Xi – Huang Gan – He Ji – Jin Lüxiang.

[3] Song Lian (1310–1381), courtesy name Jinglian, style name Qianxi, and was granted posthumously the title of Wenxian (literally culture and rites-setting). He was famous statesman, historian and literary writer at the beginning of the Ming Dynasty, and was praised by the first emperor of the Ming Dynasty as "the number one official of my Dynasty".

bewildered. When I read the *Doctrine of the Mean* in my early age, I did not agree with Master Zhu in several points. Later I found that Mr Rao Lu had the same opinion with me. What a pity that I was born too late and had no opportunity to ask him about them!" In Huang Zongxi and Quan Zuwang's comments, they both emphasized the difference between Zhu Xi and his disciples. From today's point of view it was quite natural, so long as it was not intended at attacking Zhu Xi. It is not a good student who understands the texts literally without considering the change of contexts and environment. In general, the Jinhua school was prosperous and lasted several generations, playing an important role in spreading Zhu Xi's doctrine. Though it was only a local academic school in the Southern Song dynasty, it had a critical effect in the Yuan dynasty when Principlism was spreading northward. Huang Zongxi said when introducing Wang Bai's student Zhang Xu: "Wang Bai lectured in Shangcai Academy and Zhang Xu was his student. In the middle of Zhiyuan period (1264–1294) the vice-censor Wu Manqing invited him to teach in Jiangning Official School and the gentry in midland China all sent their children to him to study the *Collected Annotations to the Four Books* or even invited him to teach in their family schools. When he went to Yangzhou, students came in even great number. All respected him and called him Mr Daojiang, named after his native place. And the imperial court ordered him to be teacher of the three families of Kong, Yan and Meng, descendents of the three ancient founders of Confucianism. The books he wrote were praised by Wu Cheng as reasoning properly and citing extensively, as if playing the role of Zhu Xi himself." (*Ibid*. p.2753) Huang Baijia, citing Wu Shidao's words, said, "Zhang Xu's learning was popular in the north, and Wang Bai became very famous because of him. It was because at that time Zhu Xi's doctrine was prevailing in north China but lacking proper teachers. That Zhang Xu was the fourth-generation pupil of Zhu Xi explained why he received so warm welcome." (*Ibid*.) Later Xu Qian was invited by attendant censor Zhao Hongwei to give lectures in Jinling for over a year, and his student Wu Shidao was engaged in the State Academy to direct the education under the banner of Zhu Xi, thus spreading the Zhu philosophy widely across the country.

Quan Zuwang said, "Principlism in north China was introduced by Zhao Fu or Mr Jianghan, in turn from Yao Shu, Dou Mo and Hao Jing. And Wang Bai was their general predecessor. The Yuan Dynasty Confucianism mainly depended on them." (*Ibid.* p.2994) Huang Zongxi described how Mr Jianghan (Zhao Fu) went to the north to spread Principlism: the Yuan army was conquering the Song Dynasty, and Yao Shu was in the army. He saved those who were familiar with the learning of either Confucianism, Daoism, Buddhism, medicine, or divination, and brought them back. At that time Zhao Fu was among the captives and prepared to drown himself at night. Yao saved him. "After arriving at Hebei Province, Zhao Fu taught students what he had learned. The number of students went up to about a hundred. At that time the traffic between north and south was blocked and Cheng Yi and Zhu Xi's books were not found in the north. It is from Zhao Fu who made them known. Yao Shu and Yang Weizhong set up the Great Ultimate Academy attached with Zhou Dunyi Memorial Temple, where they worshipped the six gentlemen Cheng Hao, Cheng Yi, Zhang Zai, Yang Shi, You Zuo and Zhu Xi. They recovered 8,000 volumes of their remaining books and invited Zhao Fu to be the instructor. Zhao thought that although the writings of Zhou Dunyi, Cheng Yi and others were widely spread, few scholars understood them thoroughly. So he drew a *Picture of Principlist Inheritance*, starting from the ancient emperors Fuxi, Shennong, Yao and Shun who succeeded Heaven to set up standards, followed by Kong Zi, Yan Yuan and Meng Zi who established Confucianism and started education, and again followed by Zhou Dunyi, Cheng brothers, Zhang Zai and Zhu Xi who inherited and carried the teaching forward; their books were listed as an appendix. Yao Shu retired to seclusion at Sumen to propagate his learning. Then Xu Heng, Hao Jing, and Liu Yin were able to read his books. Zhao Fu was respected as Mr Jianghan. Emperor Shizu of the Yuan Dynasty once asked him, 'I want to attack the Song Dynasty, could you be my guide?' He replied, 'Song is my parent country. How can I lead other army to attack my parents?' The emperor deemed it right and no longer forced him. Jianghan literary means Changjiang and Hanshui, Zhao's native place and Song's territory at that time. He was so named because he was always thinking of these places while staying in the north." Huang Baijia said, "Since the Late Jin Dynasty (936–946 AD), the northern part of China had long been in the hands of the national minorities. Although great Confucians appeared one after another in the Song Dynasty, they had not been known to the north. It was only after Zhao Fu, as a captive from the south, came to the north that Principlism became known. Scholars like Yao Shu, Dou Mo, Xu Heng and Liu Yin began to spread it, and thus started the northern school of learning, such as Wu Cheng's classics study and Yao Sui's literature study — that was really a prosperous scene." (*Ibid.* pp.2993–2994) As Xu Heng had been appointed Chancellor of the State Academy, he played a critical role in popularizing Cheng-Zhu Principlism. Quan Zuwang cited the following words from Yu Ji's *Preface to the Poem for Li Yanfang*: "Mister Xu Heng helped to make Cheng-Zhu's Principlism popular. His contribution was not to be denied." (*Ibid.* p.3002)

Huang Baijia said in his *Case Study of Liu Yin:* "The most important Confucian scholars in the Yuan Dynasty are Xu Heng, Liu Yin and Wu Cheng. Wu Cheng was a late-comer while Xu Heng and Liu Yin are the ones whom the new dynasty relied on as cultural founders. Of the two, Xu Heng made even greater contributions because for several decades many great scholars and famous ministers were his students, and through him the countrymen began to learn of the sage's doctrine. Liu Yin did not enjoy long life and his influence was not so great. But as Yu Ji said at that time, 'After Xu Heng died, his followers deemed textual study as plaything and were careless in writing, deemed problem solving as a chance to overtake others and purposely embarrassed their masters, deemed actionlessness as self-cultivation, and deemed superficial politeness as changed quality, thus outwardly deceiving the people in the country and inwardly blinding the scholars' mind. This was of course the outcome of prevalent abuses, yet Xu Heng himself was also to blame for he only saw the shallow part of the theory and the world followed him blindly. As to Liu Yin, he was much more talented and even had the temper like Zeng Dian[①]. It seems that one cannot judge which is better by the effect only." (*Ibid.* p.3030) Quan Zuwang said, "Wu Cheng was a student of Rao Lu, so he belonged to Zhu Xi school. But he studied Lu Jiuyuan's theory as well, as his another teacher, Cheng Shaokai, had once built an academy in an attempt to merge the two schools. But anyway, Wu Cheng's works were more close to Zhu Xi." Wang Baijia said more concretely, "Wu Cheng studied from Cheng Ruoyong and was the fourth-generation student of Zhu Xi. Through careful examination I found that most of Zhu Xi's disciples just studied accepted conclusions and few had real mastery of classics. Wu Cheng's *Collected Comments on Five Classics* did make contribution to classics study. He directly continued Zhu Xi's tradition, and did far much better than Zhu's own disciples like Chen Chun and the like." (*Academic Case Studies of the Song and Yuan Dynasties.* Book 4. p.3037)

Though highly respected in the Song and Yuan Dynasties, Zhu Xi's learning did not enjoy the dominant status in academic ideology. During the Hongwu reign of the Ming Dynasty (1368–1398), Xie Jin[②] proposed to edit and publish the Principlist classics by the government. In 1414, by Emperor Chengzu's decree, *Complete Collection of the Five Classics, Complete Collection of the Four Books* and the *Complete Works on Nature and Principle* were compiled by the government, and from then on Principlism became the dominant ideology of the empire. Hu Guang, Yang Rong and Jin Youzi explained their aim in the compilation of these books in their report to the emperor:

> ... so that man will all follow the right course and learning will not be led astray. When every household is reading Kong Zi, Meng Zi with Cheng Yi and Zhu Xi's explanation, genuine function of Confucianism will be acquired; when everyone keeps to morality,

---

① Zeng Dian, courtesy name Xi, father of Zeng Sen, was also a disciple of Kong Zi. He was once praized by Kong Zi for sharing the same attitude towards life.

② Xie Jin (1369–1415), courtesy name Dashen or Jinshen, style names Chunyu and Xiyi, ws posthumously granted the title Wenyi (literally "cultural and good at summarizing"). He had been the Prime Minister and was the chief editor of the great book *Yongle Encyclopaedia*.

humanity and righteousness, people's aspiration will be led towards sagehood. The society will return to the unsophisticated archaic past and be free from the long-endured corrupt custom. Fresh! Bright! Complete! And prosperous! According to our humble observation, when the Zhou Dynasty declined, Dao was discarded, and people were anxious to find a way out; only Kong Zi and his disciples were able to maintain the Dao and educate the world. There has never been an emperor like ours who is so courageous and responsible by advocating the Dao in the Six Classics, thus continuing the tradition of the ancient sages. (from Hou Wailu's *The History of the Principlism in the Song and Ming Dynasties*. Part II. p.12)

There were quite a few Confucians at the beginning of the Ming dynasty, represented by Song Lian. Because of the trend of "merging", first the merging of Zhu Xi's and Lu Jiuyuan's schools at the end of the Southern Song Dynasty, then the merging of Confucianism, Daoism and Buddhism in the Yuan and Ming dynasties, the persistence in the "pure" Principlism or Zhu Xi's scholarship had appeared out of date in academics. Xie Shan made a comment on Song Lian in his *A Note on the Portrait of Mr Song Lian,* recorded in *Case Study of the Four Scholars in North Hill* in *Academic Case Studies of the Song and Yuan Dynasties:*

Mr Song Lian received education from the four teachers of his home province, Huang Jin, Liu Guan, Wu Lai and Wenren Mengji, who in turn received education from He Ji, Wang Bai, Jin Lüxiang and Xu Qian. Tracing still back, they were disciples of Huang Gan, Zhu Xi's direct inheritor. I once said, "Zhu Xi's learning has experienced three changes during its inheritance. The first change was found in Xu Qian, who started to pay less attention to the content of Principlism than to its textual study. The second change took place in his four students from Huang Jin to Wenren Mengji who were merely literary writers. Till Mr Song Lian the third change took place, when he was relegated to those flattering Buddhism. Luckily Mr Fang Xiaoru[①] was his bright student. Mr Fang might have brought brilliance to the Zhu Xi school, or even directly continued Zhu's tradition. Unfortunately his life ended in tragedy, so we were unable to see his final achievement, and his learning was not even inherited. Nevertheless, I love the writings of Huang Jin, Liu Guan, Wu Lai as well as Song Lian, for their Confucian style, gentle and not giddy, surely benefited from their reading of the classics. Literary writing, although only of second importance to a gentleman, is what conveys one's mind and energy and not to be disguised. Mr Song, as an important minister in founding the new empire, was the first one to advocate the positive style of the Ming dynasty which lasted for 300 years. His own writing was especially full of the solemn spirit expressed in words. Is he not a great scholar of the time, who advocates justice and brightness?" (*Academic Case Studies of the Song and Yuan Dynasties*. Book 4. p.2801)

2. The Consolidation of the Status of Zhu Xi's Doctrine in the Early Qing Dynasty

When the Qing Dynasty started, the government adopted a policy of esteeming Confucianism. During the reign of Emperor Shunzhi (1644–1661), Confucian education was restored in schools and academies, and the main textbooks used included the Four Books, the Five Classics, the *Complete Works on Nature and Principle*, *A Compendium of History as a Mirror for Governance*, and so on, so that the excellent students of the Han nation thus trained could be used by the Manchu court. During Emperor Kangxi's reign (1662–1722), the worship of Kong Zi was replaced by the worship of Zhu Xi to suit the change of historical environment since the Song, Yuan and Ming Dynasties. Emperor Kangxi made special contributions in establishing Zhu Xi's doctrine as the official ideology. The *General Catalog*

---

① Fang Xiaoru (1357–1402), courtesy name Xizhi or Xigu, style name Xunzhi, but more widely known as master Goucheng or Master Zhengxue. He was a very famous scholar and minister at the early Ming Dynasty. He finally died a martyr.

of the Complete Library of the Four Treasuries recorded his decree in ordering the compilation of *Essentials of the Nature and the Principle* and the *Complete Works of Zhu Xi:*

> *Essentials of the Nature and the Principle edited by His Majesty* in 12 volumes was designated by Emperor Kangxi himself in 1717. At first, Zhu Xi's disciple Chen Chun edited *Literal Meaning of Nature and Principle*. Later Xiong Gangda edited *Collected Sayings on Nature and Principle*. The term "Nature and Principle" was thus known. During the reign of Emperor Yongle of the Ming Dynasty (1403–1424), Hu Guang et al were ordered to edit the *Complete Works on Nature and Principle* by muddling quotations of the Song Confucians, and published it together with the *Complete Works of the Four Books and Five Classics* as the official textbooks. But Hu Guang et al actually had little knowledge and their compilation was utterly a failure. The so-called *Complete Works of the Four Books and Five Classics* was a copied version of local publications with some alteration of authors' names. The *Complete Works on Nature and Principle* paid more attention on the quantity than the structure. His Majesty Emperor Kangxi continued Yao and Shun's ruling tradition, understood by heart the thoughts of Kong Zi and Meng Zi, traced the original meaning from the Six Classics and made a balance between the explanations of hundreds of interpreters. For the Song Principlist masters, he discerned their gains and losses and examined thoroughly their understanding of the Dao and the verity of their arguments. Regretting that Hu Guang et al's book was an outrageous concoction in the name of popularizing Principlism which could only do harm to the pupils with its fragmental redundancy, His Majesty ordered the Grand Academician Li Guangdi and others to make corrections to the book, and he himself proofread and finalized the version. Works such as Cai Chen's *Grand Norms Explained in Numbers* and the like had to be dismissed. Also deleted were those attachments of poems and rhymed prose as a warning against vanity writings. As to the rest sections, strict measures were

taken for the selection of possibly one tenth of the original. In this way, although the book became thinner, the meaning was more condensed and the structure more concise. Compared to the original, it was really like "gold out of the ore" as Sikong Tu[①] said in his *Twenty-four Categories in Poetry Appreciation*. Messy talking might cause confusion in understanding the sages; here we found a convincing example!

The *Complete Works of Master Zhu Xi Edited by His Majesty* in 66 volumes was designated by Emperor Kangxi himself in 1713. Confucians of the Southern Song Dynasty were fond of compiling analects, and Master Zhu boasted to have the richest content. During the period of Xianchun (1265–1274), Li Jingde eliminated all the redundancy and edited the rest into a book which still contained 140 volumes. The writers in the Southern Song Dynasty, Zhou Bida, Yang Wanli and Lu You, boasted to have produced the most voluminous works, but the volumes of *Comprehensive and Complete Works of Zhu Xi* could equal them. The recordings contained in Zhu's works mentioned above were out of many different hands, and the editions were not done at one time. Some of them might have been polished by recorders with their own understandings, and others might be imagined and added by editors in Master Zhu's name. Some, if really heard from the master, might be contradictory to each other because they were recorded at different times or spoken on different occasions. And the Confucian readers, deeply convinced in Master Zhu's authorship and thirsting for hearing more, while unable to search for the beginning or question the end, esteemed single phrases as if they were from the Six Classics. And the real meaning of Master Zhu was confused by the worshipers themselves. *The Analects of Master Zhu* mentioned that Master Zhu had left some family discourses which later became a trouble for readers for they were not well selected.

---

① Sikong Tu (837–908), courtesy name Biaoshen and styled himself as Zhifeizi. He was a poet and an important poetic critic in the history of Chinese literature.

Similarly, was it what Master Zhu had expected that the later readers read his works without differentiating truth from false or right from wrong? His Majesty, in an attempt to commend Master Zhu's doctrine, had the wise insight to know the gains and losses of the *Analects* and *Works*. He made special order to Grand Academician Li Guangdi and others to recompile the book by deleting the confusing data, retaining the essence and classify it into 19 categories. Gold becomes purer after refining and jade gets rid of flaws after chiseling. The readers of Master Zhu will no longer be puzzled by discrepancies when they get the present version as their guide. (*General Catalog of the Complete Library of the Four Treasuries*. Book I. p.797)

From the above two records we can see the deep concern Emperor Kangxi showed in Zhu Xi's works as well as his endeavor in propagating Zhu Xi's doctrine. In fact, during Emperors Yongzheng and Qianlong's reign, the official status of Zhu Xi's doctrine was always maintained. From the introduction of Zhu's four annotations to the Four Books in the *Complete Library of the Four Treasuries* compiled in Qianlong period, we can see clearly how highly Zhu's learning was respected at that time. Here is the introduction to *Textual Analysis and Collected Annotations of the Four Books*:

Textual Analysis to the Great Learning in one volume, *Collected Annotations to Confucian Analects* in ten volumes, *Collected Annotations to Mencius* in seven volumes, and *Textual Analysis to the Doctrine of the Mean* in one volume were all written by Master Zhu Xi of the Song dynasty. Note: The *Confucian Analects* was officially set as a branch of learning for academicians in the reign of Emperor Wendi of the Han Dynasty (179–164 B.C.). The *Mencius* was also officially endorsed at the same period according to Zhao Qi[1]'s inscription, but was soon discarded, so it was not recorded in historical document. For

---

[1] Zhao Qi (?108–201), courtesy name Binqing, a scholar of Confucian classics in the Eastern Han Dynasty, and annotator of *Mencius*.

The Doctrine of the Mean, two papers of *On Doctrine of the Mean* were recorded in the *Bibliographic Treatise in the History of the Han Dynasty, Notes to the Doctrine of the Mean* in two volumes by Dai Yong and *A Lecture on the Doctrine of the Mean* in one volume by Emperor Wudi of the Liang Dynasty were both recorded in *The Catalog of Classics in the Book of the Sui Dynasty*. Only the *Great Learning* had no separate recording before the Tang Dynasty. But *Zhizhai Annotated Bibliographic Records* had already recorded *Expanded Meaning of Great Learning* and *Expanded Meaning of the Doctrine of the Mean,* both in one-volume form and written by Sima Guang①, obviously before the time of the two Cheng brothers, a proof that the latter were not the first to make the two classics stand out. However, the detailed explanation doubtlessly started from the two Cheng brothers, and the name of "Four Books" was given by Master Zhu. The original order of the Four Books was *Great Learning, Confucian Analects, Mencius* and *Doctrine of the Mean*. The folk publishers combined the *Learning* and the *Mean* into one volume as both were very short, thus the *Doctrine of the Mean* was moved before the *Analects*. In the Ming Dynasty, as the Four Books were used for assigning topics in imperial examinations, they were rearranged according to the time of the authors. Thus, the *Mean* was placed between the *Analects* and the *Mencius*. But these were all of no importance; it was not necessary to return to the original order. The original of the *Great Learning* was just one piece of work while Master Zhu divided it into two parts: original classic and explanatory notes. He even reversed the original order and made some amendments. His *Mean* did not follow Zheng Xuan's classification of sections. Both his *Mean* and his *Great Learning* were generally called "textual analysis". *Analects* and *Mencius* collected different explanations in the form of "collected annotations", like He Yan's *Collected Explanations to the Confucian Analects* which had collected eight scholars' explanations.

---

① Sima Guang (1019–1086), courtesy name Junshi, style name Yusou, and ws granted posthumously the title of Wenzheng (literally "cultural nd upright"), great historian and scholar of the Northern Song Dynasty, and author of *History as a Mirror for Governmance*.

The difference lies in that He Yan had given all the names of the explanations he collected while Master Zhu did so only sometimes. Scholars might differ in their explanations of the textual study of the *Great Learning*, but stayed the same in using the original text after "Make the Thoughts Sincere", and Master Zhu's creation was to insert a chapter here. As it was not out of the so-called "eight items" and the addition was beneficial to the learners, we need not take it too seriously. His *Mean* did not follow Zhen Xuan[①]'s annotations but actually was better and more accurate than Zheng's. Now so far as textual study was concerned, the Song scholars did not do as good as the Han scholars; in terms of argumentation study, the Song scholars did better. Each had its strong side and could be absorbed by each other accordingly. For example, Zheng Xuan's annotation to the four sentences starting from "maintaining vigilance and prudence even when he was not seen" was adopted, and the explanation of the section starting from "even though he was in the position" was entirely copied. Judging from what he accepted or rejected, Zhu Xi must have a ruler or mirror in himself and one should not argue with him based on the "ancient" meaning. In his explanation of the *Analects* or *Mencius*, he also adopted quite a number of ancient annotations. For example, the dialogue about "hulian" in the Analects did not conform with *Mingtang's Position* in the *Book of Rites*, and the annotation about Cao Jiao's question[②] did not conform with what was talked about in the *Spring and Autumn Annals*. People doubted about them, but they did not know that these were not wantonly concocted by Master Zhu. The annotation about "hulian" was actually from Bao Xian[③], and the annotation about Cao Jiao was from Zhao Qi. There's even more. The "ren" in "the master's walls are several ren high" in

① Zheng Xuan (127–200), courtesy name Kangcheng, was the most important scholar of Confucian classics in the Eastern Han Dynasties who was the first one to annotate almost all the Confucian classics.
② In *Mencius*, Book VI, Part B.
③ Bao Xian (6 B.C.–65 A.D.), courtesy name Ziliang, Confucian classics annotator in the Eastern Han Dynasty.

the *Analects* was explained as equaling to "seven feet" and in "digging the well to nine ren deep" in the *Mencius* was explained as equaling to "eight feet". People were surprised at how contradictory they were. But they didn't know that "seven feet" was also from Bao Xian and "eight feet" was from Zhao Qi. Master Zhu was actually integrating many scholars' ideas instead of just giving his own opinion. If we cannot find out where each explanation was from, we would think how subjective he was. We must know that the Master exerted most of his effort in life on the explanation on the Four Books. The work on differentiation and discrimination was much more critical and harder than what he spent on explaining the *Book of Change* and the *Book of Poetry*. In reading his books, we must take a macroscopic view and consider his general meaning and subtle hints. Those attackers of Zhu since the Ming Dynasty always looked for hairsplitting facts, and his defenders concentrated themselves on trivial facts as well. They were limited in their sectarian bias and could not really understand Master Zhu's intention in compiling these books. (*Ibid.* p.294).

This introduction to Zhu Xi's *Textual Analysis and Collected Annotations of the Four Books* was one of the rare praises made by the authors of the *General Catalog of the Complete Library of the Four Treasuries*. This reflects not only the official respect for Master Zhu, but also the genuine acknowledgement and appreciation for the essence and academic value of the book. After that book, the *General Catalog* continued to introduce Zhu Xi's *Essentials of Confucian Analects and Mencius:*

Essentials of Confucian Analects and Mencius in 34 volumes, contributed by Jiangsu Governor, was written by Master Zhu Xi of the Song Dynasty. Master Zhu first collected different comments on the *Confucian Analects* in 1163 into a compilation but the book was not published. Nine years later, in 1172, he once again collected comments from twelve scholars — Cheng Hao, Cheng Yi, Zhang Zai, Fan Zuyu, Lü Xizhe, Lü Dalin, Xie Liangzuo, You Zuo, Yang Shi, Hou

Zongliang, Yin Tun and Zhou Fuxian — arranged and classified them into *Essentials of Confucian Analects and Mencius* and wrote a preface for it. At that time he was 43 years of age. Later the book was published in Yuzhang Prefecture under the title of *Extracted Meaning of Confucian Analects and Mencius*. In *Selected Works of Zhu Xi* we can find Zhu's postscript to the book:

A few years ago I edited this book and published it in Jianyang and it had long been known to the scholars. Later I studied carefully and found there were still something missing in the sayings of Cheng brothers and Zhang Zai which had to be amended, and new materials such as the four and half papers written by Mr Zhou which I got from Chen Tun of Jianyang and attached to the book. Mr Huang Mou published the book in Yuzhang and, afraid that people might be puzzled about the details of the book, asked me to write something next to the previous preface and changed its original name *Essentials* to *Extracted Meaning*.

So this was the story. Later the title was once more changed to *Collected explanations*. Nowadays the new edition retained the original title Master Zhu gave in his preface. It contained 20 volumes of *Confucian Analects* and 14 volumes of *Mencius,* as well as an outline for each of the two books, not counted in volumes. At first, Master Zhu's aim of editing this book was to explain the meaning of the classics based on Cheng's understanding. Later he extracted the essence to compile the *Collected Annotations* and gathered the difficult or doubtful points to be discussed in another book *Questions on the Four Books*. It seemed that this book was the discarded content. But in *Master Zhu's Classified Analects*, he said that the *Confucian Analects* must be read together with the *Essentials* and that the quotations in the *Essentials* should be read, memorized, and pondered constantly, so as to be understood in the future. So this book doesn't seem like the content discarded from the *Collected Annotations,* and is worthy of being preserved here. (*Ibid.* p.294)

Moreover, in the *Synopsis of the General Catalog of Extractions of the Complete Library of the Four Treasuries,* Zhu Xi's *Textual Analysis and Collected Annotations of the Four Books* was introduced together with Zhen Dexiu's *Collected Editions of the Four Books* and Zhao Shunxiu①'s *Collected Explanations of the Four Books,* which is a good example to show how Zhu Xi's Four Books Study and its propagation were valued and utilized in Qianlong's period (1736–1795):

> Your subordinates hereby note: The term "Four Books" was first used by Master Zhu Xi. Since the Han dynasty, there had been more than 180 annotations to the *Confucian Analects* starting from Kong Anguo② down to the Song Dynasty, and more than 60 annotations to the *Mencius* starting from Zhao Qi. Master Zhu reconciled the different versions and compiled the *Collected Annotations.* His understanding and appreciation was much better than those of all previous scholars. The practice of taking the *Doctrine of the Mean* from the *Book of Rites* as a separate book started in the Han Dynasty, as can be seen in the inclusion of two papers on the *Doctrine of the Mean* in the *Bibliographic Treatise of the History of the Han Dynasty.* The practice of taking the *Great Learning* from the *Book of Rites* as a separate book started from Sima Guang and continued by the Cheng brothers. Master Zhu made annotations to all the Four Books respectively. He called it *Textual Study* because he had done some changes to the chapter division of the ancient texts. His order of the Four Books was *Great Learning, Confucian Analects, Mencius* and *The Doctrine of the Mean,* in 19 volumes altogether. For the sake of convenient learning, someone changed the order by moving the *Doctrine of the Mean* directly after the *Great Learning.* Because of the imperial examinations of the Ming Dynasty, the *Mean* was placed after the *Analects,* which was effective till today,

---

① Zhao Shunsun (1215–1277), courtesy name Hezhong, style name Ge'an, scholar and official of the Southern Song Dynasty.

② Kong Anguo (?156–74 B.C.), courtesy name Ziguo, Kong Zi's eleventh generation decendent and Confucian classics annotator.

though not in Master Zhu's original plan. The book had two palace versions. One with interlinear notes was generally known as the imperial academy edition. The other was an edition in the imitation Song script with annotated words in same big characters and in single lines, which was in fact an imitation of Yongze Academy edition of the Chunyou period of the Song Dynasty (1241–1252)[①] and was especially good. The difference between the two versions lies in the usage of certain words, sometimes as many as scores in number. But since the interlinear notes version is the children's textbook in the country now, the present edition is based on it but makes some corrections in reference to the imitation Song version, so that the reader can make their own comparison.

Your subordinates hereby note: In the 26 volumes of Zhen Dexiu's *Collected Editions of the Four Books*, only the one-volume *Great Learning* and the one-volume *Doctrine of the Mean* were finalized by Zhen Dexiu. The 10-volume *Analects* and the 14-volume *Mencius* were all finished by his son Zhen Zhidao using his punctuated version and in reference with his other works: *Notes on Reading, Selected Works of Zhen Dexiu* and *Derived Meaning from the Great Learning*. Master Zhu spent his entire life on *Textual Analysis and Collected Annotations of the Four Books*, which was extremely precise and accurate. For hundreds of years it was studied by scholars word by word as their guidance. Inside the book, the textual analysis part was full of original ideas whereas the collected annotation part was a concentration of previous studies. But the reasons why he made such choices were found in his other books such as *Questions on the Four Books, Basics, Classified Analects* and *Selected Works,* which could not all be included in this book. Contained in the other books were mostly undecided sayings or casual talks that were not well recorded or considered redundant. Zhen's present book cited Master Zhu extensively from

---

① Yongze Academy mentioned here was actually founded in 1271. According to recent study, this edition should be published in 1366.

various sources to bring mutual evidence, and at times he would present his own judgment to make compromise. Zhen boasted to have contributed to selecting and complementing, which is true. Later, Zhu Zongdao presented *Attachment to the Four Books,* Cai Mo presented *Collected Interpretations to the Four Books*, and Wu Zhenzi presented *An Integration of the Four Books;* all the three were similar to Zhen's book. But as their learning was not as profound as Zhen Dexiu, their books were inferior in quality.

Your subordinates hereby note: *Collected Explanations of the Four Books* in 27 volumes was compiled by Zhao Shunsun of the Song Dynasty. Zhao Shunsun, style-named Ge'an, was a native of Kuocang, whose father Zhao Lei had once studied under Zhu Xi's disciple Teng Lin. So Zhao Shunsun could also be considered a descendent of Master Zhu so far as learning was concerned. This book cited a lot of Zhu Xi's sayings to show more clearly the intention of Zhu Xi's *Textual Analysis and Collected Annotations.* Other 13 people cited in the book were Huang Gan, Fu Guan, Chen Chun, Chen Kongshuo, Cai Yuan, Cai Chen, Ye Weidao, Hu Yong, Chen Zhi, Pan Bing, Huang Shiyi, Zhen Dexiu and Cai Mo, all belonging to the Zhu school, a proof that the book strictly followed its teachers' viewpoint. The previous scholars criticized this book for its superfluity, but different scholars could adopt different policies in classics study. For doing annotation, simplicity was encouraged, whereas for doing explanation, more facts were needed to prove the points. This book took the name of "explanation" and in its preface the author said that he was following the example of the explanation-style forerunners Kong Yingda[1] and Jia Gongyan[2]. As a book of "explanation" style, its superfluity was not to blame. Just forget this and grasp its main idea — that's enough. (*Synopsis of the General Catalog of Extractions of the Complete Library of*

---

[1] Kong Yingda (574–648), courtesy name Chongyuan or Zhongda, great scholar and annotator of Confucian classics in the Tang Dynasty.
[2] Jia Gongyan, birth year unknown, maybe a little later than Kong Yingda, also an important annotator of Confucian classics.

the Four Treasuries. pp.197–199)

What we quoted above vividly revealed the compiler's intention and how Zhu Xi was respected at that time. Because of the official encouragement, ordinary people naturally made it a popular custom to respect Zhu Xi.

There are two characteristics in the *Academic Case Studies of the Song and Yuan Dynasties* edited by Huang Zongxi and others in the Zhu Xi study: the research of the inheritance of Zhu's ideology and the diversified appreciation of Zhu Xi. The former is the book's biggest contribution to the summarization of the Zhu Xi study, which traced back to Yang Shi of Northern Song Dynasty and flew down to Song Lian of the early Ming Dynasty, thus forming a clear-cut line of the inheritance of the Zhu Xi study as well as its contribution to the country's cultural development at the end of the Southern Song Dynasty, the Yuan Dynasty, and the beginning of the Ming Dynasty. The latter can be seen from the different attitudes of the compilers towards the Zhu Xi ideology. Huang Baijia praised Zhu Xi highly:

Zhu Xi, whose father was Zhu Song, whose teachers were Li Tong, Liu Mianzhi, Liu Zihui and Hu Xian, whose friends included Zhang Shi and Lü Zuqian, and whose inheritors ranked among those not easily criticized, was endowed with exceptional talent and studied very diligently. He said to himself, "I used to study very hard and think of myself as crossing over a dangerous bridge: a careless miss would make me fall." This shows how hard he studied, and he never gave up for a second. His learning includes three aspects: setting up reverence as the foundation, exhausting Principles to acquire knowledge, and returning to oneself for practice. He read profoundly. Apart from Confucian classics and histories, he had studied and researched other branches such as miscellaneous schools' works, Buddhism and Daoism, astronomy and geography. No wonder he was the seldom-seen great Confucian of the time! (*Ibid*. p.1505)

That is a fair and level-headed praise of Zhu Xi's academic efforts and summarizes the brilliant achievements in his life.

Quan Zuwang, from an even wider angle, presented a knowledgeable affirmation of Zhu Xi's academic achievements:

> Through four generations, Mr Yang Shi's learning finally found its inheritor, Master Zhu Xi, whose academic width and depth covered a hundred generations. The Jiangxi School and the Yongjia School of East Zhejiang, though great as well, were partial in nature, which could not be denied. So a good reader of Master Zhu should read more widely so as to benefit from gathering strong points and repudiating deficient points. To stick to one and discard the rest was not Master Zhu's learning genuinely. (*Ibid*. p.1495)

Nevertheless, the chief compiler, Huang Zongxi, held a different view from the above two:

> That "self-cultivation depends on reverence and promotion of learning aims at acquiring knowledge" was the prime target set up by Cheng Yi. Zhu Xi strictly kept to it and whatever he said he never deviated from these two sentences. Comparatively speaking, Cheng Hao's words purposely encouraged people in case they stopped, and Zhu Xi's words purposely discouraged people in case they wandered about. The two had one goal. But Zhu Xi's realization was attained at his last years. Wang Shouren made "Master Zhu Xi's final verdict" which could basically stand though some of the points might have started at his early years. A scholar, knowing not how to discriminate and having not a thorough understanding of Master Zhu's intention, hesitated at Zhu's profound learning and didn't know whether to believe in Master Zhu or in Kong Zi and Meng Zi; was he whom Master Zhu was waiting for? (*Academic Case Studies of the Song and Yuan Dynasties*. Book 2. pp.1554–1555)

Huang Zongxi was obviously a believer of Wang Shouren and he fully agreed to Wang's viewpoint in the latter's *The Final Verdict of Master Zhu's Last Years* and regarded it as the final verdict of Zhu Xi. However, this was not true from the history of the development of the Zhu Xi study. Superficially Huang Zongxi respected Zhu Xi, but evidently he respected Wang Shouren even more. At the same time, we noticed that Li Guangdi, the editor of *Essentials of the Nature and the Principle* and the *Complete Works of Zhu Xi* at the order of Emperor Kangxi, at the same time respected Zhu Xi and accepted Lu Jiuyuan and Wang Shouren's ideas. And there was even a man like Li Fu to compile a book like *An All-inclusive Discussion on Master Zhu's Last Years* in defense of Lu Jiuyuan. For the research of Zhu Xi inheritance, these phenomena deserve a reasonable explanation as well as an analysis.

3. The Disputed Case of "Zhu Xi's Tendency towards the Mindology at His Last Years"

There was an academic dispute between Zhu Xi and Lu Jiuyuan brothers, which left a far-reaching influence in the propagation of Zhu Xi's thought. From the Song, Yuan, Ming, Qing dynasties down to present there have been many further disputes, supporting either Zhu or Lu, or trying to reconcile both, or comparing their differences, or just criticizing sectarianism. Among them the most prominent works are *The Final Verdict of Master Zhu's Last Years* written by Wang Shouren of the Ming Dynasty and *An All-inclusive Discussion on Master Zhu's Last Years* written by Li Fu of the Qing dynasty, both emphasizing the similarities of Zhu Xi's ideas at his last years with the ideas of Lu Jiuyuan and Wang Shouren.

Wang Shouren's *The Final Verdict of Master Zhu's Last Years* discussed Zhu Xi's thought at his last years, but the material it collected even included letters Zhu wrote in his youth or at his middle age, which aroused certain doubts. Li Fu's *An All-inclusive Discussion on Master Zhu's*

Last Years was more strict than Wang in selecting letters, but it said more frankly that similarities between Zhu Xi and Lu Jiuyuan could be seen in their youth, middle age, especially in their last years. How do we explain such a phenomenon? Up to now, few papers or monographs can answer the question to satisfaction. Here we shall discuss the problem from three aspects by analyzing concrete texts and other materials. (1) Both Wang and Li used only relevant letters they found in Zhu's works to confirm their argument. Surely that was not enough. Here we will try to make a comprehensive analysis from Zhu Xi's life at his last years to prove his tendency toward the Mindology. (2) In Li's work he only made parallel comparison between Zhu and Lu's letters with his own explanation to show their similarity. This was not a rigorous approach. What was the reason behind it? (3) Why did Wang compile Zhu's letters into a book to prove the similarity between Zhu Xi and himself when, as we know, he was mainly critical of Zhu Xi's Principlism in his *Instructions for Practical Living*? Obviously, this question has gone beyond similarities or differences. Why?

Wang Shouren's emphasis of Zhu Xi's Theory-of-Mind tendency in his letters at his last years received full support from Huang Zongxi, author of *Academic Case Studies of the Song and Yuan Dynasties,* who stood firmly on Wang's side. This support was not merely sectarian. Reading through the *Complete Works of Zhu Xi,* we may find that it is theoretically to confirm his Theory-of-Mind tendency by just citing part of letters at his last years, and based on that to deny his academic achievements in the first part of his life. If his life is viewed as a whole, Zhu Xi's Principlist ideology is a complete system, without any sudden break or turn at a certain point. So, clarifying the apparent contradiction is important for us to fully understand Zhu Xi's thought. It will also shed light on our understanding of Lu Jiuyuan and Wang Shouren's thought and the Song-Ming Principlism as a whole.

In *The Final Verdict of Master Zhu's Last Years,* Wang Shouren selected 34 letters from *Selected Works of Zhu Xi,* claiming that they revealed Zhu Xi's change of idea at his last years. The "new" philosophical ideas, equaling to Wang's Mindology, was the "final verdict" of Zhu Xi's thought. Qian Hong, Wang's student, said in the *Publisher's Note:*

The *Final Verdict* was first published in southern Jiangxi. Master Zhu suffered from eye sickness and lay still for a long time. He was suddenly enlightened of the truth of Confucianism and was sorry for the annotations he had done in his middle age, which were harmful to both himself and others, and hurriedly wrote to tell it to his friends and students. On reading these letters, my teacher Mr Wang was glad that he shared the same view with Master Zhu and copied the letters into a volume, which his students put to print. From then on, few people would talk about the differences or similarities between Master Zhu and my teacher. Mr Wang said: "I did not expect to be helped by these letters." In 1572, when Xie Tingjie was printing the teacher's complete works, he was told to include the *Final Verdict* after his own *Quotations*, so as to let people know that there was no difference between the two masters' ideas, and the orthodox thoughts of Confucianism were of the same origin. (*Complete Works of Wang Shouren*. p.144)

Qian Hong's words were actually groundless. To sum up, what he meant was: (1) Zhu Xi, suffering from eye sickness and unable to read or write, thought in recuperation and suddenly realized the truth of Confucianism. (2) Zhu regretted the annotations he did at his middle age which were harmful to others as well as to himself, and he voiced his regrets to others. (3) Wang Shouren, on reading these letters, was glad that they two shared the same view and soon published them, thus settling the quarrel about the similarities between Zhu and Lu & Wang. Following is a list of Zhu Xi's 34 letters selected by Wang in his *Final Verdict* according to the dates of writing:

1166 Reply to He Hao	1184 Reply to Liang Zhuan
1167 Reply to He Hao	1185 Reply to Lü Zujian
1167 Reply to He Hao	1185 Reply to Lü Zujian

1168 Reply to He Hao	1185 To Zhou Shujin
1169 Reply to Lin Chongzhi	1186 Reply to Pan Jingxian
1169 Reply to Lin Yongzhong	1186 Reply to Lu Jiuyuan
1169 Reply to Lin Yongzhong	1186 Reply to Lü Zujian
1170 Reply to Zhang Shi	1186 Reply to Dou Congzhou
1170 Reply to Lin Yongzhong	1186 Reply to Lü Zujian
1170 To Lin Yongzhong	1186 Reply to Pan Yougong
1170 Reply to Wu Lie	1186 Reply to Liu Qingzhi
1176 Reply to Lü Zuqian	1190 Reply to Yang Fang
1180 To Wu Ying	1191 Reply to Huang Gan
1180 Reply to Lin Yongzhong	1195 To Lord Tian Dan
1182 Reply to Liu Qingzhi	1195 Reply to Chen Wenwei
1183 Reply to Fu Fuzhong	1195 Reply to Lü Zujian
1184 Reply to Pan Jingyu	1198 Reply to Zhou Chunren

The list was made with a reference to Chen Lai's monograph, *A Research of Zhu Xi's Letters Arranged in Chronicle Order*, published in 2011. From the list we learned that the time span of those letters covered more than thirty years. There were 11 letters before 1170 when Zhu Xi was 40 years old, 3 letters before he was 50, 15 letters before he was 60, and only 5 letters after he was 60. So it is inexact to say that these letters all represented Zhu Xi's thought at his last years. What could be confirmed was that whether in his youth, or at middle age, or at his last years, Zhu Xi's thought had something in common with that of Wang Shouren, and Wang purposely emphasized that the commonness happened only at Zhu Xi's last years and he used this to deny Zhu's academic achievements before that period. Wang personally admitted the problem of the time span in the letters he selected. So we may say that Wang's conclusion was unreliable, or motivated by his own intentions. Actually Zhu Xi's thought had something in common with Wang Shouren throughout his whole life, not just at his last years. Wang Shouren said in his *Preface:*

Kong Zi's doctrine stopped after Meng Zi. 1,500 years later, Zhou Dunyi and Cheng Hao started to connect the tradition. Later, more discussions were carried out daily, whereas deviations and misunderstandings appeared daily until the true sense of Confucianism was once again covered and obscured. Why? It was disturbed by many talks of the Confucians of different times.

In my early years when I was preparing for the imperial examinations, I indulged myself in poetry creation. Later I came to know the importance of studying Confucianism, but could not find the way to study because of confusing and contradictory explanations. Then I tried to look for the truth in Daoism and Buddhism and was happy to find something agreeable, thinking that the sage's thoughts were here. But at the same time I found that their theories were more or less different from that of Kong Zi, and it was almost impossible to put them into reality. I kept half-believing, half-doubting until I was later demoted to Longchang, Guizhou, to live a difficult life among the national minorities. Through inspiration and perseverance I seemed to have understood something. With more effort I studied and experienced for more years, testifying with the Five Classics and the Four Books, and my mind was like rivers being dredged and water flowing to the sea! Then I found that the sage's way was really a broad way, and the ordinary Confucians were absurdly digging other paths, trudging along the bushes and eventually falling into the pits. Their "theories" were not even as good as Buddhism or Daoism. No wonder the clever people of the time would rather take to the latter two doctrines. It was really not the latter's fault! I had talked to my friends with my new findings, but was reproached as aspiring for curiosity. I returned and thought over and over, trying to find out whether I was wrong, only to find that I had stronger faith in myself beyond any doubt. The only regret that stayed in my mind was that my idea was also conflicting with Master Zhu's opinion. I always wondered that wise as he was, how could he not find the facts as I had found? It was not until I was assigned office in Nanjing and read Master Zhu's works again that I found that at his last years Master Zhu had realized his early mistakes and hated himself desperately for cheating others as well as himself. The *Collected Annotations* and *Questions on the Four Books* circulated in the market were in fact undecided texts he wrote when he was in his middle age; he was trying to correct them, but he had not enough time. As to his *Classified Analects* and the like, they were only recordings of his disciples done as a competition between themselves in their own ideas, so the recordings were constantly different from what Master Zhu taught in other days. And the common scholars, restricted by their own views, just followed the old sayings. Little had they heard about Master Zhu's new thoughts after he awakened at his last years — no wonder they had no trust in my words, and Master Zhu's mind had no chance to be exposed to the later generations.

I on the one hand felt lucky that I shared the same view with Master Zhu, and on the other was happy that Master Zhu had his new understanding before me. At the same time, I regretted that so many scholars only kept to the Master's old view at middle age but not the new discovery at his last years, thus confounding the orthodox doctrine and degenerating into Daoism and Buddhism. Therefore, I decided to collect those letters and privately show them to people with same ideas, so that they will have no doubt in my understanding and the illumination of Confucianism can be expected. (*Complete Works of Wang Shouren*. pp.144–145)

What was Wang Shouren's purpose of collecting those letters? From above we see clearly that he was trying to convince people that Zhu Xi's thought at his last years was the same as his, and they both had inherited the ideology of ancient sages. Obviously, considering the development of

Zhu Xi's own thought and the history of the dissemination of his ideas, it is improper to deny Zhu Xi's main academic achievements represented by *Textual Analysis and Collected Annotations of the Four Books* and *Questions on the Four Books* and proclaim his proclivity to Mindology with the proof of only thirty-odd letters. Either Wang Shouren's material and analysis, or his conclusion is questionable. But from the historical development of the Principlism, Wang's endeavor tells us a simple fact that he needed Zhu Xi to endorse his own orthodoxy and that Zhu's Principlism and his Mindology did have something in common.

What Li Fu said in his preface to *An All-inclusive Discussion on Master Zhu's Last Years* about the similarity between Zhu Xi and Lu Jiuyuan was quite the same as what Wang Shouren said about the similarity between Zhu Xi and himself. Li Fu said:

> As to Master Zhu and Master Lu's ideologies, in their early years there were equal similarities and differences; in their middle years, there were more similarities than differences; in their last years, they were almost the same. As to their comments on each other, in their early years, there were equal trusts and doubts; in their middle years, there were more trusts than doubts; in their last years, they were as irreconcilable as ice and hot coal. Master Lu's thought kept to Kong Zi's "discrimination between profits and righteousness" and Meng Zi's "seeking the lost mind" all through his life, whereas Master Zhu's thought wandered between Daoism and Buddhism at early years, indulged in textual study at middle years, and started to seek the Mind at last years. So there were still differences between them in their early and middle years, but mostly similarities in their last years. However, since there were still differences in their early and middle years, it is understandable that their comments on each other were a mixture of trusts and doubts, but why were they as irreconcilable as ice and hot coal in their last years since they held almost the same ideas? In their early years, they did not meet each other, so there were differences and similarities in their learning, and doubts and

trusts in their mutual comments; in their middle years, they met frequently, so their learning and mutual comments began to have more in common. This can be proved by Master Zhu's letter to Xiang Anshi in which he said he wished to adopt the strong points of both his and Lu's, and Master Lu's letter to Zhu in which he mentioned that "their meeting at Mount Lushan, Nankang was more friendly than in Ehu Lake[1]". When they met in Lushan, Master Zhu was 52 years old and Master Zhu was 43. Eleven years later, Master Lu died. Between the eleven years they never met again. Their dispute started from the differentiation of the Ultimate of Nothingness and the Ultimate of Extremity. Later, their disciples, strictly following their teachers, went to extremes and expanded their difference. Those who studied under both teachers came and went to convey their views, but overdid it because they didn't really know their teachers' opinions. For instance, Bao Yang talked about his teacher "constantly mentioning humanity and righteousness in his reading and lecturing". Master Zhu's request for Zhang Shi to study the *Zhou Book of Rites* made Master Lu unhappy. Then Master Zhu criticized Master Lu's ideology as similar to the "Chan sect which upheld instant enlightenment", and Master Lu criticized Master Zhu's learning as "segmental, vulgar knowledge", while as a matter of fact both criticisms were not true. *The Final Verdict of Master Zhu's Last Years*, unknown to Master Lu and copied out by Mr Wang Shouren, contained 34 letters, among which some letters to He Hao were mistakenly taken as representing Zhu Xi's view at his middle age because of similar wording. Luo Qinshun picked it out to make argument, and the ignorant Chen Jian used it to make slanders. In fact, almost all of Master Zhu's sayings were of the same opinion. I can even quote a hundred and more examples to prove it. Unfortunately, although the claim that Master Zhu at his last years ridiculed Master Lu as being similar to the Chan sect was complete

---

[1] Zhu Xi and Lu Jiuyuan met in Ehu Lake in 1175 arranged by Lü Zuqian when they had a furious debate. In 1181 they met again in White Deer Academy at Mount Lushan.

hearsay, most scholars preparing for imperial examinations were ready to believe it. Yet even those who aspired for serious study and had already learned something could not help suspecting that Master Zhu might share the same views with Master Lu in his last years.

I have made a thorough study of the *Complete Works of Master Zhu*, searched all his letters at his last years concerning learning, gathered 357 pieces with exact dates into a book, leaving out those about routine affairs, lecturing notes, or random social writings, and entitled it *An All-inclusive Discussion on Master Zhu's Last Years*. I used the word "last" to show that this was the last conclusion, and the word "all-inclusive" to show that they were not chosen to please others, so that Chen Jian and his like could have nothing to say. And scholars in the country engaged in learning would realize the sameness in the two masters' learning, and free themselves from degenerating to mere textual or word studies. Is it not helpful? People in the world have long been puzzled over the differences or similarities of Zhu and Lu. It may be difficult to ask all the scholars to study Master Lu, but it should be possible to ask them to study Master Zhu in his last years. Studying Master Zhu is in fact studying Master Lu. It's unnecessary to strive for Master Lu's name. (*An All-inclusive Discussion on Master Zhu's Last Years.* pp.1–2)

A comparison between the two prefaces will reveal that they were closely related. Li Fu's work was a continuation of Wang Shouren's book, with a relatively exhaustive improvement in the letters' time span and selection, though it was still not a strict one. What's more important is that while Wang emphasized the similarities of Zhu Xi's viewpoint to his own, Li emphasized the extreme conformity of Zhu's and Lu's thoughts. If we read through the three masters' works and their critiques in history, we might not accept the two scholars' view at once. More analysis and study are needed.

Firstly, it was obviously biased to make judgment on Zhu Xi's thought at his last years based on a part of his letters. A more comprehensive study with consideration of more factors is necessary. The starting year of Zhu's "last years" is a prerequisite to discuss his viewpoint at his last years. But Wang's attitude towards this question was vague, and Li's point that the starting year was Zhu Xi's age at 50 was not so convincing. According to the chronicles of Zhu's life and relevant materials provided in the *Complete Works of Zhu Xi,* I suggest that Zhu Xi's age at 52 be the starting point of his "last years". There are two reasons for this suggestion. One is that at the age of 48, most of Zhu Xi's academic works were finished. He edited *Analects of Xie Liangzuo* at the age of 30, compiled *Essentials of Confucian Analects* and *Confucian Analects for Pupils* at 34, edited *Posthumous Writings of Cheng Brothers* at 39, finished *Essentials of Confucian Analects and Mencius, A Compendium of History as a Mirror for Governance, Words and Deeds of Famous Officials of Eight Imperial Courts* and *An Explanation to the Western Inscription* at 43, finished *An Explanation to the Extreme Ultimate Diagram* and *An Explanation to the Book of Thorough Understanding,* edited *More Writings of Cheng Brothers' Works* and *Source and Course of Principlist Scholars* at 44, edited *Close Reflections* with Lü Zuqian at 46, and finished *Collected Annotations to Confucian Analects and Mencius, Questions on the Four Books, Collected Annotations to the Book of Poetry* and *The Original Meanings of the Zhou Book of Change* at the age of 48. It can safely be said that at the age of 30–48, Zhu's academic achievements reached a height. The other reason is that in the few years after 48 he suffered from some traumas: his wife died when he was 47, Zhang Shi died when he was 51, and Lü Zuqian died when he was 52, which all influenced his family as well as his spiritual life. The departure of his two best friends deprived him of the academic interaction, and the friendly atmosphere of academic communication later became tense and even antagonistic.

Later, Zhu Xi always suffered from poor health. Especially after he was appointed prefect of Nankang, busy affairs in dealing with natural disasters harmed his health and he was once seriously ill. Thereafter his health went from bad to worse. A proof is that in his letters to friends or relatives, the very first sentence would always be a complaint of his poor health. I checked and made a rough calculation of the letters in the *Selected Works of Zhu Xi* and found 58 letters in which the first sentence was about his poor health. This tells us about his poor health and his depressed state. In 1186, when he was 57 years old, he wrote to Lu Jiuyuan:

> My health goes from bad to worse. Last year I was hit by illness several times. These days my body seems able to stand, but my spirit is declining day by day. I am afraid that I will not live long. The lucky thing for me is that I seem to be rather strong in daily study, not so frail as before. (*Works of Zhu Xi*. Book 3. p.1571)

In 1193, when he was 64, he wrote to Chen Liang:

> I received from your special messenger your letter, your new poem, as well as your precious gift. Thanks for still remembering me and I don't know how to express my gratitude. Old and ill, I felt even sadder whenever I think of your kindness and excessively rich gifts. Please don't do so later. Autumn is coming. I wish you a good health. Old and ill as I am, it doesn't seem I will grow better. After receiving moxibustion I can eat now, but not as good as before. (Ibid. pp.1609–1610)

Such downcast spirit as revealed in the above two letters could always be found in Zhu Xi at his last years. His poor health and low spirit surely influenced his academic research. He wrote in a letter to Huang Yun in 1192, when he was 63 years old:

> It's better not to think about anything in illness, and everything should be and have been put aside. I concentrate myself in fostering my spirit. I just sat still with my legs crossed, my eyes watching the tip of my nose and my mind resting below my abdomen. Gradually this part became warm and the effect was reached. (Ibid. Book 5. p.2515)

The letter written to Huang Yun in 1198, when he was 69 years old, should have reflected the general state of his life:

Confined to bed for over a month, I thought myself dying. But when summer came, the sickness seemed lessened; only the remaining symptoms still caused some troubles. Next year I will be seventy and there shall be no use regretting that my health is worsening. But the great Dao of Confucianism is declining and waits for more friends to preserve it and carry it forward. For over a year I have found in Wu Bida a most promising scholar. Who has expected that he should have died so young! I was really sad on hearing the news, not merely for our friendship. I was told that his parents are already in advanced age. How can they sustain the loss! Letters came from friends in Jiangxi, all saying that his son is quite sensible. That may be a lucky break out of misfortunes. I wished to send someone to his family to condole on him with my message but failed. I have already written a letter. Can you find someone going there to take it as an attachment if in convenience? If it is not far from you and a return letter could be fetched back to me, so much the better. What you told me about the details of your work is clear to me now. These are unavoidable routines for being an official. As my eyesight was dim, I could not read every word very clearly in your letter, but the main idea is all known. If you can change to a post in a remote county in Hubei or Huainan to spend the rest of the years in carefree leisure, that will be the best choice. (*Ibid.* Book 5. p.2517)

Nevertheless, at his last years Zhu Xi still possessed a mind of "an old steed in a stable aspiring to gallop". He mainly did three things in his life: official business, academic debates, and writing. In his last years, he revised *A General Explanation to the Texts and Annotations of Rites and Ceremonies* at 67, finished *A Textual Study of the Complete Works of Han Yu* at 68, finished *Collected Annotations to the Songs from the South* and prepared *Collected Annotations of the Book of History* at 69, finished *The Songs from the South: Examination and Discussion,* edited *More Songs from the South: Contents,* revised *A Textual Study of the Concordance of The Zhou Book of Change,* and finished *A Textual Study of the Classic of Secret Revelation* at 70. This was like a final, all-out effort at realizing his ambition to be a sage by completing the annotations to Five Classics and making a comprehensive contribution to all four branches of traditional learning. His intermittant official life, from his post in Nankang at the age of 49, in Liangzhe at 52, in Tanzhou at 65, to other short-term posts, required him to work in illness, but also gave him opportunities to bring his administrative ability into full play and chances to contact the outside world.

Zhu Xi's academic communication after the age of 52 was mainly debating with people of the younger generation such as Lu Jiuyuan brothers and Chen Liang. In his debate with Chen Liang, as it related "the inheritance through Mind", he naturally lay more emphasis on the "Mind". Lu Jiuyuan advocated that "Man's Mind will not be worn away for thousands of years", believed in himself "giving the greatest effort which is both simple and easy", and criticized Zhu Xi's "segmented cause which will eventually disappear"[1]. From the fact that Zhu Xi did not reply to their poems until three years later, and his communication with Lu Jiuyuan, we may find that on the one hand Zhu Xi still kept to his original academic standpoint, and on the other he did have some intention to approach Lu's ideas. In my opinion, the letter he wrote in 1186, when he was 57 years old, could best reflect his basic academic standpoint in his communication with Lu Jiuyuan:

> I was told that you had asked for a post outside the capital and were not accepted. How are the things going on now? Will you still stay there? Do you have any more students? Bao Yang said in his letter that he was going to see you. Has he arrived? I met Fu Mengquan last winter. He is a rare scholar with a resolute disposition. But his prejudice might do him harm. I have given him my advice but am afraid that he might not listen to me. You must have met him already; did you give him severe criticism? Principles, though subtle,

---

[1] The above three quotations are all from Lu Jiuyuan's poem in reply to his brother Lu Jiuling's poem which was shown to , Zhu Xi did not make any reply until three years later.

do not exist outside daily life. Black or white, right or wrong, they are just in front of us. It is a great error failing to see this and trying to find something mysterious in imagination. My health goes from bad to worth. Last year I was hit by illness several times. These days my body seems able to stand, but my spirit is declining day by day. I am afraid that I will not live long. The lucky thing for me is that I seem to be rather strong in daily study, not so frail as before. It's a pity that we cannot discuss it face to face. And I am not sure if there should be similarities or differences when we meet sometime in the future. (*Works of Zhu Xi.* Book 3. p.1571)

In this letter, Zhu Xi showed concern for Lu Jiuyuan and his two disciples, especially Fu Mengquan, believing that his study was on a wrong course. This clearly reveals that he and Lu had difference in their ideology. But at the same time his mention of "daily study" and "not so frail" indicates that he was leaning towards Lu's ideas. The last two sentences, though just polite remarks, express his wish to continue discussing or debating with Lu. On the whole, my conclusion is that Zhu Xi's thought at his last years could not concord entirely with that of Lu Jiuyuan. Judging comprehensively from his health, his life, his academic achievements and his academic communications, his thought after the age of 52 did have a tendency towards the Mindology and some traces leaning towards Lu Jiuyuan's ideas, but on the whole, there was no evidence that he would completely deny his past achievements and go over to Lu and Wang's Mindology.

Secondly, when Wang Shouren and Li Fu emphasized the similarity of thoughts between Zhu and Wang or Zhu and Lu, they studied Zhu Xi's last years. But at the same time they mentioned early and middle years too, when the similarities also existed, only in different degrees. Considering the history of the development of the Principlism, we cannot say that there is a high level of similarity or overlap among the three, but from the discussion we can see the relevance of the three masters and the developing process of the Mindology. That is, from Zhu Xi's initial "governance of Mind over Nature and Emotion", to Lu Jiuyuan's transitional "Mind being the Universe or the Principle", and to Wang Shouren's absolute "no Principle or Thing outside the Mind".

Here the greatest difference between Zhu Xi and Lu or Wang lay in Zhu's ontology "one Principle, multiple manifestations". Zhu Xi held that all things under Heaven possessed the same Principle, so did all men. Their manifestations were different because of different Material Forces they had been bestowed. So Zhu's Principle included both the Principle of Things and the Principle of Mind, which were actually the same. This dualism of Mind and Thing had both similarity and difference with Lu and Wang's ideology. Thus we see that there was something inherent in Zhu's theory that was similar to Lu and Wang's theory. Since Zhu Xi lived in an environment of the development of the Mindology and he had similar sayings at his last years, it was easy for people to notice the conformities or similarities of the three.

As a matter of fact, Lu Juyuan's Mindology had experienced a process of development, which could be seen from Lu's own description of his ontology at different periods. His monism of Mindology progressed from the Principle of Things to the Principle of Mind, and was expressed with gradual clarification. Let's cite a few quotations from *Works of Lu Jiuyuan:*

This Principle exists in the universe with nothing in hiding. Heaven and Earth follow this Principle without any selfishness. How can Man, standing side by side with Heaven and Earth as one of the three realms, not follow the Principle out of selfishness? (*Works of Lu Jiuyuan*. p.142)

The Principle in this paragraph "exists in the universe"; Man is only one of the three realms and therefore must follow the Principle. Obviously, the Principle here is more of the Thing's character. Another quotation:

The Principle fills up the universe; Heaven, Earth, Ghosts and Deities cannot violate it, not to say Man. Knowing this, there shall be no selfishness. Goodness in others is the same as in oneself. Thus we have such sayings: "Seeing others to possess good quality is as he himself possesses it", "Seeing others wise and talented, and love them from his heart no less than from his mouth", and "Tell each other, care for each other, teach each other". All these are Man's emotions coming naturally from the Principle beyond any doubt. "Sincerity does not mean to fulfill oneself but to fulfill others. To fulfill oneself is humanity, whereas to fulfill others is wisdom. Both are qualities of Nature, the inside and outside of Dao" — what is to be afraid of is only that one cannot fulfill himself. (*Ibid*. p.147)

This paragraph tends to describe the function of the Mind which is the manifestation of the Principle. Knowing that the Principle fills up the whole universe, Man can possess goodness, enjoy other's wisdom and talent, fulfill himself as well as others, and be free from selfishness. Such is the evolution of the Principle along the path of the Mindology. The third quotation:

What fills up the universe is the Principle. And it is scholars' aim of study to understand this Principle. There is no limit to its dimensions. What Cheng Hao mentioned as the regret of Heaven and Earth is this Principle, which is bigger even than Heaven and Earth.

Heaven, Earth and Man all follow the same Principle, and Heaven is the greatest of the three. That's why it is said that "only Heaven is the greatest and only Yao can take it as example". The five canons are the narration of Heaven, the five rites are the order of Heaven, the five costumes are the manifestations of Heaven's decree, and the five punishments are the Heaven's condemnation. Now if a scholar can exhaust his Mind to know the Nature, he is trying to understand Heaven; if he preserves his Mind and cherishes the Nature, he is serving Heaven. Man is born from Heaven, and his Nature is bestowed by Heaven. We can say that the Principle is bigger than Heaven and Earth, but we can never say that Man is bigger than Heaven and Earth.

Both the Qian hexagram and the Kun hexagram follow the same Principle. But Kong Zi said of Qian as "Great is the Qian hexagram", and of Kun as "Perfect is the Kun hexagram". Sage kings Yao and Shun followed the same Principle. But Kong Zi said of Yao as "How great is Yao as a king", and of Shun as "How kingly is Shun". This is the natural order of high and low, just as the son cannot sit side by side with his father, or the younger brother cannot walk in front of his elder brother. They are not to be changed by personal wishes. (*Ibid*. p.161)

The difference between this and above two quotations lies in that here the sphere of Principle was already bigger than Heaven and Earth. Three realms follow the same Principle with Heaven being the greatest. Man was bestowed Nature from Heaven whereas Nature was Heaven's decree. So to exhaust the Mind to know the Nature was to know Heaven, and what he understood was the Mind. Now let's see a fourth quotation:

What fills up the universe is the Principle. The ancient sage found the Principle first. When he became king of the world, he looked up into the sky to observe celestial phenomena and looked down on the land to observe geographical features and examine colorful patterns on birds, animals and all other things that existed on earth. He selected symbols close from human body and faraway from various objects, then for the first time invented the Eight Trigrams as symbols of the brilliant and miraculous virtue of nature and as analogies of states of all things of creation under Heaven. He then used judgments, alternations, images and divinations to awaken people. The sages of later times might have experienced thousands of years, but their findings would be no different. "Their similarity was just like a closely-matched tally", or "their principles were all the same", these words could only be said by those who really understood the Principle. When this was known, people could talk about sublimating thoughts and wills of people under Heaven to accomplish all work under Heaven and find solutions for all the problems under Heaven. Since the declination of the Dao, the scholars, restricted by their own view, could not even be aware of their own brilliant virtues. When they couldn't recognize their own wills, how could they sublimate thoughts and wills of people under Heaven to accomplish all work under Heaven and find solutions for all the problems under Heaven? (*Ibid.* p.201)

This is purely Lu Jiuyuan's ontology of the Mindology.

Wang Shouren saw the Mind only, so he held that Mind could govern everything. His Mindology was more complete that Lu's. He argued that "no Principle existed outside the Mind, and no things existed outside the Mind", and emphasized that the "unity of knowing and doing" and the "arrival of intuitive knowledge" depended on the Mind. So he said:

The Principle of things is not outside my Mind. To seek the Principle of things outside my Mind ends in no Principle of Mind; to seek my Mind by leaving out the Principle of things, then what is my Mind? The entity of the Mind is Nature, and the Nature is the Principle. (*Complete Works of Wang Shouren.* p.35)

All exists in the Mind. The Mind is the Principle. The Mind, free from the disadvantage of selfishness, is the Nature born from Heaven and doesn't need anything added from outside.

With this pure Mind of Heavenly Principle, one serves his father to arrive at filial piety, serves his emperor to arrive at loyalty, and makes friends to arrive at good government, sincerity and benevolence. It needs nothing else beside working on the Mind to get rid of human desires and preserve the Heavenly Principle. (*Ibid.* p.2)

The noumenon of the Mind is what is called Heavenly Principle. The brightness and intelligence of the Heavenly Principle is what is called intuitive knowledge. (*Ibid.* p.1291)

Zhu Xi's Principlism and Lu and Wang's Mindology shared a focus on their overlapping part — the study of the Mind — and ignored the rest. This focus revealed the commonness and similarity among the three, united the three and at the same time showed the process of the development of the Mindology. Because of the dual character of the

Principle, Zhu's Principlism can include Lu and Wang's Mindology but not vice versa, and Lu and Wang's theory is a continuation and development of Cheng and Zhu's Principlism. Thus we can see clearly the continuity of the development of the Song-Ming Principlism, represented by Cheng Yi, Zhu Xi, Lu Juyuan and Wang Shouren, which is in fact the birth and progress of a new Confucian hermeneutics, as compared to the traditional Confucianism. This Neo-Confucianism is at the same time an inheritance of the traditional Confucianism and a new development in the new historical background. Such is a complete picture of the Principlism.

Thirdly, the complete picture of the Principlism represented by Cheng, Zhu, Lu and Wang means the completion of the transformation of traditional Confucianism in new period. Now how shall we describe this completed structure? Among the galaxy of Principlists and during the process of the Principlist development, various ideologies bloomed like spring flowers. Seeing this, we select Zhu Xi the Principlist synthesizer as a representative, hoping to find a creative, constructive and epoch-making system through the case study of Zhu Xi's works. Thus we found his ontology of cosmology in Zhu's *Three Books*, and his comprehensive statement of governance of Mind over Nature and Emotion, which was a synthesis of previous Confucian tradition as well as the wisdom and efforts of many Song dynasty Principlists. Explaining the Four Books in such new ontology and new understanding of governance of Mind over Nature and Emotion made it possible to turn the Four Books into a new branch of learning — the Four Books Studies. Without Zhu's *Three Books* as the theoretical foundation, there would not be such a drastic change to the Four Books. However, if we traced back the formation of the general framework of Zhu Xi's Principlism, we would find that either Zhu's *Three Books* or Four Books had come from the works of the four scholars in the Northern Song dynasty, especially the fundamental work laid by two Cheng brothers. The evolution of Lu-Wang Mindology after Zhu Xi was actually based on Zhu's Principlism, with an all-round development and a new emphasis. It would not harm the reception and inheritance of Zhu's thought, but showed the extreme development towards bipolar ends: the

Principle of things and the Principle of Mind. With that in mind, we can have a more comprehensive understanding of Principlism as a whole.

Fourthly, new thinking brought about new understanding of the past. The study into the reason why the formation of the Song-Ming Principlism should take about 700 years in the sequence of Cheng-Zhu-Lu-Wang reveals a characteristic feature of the Song Dynasty Confucians: most of them tended to trace their ideology back to Kong Zi and Meng Zi and refused to acknowledge the Confucian tradition thereafter, believing a chasm had occurred in the development. Through an objective research and analysis of the process of the development of Confucianism in the history, we could not agree with the Song Confucians. (1) The so-called division between the Han Dynasty school and the Song Dynasty school in academic studies was created by the Qing Dynasty scholars in the Qianlong and Jiaqing periods (1736–1820), in an effort to distinguish the two approaches of textual analysis and hermeneutic interpretation. It seems that the Han Dynasty textual analysis was regarded as a new period in the development of Confucianism. This viewpoint is questionable. In my opinion, the Han Dynasty Confucianism was a continuation of pre-Qin Confucianism, a revival and a recovery, not an independent stage. The political endorsement of Confucianism as the dominant ideology was only a change in the application of Confucianism, not in its development. The textual study of the classics in the Han Dynasty was the recuperation after the disastrous burning of ancient classics in the Qin Dynasty. It was neither a break with the tradition nor a totally fresh beginning, but a continuation and inheritance in the form of recovery. (2) The *Annotations to the Five Classics* of the Tang Dynasty were still textbooks used by the imperial court, which meant that Confucianism retained its dominance as the mainstream ideology even at a time of highy developed Daoism and Buddhism, though less powerful than in the Han Dynasty. Han Yu intended to recover the Confucian tradition but could not reach the goal without a new theoretical background or a new context. And it is the development of metaphysics, the introduction and sinicization of Buddhism and the development of Daoism that created the desirable conditions and environment for the renewal of Confucianism. (3) The Song Dynasty Principlism emphasized their connection to Kong Zi and Meng Zi, especially the tradition of Zisi and Meng Zi, while denying other Confucians' works in the belief that the Confucian tradition had been lost. This was surely a biased view, but it was justifiable in the historical context. That is, the humanist conceptions — the personalized way to view the world, or the principle and method to be a Man, implied in the *Confucian Analects*, the *Mencius,* or the *Survey to the Book of Change* — were emphasized and revitalized through the Song-Ming Principlism and the academic works of Cheng, Zhu, Lu and Wang. From this angle, we can re-divide the development of Confucianism into three historical stages. The first stage includes the 1,500 or so years from Kong Zi's study and his interpretation of historical classics to the *Annotations to the Five Classics* in the Tang Dynasty. The development of Principlism is the second stage. And the so-called Neo-Confucianism, starting from the beginning of the 20th century and still continuing now, may be regarded as the third stage. This new, macroscopic division is well-grounded. During the first two stages, some of the Confucian thoughts were historically justifiable, but there were certainly drawbacks. But after the development of two thousand years, the ideological cultural tradition with its ups and downs must have proved a cultural resilience, which is the precious spiritual wealth bestowed on the Chinese nation for the dealings with the complicated and changeable world. Reviewing the past history of Confucian development and looking forward to the future, we must cherish the fine Confucian tradition. And for the two historical stages of Confucian development which had already passed into history, we must always bear in mind and respect the names of the two central figures, Kong Zi and Zhu Xi.

Appendices

I. Bibliography

Works by Zhu Xi

A Brief Record of Mr. Hu Xian's Life 《籍溪行状》

A Compendium of History as a Mirror for Governance 《资治通鉴纲目》

A Complete Collection of Zhu Xi's Lost Poems and Articles 《朱熹佚诗佚文全考》

A General Explanation to the Texts and Annotations of Rites and Ceremonies 《仪礼经传通解》

A Primer of the Change Study 《易学启蒙》

A Textual Study of the Classic of Secret Revelation 《阴符经考异》

A Textual Study of the Complete Works of Han Yu 《昌黎先生集考异》

A Textual Study of the Concordance of The Zhou Book of Change 《周易参同契考异》

An Erratum on the Classic of Filial Piety 《孝经刊误》

An Explanation to the Book of Thorough Understanding 《通书解》

An Explanation to the Extreme Ultimate Diagram 《太极图说解》

An Explanation to the Western Inscription 《西铭解》

Analects of Zhu Xi 《语录抄存》

Basics of Mencius 《孟子要略》

Classified Analects of Zhu Xi 《朱子语类》

Close Reflections 《近思录》

Collected Annotations to the Book of Poetry 《诗集传》

Collected Annotations to the Four Books 《四书集注》

Collected Annotations to the Songs from the South 《楚辞集注》

Collected Explanations of the Book of Poetry 《诗集解》

Collection of Master Zhu's Posthumous Writings《朱子遗集》

Complete Works of Zhu Xi《朱子全书》

Essentials of Confucian Analects and Mencius《论孟精义》

Household Rituals《家礼》

Illustrated Sacrificial Ceremony to Kong Zi Practiced at Prefectures and Counties in the Shaoxi Period《绍熙州县释奠仪图》

Investigation and Research of Zhu Xi's Lost Works《朱子佚文辨伪考录》

More Songs from the South: Contents《楚辞后语目录》

Must-knows for Children《童蒙须知》

Perplexed to Learn and Afraid of Hearing Too Much: Miscellaneous Writings《困学恐闻编》

Primary Education《小学》

Quatrains for Educating Children《训蒙绝句》

Questions and Answers at Yanping《延平答问》

Questions on the Four Books《四书或问》

Source and Course of Principlist Scholars《伊洛渊源录》

Textual Analysis and Collected Annotations of the Four Books《四书章句集注》

Textual Analysis of the Great Learning《大学章句》

The Collected Works of Zhu Xi《晦庵先生朱文公文集》

The Original Meanings of the Zhou Book of Change《周易本义》

The Songs from the South: Examination and Discussion《楚辞辩证》

Tomb Account for Mr. Liu Mianzhi《草堂墓表》

Tomb Account for Mr. Liu Zihui《屏山墓表》

Words and Deeds of Famous Officials《名臣言行录》

Words and Deeds of Famous Officials of Eight Imperial Courts《八朝名臣言行录》

Yarrows Divination: Examination and Correction《蓍卦考误》

Zhu Xi on the Book of History《文公书说》

Zhu's Family Genealogy at Chayuan of Wuyuan《婺源茶院朱氏世谱》

Works by Other Authors

Cai Shen, *Collected Annotations of the Book of History* 蔡沈《书集传》;

> *Grand Norms Explained in Numbers* 《洪范数》

Chen Zhensun, *Zhizhai Annotated Bibliographic Records* 陈振孙《直斋书录解题》

Cheng Brothers, *Annotation of the Zhou Book of Change* 程氏兄弟《周易程氏传》;

> *Cheng Brothers on Confucian Classics* 《程氏经说》;
>
> *More Writings of Cheng Brothers' Works* 《程氏外书》;
>
> *Posthumous Writings of Cheng Brothers* 《程氏遗书》;
>
> *Works of Cheng Hao and Cheng Yi* 《二程集》

Cheng Hao, *The Works of Cheng Hao* 程颢《明道先生文集》

Cheng Yi, *Cheng Yi's Commentary on the Book of Change* 程颐《伊川易传》;

> *The Works of Cheng Yi* 《伊川先生文集》

Dai Xian, *An Actually Recorded Chronicle of Zhu Xi* 戴铣《朱子实纪年谱》

Duan Changwu, *A Collection of Explanations to Mao-prefaced Book of Poetry* 段昌武《毛诗集解》

Fan Zuyu, *Tang History as a Mirror* 范祖禹撰，吕祖谦注《唐鉴》

Fang Songqin, *Works of Han Yu* 方崧卿编《昌黎先生文集》

Hanyu, *A Reply to Li Yi* 韩愈《答李翊》

He Ruilin, *Errata of Zhu Xi's Collected Works* 贺瑞麟《朱子文集正讹》

Hong Xingzu, *Complementary Annotations to the Songs from the South* 洪兴祖《楚辞补注》

Hu Anguo, *A Supplement to the Extracts of the History as a Mirror for Governance* 胡安国《资治通鉴举要补遗》

Huang Gan, *Anecdotes of Master Zhu* 黄榦《朱先生行状》;

> *Collected Works of Mianzhai* 《勉斋集》

Huang Zongxi, *Academic Case Studies of the Ming Dynasty* 黄宗羲《明儒学案》;

> *Academic Case Studies of the Song and Yuan Dynasties* 《宋元学案》

Jin Lüxiang, *A Tabular Annotation to the Book of History* 金履祥《尚书表注》;

> *Annotations to the Book of History* 《尚书注》;
>
> *Explanations to Textual Analysis of the Great Learning* 《大学章句疏义》;

    Pre-part of the History as a Mirror for Governance 《通鉴前编》；
    Textual Study of the Collected Annotations to Confucian Analects and the Mencius 《论语孟子集注考证》

Kong Yingda, *Annotations to the Five Classics* 孔颖达《五经正义》

Li Fang, *Choice Blossoms of Literature* 李昉《文苑英华》

Li Fu, *An All-inclusive Discussion on Master Zhu's Last Years* 李绂《朱子晚年全论》

Li Guangdi, *Analects of Rongcun: Continued* 李光地《榕村续语录》

Li Mo, *Chronicle of Zhu Xi* 李默《紫阳文公先生年谱》

Lü Zuqian, *A Full Record of Historical Systems* 吕祖谦《历代制度详说》；
    Literary Anthology of the Song Dynasty 《宋文鉴》；
    Study of the Book of Poetry at Lü's Family School 《吕氏家塾读诗纪》；
    True Records of Emperor Huizong 《徽宗皇帝实录》

Shao Yong, *Supreme Norms Governing the World* 邵雍《皇极经世书》

Shi Dunshan, *Digest of Explanations to the Doctrine of the Mean* 石塾山《中庸辑略》

Sikong Tu, *Twenty-four Categories in Poetry Appreciation* 司空图《二十四诗品》

Sima Guang, *History as a Mirror for Governance* 司马光《资治通鉴》

Song Duanyi, Xue Yingjin, *Source and Course of Kaoting School* 宋端仪、薛应旂《考亭渊源录》

Su Xun, *A Letter to His Excellency Ouyang Xiu* 苏洵《上欧阳内翰书》（朱熹作"上欧阳公书"）

Wang Maohong, *A Vetted Chronicle of Zhu Xi* 王懋竑《朱子年谱考异》

Wang Shouren, *Instructions for Practical Living* 王守仁《传习录》；
    The Final Verdict of Master Zhu's Last Years 《朱子晚年定论》

Wang Yi, *Textual Analysis of the Songs from the South* 王逸《楚辞章句》

Wei Liaoweng, *Complete Works of Wei Liaoweng* 魏了翁《鹤山先生大全集》

Wu Cheng, *Collected Comments on Five Classics* 吴澄《五经纂言》

Xie Liangzuo, *Analects of Xie Liangzuo* 谢良佐《上蔡语录》

Yan Can, *Collected Explanations of the Poetry* 严粲《诗缉》

Yao Xuan, *An Anthology of the Tang Prose* 姚铉《唐文粹》

Zhang Shi, *Works of Zhang Shi* 张栻《南轩先生文集》

Zhang Zai, *Analects of Zhang Zai* 张载《横渠先生语录》;

        Correcting Strayed Ideas《横渠先生正蒙》;

        The Western Inscription《西铭》;

        Works of Zhang Zai《横渠先生文集》;

        Zhang Zai on Confucian Analects《横渠先生论语说》;

        Zhang Zai on Mencius《横渠先生孟子说》;

        Zhang Zai on Rites and Music《横渠先生礼乐说》;

        Zhang Zai on the Book of Change《横渠先生易说》

Zhao De, *Literary Anthology* 赵德《文录》

Zhao Shunsun, *Collected Explanations of the Four Books* 赵顺孙《四书纂疏》

Zhao Xibian, *Bibliographic Records: A Supplement* 赵希弁《读书附志》

Zhen Dexiu, *Collected Editions of the Four Books* 真德秀《四书集编》;

        Derived Meaning from the Great Learning《大学衍义》;

        Notes on Reading《读书记》;

        Selected Works of Zhen Dexiu《西山文集》

Zhou Dunyi, *The Book of Thorough Understanding* 周敦颐《通书》;

        The Extreme Ultimate Diagram《太极图》

Zhu Gao, *Poems of Zhu Gao* 朱樉《玉澜集》

Zhu Song, *Works of Zhu Song* 朱崧《韦斋集》

Anthology of Poems by 1,000 Authors《千家诗》

Bibliographic Treatise of the *History of the Song Dynasty*《宋史·艺文志》

Biographies of Principlists of the *History of the Song Dynasty*《宋史·道学传》

Four Divisions Series《四部丛刊》

Guizang or *The Shang Book of Change*《归藏》

Lianshan or *The Xia Book of Change*《连山》

Mao-prefaced Book of Poetry《毛诗》

Orthodox Daoist Scripture Canon《正统道藏》

Rites: An Abridged Version《礼略》

Ritual Ceremonies《仪礼》

Shaoxing Period Sacrificial Decree《绍兴祀令》

Synopsis of the General Catalog of Extractions of the Complete Library of the Four Treasuries 《四库全书荟要总目提要》
Tang Rites of Kaiyuan Period 《唐开元礼》
The Complete Library of the Four Treasuries 《四库全书》
The Confucian Analects 《论语》
The Doctrine of the Mean 《中庸》
The Great Learning 《大学》
The Mencius 《孟子》
Zhenghe Period New Ceremonies for the Five Rites 《政和五礼新仪》
Zhou Book of Rites 《周礼》
Zhouyi or *The Zhou Book of Change* 《周易》

II. Glossary

accounts/narrations 记 (jì) 1, 38

All under heaven is in tranquility. 平天下 (píng tiān xià) 124

Alternation between *Yin* and *Yang* is called the Way. 一阴一阳之谓道 (yì yīn yì yáng zhī wèi dào) 97

announcements 公移 (gōng yí) 11, 13

applications 申请 (shēn qǐng) 12, 58, 60

approaches to learning 为学之方 (wéi xué zhī fāng) 19

arousal and non-arousal 未发已发 (wèi fā yǐ fā) 116, 117, 167, 174

beam-setting addresses 上梁文 (shàng liáng wén) 11

behavior 行事 (xíng shì) 13, 34, 44, 53, 54, 57, 64, 89, 91, 104, 109, 126, 139

benisons 祝文 (zhù wén) 11, 12

biographies 传 (zhuàn) 11, 31, 38, 43, 45, 159, 164, 165

brief biographies of dead persons 行状 (xíng zhuàng) 11

restrain oneself and restore the rites 克己复礼 (kè jǐ fù lǐ) 162

reverence 敬 (jìng) 76, 92, 94, 108, 109, 115, 118, 120, 126, 127, 128, 129, 131, 133, 134, 142, 143, 144, 145, 153, 174, 188, 191, 192, 212, 213

rhapsody / rhymed prose 赋 (fù) 38

Righteousness 义 (yì) 17, 19, 51, 60, 62, 69, 86, 89, 90, 91, 92, 93, 98, 103, 104, 105, 109, 113, 114, 115, 116, 118, 126, 129, 130, 138, 139, 167, 170, 171, 183, 184, 186, 200, 220, 221

rites and music 礼乐 (lǐ yuè) 25, 33, 94, 150, 151, 162, 193

sacrifices 祭祀 (jì sì) 18

sacrificial ceremonies 祭礼 (jì lǐ) 30

sealed memorial 封事 (fēng shì) 11

silent tranquility and desirelessness 寂然无欲 (jì rán wú yù) 91

sincere intention 诚意 (chéng yì) 19

Sincerity 诚 (chéng) 43, 56, 58, 76, 81, 82, 83, 90, 91, 94, 95, 97, 98, 102, 105, 107, 120, 128, 129, 131, 133, 134, 138, 145, 149, 153, 185, 193, 229, 231

state government 治国 (zhì guó) 19, 58, 154

stone inscriptions 碑 (bēi) 38

subtlety, oneness, and keeping to the Mean 精一执中 (jīng yī zhí zhōng) 153

suggestion memorial 奏劄 (zòu zhá) 11

tablet inscriptions 碑 (bēi) 11, 159

textual analysis 章句 (zhāng jù) 18, 25, 27, 76, 77, 119, 145, 161, 163, 188, 193, 195, 204, 205, 207, 209, 210, 211, 220, 233

the constant virtue held by man 烝民秉彝 (jù mín bǐng yí) 130

the goodness bestowed by Heavenly God 上帝降衷 (shàng dì jiàng zhōng) 130

the Map and the Script 河图洛书 (hé tú luò shū) 20

the Mean, Correctness, Humanity, and Righteousness 中正仁义 (zhōng zhèng rén yì) 89, 91, 92

The metaphysical realm is called the Way. 形而上者谓之道 (xíng ér shàng zhě wèi zhī dào) 79

the purist quality of Man 人之极 (rén zhī jí) 88